Alan Fisher was converted to books when he was doing National Service and had time on his hands. Back in civilian life, he worked as a clerk in an underwriting syndicate in Lloyds, as a porter at London University, and as a clerk in Paddington General Hospital. He attended night school and entered teacher training. Teaching history in secondary schools in Sussex and Kent, he later gained a degree from the Open University and a postgraduate diploma from Sussex – but feels he learned far more from reading Arthur Koestler.

WINNER OF THE HISTORICAL NOVEL PRIZE IN MEMORY OF GEORGETTE HEYER.

Alan Fisher

The Terioki
Crossing

CORGI BOOKS

DEDICATION
This one is for my god daughter
HARRIET ESTHER WOOD

THE TERIOKI CROSSING
A CORGI BOOK 0 552 12562 8

Originally published in Great Britain by
The Bodley Head Ltd.

PRINTING HISTORY
The Bodley Head edition published 1984
Corgi edition published 1985

This book is set in Baskerville Compugraphic

Corgi Books are published by Transworld Publishers
Ltd., Century House, 61–63 Uxbridge Road, Ealing,
London W5 5SA, in Australia by Transworld Publishers
(Aust.) Pty. Ltd., 26 Harley Crescent, Condell Park,
NSW 2200, and in New Zealand by Transworld Publishers
(N.Z.) Ltd., Cnr. Moselle and Waipareira Avenues,
Henderson, Auckland.

Printed and bound in Great Britain by
Cox & Wyman Ltd., Reading, Berks.

PART ONE

1

The forest extended seemingly endless on either side of the steel tracks, running perfectly straight towards the distant frontier. Pines and birch trees reached up, silent and still, their snow-hung branches silhouetted against the near darkness of the northern winter night.

The railway track was recent in the span of things. Before, the forest had remained undisturbed for centuries and only lonely huts and occasional small straggling villages of unpainted logs marked the wilderness. There were men still living, Finns, Letts, Slavs, who could remember the spirit-breaking toil of building that link between Helsingfors and the Imperial Russian capital on the misty Baltic marshlands.

The rails vibrated to a muted rumble far to the north. The trees stirred. A pinpoint of light thickened, glinted along the snow-covered track. The Petrograd Express thundered south. Wheels gripped steel. The massive engine ran effortlessly on the flat, hauling its burden of seven hundred lives.

In an overcrowded compartment of one of the yellow, second class carriages, Helen Mirsky sat jammed up close to the window. The heat generated by so many people was oppressive. She eased her back, aware of the stickiness of her own body. Night, day, and now another night. But one had to look on the positive side. She had been fortunate to get a corner seat. If it hadn't been for the kindness of the sad, middle-aged man she might have found herself seated next to the bearded priest who was even now dipping into his copious bag for more black bread and offensive cheese. She examined her fingernails with disgust. Close continuous proximity to strangers was quite nauseating, and journeys to the toilet along the corridor cluttered with baggage had become too painful to contemplate. Better to wait now until the train reached Petrograd. The sad, middle-aged man next to her gave the appearance of sleep, but Helen suspected he was observing her thighs through half-closed lids.

The engine whistle shrieked beyond the window. There were wolves out there in the forest. She had seen their eyes. Helen rested her head against the hard padding and moved her leg slightly. Her foot touched the leg of the grey-clad lady opposite who opened her eyes, then closed them again, retreating into her faded, well-bred gentility. Only once had she responded to the middle-aged man's attempts at polite conversation. Her son was in Petrograd with the Pavlovsky Regiment. She hoped to see him before he was sent westward to the war. She was worried about all this talk of heavy casualties in the Carpathians. Now she was asleep to the steady rocking movement of the train, her head drooping, then straightening, then drooping again.

How boring they had all become. Helen could believe that she had become boring also, sitting locked in one position for hour after hour and having exhausted all possible small talk. Only the young artisan seated next to the fat priest seemed oblivious to the interminable weariness of the journey. He had large clumsy hands. He glanced up and caught her looking at him, and he smiled shyly. She returned the smile briefly then turned back to the window, determinedly cutting off any possibility of later contact. And she thought of home. The hurried visit had perhaps been a mistake, breaking her studies. Father had passed the crisis by the time she had made the long journey from Petrograd to Uleaborg. Just as well. Sick people did not bring out the best in her.

She eased her shoulders, straightening them, then relaxing. There had been the pleasurable side to the visit. Old friends, all envious in their assumptions of her romantic student life at the university in Petrograd. Yuri had, of

6

course, spoiled it by trailing around after her for the whole fortnight, dog-like in his submissive devotion. And then embarrassing her with the huge bunch of delicate, hot-house flowers as she boarded the express train to return. Such a foolish thing to do when it was obvious that the flowers would die before she reached the Imperial capital. And such a ridiculous waste of good money when their cost would have purchased three — perhaps four meals in the refectory. Of course, the flowers had started to wilt during the night, and in the morning she had scattered them from the window, a few at a time, sadly watching them blown back on the wind. Such poor frail things. And they smelled so much nicer than people. Remembering them, she felt the stickiness of her body. She took a small bottle of cologne from her bag and dabbed her wrists and forehead. She could read the Helsingfors newspaper again, but it was full of tedious military detail of the European war. After nineteen hours on a train one could hardly concern oneself with distant battles.

The sad man had begun to snore softly, his body shifting, leaning on Helen. Should she wake him? Perhaps not, because he would be apologetic then tire her further with conversation. She glanced towards the compartment door and noticed again the heavily built man frowning in his sleep. He was the only occupant of the carriage for whom she had been unable to invent a background. It was as if everything about him was deliberately indeterminate. Even his age would be difficult to guess. The only distinctive feature was an old scar splitting his lower lip. His face had hardened in sleep, as though the frown had reached deep in him, stirring something bitter.

The forest had begun to thin. Helen turned back to the window. Her stomach rumbled with hunger. When had she last eaten? She could perhaps afford supper at the working men's restaurant after she'd crossed the city to Vassili island. The train fare had cut sharply into her allowance. She frowned out into the darkness. There was barely enough to buy two cheap meals a day until end of term.

Moreover, cabbage soup at the conclusion of this journey would hardly suffice. She could go to the Zubovs' house on her way home, using the pretext that she needed a book to brief herself in readiness for tomorrow's lecture. Madame Zubov would offer a meal as she always did, and after suitable protestations she could accept. Possibly that would be the best course of action.

She dozed, dreaming of food, then woke again as the train slowed, clanking towards a cluster of lights, and there it stopped. They'd reached the frontier. Paraffin lamps illumined a raw timber station building and customs shed. The Imperial flag hung limply from a pole and soldiers with heavy swinging stride passed the carriage. A German agent had been caught here last month. Helen leaned back again, too weary to interest herself in the frontier procedure. She suspected that the Tsar's officers were more anxious to detect returning revolutionaries and agitators.

The door of the compartment rolled back and a frontier guard glanced round at them. 'Your papers.' His tone was brusque and he had the arrogant indifference of minor officials. He looked quickly at the heavily built man with the scarred lip. And that was altogether strange. As the man pulled his identity papers from his pocket, Helen thought his eyes registered a momentary fear quickly masked. Had she been mistaken? Perhaps she had. Now his head was down and he appeared to be dozing again.

'Forty minutes to Petrograd.' The guard jerked his head and the door slammed shut.

Helen took out a tiny mirror and examined herself. Second class travel tended to age one in direct relation to distance. She straightened her small hat, frowning at her reflected image. Hunger now suggested that the hat, purchased in Uleaborg, had been a wanton expense. She took her railway ticket from her bag and slid it under the palm of her glove. Only another forty minutes. The great city beckoned.

The frontier guard paused in the corridor, glancing back through the glass panel of the door at the man with the scarred lip. He made a pencilled question mark on his clip-board before moving on, pushing his way between luggage and squatting passengers. He opened the door at the end of the corridor and stepped across the gap to the first class carriage. Many of the compartments were empty. An armed Cossack in a long purple coat decorated with cartridges stood expressionless at the third door. The guard was curious. He was supposed to see the occupant even though he knew who she was. Madame Malnekov, wife of the Commander of Petrograd Military District. Should he enforce the regulations? Perhaps not. He could do without trouble from Petrograd. He moved on to the last compartment.

Hard experience indicated that it paid to show a certain deference to foreigners travelling first class. He knocked before entering. The compartment was in darkness. '*Pras-teetye*,' he apologized before flicking the light switch on.

A young army officer was seated alone in the corner by the window, his booted legs at full stretch. He looked up, squinting in the sudden light. The guard appraised him quickly and expertly. Heavy sun tan, powerful shoulders, well-worn uniform, probably poor but unlikely to be intimidated. He tried him in indifferent French. 'Your papers please. Where are you from?'

And there was a surprise. The young foreign officer replied in Russian but with a slight suggestion of the north. '*Ya priekhal eez anglee*,' and leaning forward in his seat he felt in his tunic pocket.

The guard fingered quickly through the passport before examining the accompanying document. It bore the stamp of the Russian War Ministry. He stiffened slightly as he read. Captain Michael Stern. Corps of Royal Engineers. Technical Adviser to the Imperial Russian Army. Perhaps a little more deference was due. 'We shall be in the capital in forty minutes, Excellency. Enjoy your stay.'

Michael Stern stretched out his legs again. He'd crossed Scandinavia without formality. But Finland owed alle-

9

giance to the Tsar, and he had been required to show his passport twice since he'd left Sweden twenty-two hours before. 'Thank you. Would you kindly put the light out as you leave.'

The guard nodded. 'Certainly, Excellency.' Englishmen! No matter how shabbily they dressed they all behaved like Romanovs. He moved on again to the last carriage. Crashing the door open he shoved his way unceremoniously among tired corridor squatters, glancing with a practised eye at identity papers. Was there anything left to be done? He'd impounded the packing case of subversive literature. Damned Bolsheviks. The Tsar was too lenient, they should all be hanged. There was, of course, the matter of the suspect male passenger in second class carriage Number Two, but to make an arrest on mere suspicion could land him in trouble. He pondered as he climbed down to the platform. He'd telegraph the Petrograd authorities and let them deal with it.

A soldier swung a lantern. In his darkened compartment Captain Michael Stern looked out as the train juddered and moved slowly, almost stealthily across the frontier. The lights of Bielostorov gleamed in the night. Morass and small lakes flanked the tracks. To the west, marshy flats extended to the Gulf of Finland. He felt uneasy. What a God-forsaken place. Thin wraiths of steam streamed back past the carriage window. Ahead he could see the night glow of Petrograd.

It had been St Petersburg when he'd left, on a bright cold day, his breath turning to ice. Now he'd been sent back, all the way from India. Nobody in Delhi had been able to tell him why. A sudden unequivocal order, passage to England on a reeking freighter, and nobody there had been able to tell him why either.

The train clattered over points where the branch line filtered off traffic to Novaya Derevnya. Another ten minutes and he'd be in the Russian capital, and what awaited him there? Mystery did not appeal to him. Beyond the window were darkened suburban houses, and a church, Byzantine and alien to his eyes.

He should of course try to see it all as an intriguing challenge. But six more days of travelling, by boat from

Newcastle, then on badly heated and poorly ventilated trains, had sapped any small enthusiasm he'd managed to muster. He scowled out at the night. For the past five years they'd been content to use his skills in the backwaters of empire, and for his part he had become almost reconciled to hot, squalid, barely civilized outposts and sweating male company.

The train clattered across the Vyborg district on the northern reaches of Petrograd. He could make out the black shapes of factories and chimneys looming starkly against the near darkness. He rubbed a space on the steamed up window. Cold mist from the river was beginning to freeze on the outside. His scowl deepened. He didn't like the bloody climate either.

The tempo of the wheels changed, slowing as they entered the Finland terminus, and brakes heaved and screeched. A final jolt and he'd reached the end of his long journey. He rose stiffly, hesitating before pulling his bags down from the rack. The train was still part of that other world. It had been seven years since he'd last come to this city.

Stern moved along the carpeted corridor. At the doorway of the third compartment the huge purple-tunicked Cossack gravely barred his way as a woman emerged, her pale face almost concealed by the cowl of her cloak. Stern bowed. He knew that face now. Madame Malnekov had travelled along the same route all the way from Newcastle. As she climbed down from the carriage a waiting escort of soldiers of the city garrison snapped to attention for her.

Stern hauled his bag out of the carriage and stared around him. Released steam from the massive engine shrouded the front part of the train and billowed up to the high glass roof. The platform was crowded with passengers moving towards the barrier. Two golden-epauletted officers loitered, laughing with their lovely full-breasted women. The scene was European, but with a suggestion of barbarism.

Stern adjusted his cap, setting it at a slight angle — a small, barely conscious gesture. He signalled to a stringy porter who took his bags and loped ahead of him. The

11

Tsar's police were about, standing in pairs and eyeing the crowd. Stern wondered why there were so many of them.

Ahead of him Helen Mirsky, hand pressed to her small hat, struggled out of the yellow second class carriage and joined the crowd. Stern noticed her hips. Some women, seen briefly, had a way of moving that stayed in the mind for days afterwards. The girl's bag looked heavy. She was curling the fingers of her free hand, easing her railway ticket from under her glove. She glanced round, measuring eyes searching for an easier way through, then she was almost lost to his view in the press of people.

It seemed that they were barely moving. The police were scrutinizing each traveller at the narrow exit. Stern groaned to himself. He'd have to start getting used to Russian officialdom again. The flow ceased altogether and he stood hemmed in. God alone knew what went on in the minds of Tsarist policemen.

Somebody shouted.

There was a ripple of movement at the barrier as a man with a scarred lip turned and forced his way back through the crowd. Fear on his face he clawed his way past the girl in the small hat and Stern saw her disappearing under surging bodies. She would be trampled! He shouldered his way forward and hauled her to her feet. 'You're quite safe, *dyevooshka*,' and he held the crowd off her with his back.

'My bag! Where is my bag?'

How light she was. He could have lifted her with one hand. 'That is safe too.'

Her sharp fear eased. 'Thank you. What on earth happened?'

'Somebody has been arrested. Now it is over.' He picked up her bag and steered her through the barrier.

Stern's porter had distanced himself from them, watching the police drift off in pairs. The girl brushed her coat and smoothed her hands over her hips.

'I shared a compartment with that man who knocked me over. God knows, he is perhaps a terrorist with an infernal machine in his bag. I was almost rendered unconscious when he pulled it off the rack.' She touched her hair with her hand. 'You were most chivalrous. Petersburgers are extraordinarily indifferent. I might have been trampled underfoot, to their utter unconcern.' And she gave Stern an engaging half smile. 'One wonders what other catastrophe can occur before one reaches home.'

He was amused. 'Are you quite recovered now?'

'Oh, *perfectly*.'

'Then I'll see you to a cab,' he said.

'No,' her shoulders lifted in a small, hopeless shrug. 'The horse would doubtless savage me. Anyway, I have only a short walk.'

He scratched his jaw. 'You look as though you'll manage.'

'Thank you again for your kindness.'

'I'm happy to have been of service.' And he saluted in a casual way, as if indifferent to formality.

She watched him for a moment as he moved off, large among the other people thronging the station, and apparently quite sure of where he was going. And how odd that a foreign officer should speak such excellent Russian.

Helen picked up her bag and left the station, standing aside for the horse-drawn cabs clattering across the cobbled square palely lit by ornate wrought iron gas lamps. She'd lied, of course, about the short walk. Her lodgings were miles across the city. But cab fares were outrageous, forced up like everything else by the war. She should perhaps have feigned dizziness and the chivalrous young officer would have felt obliged to take her home. However, to be trapped in a cab with a stranger and a foreigner might itself have presented hazards. Experience indicated that chivalry was often superficial.

A beggar moaned a petition, bowing low and crossing himself. Helen allowed herself one quick glance at his filthy rags and walked on. Beggars were everywhere and it was quite pointless to give them money. They only went and spent it on drink in the dens off the Siennaya Market. A boy with a bundle of newspapers was shouting something about heavy fighting in the Carpathians but Helen barely listened. Life was difficult enough merely to get herself and the bag across the city.

She crossed the Alexandrovsky Bridge and waited at the tram stop. Circles of light, evenly distanced, illumined the long curve of the French Quay. Between the lights were shadows. The river was dark and vast. On the far side black shapes of moored freighters shifted in the slow current. Some of them had been there since autumn, trapped by the German U-boats out in the Gulf.

A red tramcar, brightly lit, clanged towards the stop. Blue sparks crackled off its overhead arm. Helen hauled her bag up. The tram was almost empty now that day was over. Jolting and lurching it moved along the embankment. She counted the coins in her purse. The decision must now be made. Should she go to Professor Zubov's house or straight home? Her stomach was rumbling again. Hunger made its own decisions. Madame Zubov's *koulebiaka* surpassed mere skill, though apart from her talents in the kitchen, and a certain vacuous striving to please, she had few attributes.

A thousand lighted windows in the Winter Palace flickered like quicksilver in the dark waters of the Neva. Further on the slender spire of the Admiralty was dimly white in the light from the quay. Helen peered out at the wide river. The bells of St Isaac's ca-bonged, their sound hesitant, caught on the night breeze. Was it her own romantic assumptions, of the palaces and cathedrals and huge squares, or was it that her whole being responded to the rhythms of the great city?

The tram lumbered slowly over the Nikolayevsky Bridge and clanged its way across Vassili Island. Helen climbed down, dragging her bag with her, and she walked through the quiet streets to the house of Professor Zubov. The house was modestly ostentatious, set back from the road. The bag had become very heavy. She set it down and rang the bell. The Zubovs' servant girl answered.

Madam Zubov's pleasure was undisguised. 'Helen!' And she embraced her then stood back, her round, flat face smiling. 'How lovely! Oh, how *lovely*! Take your coat off.

Such a journey! And how is your poor father? The Professor will be so pleased to see you.' And she busied herself, taking the coat and ushering Helen into the drawing-room.

Helen smiled. It was quite impossible to resist Madame Zubov's spontaneous delight. Though the thought was there in the back of her mind that Madame Zubov's anxious compulsion to please the bright young visitors was partly motivated by her fear that Zubov would be bored with just her company in the house.

'Do sit, Helen, and tell me all that has happened. The Professor is giving another of his open lectures on the management of the war.' Her flat face was momentarily troubled by matters she could barely comprehend. 'He is kept so busy, as a Duma member, and lecturing at the university. I see so little of him. Now you *will* stay for a meal when he returns.'

'Oh, really, Madame Zubov, I don't think I . . .'

'But you must, poor dear, after all those hours on a train.'

For the sake of form she must decline once more, but not so emphatically that Madame Zubov would take it seriously. 'I came merely to tell the Professor I am back, and perhaps borrow a copy of Bogdanovitch's Journal, in preparation for . . .'

'Nonsense. You must stay. I know the Professor would want you to. He was saying only today how he hoped you would be able to assist with the hall arrangements at his next open lecture.' And Madame Zubov eyed Helen anxiously, wondering if all the requirements of hospitality had been met. 'Perhaps you would like a bath? The trains are so dirty. The Professor feels compelled to travel first class. You know how fastidious he is. I'll get Sasha to run the bath for you.' And she left, calling to the servant girl.

Helen went upstairs. If she was to help out at the next open lecture she at least deserved a good meal and the small luxury of the Zubov bathroom. How extravagant to use so much space. The bathroom at home in Uleaborg was small and cramped, steaming up almost as soon as the taps were turned. She undressed slowly, looking in the mirror at the white smoothness of her body. Surely she had much to offer? And she felt a small stab of sadness. Madame Zubov had perhaps once felt the same.

Michael Stern had taken a cab to the Hotel Astoria in the fashionable heart of the city. His room on the fourth floor overlooked St Isaac's Square dominated by the huge dome of the cathedral. He sat on the window-sill and looked down at the square. It had changed since his last visit; the hotel hadn't been here, and neither had the new German Embassy building, empty now. He could still see the beggars, limping across the thin covering of snow, like phantoms of men long dead. He'd walked in that square seven years before, with Baumler, the American. They'd parted over there, by the Horse Guards School, and Baumler had grinned as they shook hands. 'I'll see you back here one day. This city never lets you go.'

Stern closed the window against the cold night air. He hadn't chosen to come back. Frowning, he lit a long black Russian cigarette — he might as well start getting used to these damn things as well. What he most needed was a drink.

Art nouveau work ornamented the peach-coloured walls of the lounge. The furnishings were almost indistinguishable from those of the new European hotels. Stern sat with his drink and observed the comings and goings of the other guests. There were foreign officers — mainly French — and foreign business men assigned to Petrograd to compete for the war contracts. He recognized one of them; small and dark, a Zaharoff agent. He'd last seen him in Persia demonstrating a machine gun.

A few high-class prostitutes decorated the lounge. They provided an unofficial extension to the hotel service. Beautiful, jewelled-fingered, they chattered and glanced speculatively over their glasses of tea. Stern's gut tightened. How long had it been? Too damned long. He watched the red-bloused hotel boy approaching with a letter.

'Excellency Captain Stern?' and the boy bowed. 'This came for you.'

'Where the hell from?'

'A man brought it, Excellency — a foreigner.'

So somebody knew he'd arrived. He gave the boy a coin and slit the flap of the envelope. The notepaper was heavily embossed with the British Embassy letter heading. The sender was an assistant aide with an indecipherable signature, and the message enigmatic. He was to discuss the purpose of his journey with nobody. Not difficult as he hadn't the faintest idea why he was here. He was to contact Colonel H. Southgate at the Military Attaché's Office at his earliest convenience.

He reread the message. There was that feeling of unease again. He knew Colonel Southgate from his service in India. It had been — what? — five years since he and Wyatt and the Colonel had made the survey expedition, through the Khyber and across the Hindu Kush to the Mother of Rivers on the northern boundary.

Stern folded the paper and carefully slid it back into the envelope. The Colonel operated outside the regular military establishment, and that survey expedition had been a stratagem of border intrigue. But damn it, how could he have known that; he was an engineer and a surveyor, not a political officer. Even so, he'd warned Wyatt, hadn't he, as soon as he'd become suspicious, to stay clear of the Russians — small figures on the far bank.

Stern swilled down his drink and signalled for another. A courtesan paused, glancing at him and adjusting her bangle as she crossed the lounge, but he barely noticed her. Five years was time enough to reflect, and it was easy now to see what he should have done back there at the Mother of Rivers. And in any further dealings with Colonel Southgate it would be wise to assume duplicity. He'd found Wyatt exhausted on the northern bank a week after Southgate sent the boy across. Together they'd had to kill the Russian officer, and dispose of him as best they could. The memory of that was still sharp; a weighted body sliding gently under the water. Colonel Southgate had agreed that they'd had no choice and indicated that the matter was best forgotten, but his hands were clean, weren't they?

And now the Colonel was in Petrograd.

Stern left the lounge and climbed the stairs to his room. Events of the past seemingly dead and buried had a way of waiting for you in the future, and travelling round the world made no difference.

2

By December, nights were long and the city still in darkness as early trams clattered along the embankment. Fine snow swirled across the river, shrouding the moored ships and the tug hauling coal barges downstream to the Putilov Works. Beyond the Alexandrovsky Bridge the river widened, its sluggish current blocked by the Baltic tide. The wake of the barges rippled out to the marble wall fronting the Winter Palace on the south side. On Zayachiy Island across the water to the north towered the dark shape of the prison fortress of St Peter and St Paul.

St Peter and St Paul was separate from the city. Cold dampness off the river seeped through barred windows, moistening dank passageways of the Trubetskoy Bastion. Massive oak doors faced onto the passage — each with its spyhole. With the beginning of a new day the guards were making their rounds. In cell Number Forty-six the man with the scarred lip hauled himself up, hands gripping the window bars. He could see only a single tree and the grey outer wall of the bastion, but straining his ears he could hear the sounds of the city. A train. He could hear the whistle of a train far off. He hung until his fingers ached, then lowered himself and sat staring at the blotched walls of his cell. The bells of the basilica boomed the hour and were echoed by the bells of Kazan Cathedral a mile away.

*　　*　　*

Michael Stern had risen early, and left the hotel before eight o'clock. Workers were crossing the city and already there were queues straggling back from the bread shops. Food short and the winter barely begun. There were no damned cabs about at this hour. He walked the two miles to the marshalling yards of the Warsaw terminus.

A long line of ugly boxcars, white-topped with snow, rumbled across the wasteland of converging tracks. What a God-awful hour to come to this place. Stern huddled deep in his greatcoat, distancing himself from the other observers. A gas lamp flared behind him, its harsh light gold-glinting on the steel tracks. He watched critically as sweating, green-clad artillerymen struggled with a field gun, hauling it up a wooden ramp and onto a flatcar. Nineteen hundred and two model, he thought, and not much good even then.

His head ached from drinking with Baumler the night before. One brandy had led to another and he couldn't remember how they'd ended up at the all night place out on the islands. He rubbed his eyes. I drink too much, he thought sourly. Maybe I'm bored with my life. I'm waiting for something to happen.

Southgate was twenty yards away, talking with a group of foreign officers and experts from the American Locomotive Combine. His florid, expressionless face was turned towards General Paul Malnckov, Commander of the Petrograd City Garrison.

Stern returned his attention to the loading of the flatcars. A team swung their gun round and dragged it backwards towards the ramp. A wheel snagged in a rut and the gun came to a standstill. Stern watched the gunners rocking the wheel, their breath steaming in the harsh yellow light. The gun sank deeper and he reflected mordantly. A shambles. He could forgive the poor bloody gunners — they weren't supposed to know anything. The young ensign in charge had apparently never heard of levers. Old reservists and young boys. Nothing was working properly any more.

Colonel Southgate left the group and wandered over, a silver-tipped cane tucked under his arm and his hands sunk

19

in his pockets. His mouth turned upwards in a smile but his pale blue eyes remained expressionless. 'Lookin' after you all right at the Europe, are they, Michael?'

'The Astoria, sir. I'm staying at the Astoria.' That was the second time he'd told him.

Southgate's eyes narrowed as the gun slipped on the ramp, was held, then hauled up another couple of feet. 'Oh yes. The Astoria. Don't like it much. All that art *nouveau* rubbish. And you can't get a decent kipper there.' He paused as another gun was swung round. 'Like a decent kipper, do you?'

'I don't eat them, sir.'

Southgate stared at him as though he'd said something slightly distasteful. 'Well, there's no accountin'.'

Stern was getting impatient. 'I'm anxious to know why I'm here, sir.'

'Do you mean in Russia, or here specifically?'

'Both.'

'Right at this moment you just observe.' Southgate took out a gold pocket watch and frowned at it. 'Look around, Michael. Tell me what you see.'

'I see a young ensign in charge of guns and he appears not to know his arse from his elbow.'

'No, no. That's not our affair. You weren't brought all the way to Petrograd just to concern yourself with nuts and bolts.' The Colonel looked irritated. 'You were the same in India. Left to yourself you'd be on that flatcar with your coat off, like some damned coolie.'

Stern scowled. 'They'll have an accident with those guns.'

'You think like a machine. Give me a broader view.'

The railway rolling stock looked run down from excessive use. Long lines of waggons awaited repair on the sidings. Stern turned his harsh stare on the mounds of freight stacked along the outer wall of a vast shed. Boxes, crates — some broken, machine parts under wet sacking. God knows how they identified anything.

'Our Russian allies are having management problems with their railway,' he said.

'In Imperial Russia the first myth of management is that it exists.' Southgate slid the watch back into his pocket. 'It's like this all the way to Archangel in the north and Vladivostok in the east.'

'God's teeth!'

The Colonel frowned to himself. 'The railways functioned quite well for the first year of the war.' His cold blue eyes surveyed the yards. 'But now we have here the beginnings of a massive crisis. That's why I wanted you to see it for yourself. There are serious shortages of food and coal, here and in Moscow, and the agitators are busy — a lot have slipped back here from exile — stirring up the workers. There'll be trouble before winter is over. Communications are falling apart. At the front the Russian army is exhausted.'

He'd heard the rumours. Brusilov's campaign had ground to a standstill. Infantry without rifles. Guns without shells. And over a million dead since summer.

Southgate swung his cane at a pebble. 'If the army cannot be kept supplied the Russians may have to back out of the war, leaving us and the French to fight the bloody Hun on our own.' He looked up. 'Now we don't want that, do we?'

Stern's eyes narrowed. 'So we are helping to keep them supplied.'

'Yes. Quite. We're doing our best, given our own commitment. And the Americans are helping, of course. But what use are supplies if they don't reach the cities or the Russian armies? All the ports on this side of the continent are choked with off-loaded cargo — only a fraction of it is being shifted.' He poked at the snow. 'Our best hope here, Michael, is the new Murmansk railway.'

'*Our* best hope?' Stern looked at him quickly. 'Seven hundred miles of track strung out across the Karelian wilderness?'

'It links the capital with the Kola Inlet — ice-free all the year round. If we can get it working properly it will keep Russia in the war.'

'*We*? The Murmansk railway is surely a Russian affair?'

Southgate shook his head impatiently. 'We've had a hand in it from the very beginning. Conditions up there on the northern stretch are appalling. The whole damned railway has been thrown together to meet the fourteen month deadline. You take your life in your hands travelling along it. Curves are unballasted, bridges collapse. Just between you and me, they had five derailments last month alone. I've been given the job of liaising between our government and the Russian Minister of Communications. You and I have serious work, Michael. The whole link — Murmansk to Petrograd — must function efficiently.'

Stern eyed the older man cautiously. Southgate had a reputation for subterfuge and ruthlessness that went back twenty years or more. He'd opposed the Russians in Afghanistan, and in Persia where he'd narrowly escaped being murdered. Why had he been made responsible for liaison?

Southgate sensed the question. 'I'm here because these people know I get things done — one way or another. This isn't the northern boundary, Michael. The Russians are on our side.' He smiled slyly. 'For the time being. I'm pleased to have you here,' he added, shifting ground.

Stern scowled, reflecting on his new and unenviable assignment. 'I can't say I'm pleased to be here. Much of that seven hundred miles of track is above the Arctic Circle.'

'Nobody said it was going to be easy. Now we'd better drop the subject. Malnekov is about to join us.'

From pest holes in India to the wilderness of Karelia. It must be because I'm so popular, Stern thought. He watched General Paul Malnekov walking slowly towards them.

Having travelled along the same route as the fading and attractive Tamara Malnekov, Stern was mildly curious about the heavy-shouldered Cossack. He was splendidly dressed in a black greatcoat and fur hat. His spurs made a psing psing sound as he walked. The small neat Cross of St Stanislas was just visible at the throat of his tunic. There was something brutish about his movement.

Malnekov paused and lit a long black cigarette. He stared

impassively at the loading of the flatcars. 'Those guns are destined for the Carpathians.' His voice was harsh. 'If we can find some shells for them they will support my Caucasian Corps.'

'A wild and splendid body of men. They do you credit, Your Excellency. I hear that you are shortly to take up a field command.'

'Yes. I rejoin my corps as soon as a replacement can be found for me here.'

'Early morning sun on lances. I envy you, sir.' Southgate directed a probing glance at the Cossack. 'I'm sure your charming wife will regret your departure for the front. I had the pleasure of meeting her, last night at the Kleinmichael house. She told me of her journey from Paris.'

'Yes. It was tiring for her.' Malnekov stifled a yawn, indicating that the subject was closed. And Stern wondered about the shared life of Madame Malnekov and this polished barbarian from the steppes.

'If you gentlemen have seen enough of this . . .' Malnekov gestured in the direction of the flatcars.

Stern was reluctant to turn his back on the clumsy handling of the field guns. 'Your pardon, Excellency, but I suggest those artillerymen use blocks behind the gun wheels as they move them up the ramp.'

The Cossack glanced at him with a faint flicker of interest. 'Are you a gunner, Captain?' And without waiting for a reply he turned away.

Stern watched his departing back. Bloody cavalry mind, he thought. Southgate waited until Malnekov was out of earshot. 'You amaze me, Michael. Such tact. You haven't changed a bit. Never voice an opinion in front of a Russian general unless he asks for it.'

A soldier shouted and there was the raw sound of iron-rimmed wheels on wood as one of the guns rolled back down the ramp, scattering artillerymen and officers before it crashed to a stop. Malnekov glanced back, then walked on.

Stern didn't say anything.

'Have you ever wondered how many officers have been

passed over for promotion for being irritatingly right?'
Southgate swung his cane like a golf club. 'Come on. I've
got a coffee engagement at the English Club.'

They picked their way across rail tracks to the staff cars.
Stern's head was full of queries. 'How did the Russians
manage to build seven hundred miles of track across the
wilderness in fourteen months, sir? That is an almost super-
human task, given the conditions. I can hardly credit that
men could do it. Where did they find such a huge labour
force?'

'Eighty thousand men have worked on that line; thirty
thousand hired workers from the Volga region, five thousand Finns on six month contracts — they've even recruited
Chinese. Hundreds have deserted from the southern
stretches.'

And Stern was already wondering. 'You can't desert
from the north. There's nowhere to go but wilderness. By
God, it's perpetual night up there for half the year.'

Southgate had that wary look again. 'Conditions are very
bad above the Arctic Circle. They illumine the area with
huge torches — lanterns are useless in the high winds and
snowstorms. Hired men won't work on those sections, so
they have to use . . .' he paused almost imperceptibly
'unfree labour.'

'You mean convicts?'

Southgate nodded. 'Prisoners of one kind or another.'

So this was to be a very special kind of dirty assignment.
'It has been agreed with our government that I work with
forced labour?'

'It's a hard world, Michael. Obviously many men must
die. But the Russians must have that railway working properly if their empire is to survive. It is not our affair where the
labour comes from.'

'Why was I picked for this?'

'Why ask?' Southgate stared at him. 'You're used to
difficult ones, Michael. Leave it at that.'

The question had nagged at him for a long time. 'For five
years, since that expedition to the northern boundary, I've

been doing dirty jobs in every stinking pest hole of India and Persia. Now I've been brought here to shore up bridges in the Karelian wilderness, and with convicts for labour. I think, sir, that I deserve to know why.'

Southgate frowned and assumed his sincere expression. 'I did my best for you, Michael. I'd like you to believe that. Our masters are of the opinion that working prisoners in the frozen wasteland requires a particular kind of stomach.' He paused, weighing his words. 'That Russian officer you drowned. Oh, I explained, and not a word has been said against you, officially. But our masters don't like what you did. They don't like it at all. That is why you are here.'

Stern nodded. Well, he'd guessed it was something like that. He'd just wanted someone to come right out and say it.

'I see this as a great opportunity for you.' Southgate looked brisk. 'Help me to make this railway work and I promise you'll get recognition. There's something in this for both of us.'

Right now he didn't want anything that Southgate could offer. 'When do I leave?'

'You have a week or two, while I'm fixing things up with the Minister. Think of it as a small holiday. Oh, I'd like you to take a look at the Murmansk freight depot — it's half a mile down the tracks. It will give you some idea of our problems. And you can read the survey reports on the construction of the Murmansk line. You'll find copies of them in the Embassy library.' He paused. 'If you are stuck for something to do tonight you can make up a fourth at the English Club.' He stared at Stern accusingly. 'You *do* play bridge, I hope?'

Stern shook his head. He was still feeling bitter, and not particularly co-operative. 'I've been invited to some sort of function at the Meretskov house.'

Southgate's eyes opened wide in amazement. 'House! House! It's a bloody great palace! The Countess Meretskova's charity ball! For God's sake how did you get an invitation?'

'A friend of mine — Martin Baumler arranged it for me.'

'Baumler. The American trader?'

Stern considered. 'Entrepreneur.'

25

'And an odd fellow from all accounts. Mixes with all kinds. Has quite a lot of pull in court circles these days.' Southgate's eyes narrowed. 'Fancy you knowing him. You're a puzzle, Michael. A walking set of contradictions. You don't fit into any identifiable category, and that worries me a little. A slide rule for a mind. Bizarre working-class origins. Scruffy dress — I wouldn't rub my horse down with that uniform you are wearing. And you manage to get yourself invited to one of the biggest social occasions of the year.'

Stern scratched his jaw and frowned. 'I'm not sure I want to go.' He'd been more than a little drunk when Baumler had asked him. 'I suppose it must be better than reading old copies of *The Times* in the English Club.'

'Some of the Embassy people are going.' Southgate looked piqued and jerked his head in the direction of Malnekov climbing into his large black automobile. 'He'll be there, of course. Bloody barbarian.' And his pale eyes registered a momentary glint of malice. 'All that stiff-necked pride. But he's out of favour at court — some rumour of another woman in his life. Now his wife's back and he's off to the front. The Empress doesn't permit scandal.'

Southgate paused, scowling before climbing into his car. 'You haven't mentioned that northern boundary business to anybody since you've been here, have you?'

'No.' He would erase it from his mind if he could. 'Why?'

'The Ambassador had a note from the Minister of the Interior — Okhrana Section, asking if you were the same Captain Stern who took part in the 1911 Survey. It was passed to me for comment.' The Colonel pursed his lips for a moment then shrugged. 'I don't think they suspect anything. They check on all foreigners entering the country. We'll just play it down. Meet me at the Europe tomorrow — eleven o'clock sharp. We'll have a spot of lunch. Grub's quite good there.' And he prodded the driver with his cane.

Stern watched the car edging its way towards the Obvodny exit. He could have asked for a lift but he'd had enough of the Colonel for one day. Anyway, he needed to think.

He crossed the acres of marshalling yards, then out to the Obvodny canal, and he made his way towards the centre of the city. Why had he stayed in the army? He should have turned in his commission five years ago after that northern boundary business. A small pension. A cottage somewhere remote along the Sussex coast, and hills to walk, and a dog maybe. He'd intended to do that — walk those hills until he'd made peace with himself. But in the end he hadn't been able to. Something had stopped him. A penance to perform. Well, there was one ready made for him out there in the Karelian wilderness, with a life shared with criminals, prisoners of war, convicted agitators. The Tsar had a vast pool of labour.

Preoccupied with questions he hadn't asked, and with his suspicions of Southgate's role, Stern reached the Zabalkansky Prospect. A long line of cavalry in field grey approached, moving in the direction of the Warsaw Station. Hooves clattered and lances bobbed gently up and down. On the paving a few people turned to watch and Stern paused as well. That was all Russia had; just columns and columns of men, and horses, and glinting lances to charge the German artillery and machine guns. Some of the watchers looked bitter. They'd seen too many soldiers en route for the front — a prayer and a blessing before being packed into the freight cars for the journey to the south or west.

Stern walked on, fine powdery snow blowing over his boots. The bells of St Nicholas Cathedral ca-bonged the midday hour. He glanced back along Sadovaya Street. What a holy city. Three cathedrals and a dozen churches within a mile radius. He'd reached Hay Square and the area of the markets. Rubbish was strewn on the cobbles. Above the din of the crowd he could hear the strident voices of rag pickers and junk dealers. He had to edge his way between the open stalls. Reeking alleys led off into narrow, unpaved courts with rickety wooden staircases spidering up high blotched walls. It was a vast, foetid rookery extending all the way to the Fontanka. Nothing had changed since he'd last walked here.

A girl sat in a doorway. She wore an old army greatcoat too big for her, and her arm was round a small, sickly looking boy. She looked up and murmured to Stern as he approached. 'Sir, we are hungry. You may have me for three roubles.'

Twelve! She couldn't be more than twelve. He pulled all the loose coins from his pocket and dropped them in her lap. The girl's low voice had drawn an old woman to the doorway, and Stern accepted a blessing as he moved quickly on, though he doubted if God could be found in this festering place. A dazed drunk staggered past him. The Tsar's vodka edict was ignored here, where children could be bought body and soul. And a life was worth nothing.

Why am I so squeamish? he thought. I've seen worse. Only in the civilized West do we have such an exaggerated regard for human life. But a vague guilt nagged at him for that life he'd taken, five years before. There had been no time then to consider its worth as he'd stuffed rocks under the tunic and pushed the corpse out into the stream. The dead are dead. It did no good to think about it. He was still frowning when he reached the Nevsky Prospect.

Forty yards wide and two and a half miles long, the Nevsky ran straight through the rich heart of the city. It was flanked with palaces, government offices and churches. Kiosks and the entrances to noisy arcades were squeezed between elegant shops. The broad thoroughfare accommodated all; typists free for an hour, shoppers rich and poor, mill hands on strike. Stern saw girls from the Imperial Ballet, heavily chaperoned, entering the Silver Bazaar. He moved with the crowd, passing a hurried jagged slogan painted in red on a wall — JUSTICE FOR THE SOLDIERS AND WORKERS. Opulent carriages and automobiles glided confidently by.

He reached the Dvortzovaya and spent the afternoon in the Embassy library, studying the route to Murmansk on the Kola Inlet. It looked even worse than he'd thought. He leaned back and rubbed his eyes. Damn it, he shouldn't have drunk so much last night. And he shouldn't have agreed to attend the Countess Meretskova's charity ball, but he could hardly disappoint Baumler now. Wearily he closed the map case and replaced it. That was enough for one day. Tomorrow he'd start on the railway surveys.

Evening was approaching and it was bitterly cold when he left the Embassy building. Still muzzy headed, he leaned for a while on the embankment wall and looked out over the river. A bell tolled briefly from the dark shape of St Peter and St Paul. Lights glinted on the Troitsky Bridge, and other lights of vehicles passing across, all insignificant against the darkening sky. Rubbish from the moored ships drifted in the sluggish current below the embankment; a spar upjutting like a broken tooth, and a half-submerged humped shape suggesting a weighted corpse. He turned quickly away, suppressing the image.

A girl was approaching along the embankment. Her way of moving held Stern's attention, then he recognized her small hat and remembered. The girl at the Finland Station. He saluted casually as she drew near.

'We cannot continue to meet like this, *dyevooshka*. People will talk.'

For a moment he thought she was going to walk by, but she glanced quickly at him then stopped. Her mouth curved up in a half smile. 'Oh, they will soon tire of us and turn their gossip elsewhere.'

'Even so, we must be more discreet.' I've been too long out of the company of women, he thought. I hardly know how to talk to them.

Her wide eyes measured him. 'And are you enjoying your stay in Petrograd?'

'I never know how to answer a question like that,' he said. 'It depends on your criteria. But certainly Petrograd is an interesting city.'

'Merely interesting!' Now her smile was incredulous. 'Petrograd rivals Paris — or so I am told, for I have never been further west than Grodno. Possibly your sensibility is jaded by much travel?'

He pretended to consider. 'Oh, it's quite civilized here

29

since the arrival of the British Mission. They now provide knives and forks at the Astoria.'

She laughed, her breath steaming in the cold air. 'And polite anarchists double as waiters. Did you find out what happened to that man — with the scarred lip?'

'Not a word,' and he shrugged. 'I saw the police drag him away. There was nothing about it in the newspapers.'

'Doubtless he was a troublemaker. Agitation is indigenous to the Russian soil.'

'I suppose there is a lot to agitate about.'

She nodded without enthusiasm and he assumed she was not particularly interested in reordering Russian society. 'I'm getting a cab to St Isaac's Square,' he said. 'Can I give you a lift?'

'Alas, we are going in opposite directions again. Our relationship is fated.' She touched her hair. 'I am attending a lecture at the university.'

'We should at least exchange names, *dyevooshka*, for that will ensure we one day meet again. I am Captain Michael Stern, engineer and soldier of His Majesty King George the Fifth.' And he bowed.

There was that measuring smile again. 'And I am simply Helen Mirsky of Uleaborg in Finland. Goodbye, Captain Stern.'

'Goodnight, Helen Mirsky.' He watched her as she walked away.

Helen was still smiling to herself, aware of Michael Stern's gaze. He was quite handsome. And what was it about him? — an amused, wry chivalry. Rather bitter, she thought with surprise. Not that she was prepared to consider an English captain. Soldiers were invariably poor, and always going off somewhere.

Helen crossed to the north side of the river. The night wind was blowing along the broad reach and she sank her hands into the pockets of her belted coat. She would rather have stayed at home. Professor Zubov's lecture would of course run over its alloted time. He would bore her and the necessary deception of pretending smiling enthusiasm placed great strain on her facial muscles. However, keeping in with the Professor was an essential element in her plans.

At the Palace Bridge leading to University Quay, Helen hurried her pace, hugging her coat closer to her. It was bad enough merely having to go to the lecture, but selling programmes embarrassed her. And although the programme money went towards the hire charge of the hall, she still felt like a shop girl dispensing slightly shoddy goods. There was, though, the very real possibility of a free meal afterwards. Zubov was not mean, except in large matters.

She reached the Arts building and climbed the broad steps, pondering her dilemma again. How far must she allow Zubov to go in order to secure her degree? The Professor had already indicated an interest bordering on the carnal. To be successful in her studies *and* keep Zubov at bay was becoming increasingly like walking on eggs.

The large hall filled rapidly. It always surprised Helen that so many serious people should want to listen to the Professor. But perhaps there are facets of him that I do not perceive, she thought. Certainly there are men who are worried by what he says. She felt ridiculous with her bundle of programmes, but doubtless Zubov would acknowledge a small debt if her history essay was worth slightly less than a 'satisfactory' grade. She plunged between rows of seats, holding out the folded sheets and dropping money into her tin.

Zubov was approaching, moving with easy grace between the expectant members of his audience. He was dark and a little fleshy, but he had a tense charm. He nodded and smiled to those he knew, and when he reached her Helen discovered with surprise that he was nervous. He dabbed his forehead with a large white handkerchief. 'This is good of you, Helen.' He frowned around. 'Is Tuichev here? I understood he was coming tonight. How much time do I have?' And he took a watch from his waistcoat pocket. 'Another four minutes.'

Helen felt a genuine impulse to soothe him. It was alto-

31

gether odd. She could only sustain her slight contempt for him when he was absent from her. 'You will be quite splendid, Professor, as usual.' A lie. He tended to get lost in his own rhetoric, but his rich, melodious tones and expressive gestures gave his lectures a spurious impression of depth.

'I am thinking of having the lecture notes published.' And nervous as he was he managed to press his thigh against hers. 'You must join me for supper afterwards. Rodzianko will probably come also, and possibly Kerensky if he has returned to the capital.'

'What heady company you keep, Professor.' Helen did a small calculation. A few more free meals and her allowance might just last the term.

'You shall meet some of them. You may find such relationships useful in your future career, Helen.' He rested his hand briefly on her waist. 'Providing you are successful in your degree of course.'

She noticed the slight emphasis on his added comment. He has begun to bargain, she thought. At heart he really is quite contemptible. And she assumed her warmest smile. 'With so many grave responsibilities, I am grateful for your time and attention, Professor.'

'Yes. I am kept busy.' Zubov glanced round the hall and suddenly frowned. 'Not all my duties are pleasant.'

Helen followed his gaze to the slim, dark young man in a rough sheepskin coat, watching them from the rear of the hall.

Zubov's frown turned to anxious irritation. 'That man is Peter Koltsov. He wants news of his brother. I cannot talk to him now.' And he pulled a small notepad from his pocket and scribbled on it. 'Take this note to Koltsov. Tell him that is all I know.'

'But, Professor . . .'

But the Professor was already walking quickly to the steps and up onto the stage.

The applause greeting Zubov lasted for over a quarter of a minute. He stood modestly with his head slightly bowed, then raised his hand in a small graceful gesture of thanks. There was silence and he began:

'Fellow Slavs, for that is what we are first and foremost. Two years have passed since our young men left the ploughs and factories to drive the enemy from Slav soil. Tonight we must address ourselves to the question; has their patriotism been betrayed by those in government?'

Helen stared at the scrap of paper in her hand. The hastily scribbled words chilled her. 'St Peter and St Paul.' What would that message mean to Peter Koltsov awaiting news of his brother?

The slim, dark young man had followed what was happening and stood waiting, but as Helen approached he signalled with his eyes that she should follow him, out through the swing doors to the cold, empty vestibule. There he turned and held out his hand for the scrap of paper.

He looked at it then turned it over to see if there was any other word. Helen watched him. His thin hard face had been moulded as though from within; little left but determination — and passion she thought. And she was angry with Zubov for giving her this task.

'Is there anything I can do?' Her own words surprised her for she really wished that Koltsov would go away.

He shook his head. 'There is nothing anybody can do.' Koltsov's voice was like gravel. He turned and walked towards the main doors.

Helen paused in brief indecision, weighing the conflicting demands of humanity and expedience. Should she call him back and try to talk to him? No, she couldn't. Zubov would need her soon and supper was at stake. Besides, Koltsov was obviously another of the wretched agitators. Even so, he'd looked so defeated.

Helen returned to the hall and sat at the back, determinedly trying to follow what Zubov was saying. But a frown remained in her thoughts, like a small, gnawing presentiment. Until twenty minutes ago she had never heard the name, Koltsov. Yet she half suspected he had already become significant in her life. She dragged her attention back to the lecture.

Zubov should perhaps have been an actor. His voice rose

in angry condemnation of the Tsar's government and General Staff, then sank to hushed reverence as he spoke of the Russian dead. 'Tannenberg! The retreat of 1915. The Carpathians. Is there a Slav in this hall who does not feel shame and anguish for the profligate squandering of our armies?'

It was to middle class intelligentsia that Zubov made his passionate, wordy case for greater Duma participation in the conduct of Russia's badly conducted war. The elite of Petrograd society was in that hour converging on the palace of Countess Natalya Alexandrovna Meretskova.

3

Martin Baumler had left his apartment on the Liteyny Prospect and driven the two miles to the Astoria Hotel. He sat sprawled in a chair while Michael Stern frowningly shaved with an open razor.

'It will be a relatively small affair — eight or nine hundred guests.' Baumler yawned and stretched his long frame. 'Men are away at the war and a lot of families are in official mourning. Death is no respecter of rank. Six feet of earth makes all men equal.' He watched critically as the young man flicked the bright blade across his jaw. 'Tell me, Michael. Why do you use one of those old razors?'

Stern felt his face for stubble. 'I suppose I'm a traditionalist.'

'With your penchant for mechanical efficiency I would have expected you to use a safety razor.' And Baumler looked puzzled. 'You are a bit like a damned machine, you know. Ever think about that?'

'You were saying a minute ago that Sturmer has been kicked out?' Stern scowled at himself. Twice in one day he'd been called a machine.

'Well, yeah, that's what it amounted to. Rasputin and the Empress keep pushing the Tsar into changing ministers — they hardly have time to change the names on the office doors.'

Baumler took out his cigar case. 'The country is drifting towards disaster and nobody seems able to do a damned thing about it.' He sniffed the cigar appreciatively before lighting it. 'There's been a lot of trouble out there on the streets — they had to send in the Cossacks. Malnekov had infantrymen of the city garrison shot because they wouldn't fire on the crowds.' Frowning, he blew a smoke ring and watched it slowly change shape. 'God knows where it all leads to.'

Stern peered critically at his reflected image in the mirror. It doesn't look like me today, he thought. 'I'm just an engineer, trying hard not to think about the larger issues. How does all this affect your business?'

Baumler shrugged. 'I've got manganese for the British machine tool industry held up at Archangel — I won't get it out before the spring. I've got motor cycles for the Artillery Department on the wharves at Murmansk. Can't shift them either. Surprisingly I'm still making money out of war contracts. I may end up rich.'

'I thought you were already rich.'

Baumler laughed. 'All right. Richer. Mind you, mine is small change compared with some in Petrograd.'

He hasn't changed much, except for the grey in his hair, Stern thought. He still looks like a relaxed athlete. 'This ball we're going to. I take it that there will be a lot of very rich people there.'

'Right. Countess Meretskova's high charity function. I believe it is to raise money for the privately sponsored hospital trains.'

'Privately sponsored?'

'There are a number of them. They supplement the hospital trains run by the city zemstvos and the Army Medical Service. Try not to get down wind of a train full of

35

wounded.' Baumler grimaced. 'God, they reek by the time they reach the city. The Countess has a personal interest in the transport of the wounded — she served on one of the trains herself for a while back in 1915, so it's a useful topic of conversation if you meet her.'

Stern didn't even know how one addressed a member of the old aristocracy. 'Is there a Count Meretskov?'

'No. He was mortally injured at the front in the first month of the war. The Countess is his daughter — unmarried. A rare beauty even in this city of attractive women. She has a younger sister. And there was a brother who would have been head of the family, but he was drowned in an accident some years ago.'

'Drowned?' Stern nicked his face with the razor. He frowned at the small seepage of blood then blotted it with a towel. 'Where was he drowned?'

'Damned if I know.'

Stern wiped the razor clean and pulled on his tunic. Hundreds of people are drowned every year. There's nothing significant in it. 'Was the brother an army officer?'

'Yes. It's an army family.' Baumler tilted his head on one side and grinned. 'And you are looking frightfully like a British officer in that scarlet tunic, Michael. Pity the damned thing doesn't fit you.'

Baumler was right. Stern fingered his high collar. The coat was threatening to split, and it smelled of mothballs. He did up the buttons. 'Bloody thing. I haven't worn it for months — no need for it in the places I've been.' He didn't feel comfortable dressed up like this. He pinned his two campaign medals on his breast and took a last look at himself. 'Do you think I'll do? I'll have to, won't I? It's the only dress tunic I've got.'

They left the hotel and walked to Gorokhavaya Street where Baumler had parked his yellow Pierce Arrow automobile.

'You're going to enjoy yourself, Michael. The Meretskov palace is one of the show places of this great city.'

Stern nodded with assumed enthusiasm and stared out of

the window as the automobile crossed the Fontanka. Lights flickered like quicksilver on the canal. Then he noticed two policemen, large in their heavy greatcoats, hustling a shabby, bearded man with a fur hat. One of them knocked the hat off and the man stooped to pick it up, bowing low before he put it on again. Stern looked away. I need a drink, he thought.

The Pierce Arrow joined the line of vehicles moving slowly between massive wrought iron gates to the Meretskov courtyard. Pale gas lamps were outshone by the lighted windows of the pink marble palace.

Stern felt constricted in the tight tunic. The collar chafed his neck, and he was conscious that he looked dull by comparison with the brilliantly attired Russian officers. With Baumler he followed the procession up the broad steps. They could hear music from the ballroom. Liveried servants stood in attendance on the guests. Brocaded wraps and furs fell from naked shoulders.

They ascended the marble staircase. Along a corridor lined with mirrors, softly murmuring women glanced at their reflected images.

'See, Michael,' Baumler whispered, 'it doesn't matter how low cut the dresses are so long as the cleavage is compensated by an abundance of jewellery.'

The music was louder as they approached the gilded doorway. Stern was still pondering his need for a drink. What was he doing here anyway, among these over-privileged people squandering their time? But as they entered the high-ceilinged ballroom he was immediately caught up in the magic of his surroundings. His response startled him. He stood, trying to attune to the music and movement. Hundreds of dresses rustled as graceful women swirled past in the arms of their glittering officers. The colour astounded him. He tried not to stare at white perfect shoulders and slim arms.

'Where else would you see anything like this?' Baumler asked.

Where indeed? In remote and sweltering places, bereft of

anything feminine, he might have tried to imagine such a scene. Confronted with the reality he felt awkward. This change is too extreme, he thought, and edged with Baumler along the perimeter of the room.

A girl, laughing with her young officer of the Imperial Guard, clutched at the front of her dress. Her necklace had broken, scattering pearls across the floor. The officer stooped, casually picking some of them up; then they turned away, still laughing, leaving pearls behind them. Stern observed the proud, throw-away gesture. He took up a pearl from beside his boot and stared after the couple. 'Do you suppose they may all have to pay one day, Martin?'

Baumler grinned. 'What a bill that would be. Come on. Let's see who's here.' And as they moved on he indicated with a jerk of his head. 'The men in badly fitting evening dress are detectives. Thieves frequently infiltrate these great functions.'

Well, there was a rouble or two to be made here. All you had to do was bend down and pick up pearls.

Baumler seemed on good nodding terms with many people. An ancient, slightly deformed and heavily rouged lady held out a thin, talon hand. 'Mister Baumler. Shall we see you at my card party on Saturday?'

And Baumler kissed the talon. 'It will be my pleasure, Highness.'

'Who was that?' Stern whispered as they moved on. But Baumler was staring around. 'I'll tell you later. Relax. You're still frowning.'

'Habit,' he said. He had just noticed the Cossack, General Paul Malnekov, magnificent in gold and black. The woman with Malnekov had her head bowed, but Stern remembered her immediately. Tamara Malnekov, his fellow traveller on the journey from Newcastle to Russia. She had an attraction enhanced in some way by her fading beauty. Warmth was evident in her eyes as she leaned forward, nodding gravely as an elderly French officer spoke to her. She still had a fine body. Malnekov was stifling a yawn, and Stern wondered if the rumours about him were true. With a woman like that why would he need another?

Baumler peered over the heads of the dancers. 'I'm looking for the Grand Duke Serge. Very tall thin fellow. He and I have the beginnings of a deal going. Keep your eyes open for him.'

They reached the far side of the ballroom. Stern still had the pearl in his hand. He didn't know what to do with it. Full length windows faced out onto the balcony. Two were open a little, despite the chill air, and the men in badly fitting dress suits stood casually by them. Baumler was still looking for the Grand Duke. 'He's head of the Artillery Department and an honest man. Most unusual . . .' And he broke off. 'Take a look over there, Michael. It's our hostess, the Countess Natalya Alexandrovna Meretskova.'

Stern followed his gaze, to the young woman in the long white dress. Baumler was right about her. She had a rare beauty.

'Y'have to admit to life's little inequalities.' Baumler grinned. 'Imagine looking like that *and* being rich.'

'How rich is she?' Stern asked. 'Just quote me a rough figure — to the nearest million will do.'

'God knows. The family has estates at Ustreka and in the Crimea. They had a large house in Paris but sold it when the war came. In this city alone they own the mill your father worked in.'

The Countess had seated herself. She was speaking to a girl younger than herself. An officer of the Semionovsky Regiment was standing, head bowed to hear what she was saying. She gestured and smiled as the orchestra began a waltz. The officer took the arm of the younger girl and they joined the dancers.

'That's the sister, Anna,' Baumler said. 'And the young rake she's dancing with is Captain Rykov, the family escort.'

'Is the sister rich too?'

'I guess so.'

'Which one do you think I ought to marry?'

'The young one is a bit of a prig, but if you're just after

money I suppose either of them would do. As the Countess is alone for a moment we ought to seize the opportunity and greet her.'

Stern felt wary. Supposing his tunic split, or some damned thing. 'This is all a bit rich for my blood. What I really need is a drink.' But he followed Baumler. 'How do you manage to meet people like her, Martin?'

'Simple.' Baumler grinned. 'I gave a hefty donation towards the hospital she supports. Contributing to worthy causes is good for business.' And he approached the Countess and bowed.

Her wide set eyes turned to Stern as he was introduced. 'Captain Stern, from England?'

'Only briefly in England, madam. I came here from India.'

'Ah, India.' Her lips parted slightly. 'Soldiering for your far-flung empire. And the sun has bleached your hair, making you look even more English.'

Stern was aware of the distancing effect of her polite smile. He had the impression that she was skilled at opening comments designed to put people at ease. Her dress rustled softly and the star pinned below her left breast glinted, catching the light as she turned to Baumler. 'Mr Baumler has been in our country for so long, but we despair of making a Russian of him.'

Baumler stretched back his handsome head and laughed. 'No, you'll not do that, madam. But I suspect that I am more Russophile than any foreigner in Petrograd. Where else would I go? Not even in Paris will I find such splendour.' He bowed to Natalya Meretskova. 'Or such beautiful women.'

Her attention seemed caught for a moment on somebody across the room. 'I'm sure you rehearsed that speech, Mr Baumler.' And smiling, she surveyed her guests.

She's looking for somebody, Stern thought. Perhaps Baumler thought the same. He glanced round, then his face lit up. 'By heavens, there *is* the Grand Duke Serge. Would you excuse me. He and I have a matter to discuss.' And he left Stern and the Countess together, his broad back disappearing among the guests.

'What has brought you to Russia, Captain?'

'I'm an engineer, madam.' He pushed his hand through his thick hair, wondering what one should say to a countess. 'I — I build things.'

'And what do you build in those far off dusty outposts of empire?'

'Ah, well. I've recently surveyed for eighty miles of railway in northern India. It is very hot there at this time of the year.' He paused and frowned. 'Surprisingly, you get a lot of rain in the Bengal region.' What a fascinating conversationalist he was. He fingered his tight collar. 'I built a bridge over a tributary of the Ganges, high up in the mountains. The sides rose sheer, and the river thundered hundreds of feet below. Black bears used to forage around our camp at night, and wild dogs. The bridge shortened the ancient caravan route. I found a silver coin, very old, turned up by a spade. It was Greek.' And it filled me with wonder, he thought.

'Yes? Continue.'

He'd been too long out of civilized company. What else could he tell her? Of the giant rock shaped like the hand of God, or the holy man who'd told him he would kill twice? He smiled. 'I think, madam, that I would weary you as much as I weary myself. Perhaps you would care to waltz?'

She paused almost imperceptibly. 'You don't have to, Captain. I have worked all day in the charity hospital and I am rather tired.'

'Quite so.' He had a momentary image of her arranging flowers in pots.

'My sister waltzes enough for both of us,' she continued. 'But being very young she has an excess of energy in the evening.' And she glanced towards the couple.

Anna Meretskova was moving elegantly in the arms of Captain Rykov. Stern watched them for a moment. The girl's expression was imperious — mouth a little too firm to be perfect. She appeared to be arguing with her partner.

Stern noticed the covetous eyes of other girls as Rykov and Anna glided between the dancers.

'They make an attractive pair,' he said.

'Yes.'

The single word was clearly intended to end the topic, and now the Countess was discreetly scanning the guests again. 'I am surprised that you speak such excellent Russian, Captain.'

'I was raised here in Petrograd.' Should he disclose his background? Why should he not? 'My father was a mechanic. He was foreman of the Kazakhov Mill owned by your family.'

She looked startled. 'How interesting.' And she continued hurriedly as though afraid of further embarrassing revelations. 'We could not have built up our industry without the help of English engineers and artisans.'

He sensed her guarded shift and felt disappointed in her. 'Those who came out here were a tough, raw breed of men, good at their jobs.'

The Countess nodded politely. 'Unfortunately our mill and factory workers are still without basic education. They become easy prey to agitators.'

'If differences in Russian society were less obvious there would perhaps be fewer agitators, madam.'

She glanced at him coolly. 'Agitators merely disrupt progress. We are trying to drag Russia into the twentieth century but it will take time. We cannot change our world overnight.'

He ought to say something conciliatory. But he remembered the young girl in the market area, ready to sell herself for three roubles — the price of a modest meal. 'With respect, Countess, a distant utopia is of little use to a hungry worker — or a soldier far away at the front. Men and women must see a better future or they lose heart — and think of revolution.'

Her expression hardened. 'You must not assume that the aspirations of Slavs are the same as those of West Europeans.'

42

He stooped and picked up another pearl. 'Surely all people want the same things in the end.'

'Perhaps people do not always know what is good for them.' Now her tone was chilly.

Damn it, he shouldn't have provoked her like that. How to salvage the sagging relationship? 'I'm sorry, madam,' and he smiled. 'I'm marginally less irritating on the subject of bridges.'

'Then perhaps you should be offering your English expertise to our engineering officers, there are a number of them present. Please do not let me detain you.' She began scanning the guests again.

He felt stung. 'I regret that the rough and ready candour of the frontier has become habit with me. I'm not used to the conventions of your fastidious society, madam.' He bowed stiffly and left her.

His anger began to evaporate as soon as he was alone. It's a knack I have, he thought. Introduced to the most beautiful woman in the city, it took me only ten minutes to offend her. Baumler is right. I think like some bloody machine.

He wandered aimlessly around the edge of the ballroom. What he should have done was make polite chat about Russia's war effort, the way other people did. Why hadn't he been able to do that? He paused, groping with the thought. A woman like her — he'd assumed she'd expected honesty from him. Even so, it was her country he'd been criticizing.

Dancers swirled past. The evening and the music were working their magic. He watched Anna Meretskova. Gone was the imperious lift of her chin; and held lightly by Captain Rykov she closed her eyes to waltz the length of the ballroom. It was the stuff of dreams.

He edged his way towards the entrance of the ballroom. A hussar officer was laughing a little too loudly with his partner. He smelled of brandy, so the Tsar's edict was being discreetly ignored somewhere in this great palace. Stern went in search of a drink.

Blue-coated servants stood to attention, expressionless,

along the broad gallery adjacent to the ballroom. A few couples were seated, cooling themselves after the rigours of the waltz. Or maybe the evening was far enough advanced for the exchange of confidences, Stern thought.

A further stretch of gallery was lined with portraits of past members of the great house. Large among them was a full length equestrian Count Meretskov, the guns of Borodino in the background. Stern turned a corner, no longer sure of where he was going, his footfalls soundless on the thick carpet. How many servants to clean such a vast building? At what cost had these palaces been constructed on the marshlands? Tens of thousands of peasants had died turning Peter the Great's dream into reality. It was a city built on bones.

He paused startled before a painting of three children. The likeness of the girl in the centre was unmistakable. Natalya Meretskova at eleven or twelve perhaps, with long yellow plaits, her hand resting on the shoulder of a very small Anna. Next to them was a boy, slightly older than Natalya, dressed in the uniform of the elite Corps of Pages. Stern peered carefully at the young face. This then was the brother, who later became an officer and was drowned. Was there just a possibility that it was the officer he'd killed? He couldn't remember the face of the man he'd pushed out into the current of the river — he'd obliterated it from his memory. No. How could it be the same? That nagging guilt was playing tricks on him again. But now the need for a drink was becoming insistent. He moved on.

The music of the ballroom was muted by distance. Stern found the library, its doors open. He went in and looked around him. There was nobody there. The high walls were lined top to bottom with heavy ornate bookstacks. Fine leather bindings crowded the shelves; Russian, French, German. There were shelves of English writers. He slid out the poems of Tennyson. The binding cracked as he opened the cover. It had probably never been looked at.

Lower down on the stack were a dozen or more books obviously in regular use. He thumbed through a text on anatomy. Who would be reading that? There were neat pencilled notes in the margin of a cheap, cloth-backed translation of 'Notes on Nursing' by Florence Nightingale, 1859. A note book filled with the same pencilled script had been slid into the back of 'Diseases of the Urban Poor'. Stern examined it. Below the date on each page were listed names, ages, diagnosis and treatment, with sometimes an addition squeezed in the margin indicating success or failure. There was an exclamation mark beside the recorded death of a child.

Frowning, he replaced the notebook. Damn, he felt like an eavesdropper. And worse, he'd guessed who used those books. Hadn't the Countess said she'd spent the day working in the charity hospital? And he remembered now that Baumler had mentioned that she'd served at the front with a hospital train. He groaned to himself. A bloody machine. A slide rule for a mind.

He left the library, and guided by distant sounds of the orchestra began his return to the ballroom. The paintings adorning the walls of the corridor looked unfamiliar. He paused. Somewhere back there he'd missed his way. This looked like a much more private part of the palace. And it hadn't occurred to him until then that somebody might appear and ask him what he was doing there.

The music was louder from beyond glass doors ahead of him, so he opened them and stepped out onto a broad balcony extending along the rear of the palace. It was dark where he stood. Full length windows faced onto the gardens. Forty or fifty yards further on the windows were lit and he could hear sounds of laughter and a mazurka.

A couple, hardly more than silhouettes, stood looking up at the moon. He watched them as they embraced briefly before turning back towards the ballroom. When they had gone he moved quickly along the balcony, then paused again as a man emerged from where the couple had just entered. He couldn't recognize him at this distance, yet there was something familiar about the set of those shoulders.

The man lit a cigarette, then stepped into the shadows. The cigarette glowed as he turned his head, glancing quickly in each direction, then it was extinguished.

Stern watched, curious. He couldn't quite dismiss the notion that the man had been waiting for the young couple to leave before stepping out onto the balcony. Perhaps he was merely tactful. But now, damn it, the fellow had begun to walk in his direction. He seemed to be avoiding the light.

Stern edged back against a long, unlit window. The absurdity of his position was now apparent. Supposing the approaching man was one of the detectives on the lookout for thieves? He'd still got those pearls in his pocket. And what would he say if he was asked why he was in a private part of the palace? If he hadn't arrogantly offended the Countess he could walk up to that man, comment that he'd got lost, then allow himself to be led back to the ballroom. But the thought of explanations, possibly passed on to Natalya Meretskova, was too embarrassing. Wiser to step back through the window behind him and wait in that unlit room until the man had passed. He pressed the cold glass with his hand and a voice called softly from the darkness within.

'Paul?'

He heard the rustle of a dress, and the voice quite close to him. 'We have only a few minutes.'

He turned and retreated rapidly along the balcony to the glass doors.

It was fairly simple now to find his way to the ballroom and he entered through the huge, gilt doorway. The dancers seemed tireless. A liveried servant stepped quickly between couples to scoop up long strips of tulle torn by spurs from trailing dresses. Stern searched for Baumler and eventually found him standing alone.

'Michael! Where did you get to?'

'I'm not sure. I took a look round and got lost.'

'Did you see anything interesting?'

'Yes,' he said, and left it at that. 'How did you get on with the Grand Duke Serge?'

'Not so good. He's got even more problems than me, what with all the graft along the supply routes.' Baumler shrugged wearily. 'We'll leave here now if you've had enough of all this.'

'I think they'll manage without me. What do I do with these damned pearls?'

'I'll give them to the Countess — for one of her charities.' Baumler took the pearls and peered around. 'I wanted to thank her for the evening but I can't see her. Can *you* see her?'

Stern knew that the Countess wasn't there, but he scanned the room anyway. 'What do you say we go out to the islands for a drink?'

'Good idea.' Frowning, Baumler continued to search. 'I think I need one. What place did you have in mind?'

'Somewhere noisy, where people are uncomplicated.'

Baumler grinned. 'We'll go to the Lantern.' And then he looked towards the gilt doorway. 'There's the Countess.' He whistled softly and appreciatively. 'By God, where would you ever find another woman as beautiful as her?' He smiled slowly. 'You know, Michael, this modest gathering barely does her justice. I remember her, very young — sixteen or thereabouts. And her brother waltzing with her right down the centre of this ballroom, while all of Petrograd society watched.'

Stern nodded and looked at the Countess Natalya Alexandrovna Meretskova standing poised at the entrance of the room. She glanced coolly round then walked along the rim of the dancers, pausing to speak to guests.

'I'll go and bid her goodnight,' Baumler said, and he moved off.

Stern watched. The Countess smiled as her sister and Captain Rykov joined her. Her head was tilted, listening as the younger girl spoke, but her eyes were on the long windows facing onto the balcony. Baumler reached her and said something that made her laugh, white teeth perfect.

The Cossack general, Paul Malnekov, stepped in from the balcony and paused for a moment, surveying the dancers. Then he joined Madame Malnekov and the elderly French officer.

Stern wondered at his own sharp feeling of ill ease. Stupid of me, he thought. I'm distanced from these confident, exquisite people; a stranger from a far off country who accidentally stumbled on an assignation. None of this has anything to do with me. And the man I killed five years ago never danced with the Countess in this great ballroom.

4

The city census for 1897 had indicated a million and a quarter inhabitants, but by 1916 the number was almost doubled. Improvised log dwellings and cheap brick tenements straggled out over the marshlands to the south and west. In the Schlusselburg Road district eighteen mills were silent, gates locked because of the new wave of strikes, but acrid smoke still gouted from some of the high factory chimneys, fanning out over the industrial slums. Sunlight filtered through the smoke, touching blotched walls and grime-streaked windows of the Charity Hospital of St Saviour. A queue formed each day at the dispensary entrance in Kazyanskya Street.

Countess Natalya Meretskova glanced along the drab line of people. There were more of them today. Their patience puzzled her. She frowned down at her clipboard and called a name, waiting while a shapeless woman shuffled her small boy forward. Natalya was accustomed to pale, unhealthy faces but she could not get used to the smell. I lack charity, she thought. 'Come. The Doctor will see you now.'

She watched in silence as Doctor Mendel Strozhov examined the ugly eruptions on the boy's hands. Lack of elementary hygiene and poor diet, the fourth case that morning.

Strozhov glanced up and nodded to her. 'Sulphur ointment.'

The boy made no sound as she tended him, and Natalya forced herself to smile at the mother. 'You must be sure he keeps his hands clean. Put the ointment on each day. Do you understand? His hands must be kept clean,' she repeated. And she took some coins from a tin. 'Buy him green vegetables.'

There was hostility in the woman's eyes as she muttered her thanks and left with the boy. Natalya went to the sink and scrubbed her hands.

Light was poor through the narrow, high window. Doctor Strozhov squinted and poked around on his desk. 'Where have I put my glasses, Natalya Alexandrovna?'

She sighed and picked them up from where he had left them, then returned to the sink. Strozhov put the glasses on, letting them slide down his thin, Semitic nose, and he began writing in minute script on a record card. 'All this,' and he gestured. 'It disgusts you, doesn't it?' His bald head shone in the hissing, yellow gaslight.

She dried her hands and picked up the clipboard. 'Yes.'

'Why don't you work in the office instead?'

'Because I don't want to.' Untrue.

'The older I get the less I understand people. For forty years your family has maintained this hospital.' He finished writing and looked brisk. 'You have barely recovered your health after service with the hospital train. You could easily pay somebody to do what you are now doing.'

'And you can stop giving me advice.'

Strozhov's eyes glinted with amusement and he lifted his shoulders in a small shrug. 'Who do we have next?'

'A man with a filthy bandage on his upper arm. He seems reluctant to explain what is wrong.' Natalya wiped the table with turpentine and went to the door.

The man was perhaps twenty-five, collarless and unshaven. He held his right arm awkwardly as he rolled his sleeve back. Natalya carefully removed the filthy, yellow-stained dressing and suppressed the impulse to retch. The skin was stretched, crimson, round a deep, dried tear in the flesh.

Strozhov hummed softly, his eyes narrowing as he gently touched the ugly swelling. He'd seen wounds like this before, a long time ago in the wars. His wire-rimmed spectacles slid down his nose again and he went to the dispensary door and closed it. 'How did this happen?'

The young man looked down almost wonderingly at his arm, as if he couldn't quite believe that it belonged to him. 'An accident in the factory, Your Honour.' And pausing. 'Koltsov said I should come.'

'Yes?' Strozhov frowned as he soaked cotton wool with spirit. 'I'll have to open it. Sit with your forearm on the table and clasp the sister's hand.'

Natalya compelled herself to watch as the thin, shining blade touched the swelling. The man made no sound, but she felt his grip tightening as the stretched flesh split open, obscenely gouting yellow pus and blood. His face turned chalk white and sweat formed on his forehead.

Strozhov finished. 'I ought to report this, you know.' He dropped the scalpel into a tray and nodded to Natalya to clean the wound. The man wiped his dirty sleeve across his face and closed his eyes for a moment. 'If you would say it was caused by a machine, Your Honour, I would be grateful.'

Natalya tried not to let her curiosity show as she bandaged the wound. Strozhov sighed and took two tablets from a bottle. 'If you get a fever take these. Keep the dressing clean.'

'Thank you, Your Honour.' The man glanced in Natalya's direction.

'It's all right.' Strozhov looked at him levelly.

The man seemed relieved. He rolled his sleeve down and stood. 'We won't forget you, Doctor.' And he quickly left.

Natalya stared. 'What was that all about — why did you say you ought to report it?'

Strozhov shrugged. 'I'm surprised it wasn't obvious to you. A sabre wound. He's been in a brush with the

Cossacks. Did you see his hands? He's a steel worker. Probably one of the strikers from Aboukov's.'

She gaped and gave a small incredulous laugh. 'A sabre wound! You mean he's an extremist — a political agitator?'

Strozhov groped around. 'Where did I put my glasses?' He found them again and began filling in a record card. 'Political agitator? What does that mean in Russia today? A man trying to get a living wage for his family.' His pen scratched. 'We'll call it an industrial accident.'

The gas lamp hissed. Natalya looked at him for several seconds. 'You are so sure I will say nothing?'

He nodded. 'Yes, Natalya Alexandrovna, I am sure you will say nothing. Now, who is next?'

She paused as if about to speak, then changed her mind and went to the door.

They worked steadily through the afternoon, until the last patient had been treated. Natalya began to scrub her hands again. 'In the course of time we shall change Russia.' She frowned. What had that arrogant English captain said? A distant utopia is of little use to a hungry worker. 'Meanwhile, if we have any more sabre wounds I would rather you didn't tell me.'

The doctor grunted to himself. 'Very well. But if you work in this part of the city you have to give these people your love in return for their trust.' He began writing again. 'You give them everything but that.'

Natalya stared down at her hands. I can never get them clean enough, she thought. 'Are you saying that I shouldn't work in the hospital founded and maintained by my family?'

Strozhov put down his pen and looked puzzled. 'It is not that I want to lose you, Natalya Alexandrovna. With all your experience you have become an excellent nurse. And God knows, with so many away at the war you are needed here. But your distaste for the work makes me wonder why you continue so determinedly.' He glanced at the sensual curve of her body. If I were a young man again . . . He let the thought tail off. 'If you did not come here I would miss you.' And he shrugged. 'Who else would remember where I put my glasses?'

'And who else would put up with you?' Natalya paused for a moment and bit her lip. 'I shall have to spend more time here. Katyn Lesechko and two other nurses are joining the Army Medical Service. And we are now committed to taking in wounded from the front — the Alexander Ward is being cleared in readiness.'

He frowned. 'We are already overstretched. When are the wounded expected?'

'Soon — before Christmas. The military hospitals are overcrowded. With Katyn leaving, I must take charge of the Alexander Ward.'

'I'm not sure you should do this, Natalya.' Strozhov shook his head.

'There really is nobody else.'

'Your last tour of duty with the hospital train — right through the retreat of 1915. It took too much out of you. I suspect you are still not completely recovered.'

'It will only be until somebody else can be found.'

'And your bouts of sickness?' Strozhov was still concerned. 'You were vomiting every day, even after your return from the front.'

It was revulsion, she thought, a conditon of the mind. 'You examined me yourself and found nothing physically wrong. If it is necessary for me to take charge of a ward full of wounded, then I'll manage. Now let us change the subject — please.'

'Very well.' Strozhov sighed. 'How is that sister of yours — Anna? We don't see much of her. Does she still drink a pint of water each day as I told her?'

Natalya smiled to herself. 'Yes.'

'Flushes the system through. Coarse bread is similarly good for the bowel movement.'

'You take perverse pleasure in embarrassing her. And now you ask why she doesn't visit the hospital.'

Strozhov's eyes glinted. 'Well, she is rather imperious for one so young.'

'And you told Nina Nicolaievna not to wear stays.' Natalya paused, and because she was fond of the old man she added a note of caution. 'You also tend the wounds of political extremists. If you continue in this way you will be barred from practising.'

'I am a Jew, and in Russia that means I am merely tolerated.' Strozhov rested his chin on his hands. 'Why would they need an excuse to bar me from practising? And I am getting too old to care what happens to me. But I do care about you, Natalya Alexandrovna. May I give you one last piece of advice?'

'If you feel you *must*. And I am sure it will not be the last.'

Strozhov had taken his coat from its hook and was pulling it on. 'Make peace with yourself,' he said.

The smile faded from Natalya's face. 'Goodbye, Doctor.'

Make peace with herself? Peace comes with the absence of passion. She put the bowls and instrument dishes in the sterilizer ready for the next day, and turning, caught her reflected image in the glass door of the wall cabinet. She stared at herself, touching her face with her fingers. How strange that she should still look the same — as that other time before she knew the fierce need that still shocked her with its suddenness. Remembering, her cheeks burned and she turned quickly away. Three days and no word from Malnekov. It did no good to think about it. She dragged the bin of filthy dressings out to the corridor. Love — lust. How to separate them in the mind when one seemed so much part of the other?

Natalya looked round the dispensary. There was nothing left to be done. She turned out the flickering, hissing gas lamp.

Peter Petrovich was waiting with the carriage and grumbling softly at the horses. 'You are late again, young Highness. It is all wrong. In the old Count's time young women spent their mornings with their hairdressers.' He opened the door of the carriage for her. 'Two more of the stablemen have been recalled to the army. I suppose you will expect me to do their work as well.'

Captain Gregory Rykov, escort to the Meretskova sisters, was asleep in the carriage. He woke as Peter Petrovich helped Natalya in. He was twenty-eight years old, but faint indications of dissipation were already evident in his thin, handsome face. 'My apologies, Countess.' He blinked and straightened himself. 'I dozed a little.'

Natalya settled herself in the corner seat. 'Were you at the card tables all night, Captain?'

'Some of the night,' and he politely stifled a yawn.

'But you managed to drag yourself from your bed in time to take Anna riding?'

'You know I live to serve you both, Countess.'

Natalya smiled very slightly and looked out of the carriage window.

Old Peter Petrovich clicked at the horses and they moved off towards the Liteyny.

'Your sister wishes to attend the Maryinsky this evening, with Ryjitsa and one of the Hitrovna girls — Karsavina is dancing in "Sylvia".'

'Will you go with Anna?'

Rykov gave an almost imperceptible sigh. He hated the ballet. 'Yes, of course. Unless you need me.'

'Anna is concerned for you.' Natalya eased herself and stretched her legs. 'Major Ryjitsa says you won from everybody at the Lantern then lost it all the next night.'

'Is she concerned because I won, or because I lost?'

'I am too weary for subtlety.' Natalya leaned her head back on the velvet upholstery. 'Have you examined the accounts of the Ustreka estate?'

'I did it yesterday.'

'And Tarkhankut?'

'Last week.' He coughed into his handkerchief and paused to recover his breath. 'Expenditure is up, as I told you it would be.'

'Are you well?'

'I'm well enough, madam.' He smiled. 'This raw weather.'

She glanced quickly at him. Rykov's organization of

Meretskov affairs was faultless. Was his boredom a pose? She had recently begun to notice his eyes on her body, but assumed it was a passing interest. Now he seemed preoccupied, staring unseeing out of the window. Natalya closed her eyes and her thoughts returned inevitably to Malnekov. Why had he sent no word? For the sake of self-respect she must repeat to herself that he was too busy with the demands of the city garrison. But it wasn't true, and she knew it. The Empress was displeased. Malnekov was afraid of the consequences. And, oh God, was it worth all this worrying?

She breathed deeply now that she was free from the stale, tainted air of the hospital. Could she ever be *completely* free of it? It is in the mind, she thought. Yes. Why else did she sometimes wake in the night with the foul odours of the dressings in her nostrils? Illicit desires, fulfilled, must be paid for one way or another.

Gregory Rykov watched her and wondered. She would fall asleep before they reached the Liteyny. She goes to that hospital four days a week with the same cheerless resignation that I go to the gaming table. In my case it is because I do not know what to do with my life. In her case it is guilt. He coughed into his handkerchief again. That lung wound from Tannenberg might kill him yet.

The carriage clattered into the courtyard of the Meretskov palace. Rykov and Natalya climbed the broad steps and entered the colonnaded entrance hall.

'Facilities for the wounded have been seriously stretched by Brusilov's campaign.' Natalya took off her fur hat and shook out her hair. 'The Empress has suggested that we turn more of the large estate houses into convalescent hospitals. Ustreka could be easily adapted.' She shrugged very slightly. 'But part of me wants to keep it just as it was when Father and Ivan hunted there.'

Rykov nodded. 'I think your father would approve of the change.'

'The dogs still miss him.' Natalya paused at the foot of the stairway, frowning to herself. 'Ivan dead, then Father killed in the war. I must make all the decisions, good or bad.' She took the letter from the tray held out to her by Vasya, the house servant. 'Sometimes I miss Ivan dreadfully. I find myself asking him what I should do, even though I know he cannot tell me.'

'I miss him also.'

'To drown so far from home. Even after five years I can hardly believe it, and I half expect him to walk through that door.' She stared down at the handwriting on the envelope, then continued slowly as though her thoughts were really elsewhere. 'Foolish of me, of course. The dead do not come back. We cannot tell what sense they would make of our actions, or what they would urge us to do.'

With sudden insight Rykov wondered if her last comment was prompted by the handwriting on the unread letter. 'We must assume they understand our human frailty,' he said. And he watched her as she ascended the stairs. The smell of the hospital was in her hair and clothes, but she was still the most desirable woman he knew.

Rykov went into the old Count's study and poured himself a brandy. Anna would be too busy to seek him out with her probing questions. He speculated on probable activity in the upper part of the palace. Anna would be chattering and comparing white dress against yellow dress against blue, whilst Natalya wearily stripped off her clothes. Stirring, he was momentarily unwilling to suppress the image of her body. He downed the brandy in one gulp and went to the window, staring out across the courtyard to the traffic on the Nevsky Prospect.

Natalya had read the letter, and she reread it in the brief moment when Anna left to change her dress. Malnekov would be waiting for her tonight. She lay back in the marble bath and stared at the ripples of reflected light on the ceiling. It was strange that her flesh should tingle with expectation, quite independently of her already doubting mind. There was an urgency behind his hastily scribbled words. Something had happened — some change in his circumstances. God knows, she knew him well enough. Frowning, she bit her lip. What a fool she had become, her life no longer her own. And she smoothed her hands over her thighs.

Anna returned carrying a blue dress. 'Oh! You are still in your bath. I wondered if I might borrow your ruby pendant tonight. I have contrived that Major Ryjitsa and Elizabeth should attend the ballet with Captain Rykov and me. Natalya, you are not listening.'

Natalya rose and took the towel from Anna. 'Yes, I am. You are saying that you intend to meddle in the lives of Major Ryjitsa and Elizabeth Hitrovna.' And she wondered for the hundredth time, should she summon all her will and end the affair with Malnekov?

'But it is entirely for their own good, Natalya.' Anna's firm mouth tightened determinedly. 'The Major is so shy. Unless he and Elizabeth are pushed together, nothing will happen. The Major's wounds were not as serious as those of Captain Rykov and he may shortly have to return to his regiment.' She glanced at her sister. 'Of course, Captain Rykov cannot be sent back to the front — not with his damaged lung.' She paused, frowning. 'He never talks about what happened to him, and I do not feel that I can ask. Is it true, that story, about Father taking the St George Cross from his own tunic and pinning it on Captain Rykov?'

'Yes, it's true.' Her thoughts were really elsewhere. Natalya pulled on her bath robe. Working with the wounded again would drain her of energy — drain her of desire? There would be little time to think about Paul Malnekov. 'You seem to have become very concerned about Captain Rykov.'

Anna stiffened. 'Really, Natalya. What a ridiculous notion, that I should be in any way interested in the Captain. His family are mere merchants. They trade in timber.' She paused, reflecting. 'They also have a small paper mill in Viacta.'

'*I* didn't know that.' Natalya selected from the clothes put out for her by her maid. Why do I always assume the worst? she wondered. Because I love Malnekov but do not entirely trust him. And there remained the problem of how to get to his villa on Krestovsky Island.

'Captain Rykov is quite impossible,' Anna continued. 'He frequents the Lantern. A very low class of person goes there — so I am told. And Baroness Klienmichael told me he left her supper party in the company of the daughter of that awful painter — the one who did the portrait of Alexander Michaelovich.' She looked in the mirror and touched her hair. 'I cannot imagine how he justifies squandering his life in this fashion.'

'It is his life.'

'But he serves this house.' Anna's mouth tightened.

'Captain Rykov was Ivan's friend. He brought Father's body home. And it was the Tsar who appointed him to the service of our family,' Natalya said. 'But we do not own him.' She would have to go to Krestovsky after dark to avoid being seen. Peter Petrovich was too old to take her so far at night in the coach, and if she used the car the chauffeur might talk. Who then would drive her? She pondered then turned to Anna. 'Would you mind very much if Captain Rykov does not attend the ballet?'

'But why?'

Natalya began to dress. Now she would have to tell a half lie. 'It is to do with the hospital. Katyn Lesechko is leaving for the front. I will have to take her place for a while and work with the wounded.'

'Natalya, you shouldn't!' Anna was shocked. 'You lost pounds when you served with the hospital train!'

'Somebody has to do it.' Natalya bit her lip. 'I worry about you though. I'll have little time to spare for you.'

Anna sighed. 'Oh, I will be perfectly all right. Bored. Safe. Fussed over by Vera, Vasya, and Peter Petrovich.' She pouted at herself in the mirror. 'The demands of this war are monstrous. Of course, Captain Rykov will be here each day. He is irritating, but one does get used to a person.' And she considered for a moment. 'I am sure he could be useful to you — at the hospital I mean. Organizing is one of his talents. Is that why you require him tonight?'

Natalya evaded her sister's glance. 'There are decisions I have to make. I need the Captain to drive me to Krestovsky.

I'm sorry to upset your arrangements.'

'It doesn't really matter — he can ride with me tomorrow.' Anna shrugged. 'He becomes dreadfully bored at the ballet and invariably falls asleep. I'm sure I'll be more successful matching Elizabeth and Major Ryjitsa without him.'

'Very well.' Natalya smoothed her hands over her dress. 'I will talk to the Captain now.'

Alone, Anna returned to the problem of what she should wear. She held one dress and then another against herself. Perhaps the blue one? If only she was as well endowed as Natalya. And she remembered the ruby pendant. Natalya hadn't given an answer.

She ran quickly to the head of the stairway and looked down to the colonnaded hall. Something covert about the tableau made her pause. Natalya was standing quite still, head bowed and her hands lightly clenched, and Rykov was in the open doorway staring out across the courtyard. They remained so for several seconds, then Natalya began speaking softly.

Anna had not seen anger in Rykov's face before. He seemed suddenly a different person. She was conscious of a small, puzzling apprehension. What was it Natalya had said? We do not own him.

She returned to her room and watched from the window as Rykov crossed the courtyard.

5

When darkness settled over the city, Rykov returned to the Meretskov palace to drive Natalya to Krestovsky Island. The French automobile moved with the sparse night traffic across the Dvortzovi Bridge. St Peter and St Paul loomed massive in the glow of the lights beyond. Rykov drove northwards across the first of the islands. It began to rain, turning to sleet, streaming down the windscreen and obscuring Natalya's view. What would she say to Malnekov? Her carefully prepared questions seemed inappropriate. Once more reason had deserted her.

The headlights of a passing car slashed harshly, briefly illumining Rykov's face. Natalya bit her lip. 'Captain, your silent disapproval makes me feel slightly unclean.'

Rykov blurted out his thoughts. 'I have watched you grow up, from your thirteenth birthday. When you involved yourself so unworthily with that Cossack I thought that sooner or later you would come to your senses and recognize your tawdry little affair for what it is.' His face twisted in disgust. 'But now you have dragged me into the fringe of this squalid business. You are right, lady, to feel slightly unclean. I feel unclean also.'

She was shocked, then angry. 'As you find this so distasteful I give you leave to seek service elsewhere.'

But she sensed something more in his bitterness. For a while they were silent, then she said, 'I didn't mean that. I'm sorry.'

Rykov swung the car onto the verge and stopped. He turned to face her in the darkness and she could just make out the shape of his coat collar pulled up, and his peaked cap set at an angle.

'Good and gracious Countess. Think well. No good can come of this. You are finer than you know; too fine for Malnekov. The man is nothing but a butcher. There is still time for us to turn back.'

She stared at him in amazement. 'A butcher! How can you say that?'

'Last week he had thirty men of the city garrison shot for refusing to fire on the strikers. And Chita, lady, 1905. A dark year with a dark ending.'

'He put down the army mutiny — his necessary duty.'

Rykov sighed, defeated. 'He did more than his duty. You were only thirteen then. You do not know. He flogged men's backs and he hanged mercilessly. I beg you once more. Let us turn back.'

'No. I cannot.'

Rykov said nothing. He drove onto the road again.

Near the northern extremity of Krestovsky they came to a large remote villa set among trees. A light burned in one window. The car crunched up the drive. Paul Malnekov stood silhouetted in the doorway.

Rykov climbed out and opened the door for Natalya. Malnekov seemed barely to notice him. 'You can go, Captain. I will see that the Countess returns safely.'

Natalya turned to Rykov but he didn't look at her as he climbed back into the car. No time even to thank him. The car swung round, returning the way it had come, its tail light winking in the sleet.

Rykov badly needed a drink. Out on the islands night life began after the theatres and formal parties of the city ended. Between eleven o'clock and dawn one could carouse and watch the gipsy dancers.

At the Villa Rode he drank with steady determination, slowly obliterating the image of Natalya bedded with Malnekov. Then he left, driving unsteadily to the Lantern which was smaller but more exotic.

Berdichev, the fat proprietor, greeted him as he edged through the crowd. Rykov scooped a bottle and a glass from the tray of a passing waiter, and he sat alone at a corner table, unaware of the noise and the heat, or even of the naked girl playing the piano. He was sick with impotent, jealous anger. I want Natalya Alexandrovna for myself, he thought. That is what it is really all about. Over the years he had charmed many women — and used some, so he must now concede a certain rough justice. He swallowed more wine and sat staring down at the glass. Perhaps he could have continued, safe behind the façade of bored, efficient servant to the house of Meretskov. At least that way he shared a small part of her life. Maybe that would have been enough for a little while longer. But now she'd used him to take her to that strutting ox Malnekov whose greatest asset hung between his legs. I made the vast error of revealing my feelings, he thought. I should never have done that. What was now left to him?

Somebody at a nearby table called his name and he looked up.

'Captain Rykov? Would you care to join us?'

Rykov slowly focused. It was the American trader, Baumler; and that large, badly dressed English captain. He raised his glass in salute. 'Thank you, gentlemen, but no. I am erasing an illusion. It requires determined, solitary drinking.'

Baumler grinned. 'We'll pick you up and take you home if you pass out,' he called. And he turned back to Michael Stern. 'Crazy Russians. Funny. He's a very sharp card player and doesn't usually drink·this much. We'd better keep an eye on him.'

'He coughs a lot.' Stern frowned at the half-slumped figure.

'He caught a lung wound at Tannenberg and was sent home. The Tsar appointed him to the Meretskov house and he's been serving the two sisters ever since.'

'Maybe that's why he's drinking.'

Baumler laughed. 'And what is *your* excuse for constantly reaching for the bottle?'

He shrugged. 'It blunts the sharp edges of my thoughts.' Or maybe I'm just waiting for something to happen, he thought and glanced sideways at Rykov, curious about his relationship with the imperious Countess. Everything he had heard about the Meretskov house puzzled him.

'The brother — the one who was drowned. How old would he have been?'

'About the same as you, and Rykov.'

Stern pondered. He should ask no more questions. He should leave it while he could believe in coincidence. 'Can you remember his regiment?'

'No. Yes. Knights Guards. Aren't you a little over-interested in that affair?' Baumler's eyes were questioning.

Stern felt his gut tightening. 'Knights Guards you say?' It

could still be coincidence. 'No, I'm merely speculating. Do you ever wonder, though, about the compound effect of the loss of just one man? It's a game you can play inside your head. Supposing Bismarck had been killed in one of his duels while he was still at university?'

'Or if Napoleon had died of pneumonia at the age of twenty?'

'How different history might have been.' Stern frowned. He should never have started this. 'And what of the sisters Meretskova — would their lives be quite different if the brother hadn't drowned?'

Baumler stared at him blankly for a moment. 'All right,' he said. 'Let's *play* this game. Supposing your ship had been sunk by a U-boat while you were on your way to Russia. How might that small amendment to history have affected my life, and the lives of all the other people you've met since you arrived in Petrograd?'

Stern shook his head. 'It's like playing chess on three dimensions.' He looked up as a drunken man pushed between the tables. 'I never get far beyond the opening questions. What is that fellow doing?'

The drunken man was large, with a long black matted beard and straggling hair. He stood, swaying and peering round at the watchers who were briefly silent. Then he saw Rykov.

'My dear Captain!'

Conversations at the other tables were resumed, falsely loud, as though nobody wished to draw the man's attention by seeming to observe him. Berdichev had signalled to his waiters and they gathered at a distance.

They are afraid, Stern thought, and he watched, curious.

The man's clothes and felt boots were filthy. He had a heavy, offensive odour, Stern could smell him from five paces as he sat himself opposite Rykov and began to speak in a deep, gentle voice.

'Your spirit is heavy with anger, Captain. I can tell. I know all things. I shall drink with you. We can talk a little, then find ourselves gypsy girls.'

'Leave me, *moujik*.'

'But why? We have common desires. Why haven't you brought the beautiful sisters to my house? I would like to pray with them.' He bellowed with laughter then turned his dark eyes on a waiter who had approached too close. The waiter retreated.

Rykov's hand tightened on his glass. 'I told you to leave.'

'Why are you so unkind? You need me. You are sick, Captain.' He leaned across the table and looked at Rykov's face. 'Death is lurking behind your eyes, but I can save you. I have powers given me by God. Come to my house and bring the Countess Natalya. With her a man could lose himself — sink down and down to his original innocence.'

Rykov's pent up anger found release. He grasped the man's filthy coat. 'Never mention her name. Do you hear? Never even look at her! *Moujik*, you are corrupt!'

'Unless we sin, how can we be saved?' Still the man's voice was gentle and persuasive. His dark eyes widened. 'I would like to save the Countess before they kill me.'

Rykov lurched clumsily to his feet. Face flushed, he stood swaying. 'By God, I'll kill you now!' and he pulled his revolver from its holster.

Stern kicked his chair back and cleared the distance between the tables in two strides. He wrenched the gun from Rykov's hand. 'Easy now,' he said. 'Relax, Captain.'

The dark man laughed harshly. 'You should have let him shoot me, *yoonasha*, it would have saved others the trouble.' And he rose and elbowed his way out.

Stern stared after him. 'Who the hell is he?'

'Rasputin,' Baumler said. 'The Court *starets*.'

'Well, I'll be damned!'

'Maybe,' Baumler grinned and took Rykov's arm, steering him between tables. 'Come on, Captain. Time to go home.'

They went out into the night and Berdichev followed, clutching Rykov's cap.

Rykov stood for a moment and breathed deeply. 'I'm sane again. You can leave me now.' He shook Baumler's hand away and walked unsteadily to the Meretskov auto-mobile. Stern followed him and handed him the revolver. 'You had the safety catch on.'

Rykov shrugged. 'Thanks, Englishman.' He hauled himself into the car.

'Captain, you cannot drive in your condition!' Berdichev implored. 'Be sensible. Stay. You can have a room — and a girl if you want one.'

'He's right,' Baumler called. 'You'll kill yourself. Take Berdichev's offer.'

'No more girls.' Rykov pressed the starter. The engine burst into life and the headlights flashed on.

Berdichev leapt aside as the large automobile spurted wet gravel and swung out onto the road. 'Take care, Captain!'

'Crazy Russians.' Baumler watched until the car disap-peared, and he spoke to Stern without turning his head. 'Who can tell how history might have changed if you'd let him kill Rasputin?'

Who indeed. Stern smiled. 'I told you. I can never think beyond the first few questions.' His breath steamed and he sank his hands into his pockets.

Together they went back into the Lantern.

Rykov drove with clumsy abandon. Snow began to fall, fine and powdery, settling over wooded slopes. That part of the island was sparsely inhabited. Within living memory wolves had strayed south one winter and killed a groom on the Oldenburg estate.

The white-covered road was deserted. Rykov felt drowsy with the sweeping movement of the windscreen wipers. He peered through the flurries of snow but didn't slow the car. All sense of danger had left him. He skidded on a bend but was barely aware of it.

Damn my luck that I ever met her, he thought dully, and pushed his foot down hard on the accelerator. Twelve years of my life. A chance invitation. A summer month at Ustreka — she was thirteen then. And I was trapped; caught up by her innocence. Our lives are shaped by chance. Twelve years, and despite Malnekov I'm still caught — by her innocence. The wipers purred back and forth across the glass. A man might fall asleep.

The car mounted the verge, bouncing and juddering him back to consciousness. He spun the wheel too late and the car crunched into a tree.

Slowly he stirred. Blood was trickling from a cut over his eye. He coughed, aware again of the copper taste in his mouth. He could freeze to death here, or that old lung wound would get him later. What did it matter? He rested his head on the steering wheel. Five minutes, he thought. I'll rest for five minutes.

But he woke bitterly cold and shivering. The windscreen was finely covered with snow. In God's name what was he doing here? Slowly he remembered. And I'm still drunk, he thought. It must have been hours since he'd left Natalya. Groping clumsily and still shivering, he started the car and reversed back to the road.

The streets were almost deserted when he crossed from Vassili Island to the heart of the city. A milk cart moved slowly up the Nevsky ahead of the car. Early morning street cleaners were out, sweeping up the rubbish of the previous day. A beggar was asleep, huddled on the steps of Kazan Cathedral. Rykov glanced back as he drove past. Perhaps the man was dead. Or drunk like him. He swung the car into the courtyard of the Meretskov palace.

Summoned by Rykov's insistent ringing, a sleepy servant opened the door. Rykov straightened up, swaying. 'I have returned the Countess's automobile, barely marked.' And he gestured to the crumpled mudguard and smashed headlight. 'I shall now go to the old Count's study and pour myself a nightcap.'

'But Excellency! It is half past four in the morning!'

Rykov nodded firmly and patted him on the back. 'Best time of the day.'

'But Excellency . . .'

Rykov walked unsteadily across the hall, then stopped short, peering up at the marble staircase.

Anna Meretskova was looking down at him. Her hand moved up to the lapels of her dressing gown, carefully pulling them together. 'Go to bed, Vasya. I will look after Captain Rykov.'

The old servant shook his head and tutted to himself as he went away.

Rykov groaned softly as Anna followed him into the study and closed the door. She leaned with her back against it, watching as he splashed brandy into a glass and poured it down his throat in one movement.

'The Tsar has asked that we refrain from drinking until the war is over.'

'To hell with the Tsar.' Rykov rubbed his hand across his eyes. She's begun already, he thought. Probing questions will surely follow. 'I very nearly killed Rasputin tonight.'

'It is morning.'

But he continued. 'The story of my life. I've *nearly* done a lot of things.' And he reached for the bottle again.

'Don't!'

He paused, then half filled the glass. 'That fair-haired English captain stopped me — pulled the gun from my hand.'

'Look at yourself! How could you get into such a condition?'

'It wasn't terribly difficult,' he said.

'It would be better to sit before you fall down.'

So now she was going to preach at him. 'I'm perfectly . . .' he frowned, groping for a word '. . . perfectly stable.'

'I think not.' She crossed the room and sat in a chair facing him, carefully arranging the dressing gown over her knees. The small movement irritated Rykov. Eighteen, and she's like some prim school marm, he thought.

'You seemed upset yesterday, Captain. Perhaps that is why you have been drinking? Tell me.'

He shrugged and gulped down the brandy. 'I was angry with myself, but it is nothing.'

'It must be *something*.'

God, how his head was aching! He sighed and spoke

almost to himself: 'I have become a man without dignity.'

'You don't have to be without dignity. Oh, I know you cannot return to the front and fight as other men are doing, but there are things you could do here at home . . .'

Rykov held his hand to his head. Not only is she preaching and priggish, she is completely tactless. Soothing, emasculating reason flows ceaselessly from her attractive mouth.

'. . . and you look quite ill. How on earth did you get that cut over your eye?'

'I had a small accident with the car.' Rykov touched the dried blood on his eyebrow. 'Do not concern yourself.' And he prepared to go.

Anna rose and came over to him, peering critically at the gash. 'Natalya says a cut, no matter how small, should never be ignored.'

'I'll look to it when I reach my rooms.'

'No. I think I should dress it.' Frowning, she touched the dried blood with the tips of her fingers. 'I do not think it requires stitches.'

Her dressing gown had slipped open a little, revealing the smooth white vee of her breasts. Rykov tried to turn away but her fingers were gently probing at the cut. 'After I have attended to it you must go home and sleep for several hours. You have been acting most strangely recently . . .'

Her unceasing flood of comment and instructions muddled his thoughts. How could one so young keep on so? There was only one way to stop her. Rykov put his arms around Anna and kissed her firmly on the mouth, feeling again the surprise that is never a surprise. How soft her body is! And for a moment she seemed quite helpless. Then she struggled, forcing herself free of him, her face white with shock.

'How *could* you!' She slapped him hard across the mouth, then stood back gasping. 'How could you! Did you think that I would submit to you as do those — those whores you go with?'

He grinned foolishly, touching the white marks on his

face and suddenly sobering. For God's sake what had he done! What a stupid thing! 'I am sorry. My intentions were not as you think. I merely . . .'

'You *merely*! How dare you!' She quickly pulled the dressing gown together, holding it at the throat. 'That you should presume to — to . . . Why, you are nothing more than a servant here!'

Rykov stiffened. Then he bowed. 'Quite so. A servant. Again my apologies.' And he turned and left the room.

Anna remained staring at the door. Slowly she touched her lips. He had kissed her. In his drunken, dishevelled condition he had kissed her.

Dazed, she left the study and returned to her bedroom, then sat before the mirror looking at herself. He had actually *kissed* her. And she had slapped his face and insulted him, choosing in that moment the most hurtful thing she could say. She bit her lip. Oh God, why had she said *that* to him?

She went to her bed, and pulling the covers over herself she lay looking up at the ceiling. He would come back — at ten o'clock as he always did. She would put it right then.

Anna dozed, then woke, then slept soundly; waking late in the morning to the sounds of hundreds of boots crunching in step along the Nevsky Prospect. She slid out of her bed and went to the window. Recalled reservists marching to the Warsaw Station half filled the broad thoroughfare. Alternate companies were without rifles. The column stretched back nearly half a mile and the watching people were silent.

Was it ten o'clock yet? Was Rykov already here? Anna began hastily pulling on her clothes. And she stopped suddenly, the stocking halfway up her leg. I love him, she thought. I've always loved him. She finished dressing and almost ran along the thickly carpeted gallery to Natalya's room.

Natalya was on the balcony, watching.

'Oh, Natalya! I'm so pleased to see you back. Where were you?' Then hastily. 'What time is it? Is Captain Rykov here yet?'

There was a faint tinge of blue under Natalya's eyes but otherwise she seemed no different. 'No. Captain Rykov has sent word that he will be late.'

'Oh.' Anna looked down at the soldiers and the hundreds of watchers lining the paving. They don't cheer any more, she thought. 'I fear that I have offended the Captain. I was so utterly stupid. I so much want to put it right.' And she sighed heavily. 'If only I could be calm and rational like you.'

How deceptive are appearances. Natalya frowned. And how could I have been so determinedly wrong after Rykov's warning? 'I also want to see the Captain,' she said. Years of taking him for granted. His loyalty had been like a rock. Then last night he'd tried to prevent her graceless act. But I used him anyway, she thought. And I feel numb, no excuses left to me. That she had in turn been used by Malnekov was unimportant now. Malnekov was off to the front, to his close brotherhood of Cossacks of the Caucasian Corps. He'd known it for weeks and he'd kept it from her, until last night. Not one small excuse left. Even after he told me I surrendered; willingly and unconditionally. Love. Lust. I know which it is now.

She stared down at the long column of men. I'll change my life, she thought. Without love perhaps I can be really useful again. 'Princess Scherbatova has telephoned. The hospital train of Alexandra Lvovna is arriving from the southern front on Thursday. St Saviour's charity hospital will take sixty of the seriously wounded.'

Anna interrupted. 'Please let Captain Rykov help you. Oh, let him! He needs to feel useful again.'

'Yes. I will ask him.' She owed him more than that.

Together they waited in the library, and just before midday Rykov was announced. His face was pale and he had a sticking plaster over his eye. There was a tension in him that Anna felt immediately and her unthinking stupidity of the earlier meeting appalled her.

Rykov bowed stiffly. 'I regret that I am late. A matter of some importance delayed me.'

'You seem . . .' Anna faltered. 'You seem yourself again, Captain.'

'Yes.' He nodded slowly. 'I suppose it could be said that I am at last myself again.'

Anna's face flushed. She must talk to him, later, alone. 'Natalya has a service to ask of you.'

Rykov turned to Natalya. 'If I can, Countess.'

'Your help, Captain, at the hospital. We are taking in wounded and I need you to take care of the administrative work.'

If only she had asked him yesterday. If only yesterday had not happened. 'I regret that my services will not be available after today, Countess. Before coming here I requested a return to the active list. At midnight I must leave from the Warsaw Station with the Third Reserve Battalion of the Semionovsky Regiment.'

Anna froze. 'But you cannot! Your wound from Tannenberg! You are unfit for service at the front.'

He smiled wryly. 'Oh, I am fit enough. There is a desperate shortage of experienced officers. And it has been a long time since I have felt really useful.'

'But you are needed here. You were appointed to our household by the Tsar!' Anna exclaimed.

Rykov shook his head. 'One servant less in the house will hardly matter. Truly I mean no offence. My intention in coming here was to thank you both.' And to Natalya he added, 'I am sure you will recognize that I have taken the only honourable course open to me.'

Natalya nodded slowly. 'If that is what you feel you must do.' I have forced him into this, she thought. All my smug and oblique reproaches, about his gambling and his women; all my gentle mockery, casual and without real concern for him. Yet he is nobler than I. Almost hesitantly she said, 'Anna and I would be grateful if you would allow us to accompany you as far as the Warsaw Station, Captain.'

'There is no need.' Rykov sighed almost imperceptibly. 'But if it pleases you, ladies.'

*   *   *

71

Nearing midnight, the Warsaw Station was as busy as at midday. From here traffic rumbled ceaselessly along the rail links to the far off war. And trains returned, reeking, crammed with wounded. The station smelled of disinfectant, and smoke from the huge locomotives. Harsh flaring gas lamps cast a yellow, alien light on the platforms strewn with rubbish, and on the long line of soldiers laden with packs and blankets — the lucky ones had rifles and the others would take theirs from the dead. They filed past the mitred priest and each knelt quickly for a hurried blessing before climbing up into the freight cars.

There were few civilians in the station at that late hour, and the ticket collector bowed as the two attractive fur clad young women passed through the barrier with the Semionovsky captain.

The three walked in silence along the length of the train. Night wind made the gas lamps flare and Natalya was aware of faces, yellow and unnatural. Such a dreadful hour to begin a journey, she thought. The spirit ebbs, and in this drab wasteland I see only hopes ending. And Rykov is hurrying, anxious to be gone from us.

Rykov reached the door of his compartment and turned to face them. 'Well now,' and he smiled gently. 'It is cold. There is little point in you waiting.'

'We will stay until your train leaves.' Anna's face was set determinedly against tears. 'I have a gift for you. It belonged to our brother.' And she held out a small icon.

He took it in his gloved hand and looked at it. 'I remember this. I shall keep it safe.'

'Be sure . . .' Anna faltered. 'Be sure you bring it back.'

He nodded and slid the icon into his greatcoat pocket.

The reason for Anna's unhappiness was now obvious. Suddenly I hardly know either of them, Natalya thought, and she was aware of a sharp sadness. Anna is a separate person with thoughts and feelings I know nothing of.

Midnight sounded from St Nicholas Cathedral across the dark acres of converging tracks. The train juddered and Rykov frowned quickly round. 'I must leave you, ladies.'

Anna bit her lip, then murmured quickly, 'I'm sorry. I'm sorry for what I said.'

'Don't be. It was really about nothing.'

'I don't want it to be about nothing.'

'But it was.' He smiled at her.

'Is there anything I can do?'

'Pray to St Anne for me.' He turned quickly to Natalya as the engine whistle shrieked. 'Goodbye, lady.'

'God is good.' Natalya clasped his hand. 'We shall meet again soon.'

'I hope so.' Rykov was pale. He looked at her for a moment longer then swung himself up into the carriage. The train jerked and began to move, rumbling slowly out of the Warsaw Station.

'It is you he has left,' Anna said.

Natalya didn't answer.

6

Michael Stern slept badly on three successive nights. Even in the dream he knew it was the third night. He tried to will himself into consciousness but the dream kept dragging him back. The upturned face was just below the surface of the water, bubbles trickling from the nose and mouth. He groaned, turning in his bed. The face was never clear in the dream but the eyes were open, accusing, as he pushed the head down again. He'd have to go right through it, watch the body float out into the stream, and then he'd wake in the hotel room.

Something disturbed the pattern — sharp sounds beyond the window. He woke, relieved, and sat up. Pistol shots? Two — no, three, quite close by. He switched on the bedside lamp, listening for other sounds, then rose and went to the window. The snow had stopped but St Isaac's Square was white-covered and deserted. Solitary wheel tracks of an automobile marked the Morskya on the south side. Had the shots been part of the dream? He was about to turn away, then noticed a moving shape. A man limped rapidly, trailing blood as he passed across a circle of light cast by a street lamp. He glanced back, then limped on round the corner. A minute later a black automobile moved slowly up the Morskya, its headlights following the red stains. Stern watched until it disappeared. Again there was silence. He stared for a while at the snow-covered square then returned to his bed.

It was nothing to do with him. Pistol shots at night were not that uncommon in Petrograd in the winter of 1916. He was a stranger here. He lay with his hands behind his head, staring up at the dark ceiling. If he fell asleep would he have to complete the dream? The night seemed endless, with questions of purpose nagging at him. He peered at the luminous dial of his wrist watch. Three a.m. Unwise to think about one's life at this hour of doubt. A stranger in a tense city. Fifteen days since he'd crossed Scandinavia. Was it really only fifteen days?

The memory of arrival at the Finland Station evoked an almost immediate image of Helen Mirsky ahead of him on the platform. Some women stay in the mind. It was the way she moved; sensual, and with an unconscious assertion of life. He felt drowsy again, purpose momentarily unimportant, and despite his unwillingness to attempt sleep his eyelids closed, and he dozed.

Soft sounds of hotel servants in the passage woke him at five thirty. Day sixteen began. He felt the stubble on his chin and rose to stare critically at himself in the mirror.

There were no other guests in the dining-room. He breakfasted alone with the three Petrograd morning papers, then with the second cup of coffee he began to think about his day. There were still bridge survey reports to study. Four notebooks already filled. And Southgate was getting insistent about the completion of month by month freight figures for the Murmansk route. He pondered. Those figures suggested that it was time he visited the Murmansk freight depot across the city. He'd been putting it off. Now it seemed a good idea. It would get him out of the stuffy Embassy library. And maybe he'd find out what the bloody depot manager thought he was up to.

The dining-room was filling up; foreign business agents making an early start. The Zaharoff arms salesman, small and dark-haired, passed Stern's table, glanced with a flicker of recognition and nodded. Does he remember that we last encountered each other in Persia? Stern wondered about the expanding market for machine guns. That man must be getting rich.

He fetched his greatcoat and cap from his room, and as he returned across the reception area a tall, grey-haired Russian army corporal approached and saluted.

'Excellency, Captain Stern?'

He wondered how long the corporal had been standing there. 'Yes. I'm Captain Stern.' Then he remembered, groaning softly to himself. Southgate had warned him that he was to expect a servant-driver-guide. All military advisers had them — even captains. 'You've been told to look after me?'

The corporal stood rigid, expressionless. 'That is my instruction, Excellency.'

'Very well, Corporal. Our first duty today takes us to the railway depot.'

Early morning, and the station was busy with local traffic. Harsh yellow lamps burned until the late beginning of the daylight hours. Snow ploughs had cleared the tracks west, and east as far as Lake Ladoga. Stern checked on the scheduled arrival time of the Murmansk freight train. He knew it would be late.

'Even the large American engines are inefficient if they are burning inferior coal and hauling heavy loads.' He glanced quickly at the old corporal striding to his left but half a pace behind him. 'The coal cannot generate enough heat. Do you understand?'

'I understand, Excellency.' The corporal nodded, frowning. 'Like a man fed on thin soup.'

'Yes.' Stern smiled. 'That's it exactly.' And he led the way through the terminus building.

His identity document served for both of them and they passed the Railway Battalion checkpoint that gave them access to the Murmansk freight depot half a mile down the tracks. The marshalling complex was vast; steel threads converging under signal gantrys and curving in elaborate patterns round islands of snow-covered sheds and workshops.

An empty hospital train had been shunted onto a siding. Stern and the corporal walked along its length. Cleaners were still working, emptying latrine buckets and scrubbing out the waggons with disinfectant.

'God's teeth! I didn't know they reeked so.'

'It is the end of the journey, Excellency.' The corporal seemed unaffected.

Stern pulled his scarf up over his face and walked faster. Nine days to the field hospitals of the south, five perhaps to those of the west. Countess Natalya Meretskova had had charge of such a train during the retreat of nineteen fifteen. How to equate that beautiful woman in the palace ballroom with these reeking waggons?

Two orderlies were lifting out a long steel box and edging it onto a handcart.

'It contains amputated limbs, Excellency. It has to be emptied at each stop along the route.'

Stern glanced curiously at his newly appointed servant. 'You've travelled on one of these trains?'

'Yes, Excellency. I was wounded on the Austrian front.' The corporal's lined face was impassive. He moved with an easy swinging stride. 'As you can see, I am now past the age for service in the line.'

'What do I call you?'

'I am Rantalla, Excellency. Corporal, Second Battalion, Finland Regiment.'

'Right, Rantalla. We are about to harass an incompetent

76

official, so do your best to maintain that rigid expression.'

The corporal's eyes registered a faint flicker of amusement. 'It is habitual with me, Excellency.'

They reached an ugly, blind-faced building on the far side of the tracks, its brickwork smudged with coal dust and daubed with the familiar slogan — BREAD PEACE FREEDOM. Labourers clad in coarse ragged expediencies to keep out the cold were off-loading freight from trucks on the snow-covered siding. Their movements were slow, pausing overlong between hauling down wooden cases. Damn, another train arriving and this one not yet cleared. Stern watched them. Morale is low, he thought. Men work like that when they harbour grudges.

Two soldiers of the Railway Battalion, bayonets fixed, squeezed their way between waggons and paused. The labourers didn't talk to them. Stern went into the depot. With the huge wooden doors slid back it was almost as cold inside. Rubbish was strewn in the gangways between boxes and sacks. Rolls of rusting wire were heaped on spades and pickaxes.

'Oh my God!' Stern rubbed his short beard and surveyed the interior with disgust. Water had seeped across the floor, soaking bales of flax. Workers were slouched idle between the bays, trying to keep warm.

'Right, Rantalla. Start to look official and disapproving.'

They climbed rickety steps to a catwalk running along the interior length of the vast shed. Recently before the war the building had been used by a German electrical component firm and the shelving remained at one end, with the office high above. They reached the office door and paused, watching a rat as it ran along the rafters and dropped like an acrobat onto the high piled bales.

'Give me five minutes alone with the manager, Rantalla, then we'll examine this disgusting mess. See how many rats you can count.' Stern knocked.

'Come in! Come in! Close the door.' The depot manager was huddled by the small stove, his fur coat fastened up to the neck. He smelled of cheap spirit. 'This place is wretchedly cold. You are the English captain?' A small nerve above his eye twitched. 'Have that chair. Tip the files on the floor.'

Stern sat and undid his greatcoat.

'I have no assistance. I have to do everything here.' The manager poked at the stove. 'They will not give me coal. I have to burn damp wood.'

'There is only three days' reserve of coal in the city.'

'Three days, eh! Well, things are getting bad all round.' The man pulled a bottle of spirit from his drawer, looked at Stern, then changed his mind and replaced it. 'I do my best here but I get no support.' The nerve above his eye twitched again. 'I'm not used to working in these conditions. For fifteen years I have loyally served the Tsar. And this is my reward.' He stoked ineffectively at the stove. 'I am scandalously served. I was informed you were coming, but nobody told me why.'

'To expedite.' Stern lit a cigarette and frowned. He knew already that he'd never get this man to change. 'There's a hold up here with return of freight waggons. Can you see that?'

'Those lazy stupid oafs out there! They will not work any faster!'

'There are not enough freight waggons so the ones we have must be used to the maximum.'

'The labourers are all thieves and Bolsheviks!' The manager lowered his voice. 'Did they tell you I have Koltsov working here? Here! In my depot!' He held his hand to his eye to conceal the twitch. 'And the Ministry expects miracles of me.'

Stern sighed to himself. If he had the authority he'd get rid of the incompetent idiot. 'The freight waggons must never stand idle.'

'Look at all this paperwork! Directives. Complaints. Freight manifestos. I cannot keep up with it.'

'The war could be lost if the railways do not work efficiently. Off-loading and on-loading must be conducted as rapidly as possible. It is all a matter of organization.' Stern

78

crushed out the cigarette and stood. 'I will spend two days with you. That is all I can spare. Let us look round the depot.'

He went out to the high, rickety catwalk and the official followed complaining loudly.

Rantalla was leaning against the rail, his long hard body curving as he looked down. Red evil eyes of rats glinted in dark recesses below.

'How many did you count, old man?'

'A dozen or more, Excellency. They are fat and audacious.'

'I daresay they are well fed.'

The depot manager peered down. A slim man in a sheepskin coat was pulling a long box from the top of a pile. 'Lazy thieves I have working for me. They are infected by the strikers in the city. And they play tricks on me. Oh yes, they are cunning. You there!' he shouted to the man below. 'What are you doing?'

The man glanced up, his thin hard face questioning, and he let go his hold on the box. It crashed down on one corner and the wood splintered.

'That was deliberate, you swine!'

'An accident.' The man stared, expressionless. 'It slipped from my hands.'

'It was deliberate damage!' And the manager turned to Stern. 'You saw it! He let it go on purpose.'

Stern wasn't sure.

Together they descended to the depot floor, and the manager muttered as they walked over to the damaged box, 'That man is Peter Koltsov, a troublemaker well known in the railway yards.' And to Koltsov he bellowed, 'Vandalism! And who told you to move these boxes? I said they were to stay here until they are collected by the Prefect of Police.'

'We thought there was a mistake.' Koltsov's cold gaze was on the pile of boxes. 'They are marked "Books" but that is not what they contain.'

'It is none of your business what they contain! They are for the Prefecture. That is all you need to know.'

79

'But the Prefect of Police would not want all these cases of books. See. It must be a mistake.' And Koltsov pulled at the splintered lid.

'Don't! I forbid it!'

The manager's hoarse shout came too late. The lid was off. Stern stared down at a Vickers machine gun.

God's teeth! It was brand new; gleaming, oiled. Straight from the factory in England. And there were two dozen more crated guns in that pile. Stern stared at them in astonishment. So the police were preparing for insurrection. He looked quickly at the hard-faced depot worker. Koltsov was counting the boxes.

Groping clumsily, the manager replaced the broken lid. 'Do you realize what you have done? You have knowingly broken open a case in transit. But there are laws. Oh yes. There are laws. This is a prison offence.' He turned to Stern. 'You witnessed this man's crime, Captain.'

Why do I hesitate? Stern thought. This has nothing to do with me. It is obvious that the worker, Koltsov, suspected the box contained a gun and smashed it to find out. And that, regrettably, is a crime. His own reply surprised him. 'I saw the box slip from the man's hands. That is all. Corporal Rantalla, what did you see?'

'Nothing, Excellency.'

The manager stared at them. 'But . . .'

'I think we'd better get on,' Stern said, and he moved along the bay. 'Now where do you store the Murmansk-bound freight? You must have it stacked ready for rapid loading. And you need trolleys. It is ridiculous to over-burden your workers by making them carry everything.'

Two days. He could spare this idiot two days.

He scribbled in his pocket book as he went round, and by midday he'd seen enough. Rantalla watched, curious, as he drew a diagram of the depot.

'Come on, Rantalla. We'll return tomorrow and start work.'

A ragged labourer rolled the great door back for them. 'Koltsov thanks you,' he muttered.

Stern didn't reply.

They strode through the deep snow, back the way they had come, but found their way barred by a line of red boxcars. Stern squeezed between two of them. 'The labourers in that depot are idle, cynical, and probably hungry, Rantalla.'

'Men need a good leader, Excellency.' The old corporal followed him then stood staring at the boxcars.

'Yes. Somebody who makes them work but cares a little for them. They do not even have suitable clothing.' He noticed that Rantalla was only half listening, and he looked with him at the ugly, red-painted waggons. 'What are those used for, old man?'

'They are for transporting convicts, Excellency. Red is the identifying colour.'

The boxcars might have been designed for the movement of cattle. Each heavy timbered container had a small barred window high up. Thick, long iron bolts secured the doors.

'They make vast journeys, Excellency, to the penal colonies. An unpleasant duty for the soldiers who have to accompany them as guards. Happily I have never drawn that service.'

'I wouldn't even put animals in them.' Stern scowled up at the barred window, then he turned away and moved on. 'You don't seem like an officer's servant, Rantalla.'

'Quite so, Excellency.' Rantalla held himself erect. 'I am — I was a line soldier. But as I know this city quite well I was given the task of looking after Your Excellency until your departure for Karelia.' He frowned slightly. 'Then I am to be discharged from the army, my service completed.'

Stern nodded, noticing that Rantalla was no longer walking the customary half pace to the rear. He felt oddly flattered. 'That man Koltsov. What do you know about him?'

'I hear his name, Excellency. He is on a workers' war relief committee. The Okhrana has an interest in him because he has organized a trade union for unskilled railwaymen.'

'Yes. I can imagine that the Tsar's police would keep an

eye on him.' Stern had the impression that the old man knew more. 'Tell me honestly. Do you think Koltsov dropped that case deliberately?'

'I saw it slide through his hands.' Rantalla shrugged his heavy shoulders. 'God alone would know Koltsov's true intentions.'

Odd that he should choose that moment, while I was watching, Stern pondered. Unless time was running out and that was his last opportunity? 'If it was deliberate, it was a reckless thing to do. A man like that ends up in trouble.'

More red boxcars were trundling slowly along the tracks to join with the others. No, I wouldn't even put animals in them, Stern thought. Were they to transport some of his labour force? Those awful boxes would crush hope out of a man long before he reached the wilderness. He looked up at the heavy, threatening sky. And to make such a journey in this weather.

The daylight hours had already passed. The first heavy snowfall of winter delayed traffic from the south and west and Alexandra Lvovna's hospital train was late arriving at the Warsaw terminus. Wounded were despatched by horse-drawn ambulances to the hospitals of the city, but fourteen bundled shapes, each covered with a blanket, remained on the station platform, no longer concerned about their last journey.

The snow had stopped falling by midnight and labourers of the Petrograd Zemstvo were already shovelling to clear the main thoroughfares in readiness for the day.

At the Prefecture of Police on Gorokhavaya Street the cleaners were grumbling because their changing room had been filled with long wooden boxes and locked. For the love of God, what did the Prefect want so many books for?

7

The coal shortage was affecting even the smart hotels. At the Astoria the hot taps were running tepid for the third day. Michael Stern fingered his razor. British officers were not permitted to wear beards and until that morning he'd fully intended shaving off the close-cropped stubble. But now? He spoke without turning his head. 'Go on, Mister Popov. I'm still listening.'

Popov was seated on the edge of the elegant but uncomfortable hotel chair. He had a grubby notebook open on his fat knees. His eyes were almost comically large behind thick, pebble spectacles. 'It is merely a routine enquiry, Captain.'

Stern frowned at his reflected image. Indecision over the beard was symptomatic. Since arriving in the city he'd become less sure of who he really was. 'You were about to tell me the name of your employer, Mister Popov.'

Popov shrugged deprecatingly. 'A minor agency of a government ministry, of no great interest to a visitor as distinguished as yourself.' He took out a stub of pencil. 'May I compliment you on your excellent spoken Russian? It is rare. Few foreigners bother to learn our language.'

'I was raised here in Petersburg.' Stern rubbed his hand over his face again.

'And you returned to England in 1905.' Popov peered myopically at his note book. 'To a place called Woolwich. And then a place called Chatham.'

Popov seemed to know a lot. Stern glanced quickly at him. 'Right. The schools of British Army engineers.'

'And you served in India and Persia.' Popov turned a page. 'Boundary Survey of 1911.'

'Correct again. I am also a surveyor.' He'd begun to feel a little wary. 'And, Mister Popov, I have an appointment so I would be obliged if you would tell me who you are employed by and what you want of me.'

Popov blinked several times, and he hesitated. 'I work for the Ministry of the Interior, Captain.' He glanced round as if out of habit. 'We are interested in matters of internal security.'

Secret police! He's a bloody Okhrana agent! Stern didn't allow his expression to alter. 'Yes, go on.'

'For three days you have gone to the Murmansk freight depot. The manager says you refuse to corroborate an act of vandalism by one of the workers there.' Popov looked apologetic. 'The manager says you have had two brief conversations with that worker.'

Stern busied himself putting the razor away. Popov's appearance had misled him. 'The manager is an incompetent halfwit. But, yes, I have spoken to many of the workers, including the man who accidentlly dropped a wooden case.'

'Captain, that man is Peter Koltsov.'

'Is that important?'

'Yes. Would you please tell me what was discussed?'

'We talked about re-locating some of the northbound freight.' I don't even have to lie, Stern thought.

'Perhaps he said something else — some small thing?' Popov wheedled.

'I don't remember. Why are you interested in him?'

Popov assumed a look of concern. 'Peter Koltsov is misguided, Captain. The poor fellow is confused — has dangerous thoughts. We would like to help him.'

'I'm sure you would.' Stern set his peaked cap at a slight angle and pulled on his greatcoat. 'But as no unhealthy thoughts were expressed, I'm afraid I cannot assist you.'

Popov trailed behind him as he left the hotel room and descended to the lounge. 'Are you absolutely sure that nothing subversive was said, Captain?' He lowered his voice. 'You may tell *me*, Popov. No harm will come to you. Your name will not even be mentioned. You have my word as an honest servant of the Tsar.'

Stern stopped and turned to him. 'Mister Popov, why should this man Koltsov speak subversion to me? I am an engineer, brought here to Russia to advise on certain transport problems.'

Popov's face screwed up in embarrassment. 'Captain, my employers cannot believe that your connections with Koltsov are coincidental.'

'What connections, for God's sake?'

Popov blinked rapidly. 'Peter Koltsov's brother, Dmitry, worked at the Kazakhov Mill owned by the Meretskov family. He was known to your father who was foreman there — they played chess together.' He glanced anxiously round him. 'Dmitry was a member of the treasonous St Petersburg Soviet. He was convicted and sent to Siberia, but escaped to London in England in 1907. There he met with Maxim Gorky, and Vladimir Ilyich who calls himself Lenin. Do you see now, Captain, why my employers are concerned?'

'No, damn it, I don't. You're saying my father had a tenuous link with a Russian who became a political exile. The cities of Western Europe are cluttered with such men; mostly lost, harmless pamphlet writers.'

'Dmitry was never harmless!' Popov's eyes were large behind his thick spectacles. 'His organization in London smuggled guns and subversive literature into Russia. Our records are meticulous. He was funded by the proceeds of the Tiflis bank raid — June, 1907. His brother, Peter, was known to be in Tiflis during that month.'

'Are your employers seriously attempting to connect me with the Koltsov brothers?'

Popov had begun to sweat. 'You arrived in Petrograd on the same train as Dmitry — we arrested him at the Finland terminus. And you have twice spoken to Peter Koltsov.'

'A coincidence.' Despite his irritation he was puzzled by the strangeness of lives touching and crossing.

Now Popov looked pleading. '*Please*, Captain. My employers do not believe in coincidence! Try to remember everything that Peter Koltsov said.' He pulled a page from his grubby notebook and scribbled a number. 'You can contact me here — just ask for Popov.'

Stern didn't take the piece of paper. 'We really have nothing to talk about.' He walked quickly out of the hotel and beckoned a waiting motor cab. As the cab moved away he glanced back. Popov was standing on the hotel steps, still clutching the piece of paper.

That the bizarre Popov should be an agent of the dreaded Okhrana seemed barely believable. But experience suggested that unlikely little men are sometimes more dangerous than they seem.

Stern stared out of the window at the Prefecture building on the busy Gorokhavaya. So there was a file with his name on it in some Okhrana office. It meant little. What could the Czar's secret police have on him? Yet the possibility remained, like a small frown on his thoughts.

The cab turned off, moving towards the Nevsky. There was a long queue outside a bread shop and the mood of the waiting people was ugly. Somebody was banging on the shop door. Sometimes the bakers only opened for an hour or two. Sometimes not at all.

On the Nevsky Prospect the cab passed the massive wrought iron gates of the Meretskov palace then filtered left at the Mikhaylovskaya. Stern paid off the driver at the far side of the square. Wind whipped the snow in swirling patterns. Baumler's gleaming yellow Pierce Arrow automobile was parked a few yards down from the Europe Hotel, and Baumler was waiting in the thickly carpeted Oriental lounge.

'I've ordered lunch. They'll tell us when it's ready.' The American trader was scowling. 'Where the hell have you been?'

'An unexpected visitor. What's put you into such a good mood?'

'A damned tax official has been looking over my books. What'll you have?'

'Brandy.' I'm drinking too much, he thought. 'Why would a tax official worry you?'

'Some items in my books are hard to explain.' Baumler

grinned sourly. 'Little sidelines I have. You can't trade completely honestly in this country, for God's sake. I've got flax waiting shipment out of Murmansk. But the ship won't take the flax because it can't off-load incoming cargo onto the choked docks. And the docks can't be cleared because the single track railway is totally inadequate to cope with the traffic. So you see I have to have alternative trade lined up all the time. I hope you're going to do something about that railway, Michael.'

'I'm leaving for Karelia in a few days.' Michael Stern frowned to himself. Strange as he felt in this city, part of him wanted to stay here. 'We hope to get the line working efficiently after the spring thaw. What's this about alternative trade?'

Baumler was pensive, wheeling and dealing inside his head. 'One of the few pleasures left to a fairly honest trader is outwitting Russian officialdom. I've got some quick-witted couriers making regular trips to Archangel for me. They bring back small stuff — one or two suitcases at a time. Not likely to win the war, but I'm making money. It's getting a bit dangerous though I've upset too many officials in the Technical Department. They're not getting a rake-off from me. That's why the tax official is breathing down my neck.'

Stern thought for a moment. 'How about the Okhrana — have you ever had any dealings with those fellows?'

'No thanks! It's a damned sinister organization. Okhrana agents are everywhere — even abroad. London. Paris. Anywhere you find Russians congregating, there'll be Okhrana agents among them. They are answerable only to the Minister of the Interior.'

'Do you think my father might ever have had anything to do with them?'

Baumler frowned. 'God, Michael, how could I know? Those last few months of his life we didn't see much of each other. I suppose that although he was poor, he'd moved on from me, all that Ruskin and William Morris he read. He was thinking of the socialist state and I was still out for a fast buck. Your father never really approved of the way I made my money.' He shrugged but looked a little uneasy. 'Last time I saw him we had an ugly row. I wasn't going to tell you that.'

'When was the last time you saw him?'

'Two days before the accident.' Baumler stared down at his drink. 'Every month or so I go and put some flowers on his grave.' He grinned wryly. 'When guilt becomes intrusive.'

Stern nodded. 'Guilt is an inevitable consequence of living. Don't worry on my account. I know the old man was a bit dogmatic in his views.'

'You're a lot more tolerant than him, Michael. And you never shared his passion for political theory?'

'No. I can't summon enthusiasm for mankind as a whole. I suppose I'm only curious about the journey of the individual.'

'That must be why we get along.' Baumler had recovered his good humour. He lit a cigar and looked casually round the lounge. 'You can still get a decent meal in this hotel, Michael, and there are always attractive women to look at.'

Stern glanced round as well. None of them interested him very much. He wondered why his thoughts returned so repeatedly to Natalya Meretskova. 'Have you seen the Countess since the night of the ball?'

'Briefly.' Baumler leaned forward and lowered his voice. 'You know there is a serious shortage of drugs in the city? Imagine it, in this day and age. At St Saviour's they sometimes have to operate without anaesthetic. I told her I'd do what I could.'

'You mean you're going into the business of running drugs?'

'Morphia. Just for the hospital.' Baumler considered, frowning. 'One of my couriers is going to try. I've given him enough money to placate the officials on the Finland route.'

'This is not like you, Martin. Where's the fast buck?'

Baumler looked almost embarrassed. 'You could say I'm ploughing back some of my obscene profits. Anyway, helping out the aristocracy is good for business in the long term. And I like a little excitement in my life, it keeps me from feeling old.'

'It could be bloody dangerous for you if your courier gets caught.'

'We-ll.' Baumler scratched his fingers through his thick hair. 'Aiding the Countess is worth a little risk. And I can always buy my way out of trouble.'

Stern wasn't too sure about that. In wartime Russia they'd been known to hang smugglers.

'How is the Countess?' he asked casually.

'Beautiful. Looks thinner. Tired. She works long hours in that hospital. I met her by chance at Fabergé's. She was with her sister.' Baumler's face creased, puzzled. 'Young Rykov has returned to the active list — a damned foolish thing to do with that lung wound of his — and he's on the southern front with the Semionovsky Regiment. And Anna tells me she's taking up nursing. It surprised me that she can now bring herself to talk to a mere American entrepreneur. Odd, isn't it, the way people shift — their values changing slightly all the time.'

Sometimes not so slightly. Stern pondered his persistent curiosity about the Countess and her family. He wished now that he hadn't searched the Russian Army lists. It had been an impulse, seeing them there on the shelves of the Embassy library. 1910 and there was the name, Ivan Alexander Meretskov, Captain, Knights Guards. There had been no entry in the list for 1911.

Baumler never missed anything. 'You are noticeably silent. I have the distinct impression you are interested in the affairs of the Meretskovs. Two beautiful rich young women?'

'I was wondering which of them would settle for life in married quarters at Aldershot or Woolwich. Two rooms, kitchen, bathroom. Could be quite snug.'

'Can't you offer a little more than that? I mean, where would all the servants sleep?'

'No servants. She'll have to make do. Naturally I'd be too proud to touch her millions.' Perhaps I really do owe the Countess and her sister a life, for that brother of theirs, he thought. The 1910 list had located Captain Ivan Meretskov at Samarkand, only a few days' ride from the northern boundary.

'Seriously, Michael, I think you ought to squander a little time in feminine company. I know just about everybody in this city. Why don't you let me find you a nice girl before you go off into the Karelian wilderness?'

'I've just seen one I know,' he said and stared with pleasure at the sensual movement of the girl crossing the lounge towards the exit. What was Helen Mirsky doing in the Europe Hotel?

Baumler followed his gaze. 'Well don't just sit there. Ask her to join us for lunch. I'd rather look at her than at you.'

Stern rubbed his chin. 'All right, damn it, if it will raise the level of conversation above your wheeling and dealing.'

He crossed the lounge and caught up with Helen Mirsky as she reached the heavily ornate doorway. 'Where will I find you next, *dyevooshka*?'

She turned, startled. He thought he detected a momentary alarm in her eyes.

'Captain Stern?' Her mouth curved. 'Perhaps I should feign astonishment. I thought foreigners frequented the Astoria, it being more conventionally Western.' She touched her hair with her finger tips. 'I came in hope of seeing a friend.' She had in fact pretended to be looking for somebody in order to use the luxurious hotel toilet. And to filch a piece of soap. 'Isn't it quite dreadful the way standards are falling? Everything seems so hurried here.'

'Even so, as you are here you might as well join my friend and me for lunch.'

'Oh, I really don't think I should.' She touched her hair again, and she waited.

Stern smiled. 'Our long association demands it.'

Baumler managed a steady barrage of comment and question while they ate.

'What do you do, Miss Mirsky? A student at the university! Well, good for you! I never got beyond high school back in the USA and I was working in a fish canning factory when I was fourteen. An all pervading aroma of fish is a powerful incentive to get on and better oneself in the big world.' He laughed, and Helen smiled as she hurriedly ate.

'And have you now become a shark, Mister Baumler?'

He tilted his handsome head and considered. 'More of a barracuda.'

'What do you study at the university, *dyevooshka*?' Stern asked.

'Literature.' A small suggestion of a frown crossed her face. 'I must also gain satisfactory grades in Ancient Philosophy and History. Alas, an imaginative approach to these subjects is not expected of students.' Her frown deepened. 'Professor Zubov feels that I would be better employed writing historical fiction — of the more sensational kind.'

'Zubov? He's a Duma member, isn't he? Just a bit Red.' Baumler pondered. 'You must never take the truths of academics too seriously.' He held up the wine bottle and smiled at the label. 'Montrachet. That is real history, Miss Mirsky,' and he refilled her glass. 'You know it's real because you can taste it. I know of no better indication of truth.'

Helen held Baumler with her eyes, and her mouth curved upwards.

Stern watched them both and thought how alike they were. He half listened, his mind drifting back to the meeting with Popov. And there was that nagging doubt again. The foreman of the Kazakhov Mill plays chess with a revolutionary, and ten years later the revolutionary attempts an illicit crossing of the frontier on the same train as the foreman's son. An acceptable chance occurrence. But then the son has a significant encounter with the revolutionary's brother in the Murmansk freight depot. Stern speculated on the strangeness of lives touching in a way inconsistent with his belief in a world determined by probability. The connections had to be coincidental. If he doubted that he'd have to admit the possibility of a pattern secreted somewhere in the converging threads, and that was ridiculous. Wasn't it?

Helen laughed at something Baumler was saying, and she turned. 'And how do you measure truth, Captain Stern?'

He smiled. 'In the past I've always used a slide rule.'

What now? I'm not even sure that the old man wasn't involved with revolutionaries. Maybe he did more than just play chess with Dmitry Koltsov. The Okhrana had clearly kept a watch on him, they didn't believe in coincidence, and now they were out to get Koltsov. Maybe I ought to find out more about Peter Koltsov and his brother, and that tenuous link with my father.

They lingered over coffee then left the hotel, pausing for a moment on the steps to watch the thick snow swirling across the Mikhaylovskya.

'I love it,' Helen said. 'The first really heavy fall, and all those sharp memories of one's childhood.'

Baumler pulled his fur hat over his ears. 'I guess I'm too old to recall them.'

'You are certainly not old.' Helen continued to stare at the bright whiteness. The slight frown had returned to her face. 'But I suppose that in time innocence fades to the barely remembered. How sad that it must be so.'

'I'll settle for the compensations of well-heeled middle age, Miss Mirsky.'

She gave Baumler her most engaging smile. 'Thank you for the meal.' And she lowered her eyes modestly. 'And for the conversation.'

Baumler grinned. 'My pleasure. I'll see you again.'

She looked up quickly but he had turned to Michael Stern. 'You keep looking around, Michael. Who do you expect to see?'

A little fat man with thick spectacles, Stern thought, and he surveyed the passers-by. 'Nobody,' he said. 'Nobody in particular.' He bowed to Helen. 'If our innocence is ever lost, *dyevooshka*, I suppose it can always be found again if we search hard enough.' And he smiled. 'At least, that is my hope. Now our paths separate once more, but fate will surely reunite us.'

'Be careful, Captain Stern. I shall suspect that you are a romantic.'

8

Helen left the two men and walked up the Nevsky Prospect. The snow was already deep, covering her suede boots. I look a shabby hag, she thought, and the interesting Mister Baumler is obviously rich. The studs in his shirt cuffs could only have come from Fabergé's. If she'd known she was going to meet him she would have worn the red dress, and used the last of the cologne.

Lunch at the Europe Hotel had provided her with another tantalizing glimpse of the full, comfortable life she aspired to. She frowned. Last year poverty had stiffened her will. This year it was merely demoralizing. Her allowance remained the same but prices were rocketing. She had had to forsake the few small luxuries, like the single pastry once a week from Eleisef's, and the occasional bottle of scent. Even soap had become a problem. If this dreary situation continued she would end up smelling like a carthorse.

Determinedly Helen calculated the saving consequence of a free meal and the piece of soap filched from the hotel cloak room, then returned her thoughts to the now insistent questions. The whole object of a good education was to gain access to Petrograd's upper middle class, there to find a rich and purposeful husband. Like Martin Baumler. What of all her hopes if she could not graduate from university?

She was barely aware that she had reached the tram stop. Her thoughts followed the familiar spiral of plus and minus. Nineteenth-century literature she could manage, even though her favourite lecturer, Serebrov, had blushingly confided his intention to enlist in the defence of Holy Russia. What a sinful waste of a fine mind so easily obliterated by an impartial bullet. A 'satisfactory' grade in Ancient Philosophy seemed within her grasp now that wartime contingencies had resurrected the geriatric Professor Shcheloskov with his less exacting demands. But unless she managed better grades for Professor Zubov she would fail her degree; and return to dull, provincial Uleaborg would surely follow. It was too depressing to contemplate, and there remained only one sure way of moderating Zubov's stringent academic requirements.

Helen boarded the tram and was still deep in thought as it rattled and swayed across Nikolayevsky Bridge to Vassili Island. She must now capitalize on Zubov's carnal interest in her. The eventuality had always been there, waiting. It wasn't that she had any deep-rooted objection to the abandonment of her honour — far from it. The notion was breathtakingly intriguing. But she would have preferred that in the first instance the pleasure should not be the Professor's. With a man like Martin Baumler, or even the wry Captain Stern, the decision would have been easy. Life was seldom that generous. Perhaps we only get what we deserve, she thought. But that possibility was even more depressing.

Helen alighted from the tram and walked the last part of her journey. Vassili Island was only partly academic. She lived in the poorer district because the rents were cheap. Mean streets led off to factories, and the huge Baltic shipyards with their cranes soaring into the snow-filled sky. The working men's café smelled of cabbage soup and cockroaches. She would have eaten here today if Captain Stern had not called to her in the lounge of the Europe Hotel. Pondering the sharp contrast she glanced in as she passed, and almost stopped in her tracks.

A man in a heavy sheepskin coat was seated near the window. His head was lowered as he talked to two workers, but she had instantly recognized his thin face and hard, certain eyes. Why should she be surprised that Peter Koltsov was here? She walked on quickly. The steel workers were organizing for a strike — she'd heard it from Moosha in the room above hers — so of course the agitators were gathering. Even so, it is a puzzle, she thought. With a brother in the prison fortress of St Peter and St Paul, why would Peter Koltsov risk trouble with the police? People who acted against their own best interests disturbed her. One could never be quite sure of where one was with those whose rules were different.

Helen returned to her problem as she reached her own narrow street of cheap tenements, once peopled with minor technicians and skilled artisans, but now in an indeterminate state of decline. The glinting white snow had blurred the street's ugliness, reminding her again of childhood in Uleaborg. There was still time to change her mind. She could tell Zubov she had one of her migraine attacks. He would not believe it. He'd planned this day for too long.

She entered the house and groped along the dark passage. Smells of cooking and damp washing hung in the air. Helen could hear Krillo coughing; he'd worked for ten years in the asbestos factory and now he was finished, old while still young. She climbed the stairs to her room on the first floor, still pondering the surrender of her virtue. Clearly such a weighty question could not be discussed with Irene, the other unmarried girl in the house, who would urge that they should save themselves for love, or some such. She wished she could talk to Moosha — just talk about what he was reading. But he worked the long night shift in the telegraph office and slept for much of the day.

Helen's room faced onto the narrow street. She kept her coat on while she lit a fire — another sacrifice for her degree, she'd hoarded enough coal to keep the room warm for a possibly protracted evening with Zubov. How long would he stay? How long did this sort of thing take? Helen reflected despondently on her abysmal ignorance. The day before she had toyed with the notion of asking Nina Myshkino, who supplemented the near starvation wage of her clerk husband by occasional whoring, but rejected this possibility on hearing Nina's harsh, brassy laugh from the floor above.

Helen surveyed the cheap, fading wallpaper and the drab bedcover. Her books, and the framed pictures of Lermontov and Blok now seemed small sad reminders of last year's hope and determined academic endeavour. And this was to be the setting of her seduction. She stood quite still for a moment. I had always envisaged it quite differently, she thought, then briskly took the piece of soap from her bag. Virtue was an asset, to be traded when circumstances demanded. She must wash and change. Zubov would be here in just two hours.

In the Tauride Palace on the eastern reaches of the city centre, Zubov was steeling himself to address the Duma. Over three hundred deputies had remained to hear his speech. Although not yet prominent, his open lectures directed against mismanagement of the war had begun to interest many of the members. There was subdued excitement as he walked to the rostrum and faced them. He gripped his notes tightly, afraid that his hands would shake.

'Fellow deputies. We, the elected members of this Duma, know who is responsible for our country's dark hour. Let us not deny that our empire is exhausted. But we have made a gain. The situation has been clarified. Here at home our people are hungry and disillusioned. And at the front our guns are without shells and our soldiers without rifles. An impression of strength has been shattered and all members of this body agree on the diagnosis. The incompetence of the Tsar's government is now manifest. Never before have we seen such a crowd of irresponsible people in power; a regime of favourites, conjurors and clowns. We are being led towards complete defeat abroad and total collapse within.'

For a moment Zubov's voice was drowned by applause and shouts of agreement. He waited, certain now that he would not need his notes, and he raised his hand slightly.

'Should we say that we are no longer ready to keep the

peace? We cannot continue to be loyal until the Tsar appoints ministers answerable to this body. To call for strikes and cause more unrest is a course of action which we fear. But if we continue to do nothing to limit the Tsar, even the *moujik*, Rasputin, may become Prime Minister.'

There was another roar of agreement. Members rose to their feet and clapped for half a minute. Zubov glanced round quickly to gauge the response of the hooded-eyed Deputy Kerensky, and before he resumed his speech he allowed himself to speculate briefly on the exhilarating possibilities of power.

Later, as he left the chamber, Zubov was light-headed with his success. Kerensky had remained behind to congratulate him, and even the fat, cautious Rodzianko, President of the Duma, had talked to him for ten minutes. His steps were springy as he crossed the great hall. Tomorrow news of his address to the Duma would be all over the city. He would be recognized as a formidable deputy. And if power should slide to the Duma . . .? The stress of the afternoon had left him wet with perspiration. All those months of work and he was surely now entitled to a small diversion. He wished that Helen had been there to hear his speech. In just a short while he would be with her. That faint mockery in her eyes would dissolve — he would see to that.

As he reached the great doorway of the Tauride Palace a small fat man with thick spectacles sidled up to him. 'Deputy Zubov?'

'Yes.'

'I would be grateful, sir, if you would spare me just a few moments.'

'I'm sorry. I'm in a great hurry. Try to see me tomorrow.'

'It is important.' Popov held out a battered identity document, and he blinked.

'Okhrana!' Zubov was startled. That they should send one of their slimy operatives to him! Was it because of his speech? No, he couldn't be held accountable for anything he said in the Duma chamber. 'Please be brief.'

'Certainly, Professor.' Popov fumbled in his pocket. 'May I say what a great pleasure it is to meet you. I have read your speeches — every one.' He pulled out a grubby notebook. 'You met a prominent Bolshevik named Peter Koltsov on Wednesday. At the Bear Café. Three-twenty to four-fifteen.'

He'd been watched! Zubov stifled his anger. 'That is correct. Koltsov and I are members of the Workers' War Relief Committee — it is non-political. We had business to discuss.'

The fat man looked at him expectantly.

Zubov shrugged, determined to appear unconcerned. 'That is all. That is all we did.'

'You are aware that Koltsov holds extreme views?'

'Yes, of course. But in his capacity of committee member his politics are of no concern to me. As it happens he said nothing to me in the nature of . . .' Zubov searched for an appropriate word.

'Treason?' Popov suggested gently.

'Certainly not! My position is well known to all. I am opposed to certain members of the Tsar's government but I am not opposed to the principles of autocracy. I want only the good of Russia.'

Popov nodded seriously. 'A worthy sentiment, Professor. But we suspect that Koltsov and his fellow conspirators intend the destruction of government *and* our noble Tsar. He is careful what he says in public. Perhaps you recall some small comment made by him that would be useful to us?'

Zubov's hands had begun to sweat. 'I've told you. We met merely to decide the order of business for the next committee meeting. You are wasting my valuable time.'

'I apologize, sir.' Popov sighed and closed his notebook. 'When we question Peter Koltsov he will, of course, confirm that you only discussed committee business.' He creased his fat body in a small bow and turned to leave.

Zubov felt a twinge of fear. 'Wait!' Was the fat little man bluffing, or should he be taken seriously? Supposing the

Okhrana really did intend questioning Koltsov — the truth of what was said might then come out. 'It is *possible* that I may remember something else,' he said, and glanced quickly round. 'But I would prefer that you do not contact me directly.'

Popov lowered his voice. 'Professor, you may count on the discretion of my department. Your name will never be mentioned. You would not wish to be associated with the Okhrana — or with traitors. A telephone call to Number Five Panteleimonskya will reach me. Just ask for Popov.'

'I'll think about it.'

'Very wise. I am grateful for your time, Professor — a man with such a heavy burden of public responsibility.' Popov blinked. 'And your day not yet complete.'

What had he meant by that? Zubov left the Tauride Palace and caught a cab across the city. I am entirely without blame, he thought. I have been party to no treason. Though it would, after all, be wiser to tell Popov the substance of Peter Koltsov's insane suggestion. He frowned out at the snow. It had been imprudent to be seen in the company of that Bolshevik — he'd known it as soon as Koltsov had made the proposal that all factions of the Left denounce the war, call for immediate peace, and work towards toppling the government, by civil war if necessary. Zubov shivered slightly. Peter Koltsov would end up like his brother. Yes. Better to inform the Okhrana in this instance. After all, it wasn't really a betrayal. Koltsov was too far to the Left.

As the cab approached the poorer quarter of Vassili Island all thoughts of Peter Koltsov left his mind. Zubov took the precaution of paying off the cab driver several streets from where Helen lived. As he walked he felt a small guilt over Madame Zubov. She suspected, of course; he'd read the anxious and injured expression in her round flat face. But she would forgive him. He frowned to himself. She always did.

Alone in her room, Helen felt increasingly nervous at the prospect of Zubov's arrival. He was already late. She turned, startled at a tap on the door. Irene, the other unmarried boarder, had come to borrow notepaper. And she hovered, chatting in the hallway, reluctant to leave and curious because Helen wasn't inviting her in. It took Helen five minutes of determinedly unresponsive answers to get rid of her.

Helen closed the door and leaned against it, weary from the necessary deception. Her curiosity about the forth-coming experience with Zubov had completely evaporated and her mind was filled with doubts. It was clearly impor-tant that the Professor should derive some satisfaction from the evening, but not so much that he felt encouraged to make a habit of it.

She began fiercely brushing her hair. The experience would be of no real significance, and the world would not end merely because she had forsaken the path of virtue. She must think of the evening as a form of insurance. A 'satisfac-tory' grade in History required only a satisfied Zubov. So why did she not like looking at herself in the mirror?

Zubov arrived a few minutes later. Helen wondered how they could be so ridiculously formal, exchanging greetings as she took his coat. Her hands trembled as she hung it up.

Zubov was still buoyed up. 'I have had a successful day.' He smiled, sure of himself, and sat, tensed, in the only good chair. 'What a — a quaint little room. Are you staying here over the vacation, or are you returning to . . .'

'Uleaborg. I haven't made up my mind.'

Now that the long-planned ravishment of Helen was imminent, Zubov felt free to coolly appraise her figure. Some women have a magic about them, he thought, and it has nothing at all to do with their tiny minds or trivial aspirations. Helen's bare, tacit acquiescence he interpreted as modest anticipation of fulfilment.

Helen stood quite still for a moment, uncertain what she should do. She swallowed hard. 'Would you care for some tea?' Now she didn't know what to do with her hands. How on earth did one conduct oneself on these occasions?

Zubov shook his head slowly and smiled. He rose from the chair and took her shoulders in his hands. 'You are

100

trembling. Do not be nervous. I will give you such pleasure.'

Even in her anxiety she wondered that he could irritate her so with his vast assumptions. 'I suppose I should undress,' and she began undoing buttons. 'Shall I remove all my clothes?'

Zubov was a little vexed. Months of waiting, and now this mechanical surrender. He rejected the fleeting possibility that she really didn't want him, and he slid her clothes from her shoulders down to her waist.

Helen felt shocked. She had to suppress the urge to cover herself. Zubov stared at the smooth-curving whiteness of her body. Even better than he had so repeatedly imagined. 'Did it occur to you that you would perhaps pass your degree examinations anyway?'

Helen raised her eyes, measuring his expression. 'Then again, perhaps not.'

'Then again, perhaps not.' Zubov ran his hands down to her bare waist and drew her to him.

It was ten o'clock when he left.

Helen sat before the mirror and looked at herself. A few bruises — Zubov was a selfish lover. And she had an odd feeling of loss that she had not anticipated. I look no different, she thought. The degree was safely hers. But why did it suddenly seem so empty?

She washed herself slowly and prepared for bed, then paused, kneeling in front of the fire. What was it that Captain Stern had said? Innocence can be found again if we search hard enough for it. Or such was his hope. Perhaps that is so, she thought, and one had to look on the positive side. She had learned something about herself tonight. Not for a million roubles would she marry a man like Zubov. She rose from her knees but continued to stare into the fire for a moment longer. How odd it all was. Right at the crucial moment with Zubov she had felt sorry for him.

Helen lay wide awake in the darkness, listening to the muted night rumblings beyond the window. And for the first time it seemed to her that she was not responding to the rhythms of the city. It would all seem the same again when morning came. And in the morning she would have to decide whether or not to go home to Uleaborg for Christmas. She frowned, remembering her surprised feeling of not belonging in the small provincial town. I don't want to go home, but neither do I want to stay here, she thought. Perhaps I'll go to Terioki for a while. The half-decision, briefly considered in odd moments, suddenly hardened into certainty. Yes, she would go to Terioki, and the small house by the harbour, cluttered with fishing tackle and smelling of the sea. Grandmother would spoil her. Cousin Erik would flirt with her, and Cousin Paul would tell her stories of smuggling while he worked on the nets. Nobody would talk about the war or shortages, or examinations. And there perhaps she would recapture that feeling that comes with the first heavy fall of snow.

Helen fell soundly asleep.

9

'I can see that our dress is appropriate, Excellency.' Corporal Rantalla frowned out of the tram window at the narrow ill lit streets leading off the Nyustadlskya. 'But I must question the wisdom of our purpose.'

'We're attending a union meeting — no law against that. So we dress as workers.'

'You will forgive my concern for Your Excellency. This part of the Vyborg district is unstable at night.'

'It looks quiet enough now.' Stern pulled his feet back out of the icy draught from the tram entrance.

'My cousin will not bring his cab here after dark.' Rantalla considered. 'He is a cautious man when sober.

The police have been active. They opened fire on demonstrators two days ago.'

'*Another* demonstration?'

'There was no bread, Excellency. So the crowd started to pull down telegraph poles. Acts of desperation. Two people were killed, four wounded by police bullets.'

'Things are getting worse. What do you think about it?'

'No doubt God recognizes the Tsar's honest intentions. If our Little Father can rule, then I say let him. But . . .' The frown on Rantalla's lined face deepened. 'But you and I know that the Prefect of Police has English machine guns — we saw and condoned when Peter Koltsov smashed that case. Who will forgive the Tsar if those guns are used in the city streets?'

'They are being saved, old man.' Stern scowled to himself. 'For some other day.'

Two workmen, dressed like Stern and Rantalla in padded cotton coats, boarded the tram. They lit cheap 'Irina' cigarettes and coughed hugely. The tram heaved and moved off slowly. Beyond the window a woman picked at rubbish in the snow. Splashed behind her on the brick wall were angry jagged words mixed with sad reminders of a hungry Christmas just past. GIVE US BREAD — CHRIST IS BORN — GIVE US PEACE.

Stern watched the woman pushing scraps into her pockets. What would I do if I were a Russian worker? he wondered. 'How much further?'

'Beyond the viaduct, Excellency. Then we must walk.' The corporal paused. 'Your Excellency will pardon a question?'

'Try me.'

'You leave for Karelia tomorrow. This seems a strange way to spend your last night in the city. Why do you wish to hear Peter Koltsov address a meeting?'

'Curiosity.' That tenuous link revealed by the fat little Okhrana agent. He needed to find out about Koltsov before he left Petrograd. 'You disapprove, old man?'

'Turning a blind eye to a smashed case is one thing. This is something else.' Rantalla looked uneasy. 'We are soldiers, Excellency. Politics — unions. These are not our concern.'

Stern nodded. 'I suppose this could be unpleasant for you — a Russian soldier. I've been thoughtless and I understand your reluctance. Better that you show me where the hall is and then return.'

'And what will you do if there is trouble? Your Excellency has a way of making retreat seem unthinkable. I will come with you.'

Stern smiled to himself. 'Very well. But if there is any indication of unpleasantness you must leave immediately. I don't want you caught by your own police.' He thought for a moment. 'Tell me though. You're just a bit curious about Koltsov yourself, aren't you? You found out about this meeting.'

'My cousin mentioned it.' Rantalla sighed then continued in a lowered tone. 'Of course, Excellency I am an old hand and I do not believe everything that is said. But it seems that Koltsov was once religious — he walked as a penance, all the way to a monastery in Greece. Then walked back an atheist, God forgive him. After that he was a soldier, just as we suspected. He served in the war against Japan. And his back is badly scarred from a punishment.'

'A flogging?'

'The knout, Excellency. Its use is now prohibited by civil courts, but soldiers may still be flogged. I have witnessed this on mercifully few occasions.'

'I wonder what he did to earn that? What else have you heard about Koltsov?'

'Active in unions. He addresses meetings and is on committees — all seemingly within the law.'

'Seemingly?'

'Again rumour. My cousin hears much, it being in the nature of his profession. It is said that Koltsov killed an Okhrana agent but there is no proof against him.' Rantalla looked out as the tram approached the viaduct. 'One thing is certain. The man can be dangerous. And this is his home

104

ground. We get off here, Excellency.'

They walked through the unsavoury quarter. Reeking alleys led off. There was no paving and trampled snow covered the hard, rutted mud. Rubbish was piled by narrow doorways, spilling over onto the street.

'An unhealthy neighbourhood, Excellency. It breeds cholera in the summer.'

'And revolution in the winter.'

They found the small, dingy hall and went in. It smelled of unwashed bodies and cheap tobacco. Aboukov found-rymen and women machinists from the mills had filled the close-packed benches, and more stood along the sides. For a while Stern could barely see for the smoke stinging his eyes. Bare electric bulbs lashed to the rafters cast a dim orange light. A man in dirty working clothes was addressing the meeting from a table at the far end. A girl with blonde hair severely pulled back sat on the right taking notes. Peter Koltsov was between her and the speaker.

The meeting appeared to be about cuts in the working rates for the women machinists. Stern had difficulty following the speaker's earnest, clumsy argument. The poor devil kept repeating himself. Koltsov sat, arms folded, staring at the table. From time to time he murmured something to the girl taking notes, then glanced round the hall. He noticed Stern. One eyebrow lifted in surprise and his thin, hard mouth curved very slightly, then he returned his gaze to the table.

The crowd politely nodded their agreement as the speaker laboured his point. The scene had an odd dignity that Stern hadn't expected. He muttered to Rantalla. 'What do you make of it, old man?'

'I feel uneasy, Excellency.'

It all seemed orderly. Stern rubbed his eyes, still stinging from the tobacco smoke, and in that moment he noticed the small fat man with the pebble glasses. Popov! What was he doing here?

The Okhrana agent was seated on the end of a bench on the far side of the hall. Two men in bulky overcoats were standing by him. One of them glanced across and nodded almost imperceptibly to others in the crowd.

Stern whispered. 'You were right to feel uneasy, Rantalla. There's going to be trouble. Edge your way out of the hall. Wait for me by the viaduct. I'll follow in a moment.'

Rantalla paused, expressionless. 'Do not delay too long, Excellency.' And he turned away casually.

The speaker thanked them all for listening, announced that Comrade Koltsov would now address the meeting, and screwed his notes into his coat pocket while they clapped. Across the hall the fat little Okhrana agent took out his watch and blinked at it. He's waiting for something to happen, Stern thought, and began to ease back. Had he left it too late?

The main door at the rear of the building crashed open. 'Everybody remain still!'

Damn, he had.

Policemen pushed their way in. A full-bearded officer stumped towards the desk at the far end.

'Nobody is to move. This meeting contravenes the city ordinances for the maintenance of public order,' he barked. And stopping at the table he turned to face the crowd. 'The Prefect of Police recognizes your probable ignorance of the law. Those who called the meeting, and certain others, will be detained briefly for questioning. The rest of you will be permitted to leave quietly in a few moments.'

Women began to mutter angrily, and a foundry worker somewhere in the crowd bawled, 'Bugger the Prefect! We want a living wage.'

Stern groaned to himself. How could he explain his presence here? If Popov saw him there could be no pleading coincidence. But he still wanted to see what would happen. It was Koltsov they were after, and maybe the crowd knew it. The bolder of the women were standing and they began to shout. 'Police jackals! Leave our people alone!'

Popov blinked anxiously, nodding to the two bulky men by him, and the pair moved towards the table. Koltsov stood tensed, glancing quickly at the exits.

Stern peered up at the dimly glowing electric bulbs. The loose hanging cable was strung down to a switch on the wall just behind where he stood. He leaned back and edged the switch with his shoulder. The lights went out.

Glass shattered in the darkness. Immediately the crowd stampeded, kicking over benches and pushing their way through the door. Stern was shouldered along with them, out into the narrow street. He fell over a bundled figure in the snow. The man cursed loudly and ran off in the other direction. Dark shapes moved confusedly, calling to each other in the night, and a sudden pistol shot echoed dully off the buildings.

Stern lurched along, keeping close to the wall of the hall. The old corporal had been right; soldiers should stay clear of politics and unions. Torches were flashing ahead of him. He groped round the side of the hall, feeling his way along the rough timber, and came to an alleyway. His boots crunched on broken glass at the back of the building. He stumbled, falling clumsily into a mound of stinking rubbish. 'God's teeth!'

'Keep down!'

The voice was close by, muffled in the rotting pile. He burrowed hastily, suppressing his nausea as squealing rats scuttled over his hands. A dung heap! The accumulated filth of months! Foul odours caught at his throat.

Torches flickered from the direction he had come, and he lay quite still. Vague shapes of men moved cautiously along the alleyway and the shafts of light licked along the timber wall. He held his breath.

'Blood in the snow; look here.'

'And more here!' Another man called from further on. The voices receded along the alleyway.

Stern began to ease himself up, but paused on the hoarse imperative whisper close by. 'Wait a moment longer!'

He waited, certain that he would vomit, until the man sharing the heap rose slowly to his feet. 'Now we move.'

'Peter Koltsov?'

'Yes. Follow me.'

They returned round the side of the building to the dimly lit street. Silent now, there were only small indications; a woollen cap, a glove, of those who had scrambled out of the hall.

Koltsov leaned against the wall, hugging himself with his arms. 'Was it you who put out the lights?' He groaned.

'Yes. Are you hurt? I heard a shot.'

'My ribs are broken. That was Zersky's blood on the snow — he jumped through the window and took most of the glass with him. I followed but fell clumsily.' Koltsov leaned his head back and closed his eyes. 'Wiser for you to go, Englishman.'

Wiser, but not a thing he could bring himself to do. 'You need a doctor.'

'I can't go to the house of a comrade, they'll all be watched.'

'If your ribs are badly broken you could puncture a lung. Quick! Think now. Where can I take you?'

'The Charity Hospital of St Saviour.' Koltsov moved slightly and gasped. 'Doctor Strozhov. He'll ask no questions.'

'Are you sure he'll be there?'

'He'll *be* there.'

Stern nodded and peered along the dark street. 'Tread carefully. Don't jolt as you move. Lean on me if you need to.'

I'm crazy, he thought, as they moved slowly towards the viaduct. The approach to each street corner forced up his pulse rate. What the hell do I do if the police are round that corner?

'Why did they raid the hall tonight?'

'They could arrest me among others there, just on the charge of breaking the city ordinances. But they wouldn't have bothered if they hadn't accumulated other evidence that will stick. Somebody has betrayed me.' Koltsov winced and clutched his arms tightly round himself. 'I wonder who it was?'

Stern allowed brief speculation on his own predicament.

If we are caught, Southgate will certainly let me rot in a Russian prison cell. And I still know practically nothing about Koltsov, except that he's an agitator, probably dangerous, with a murder to his credit. But in that last respect we may have something in common.

Bright moving lights made them hurry into a doorway. They waited while a car went by, then moved on.

Rantalla was waiting in the small circle of light cast by a bracket lamp set in the grey, dirty brickwork of the viaduct wall.

'Excellency.'

'Thanks for being here, old man.' Stern glanced round. Late now, there was little traffic, and only a few nightworkers on their way to the power station. 'I have to get Koltsov to the hospital of St Saviour.'

'Your Excellency enjoys a challenge.' Rantalla's face remained impassive. He looked quickly at Koltsov, then sighed almost imperceptibly. 'You will not manage on your own. I will go with you.'

'How do we reach St Saviour's from here — a cab?'

'Your pardon, Excellency. You smell worse than gravediggers and cab drivers are suspicious men.' Rantalla frowned to himself. 'A tram to the Schusselburg, but it is a workers' district and heavily patrolled at night.'

'We'll worry about that when we get there. We must keep moving.'

They continued, through backstreets and avoiding the light, and they waited near the Alexandrovsky Bridge. Koltsov leaned against the wall and closed his eyes.

'Why are you doing this? It is not your affair.'

Stern didn't know. He shook his head. 'God knows!'

'There is no God. Why did you come to the meeting?'

'Because I'm mad.'

'His Excellency is English,' Rantalla added as explanation, and he paused, listening.

'He's not mad. He has a reason.' Koltsov stared at Stern. 'There is always a reason.'

In that moment Koltsov's reasoning seemed chillingly

like that of the Okhrana agent, and Stern was aware of a puzzled foreboding. 'The tram is approaching,' he said. 'We'll talk of repairing sewers. The smell should add conviction.'

The tram was empty, on its way back to the Schusselburg depot. Koltsov sat between them, his face white under the smears of dirt. Three shabbily dressed women, with shawls pulled tight round their ears, climbed on at the Shpalernay stop on the south side of the river. They grumbled as they moved up the gangway.

'The police are everywhere, searching people. One of them touched me — here.'

'You liked it.'

'My Boya can't get leave — I haven't had him for ten months.' Her cheeks were pitted by smallpox.

'Ten months! The Empress would copulate with Rasputin when the Tsar is at the front, and he's only a *moujik*. Get yourself a garrison Cossack to shaft with, they're like bulls.'

And they laughed hoarsely, faces grey in the dim light. The one with the pitted face coughed and spat, then held her nose as she looked around at the three men. 'I'd even have them.' Her eyes narrowed as Koltsov breathed painfully. 'What's wrong with him?'

'He's got a belly ache,' Stern said. 'We're sewer workers.'

She looked at Stern's filthy clothes and her pinched mouth curved in invitation. 'I thought you were a grand duke.'

He grinned back at her. 'I am. Cleaning sewers is my hobby.' They were like the crones from Macbeth.

But the first woman was peering closely at Koltsov. She nudged the other two and they muttered together.

Damn! They'd recognized him! Stern thought quickly — should they get off the tram and lose themselves in those dark streets?

The woman turned again, her eyes sharp. 'It's him, isn't it — Peter Koltsov, the man they're after?'

110

Koltsov nodded. 'Yes, old mother. I'm Koltsov.'

Her face softened. 'It *is* him!'

And the three whispered urgently. 'Let us help! — Tell us what to do.'

Stern was astonished, and shamed by their immediate and unquestioning response. 'We have to get to St Saviour's hospital,' he said. 'We'll get off the tram at the next stop, and you walk ahead of us. If the police are about, distract their attention.'

The women were like accomplished small part actresses, bantering and grumbling as they trudged through the snow. Not once did they look back.

The lighted windows on three floors of the charity hospital outshone the dim street lamps of Kazyanskya Street. Stern almost sighed with relief. We've got this far safely enough. And in that moment two policemen moved into the light. Bulky in their overcoats and with revolvers strapped round them, they watched as one of the women shouted an insult and hit out at her partner. The third tried to separate them, then cursed the policemen for laughing.

'Pigs! All men are pigs — betrayers! For the love of Christ, save my sisters from killing each other!'

And even then, none of them glanced back.

Stern wished he could thank them.

'Through the side way, to the dispensary,' Koltsov grunted. 'Get word to the Doctor, then leave. I'll manage the rest on my own.'

'We'll see.' Stern pushed open the door, and they entered the echoing, polished, brightly lit corridor of the hospital. The door banged to behind them.

10

'We agreed sixty. Now we have one hundred and thirty-two.' Natalya stood in the doorway of the Alexander Ward and looked along the rows of closely packed beds. She eased her back. 'There is barely ten inches between each of them.'

Rearrangements had taken much of the day; head, neck, and chest cases moved on the rubber-wheeled trolleys to the hastily cleared adjoining ward, while new arrivals — an overspill from the military hosiptal — filled the vacated beds.

'Even the corridor is full. We cannot receive more.'

Thin-faced Surgeon Litchitski murmured, 'At least five of these will not live much longer.' He speculated. 'And four from the Nicholas Ward. That will give you a little more room.'

And the young ensign in the side ward, Natalya thought. That will make ten. 'Have you sufficient assistance in the operating theatre? I can spare the orderly, Dimitriev. He has a strong stomach.'

'Has he strong arms?' Litchitski shrugged hopelessly. 'We are almost out of morphia.'

'Medical Services say the shortage is temporary.'

'Temporary? They must think we are fools!' He rubbed his hand wearily across his eyes and turned away. 'We'll manage somehow. I'll operate through the night.'

I am spared that, Natalya thought. I am spared watching while he cuts without anaesthetic.

It was nearly ten-thirty. Small sad reminders of Christmas still decorated the darkened windows. Natalya had barely noticed its passing. The old priest had blessed the wounded, solemnly intoning the words through his great beard. She had left a small gift on each man's bed. They had sung hymns, moving her with their deep, sad voices.

Natalya began her last round of the beds, smiling briefly

at each soldier. The trick was to keep part of oneself detached. Most of the time it worked, but not always. She knew it wouldn't work at the end of the duty; when each night she visited the dying ensign in the side ward. It never worked then.

'Can't I be sent to a hospital near home, Sister?'

'Not yet.' Natalya adjusted the harness supporting the man's shattered arm. There was a basin beneath it to collect the dripping pus. 'We have to mend you. You'll need both arms to embrace your wife.'

'They'll make a box to send me home in.' The grey-bearded soldier in the next bed pushed himself up on his elbow and grinned cheerfully. 'Cheap pine and no brass handles.'

Natalya smiled at him. 'No, they won't. They cannot afford boxes. They'll send you home in a sack.'

'A fine thing! A man gives his life for the Tsar, and they send him home in a sack.'

'You're not going to die.' A guardsman with a face the colour of putty, groaned and arched his back. 'We'll get justice when the Tsar bleeds like us. Something for the pain, Sister?'

She squeezed his hand tightly. 'I'm sorry, soldier. We are desperately short of morphia.'

'For the love of Christ!' he snarled. 'Officers get it all!'

The grey-bearded soldier stared at him. 'Patience, brother. We're men, not boys.'

'I've got a gut wound going bad — I piss blood. You've only lost a leg.'

Grey-beard looked down at the flatness where his leg should be. 'I'd still have my leg if I'd deserted, as others did. But in the end I couldn't.'

Natalya remembered the leg coming off. A tourniquet had been put on at the front and nobody had had time to loosen it. Surgeon Litchitski had cut high because of the gangrene. The bright saw blade, flecking blood, hacked rapidly through the bone and Natalya had felt the heaviness of the leg in her hands. 'Yes. It's only a leg. And now you

113

can invent stories about how you lost it.'

He put a cigarette between his lips. She scratched a match on a box for him.

Only a leg?

Tiredness numbed one almost to indifference.

Grey-beard dragged on the cigarette, watching her. 'You've been good to us, Sister.' Was that all he could say? Yes, that was all. She had not spared herself in her duties. She pondered where duty ended and love began.

Natalya hadn't noticed that she was being closely observed. She took the board from the bottom of Grey-beard's bed. 'I see you were with General Malnekov's Caucasian Corps.'

'A survivor, Sister.' He shrugged. 'His High Excellency moved his finger across the map, and we were thrown like lead into the furnace. There are few of us left to complain.'

Natalya felt guilty, as if she were Malnekov's accomplice. 'Is it better to thank God you are still alive?'

'Perhaps, Sister.' Grey-beard's eyes were wide and totally innocent. 'The General lost a battle. I only lost a leg.'

She bit her lip. What would I give up to make them whole again? — a palace? — half my wealth? — all my wealth? One thing I cannot do is love them.

Grey-beard smiled at her. 'Don't be sad for me, Sister. I'm a carpenter. I can make myself a peg leg. And you shouldn't be sad tonight. It's New Year's Eve.'

'So it is.' Natalya smiled back. 'I keep forgetting.' And she moved on, checking each patient. Four Semionovsky of Rykov's battalion in the ward, all from the lost battle on the southern front. Malnekov's reputation had slipped badly with that small disaster. Natalya's eyes ached and her limbs felt heavy. There was just one compensation in working twelve hours a day — it left little time to miss Paul Malnekov. She adjusted a pillow and smiled mechanically at the wounded guardsman before turning away. Desire remains.

Had love for Malnekov been an illusion — nothing left now but a hunger? The thought disturbed her. If she hadn't loved Malnekov, then she'd never loved anybody.

Now the day was almost over; one duty left. Natalya went into the toilet and quickly examined herself in the mirror. Old, she thought. My face looks old. Without knowing why, she was aware it was important that she appeared attractive for the dying ensign. One more night — perhaps two. She let down her hair and combed it, then pinched her cheeks to bring colour to them.

The side ward smelled sickly, cloyingly sweet of gangrene. The ensign was alone. His face and closed eyelids had a faint blue tinge. Natalya took his hand.

He opened his eyes slowly and whispered, 'I thought you would not come.'

'I always come.'

He looked puzzled and stared unseeing at the white wall. 'The ballroom is so crowded. I searched everywhere for you.'

'I went to change my dress — for the white one, the one you like. Now I'm here.'

'How beautiful you are!' Exhausted, he closed his eyes, then frowned. 'I had a dream. The palace was burning. Red! Everywhere was red. There was blood on the snow.'

'It was only a dream.' Natalya spoke softly. 'The snow has gone. Now it is summer. Can you see the wheat-fields?'

He strained with his eyes. 'I can see them!'

'And soon you will be well.'

'And you will save me a waltz.'

'Yes. I will save you a waltz. Now close your eyes. And sleep.' And please God don't let him wake.

Natalya left and went to fetch her army greatcoat. She held it close to herself for a moment, feeling the rough, green cloth, worn now after her service with the hospital train all those months ago. It comforts me, she thought, more than all the silk and furs. And she wondered at the changes in herself, and where they would lead her to.

She passed the beds of the less seriously wounded, crowded along one side of the corridor, and bade soldiers goodnight before descending the stairs to the ground floor.

Peter Petrovich would be waiting with the carriage, and he would grumble and fuss over her. And how comforting that was.

She walked quickly along the silent, empty passage towards the side exit, but paused, noticing a light behind the frosted glass door of the dispensary. Who could be in there at this hour of the night?

Natalya opened the door and looked in.

There were two men in the small room. One had his back to her, arm stretched up adjusting the flame of the hissing gas lamp. The other man was stripped to the waist, seated on the table and facing the door.

'Oh! Is somebody looking after you?' She was aware in the same moment that they shouldn't really be there. 'I thought Doctor Strozhov had left.'

The man adjusting the lamp turned to her. 'Madam.' And he bowed. 'The Doctor will return in a moment.'

'Do I know you?' She looked at him and frowned. 'Yes, I think I do.'

'Michael Stern, madam.'

'Ah, yes.' Now she remembered. It was the young English officer who had irritated her that night at the ball. And why was he wearing filthy workingmen's clothes? 'What are you doing here?'

'Here?' Stern looked round him, as if surprised by his surroundings. 'This poor fellow has had an accident — a fall. He fell, you see. Getting off a tram. And as we happened to be near the hospital . . .' He tailed off.

The explanation sounded impromptu, even more so to Natalya as she noticed the wary expression of the seated man. She stared hard at them both. 'And your clothes? What did you fall into?'

Stern looked solemn. 'Alas, the sanitary arrangements for this city are quite appalling.'

The other man's laugh cut short, and he hugged himself in pain. 'This Englishman found me in the snow. The filth has rubbed off my clothes onto his. That is why he smells. I am a Russian worker so of course I smell all the time.'

116

The sneer in his harsh voice shocked her. He doesn't know who I am, she thought with surprise, or he would not use that tone. He thinks I am just another nurse. 'And Doctor Strozhov knows you are here?'

'The good doctor will return in a moment,' Stern said.

Natalya's suspicion hardened into certainty. And why, in heaven's name, has the good doctor involved himself yet again? she thought angrily. This man is another wretched agitator, and the arrogant English captain has blundered into something he shouldn't have. 'I think you have come to the wrong place.'

Stern stared at her.

I haven't the time or inclination to worry about his opinion, she thought, and turning to the seated man she added, 'Go to your own people. Let them look after you.'

Strozhov appeared in the doorway, the light from the hissing lamp shining on his bald head and thin Semitic nose. 'I'm sorry, Countess.'

Natalya steered the Doctor out into the corridor and closed the door behind her. 'You must not *do* this!'

'The man has fractured ribs.'

'And is no doubt in trouble with the police.' She sighed, exasperated. 'We have the sick to look after. And soldiers wounded in the service of Russia. And you persist in tending troublemakers.'

'But, Natalya Alexandrovna, he is not just a troublemaker. He is Peter Koltsov and he . . .'

'You jeopardize the reputation of the hospital. I cannot permit you to continue in this way. The man must go elsewhere.'

Koltsov must have heard her, she knew it as she opened the door. He stared coldly. 'I had not realized I was in the presence of aristocracy. I'll leave.'

As he turned stiffly, reaching out to pick up his shirt, Natalya saw the scars of the lash on his back.

'Oh, my God!'

Her exclamation was quite involuntary. The scars were old, purple, obscene; deep grooves crossing and completely

117

covering him from shoulders to waist. She stared in revulsion. How could anybody do that to a living being?

Michael Stern had taken the shirt and was helping Koltsov with it. 'Careful now. Left arm up slowly.' And he addressed Natalya without looking at her. 'My servant is out finding a cab for us, madam. We'll leave as soon as he returns.'

I cannot do it, she thought. I cannot turn away a man who has been marked like that. And she turned to Strozhov. 'How many ribs?'

'Lower three, left side.'

'Let us do it quickly.' She pulled off her greatcoat.

A suggestion of a smile on Stern's face irritated her. 'You can make yourself useful, Captain. Fetch the wide sticking plaster from that cupboard.'

'Three — possibly four ribs.' Strozhov frowned and his wire-rimmed glasses slid down on his nose. 'I will take care of this, Countess. You go home.'

'And what else will you get up to when I am gone?' Fond of him, she rested her hand on his arm. 'Leave it. I'm better at it than you.'

'Very well. Bind the rib cage tightly.'

Natalya felt Koltsov's lower ribs, and his eyes registered pain. 'I'm sorry. This will hurt a little.'

'Don't worry. Just get on with it.'

She was astonished by his cold hostility. People do not talk to me that way! She pulled the plaster tight, aware again of a feeling of repugnance as her fingers touched the deep-ridged scars. Was it his sneering contempt that earned him that awful flogging? His clothes stank and his hands were ingrained with filth. He is barely like a human being, she thought. 'I can see from the marks on your back that you have a strong constitution.'

'Pretty, aren't they?'

'How old are the scars?'

'They date back to Chita, eleven years ago.'

1905. What was it Rykov had said? A dark year with a dark ending. 'The army mutiny?'

'Yes.' He watched her face. 'They could have hanged me, of course, along with others, but General Malnekov showed clemency because of my youth.' And he smiled thinly. 'Besides, a flogging is a more vivid deterrent.'

And that is how Malnekov so efficiently crushed the mutiny.

Stern passed her the scissors and Natalya cut the sticking plaster. Awful as the scars were, it was not for her to judge. Malnekov had surely done what he had to do. Mutineers had to be punished — examples made. Even so, to do that to a man — or a boy. Koltsov couldn't have been more than seventeen or eighteen then.

Strozhov felt Koltsov's bandaged ribs and nodded. 'I am sorry, Countess. Not for what we have done, but for involving you.'

She didn't look at him. How do you deter an old doctor from his folly? 'You and I must have a talk tomorrow.'

'And we will leave you now, madam.' Stern wrapped Koltsov's coat round his shoulders. 'I will take Peter Koltsov to his friends.'

She looked at Stern sharply. 'I do not want to know what you do with him, Captain.'

'I meant, madam, that we will embarrass you no further.'

'For that I would be grateful.' And why has an English captain got himself mixed up in this? she wondered.

'My servant should be outside with the cab.' Stern paused briefly at the door, and he frowned. 'I'll take a look around and make sure the way is clear.'

When he had gone, Koltsov fingered a cigarette from his coat pocket and lit it. 'You know him — the Englishman?'

'Very slightly.' Natalya wondered why she even replied. It must be because he puts me off balance, she thought. I'm not used to Koltsov's rules. 'You shouldn't smoke.'

'He's a strange one.' Koltsov frowned, then he coughed and winced.

'The English are a strange race.' Strozhov took off his spectacles and rubbed his eyes.

And Koltsov continued, puzzled, 'He must have a reason for doing this.'

'Would nobody else have helped you?' Natalya asked.

Koltsov shrugged very slightly. 'Some out there would. Many wouldn't — you see, they suspect that what I tell them is the truth. There are no rewards in heaven. The here and now is all.' His thin mouth twisted in a smile but his eyes remained expressionless, watching her.

'And you are out to change the here and now?'

He didn't answer.

I find him disgusting, and rather frightening, Natalya thought. And I suspect he is aware of my feelings.

There was a knocking on the frosted glass panel and Strozhov rose to answer it.

'No, Doctor. If it is more bullet wounds or cracked skulls then they must be taken elsewhere.' And Natalya opened the door.

Three men in thick overcoats faced her. For a moment she assumed they were friends of Koltsov's and she was angry that they should come here. 'What is it that you want?'

The oldest of them took off his fur hat and bowed. 'My apologies, Your Excellency. Police Inspector Kazimov, Rozhdestvenskya District. We are informed that Peter Koltsov is here. We have a warrant for his arrest.'

So there are police informers on our staff, Natalya thought numbly. There is nothing left to surprise me tonight. 'You mean to arrest him here, in the hospital?'

The officer looked over her shoulder at Koltsov still seated and he murmured softly, 'The man is dangerous, Your Excellency. We bring a charge of treason. If you will just step aside, we will take him, and no bother to yourself.'

'I suppose you must do your duty.' Natalya let them pass, but seeing them move determinedly on Koltsov she added quickly 'Please be careful! He has fractured ribs.'

The youngest of them grinned, brutality coming easily to him. 'He'll get all our attention when we get him to the Predvarilka.'

Koltsov stared down at his wrists as the steel manacles clicked.

'Is that really necessary, Inspector? He cannot possibly struggle or run.'

The Inspector nodded, misinterpreting her concern. 'Do not worry, Excellency. Nobody in the hospital will see him handcuffed, we will take him out by the side door.'

'I meant . . .' And she stopped.

With a glimmer of understanding, the Inspector's deference hardened very slightly. He glanced first at Strozhov and then at Natalya. 'I am of course assuming that Your Excellency was quite unaware that this man was injured escaping from the police.'

'Idiot!' Koltsov snarled. 'Do you suppose I would have told them that?'

'And the two men who brought you in here?' The officer's eyes narrowed. 'Two tall men; one young, one old. Where are they?'

'They found me in the snow.' Koltsov shrugged. 'A pair of do-gooders, full of stupid questions. I was glad to see the back of them.'

The Inspector nodded. Well, it didn't matter. It was late, and they'd got Koltsov. It didn't even matter if this imperious Countess knew what she was doing. Best to show respect — she could make trouble for them. The Okhrana could check later. He bowed low. 'Again my apologies, Your Excellency. We have difficult work.' Natalya didn't answer, and he jerked his head to the other two. 'Bring him.'

Peter Koltsov stood and his manacles clinked. The young policeman pushed him in the back and he winced, but paused, staring at Natalya for a moment. She felt her face flush and turned away as they led Koltsov out.

In the corridor they passed Michael Stern returning. Koltsov didn't glance at him and Stern walked on without turning back.

He found Natalya pulling on her army greatcoat. Strozhov was seated at the desk, filling in a record card.

'Well, it ended badly. But I must complete this card in case the police come back.' Strozhov frowned and read over what he had written. 'Name, Petrovich. Age, approximately thirty. Three fractured ribs sustained falling from a tram. Other identifiable injuries?' He paused then wrote again. 'Old scars, shoulder blades to waist. Date, 31st December, 1916.' And he looked up. 'A strange way to end the year.'

Natalya peered over his shoulder at the card. 'It seems so little to say of a man.' She frowned, puzzled, and Stern thought that her face in profile seemed oddly innocent.

Strozhov took off his spectacles. 'He's been trouble for the authorities for a long time. Now they have a case — the Okhrana must have found somebody who would talk.'

'What will happen to Koltsov?' she asked.

'Treason? They could hang him, but I doubt if they will do that. It will probably mean penal service as a convict.'

Natalya determinedly fastened her coat. 'It is not our affair. Do you hear me, Doctor?' She rested her hand on his shoulder and added gently, 'We have a hospital to worry about. That is *our* duty.'

Strozhov touched her hand on his shoulder. 'Perhaps you are right, Natalya Alexandrovna. But I am old; less certain now where duty will lead me in that grey area between right and wrong.'

You don't have to be old to lose your certainty. Stern watched Natalya as she stretched, half-turning, the army greatcoat pulled tight across her breasts. But she appears to have no doubts. What is it about her? he wondered. Her face is drawn with fatigue and her hair lifeless. Yet she retains an imperious sensual attraction, and a cool certainty of what she is.

'If there should be further questions from the police, I am entirely responsible for what has happened,' he said. 'I am anxious that you should be troubled no further.'

'Are you concerning yourself with my reputation?'

'Yes, madam.'

She held him with her steady, guarded gaze. He wished she wouldn't do that.

'Chivalrous of you, Captain Stern, but quite unnecessary. That agitator has completely disowned us.' And she looked at the clock. 'We really should leave here.'

She has cut me down again, Stern thought. She's assumed inevitable male interest in her and rejected it. And damn it, my intention is merely to protect her. But almost immediately he wondered if that was entirely the case. To what extent was he influenced by the possibility that his destiny had touched hers five years before, on a river bank two thousand miles away?

'Nevertheless, madam. And you, Doctor Strozhov. The police *may* come back here. Peter Koltsov has lied to save us from further questions. But he may be persuaded to say more than he intends. If that happens you will please indicate that it was I who brought him here. I can be contacted through the British Military Attaché's office.'

'Might they persuade him?' It seemed that brutal interrogation of Koltsov had not occurred to her. 'Poor man.' She bit her lip. 'Even if that is so, the police are hardly likely to question anything I say. However, your position is less happy, Captain. The British Government and your War Office — will not be pleased if they learn of your association with an agitator accused of treason.'

'I've displeased them before.' Stern shrugged and his jaw tightened. 'That is why I'm here. And it hardly matters. Tomorrow I leave for Karelia and the Murmansk railway. There is nowhere worse they can send me.'

'The Murmansk railway?' Strozhov was staring at him. 'Hell might be more congenial. I do not envy you.'

Natalya looked curiously at Stern. 'Then you really have displeased somebody.'

'It is a knack I have, madam.'

She smiled very slightly. 'We have noticed, Captain.'

And it seemed to Stern that she was seeing him as a person for the first time.

Rantalla knocked on the door. Natalya opened it and glanced suspiciously at his dirty clothes. 'I hope your ribs are not broken.'

He bowed. 'No, Sister. I am searching for my captain — the English Excellency. I have a cab.'

'Your captain is here.' She turned her head to Stern. 'And I think he is about to leave.'

Michael Stern rubbed his hand across his face. Perhaps he wouldn't see her again. He wanted to say something — indicate in some way that meeting her had been important to him. He scowled to himself, unable to think of any appropriate words. 'Again my apologies.'

'Worry about yourself.' She sighed and smiled wryly. 'Karelia is harsh country in the dead of winter, Captain. God protect you.'

'Goodbye, madam.'

Stern left with Rantalla. He noticed the waiting black carriage, and the sleek Meretskov horses pawing the snow under the dim street lamp. The cab was further along and he told the driver to take them to the Nevsky Prospect.

'Our efforts came to nothing, Excellency.'

The cab trundled slowly, wheel sounds muted by the deep snow.

'We did all we could.' Stern was wondering about the Countess. Half an hour and she would be back in her palace, distanced from that grey brick building, and Koltsov. And himself.

'There is a lot of anger in Peter Koltsov,' he said.

'Perhaps he is angry with God, Excellency?'

'You said he rejected religion, in Greece. You said he walked back from that monastery an atheist.'

Rantalla shrugged slightly. 'That is only a story I heard, Excellency. And you have to be a religious man to reject God.'

'Of that I'm not sure, old man.' Stern looked out at the snow-covered street. 'What will you do now that I'm leaving Petrograd — do you have another officer to serve?'

'No, Excellency. Tomorrow the army is discharging me.' Rantalla pondered. 'New Year's Eve. A time for decision. I may go back to Finland.'

'Yes? A man should go home in the end.' And where is home for me? Stern wondered. A cottage on the Sussex Downs? I invented it inside my head. Hills to walk and the sea. I even invented a dog to run over those hills while I walked.

'How long since you last saw home, old man?'

'Many years, Excellency. When I was sixteen I worked on the boats in the summer, and I smuggled in the winter. I was caught and the judge offered me life as a convict or life as a soldier. I have been home only twice since then.'

'God's teeth! That must be forty years or more?'

'There seemed little to go back for. Soldiering separated me from that other life. I have marched across deserts and mountains. I've fought Koreans, Turks and Japanese. I was with Cherniev's Corps in Poland, fighting the Austrians. I am even familiar with Karelia — I served with the border patrol in 1902.' He frowned to himself. 'One becomes a stranger to one's own land. Perhaps I'll stay in Petrograd. My cousin has offered me a half share in his cab.' And he paused. 'I shall miss Your Excellency.'

Stern wondered, This straight-backed old corporal wants to come with me. Karelia is the edge of the world. Perhaps he's a little crazy. But I've grown to like him. 'Stay with me if you wish,' he said casually, 'though we'll be months in the wilderness.'

Rantalla appeared to consider. 'Well, as I said, Excellency, I had made no definite plans. My cousin can manage the cab without me. Oh, we get along well enough, but he is a man comfortable with empty conversation and crowded streets.' He rubbed his jaw. 'Possibly I could be useful to Your Excellency. I cook a good stew. And I have watched engineers at work.'

'Then you have a job, though God knows why you want it.'

'God, of course, determines our destinies.' A suggestion of a smile crossed Rantalla's leathery face. 'But Your Excellency puzzles me; he has a purpose locked up somewhere inside his head. If I do not go with you I will keep wondering what it is.'

Stern stared at him. 'Purpose? I'm not aware of one.'

'Then we must see what Karelia offers us.' Rantalla looked thoughtful. 'The wilderness has a certain harsh wisdom, and Petrograd is just a city after all.'

Was it just another city?

The cab moved past the yellow-columned Tauride Palace and alone Shpalernaya Street. Stern looked back at the Petrograd Regional Law Court and the grey blind wall of the prison. Koltsov would have been taken there.

No, Petrograd wasn't just another city. Since his return he'd been aware that fragments of his life were here coming together. He partly feared this though he was reluctant to leave. The Countess Natalya Alexandrovna Meretskova had become important in his life but he was not certain why. One shakes the kaleidoscope and new patterns emerge out of the old pieces, he thought, and watched as a group of patrolling soldiers paused cautiously at a street corner before moving on.

The bells of Kazan Cathedral boomed midnight and were echoed by the bells of St Isaac's.

'It is a new year, Excellency.'

'Yes. The first day of 1917.'

'The Tsar is still on his throne.'

'And the streets are quiet again.'

'Who can tell what this year will bring?'

Who indeed.

11

In the tea room of the Astoria it was still almost possible to believe that nothing had really changed. At mid-afternoon musicians played in a jungle of potted palms. The rich met here, warmly insulated from what was happening out there in the streets.

There were more foreigners using the hotel. Natalya

could pick out the Americans even without the little stars and stripes buttons in their lapels.

'Mr Baumler is late. It's unlike him.'

'You have changed the subject.'

Natalya sighed. 'Anna, it is pointless to pursue the matter. Even if you had completed your nursing training the Empress would not permit you to go.'

'I can't see why.' Anna frowned and toyed with her spoon.

'You are too young to join the volunteer nurses; it is only for the fittest and best qualified.' Natalya smiled and inclined her head very slightly as a tall, grey-haired Dane bowed to her, monocle glinting, then moved on. 'And it takes a stout heart to serve in Austria. Ask the Count, he'll tell you.'

Anna glanced at the Dane's Red Cross armband then turned almost angrily. 'It would make no difference. It's a duty. Some have to go.'

'But not you.' Natalya scanned the guests to see if Baumler had arrived. 'You are not used to such hardships.'

'You served on a hospital train. The Empress didn't forbid that.'

'I was twenty-three then.' Dear God, how old I'm getting, Natalya thought. 'You are only eighteen. And bad as the trains are, at least we were among our own people. In Austria you would be considered an enemy even though you nurse, treated with little more respect than the captive Russian soldiers. Conditions in Austrian prisoner of war camps are appalling.' Damn! She shouldn't have said that. Now Anna looked more determined than ever. 'I know it's hard for you but you must try to be patient. At the moment we know only that Captain Rykov has been taken prisoner. He could be in any one of a dozen camps.'

A loudly talking group passed the table. Anna clasped the glass of tea with both hands, pressing it hard on the table. 'I can't bear to think of him; wounded or sick, dying perhaps, with nobody to nurse him. He was unfit but felt impelled to leave us and return to active service. I was shamefully rude to him, but it wasn't that.' She looked up. 'I suspect, Natalya, that it was something you said or did.'

Why am I always made to feel guilty? Natalya wondered. 'You shouldn't under-rate Captain Rykov. Neither of us is responsible for the decision he made — it was his alone. He is a *man*, answerable to himself. If he were anything less, how could you love him?'

Anna stared at her. 'Sometimes I wonder if you understand what love means.'

That was a little too close to the truth. Natalya stiffened. 'So I don't know what it means.' Perhaps I haven't yet met a man I can really love, she thought. Perhaps there isn't one.

'I'm sorry.' Anna bit her lip. 'I shouldn't have said that.'

'Better that you say it than just think it.' Natalya shrugged. 'It doesn't matter, as long as you know I love and care about you.'

'I know it.' Anna frowned down at the table. 'You puzzle me. You work so hard at the hospital but you hate what you have to do.'

'That's something else again.'

'Nobody works harder. And now you are sleeping badly. Vera told Vasya that you were reading at two this morning.'

'It wasn't just the work yesterday.' Natalya felt the frown on her thoughts again. How to explain that restless dream, even to herself? 'A man we tended at the hosiptal. I keep remembering him. He filled me with revulsion. His back was hideously scarred from a flogging. The police came and arrested him.'

'What had he done?' Anna leaned forward, curious.

'I'm not really sure. A Bolshevik of some kind. Slight build — the policemen towered over him. His wrists were manacled and his ribs were broken. But as they led him away he seemed . . . he seemed bigger than them, almost as though he could tear our world down.'

Anna stared. 'Really, Natalya. You sometimes have the strangest notions.'

Baumler approached; smiling, large among the other guests, and a waiter hurried to serve him.

'Ladies.' He bowed, looking pleased with himself. 'I'm sorry I'm late.'

'We knew it must be something important that delayed you, Mr Baumler.' Natalya watched his face. Had he managed to get the morphine?

He leaned forward, glancing round quickly to ensure that he could not be overheard. 'I have a package for you, Your Excellency — just arrived from Helsingfors. It is flat inside my newspaper. Better that nobody sees me hand it to you. In a while I will place the newspaper on the table. You take it with you when you leave.'

Natalya nodded.

'I'm making a short journey to Finland fairly soon,' he added. 'I'll bring back more.'

'Do not take too many risks.'

'I'm just beginning to enjoy myself.'

Yes, he probably is. Natalya smiled slowly. He is like a boy who has just discovered a new and exciting game. 'How can I repay you?'

Baumler appeared to ponder. 'Call it a gift, Countess.' He'd never get the payment he'd most like from her. 'My contribution to your war effort.'

Natalya sensed his surge of interest. With virile Americans one has to phrase questions differently, she decided. 'You are generous. Was it difficult — bringing the package in?'

'We-ll.' He thought for a moment. 'These days nothing is easy. I fight my own private war with the Russian Technical Department. Happily for you I'm not entirely honest — you can't be and survive here. Many of the independent traders have been forced out, or swallowed up by the big sharks.'

'But you remain.'

'I'm just a shade too big for the sharks to swallow.' He grinned and placed the folded newspaper on the table. 'Have you seen the news? They are still looking for Rasputin. Rumours abound. He could be bedded with somebody's wife — if you'll pardon the observation. God knows, he's done that often enough. But the hottest rumour is that he's dead — murdered by Prince Yusupov and friends and dumped somewhere.'

Natalya edged the newspaper towards her, feeling the fatness of the package between its pages. She quickly read the column recording Rasputin's disappearance and felt a small flicker of relief. The monk had frightened her. 'What of his prophecy?'

'Oh, that.' Baumler shrugged. 'If he dies at the hands of the nobility the war will be lost and the Tsar and his family swept aside.'

'Along with the rest of the aristocracy.' Natalya's eyebrow lifted.

Baumler pondered. 'Funny thing. Young Captain Rykov very nearly shot him, one night at the Lantern.'

'And Captain Rykov is not of the nobility.'

'Don't worry, ladies, we needn't take Rasputin's prophesying seriously. He's probably sleeping off his excesses somewhere, and the war isn't yet lost.' And he said all the things they wanted to believe; Austria was sick of the war and would sue for peace, Russia could get through the winter, aid was pouring in — if only they could get the railways working properly.

Natalya half listened. How many times had she heard it all? Yet the Tsar becomes more remote, and the Empress is hated — even the nobility are speaking openly against her. So much unrest in the city, with demonstrations almost a daily event. If the railways are made to work and we win the war we've lost a whole way of life, she thought. How can we ever go back to what we were?

'Your friend, Captain Stern. He's working on the Murmansk railway, isn't he? Have you heard from him?'

'A letter from Kandalaksha. Michael is the only British officer on the northern stretch.' Baumler's face creased in a frown. 'He's an uncommunicative fellow — doesn't reveal too much of what he's thinking. But it must be hard for him. It isn't in his nature to work convicts and prisoners of war to death.'

130

Anna stiffened. 'I'm sure Russia treats captive soldiers more humanely than does Austria or Germany.'

Natalya was no longer so sure about that. 'Why would Captain Stern's government allow him to be used in this way?'

'I guess they are making him pay for something he did.' Baumler looked puzzled then quickly changed the subject.

'A charming hat,' he said to Anna, 'and it graces the head of one of the two most beautiful young women in Petrograd. How are you enjoying nursing?'

'I'm not very happy at the sight of blood and I've learned how clumsy I am. Doctor Strozhov is convinced that I'm a paid agent of the Kaiser.'

'But you keep at it?'

'Yes.' Anna's near perfect mouth tightened. 'Even Doctor Strozhov concedes that I am strongly motivated.'

Baumler nodded. He knew about her and Rykov but he couldn't bring himself to mention it. 'I must leave you, ladies. For less attractive company.' And he rose and bowed. 'Your Highness. Don't forget your newspaper. I'll contact you again when I return from Finland.'

Anna watched Baumler's broad back as he moved between the tables. 'What a forceful man he is.'

'Yes.'

'Baroness Klienmichael told me a strange story about him. Baumler is not his real name. He arrived in St Petersburg from a Greek ship and with only one suitcase, and he remains in Russia because he doesn't dare return to America.'

'The Baroness is an awful old gossip.' Natalya had heard that story too.

Baumler made his way into town. Most of his money was deposited in the Assignatsiony on Sadovaya Street but he retained an account under the name of Larsen in a small bank in the Rozhdestvenskya District. The account was used mainly for bribe money. He drew out cash to pay off Colonel Nevisky in the Technical Department. I must have

131

bribed damn near every official in the Tsar's service, he thought. I used to take perverse pleasure in knowing my way round this jungle. Now it disgusts even me.

The only thing he'd felt good about recently was smuggling in the morphine. Winthrop in the consulate office had twice warned him, but he knew he was going to go on doing it. And it wasn't just the feeling of having done something really useful for a change. It had excited him. The staff of the Technical Department might get rich at his expense, but he wasn't going to let them stifle him. So smuggling is dangerous. Let them try and catch me at it.

Snow was swirling across the street as he left the bank, white covering his Pierce Arrow automobile. Preoccupied with his thoughts he drove towards the river. The heavy car crunched freezing snow as he turned along the embankment. He'd have to start thinking of new routes in, for small, easily transportable contraband — why stop at morphine? There were the overland sledge routes but traffic was carefully monitored. Gunderson the Swede had tried smuggling by sledge from Skibotten. Now he was in jail and they'd thrown away the key.

Torch lights were flashing along the embankment and dark figures moved warily on the thick ice of the frozen river. A police van, rear doors open, backed towards the embankment wall, blocking the road. Baumler cursed softly as he slowed the car to a stop. He climbed out, pulling up his fur collar. His breath steamed. Men were hauling a bundled shape up over the wall. He watched them until somebody gently touched his arm. 'Better that you move on, sir.' A small fat man with thick spectacles blinked apologetically.

'What the hell is going on?'

'An accident. The poor fellow has been drowned. Dreadful. Quite dreadful.' And the fat man blinked again. 'Better that nobody sees him.'

'Right.' But Baumler looked quickly at the corpse as they began draping it with a blanket. One boot was missing. The long black matted hair and beard were frozen, stiffening. Rasputin! There was no mistaking those staring, ice-encrusted eyes.

'You should move on, sir.' The gentle voice was more insistent.

'Yes. Yes, I'm going.' Others, curious, were being herded back by the police as Baumler got into his car and edged round the police van. That was no accident, he thought.

He drove along the embankment and turned off at the Liteyny Prospect, parking the car just beyond the Moslem mosque. No, it was no accident. A man doesn't smash a hole in the ice then fall in. There's a deep, savage undercurrent in this city, getting worse. And there was that ominous feeling that things were falling apart — the *moujik's* death now just a symptom. For years he'd been hated and feared. If Rykov had shot him that night at the Lantern it might have made a difference — like in that game Michael Stern played inside his head. Imagine Rasputin removed from the scene two months earlier, how significant might that small amendment to history have been? It was Michael who had intervened — pulled the gun from Rykov's hand.

Baumler remained seated in the car for a moment longer, pondering the strangeness of chance. What unspoken deed had brought Michael to Russia anyway? Dammit, I miss him, he thought. The snow was falling heavily, large flakes piling up on the car windscreen. And he remembered that day, leaving the Astoria with Michael and the girl, and the bright whiteness all around them. The first heavy fall of the winter; reminding her of her innocence the girl had said. What the hell was her name? Helen. Helen somebody.

12

Helen Mirsky had left Petrograd five days before, travelling thirty miles up the Gulf to the small Finnish town of Terioki. And it was altogether strange. In the city she slept lightly, waking in the night if somebody passed in the street. And early movement in the house always stirred her from her bed, whether or not she had a lecture to attend. But here in the cottage of her grandmother it seemed that she merely rested her head on the pillow, and instantly sank into a heavy slumber from which even the noisy departure of her cousins rarely woke her.

Helen rose in the middle of the morning and breakfasted slowly, her face still dreamy with sleep. 'Where did Erik and Paul go the other night, Grandmama?'

'None of your business.' The old lady leaned over and filled her plate again. 'There. Eat that. You don't look after yourself properly.'

And that was another thing, repeatedly puzzling Helen. Here, no matter how much food she shovelled down herself, she could always eat more. Perhaps it was the sea air? She said so to her grandmother.

'But you get no fatter! Look at you — skin and bone. Young girls today . . .' And she clucked and shook her head.

Helen looked down at herself. Her waist remained slim no matter how much she ate. 'But surely I curve satisfactorily in the appropriate places?'

The old lady looked at her, almost disapproving. 'Yes. You are very trim. Like your mother. There's a lot of her in you.' She began to wash shirts in the sink, then stopped suddenly, peering down at her hands in the water. 'Your mother would have been happier if she'd stayed here. It's still her home — and yours. All your roots are here, girl.'

Breakfast over, Helen left the cottage, walking past the old Russian church and down to the beach. Perhaps I *do* belong here, she thought. Certainly it is more home than dull, provincial Uleaborg.

The Gulf was frozen over; ice beginning on the shingle and stretching out, a vast grey-white stillness as far as the distant horizon. The wind stung her face. She peered southwards. Petrograd was too far off for her to see, beyond the headland of Lissy Nos. It was always the great city that beckoned her back. What a pity the Tsar had changed its name. St Petersburg. It had a fine and romantic ring, evoking the memory of its giant Romanov founder. Tsar Nicholas's gesture, of giving the city its new, Russian sounding name had been patriotic, but lacking in imagination. Like the man himself.

The wind roared across the ice. Helen sank her hands deep into the pockets of her coat and walked towards the line of beached boats. The old people would never get used to the new name. It would always be Petersburg to them.

Further along, men were scraping hulls and repairing boat timbers ready for the spring. There was an alternative cottage industry — wooden spoons, baskets — but many of the men left in the winter for work in the larger towns. Some went smuggling overland, or so she had heard.

Her cousins' boat was heeled over on the shingle. It was old, clinker built, but in good repair and sleek looking. Cousin Erik claimed it was the fastest on their stretch of the coast. Helen smiled to herself. Erik always boasted. She waited for him, leaning against the hull out of the wind. A heavy tarpaulin covering the rear decking and cockpit had torn loose, flapping loudly.

Helen was intensely curious. Two nights before, Erik and Paul had left with the sleigh and had not returned until the following night. Grandmama had been determinedly reticent about the whole mysterious business. And what was also interesting, now that she had begun to think about it, was the modest affluence of the family. Fishing surely didn't yield much, and neither would odd-jobbing in the winter months. And she remembered stories of Finnish contrabandists told by her mother.

She watched fishermen, small figures, building a fire on the beach further to the west where the coast curved round to Fort Ino. They were a tough breed of men here, sturdily clinging to Finnish autonomy despite the Tsar's efforts to drag them back under the Russian yoke.

Erik was trudging along the frozen shingle. He carried a coil of rope slung over one shoulder and a long, leather-sheathed knife hung on his belt. His sea boots crunched the beach. Seeing Helen, his mouth curved, fair beard upjutting, and he began talking before he reached her. 'So you braved the weather. I thought you'd sleep all day.'

'Grandmama prodded me.' She paused. 'Are you working on the Mayor's house this afternoon?'

'No. Not today.' He shook his head and dropped the coil of rope. 'I'll have to fix this,' and he caught the flapping corner of the tarpaulin. 'Then Paul and I will have to repair the sleigh, a runner has splintered.'

'Did that happen on your mysterious expedition the night before last?'

'Not *so* mysterious.' He hauled on the loose sheet and frowned. 'The wind finds all our weaknesses.'

He's evading, just like Grandmama. She watched his face. 'Where did you go?'

'When?'

'Two nights ago, with the sleigh.'

Erik smiled, enjoying her curiosity. 'Paul and I went for a little ride, up the Gulf to Vysotsk,' he paused, 'to fetch some things.'

'What sort of things?'

He squatted on his haunches and began cutting the shredded rope. 'Just things.'

'You are infuriating.' She assumed her attractively cross look.

'And you are very pretty, and greedy, and cat-like.'

'Cat-like?'

'Yes.' He glanced up at her, his white teeth wolfish through his fair beard. 'You came out of the hut where Paul and I had hidden the boxes, and you looked like a sleek, smiling, charming cat.' He stretched out his large hand and caught her ankle. 'And I don't know why you want to go back to St Petersburg when you could stay here and marry me.'

She struggled, not too seriously, to free herself. 'Petrograd. It is called Petrograd now. And I didn't know that you had anything as serious as matrimony in mind.'

He released her and returned his attention to the tarpaulin. 'But you still intend going back tomorrow?'

She knelt down next to him, watching his hands as he worked. 'Yes. I have to. I have to get my degree.'

Erik shrugged. 'Studies! What good do they do you? See that big house up there — next to the church? I will own that one day, but not by studying.'

'By bringing "things" from Vysotsk?'

'Partly.'

'And where do you take them?'

'Never you mind.' He shrugged again. 'Somewhere near St Petersburg.'

'Petrograd. What sort of "things" are in those boxes?'

He sighed and began fastening the new rope to the tarpaulin. 'You see, you really are cat-like. Always curious. If you don't marry me I shall marry the Mayor's daughter.' He frowned, considering. 'She is very good in bed but I would prefer to marry you.'

Helen pretended to be shocked, and in fact she was tingling slightly at the thought, quickly stifled, of bed with Erik. She pulled on the sheeting for him while he knotted the rope. 'Why would you prefer me?'

'You are unpredictable — except when you are greedy. And you make interesting conversation. Though you are not quite so . . .' he cupped his hands over his chest 'so well-endowed as the Mayor's daughter.'

Helen was slightly disconcerted. She glanced quickly down at herself, then seeing him smile she looked up self-consciously to the large house by the church. 'You really plan to make enough money to buy that house?'

'Yes.'

'From the profits of the "things" you sell in St Petersburg?'

'Petrograd,' he said. 'You are beginning to look greedy again.'

Helen *felt* just a little greedy. 'I am sure I am not. I am merely speculating what could yield such profits.'

He enjoyed letting her guess.

'The boxes are quite heavy,' she said, probing. 'But they are not very long. Precious metal?'

He burst out laughing. 'Precious metal! Bullion is being sent *out* of Russia, not in. The Tsar is purchasing the necessities of war with gold. But the routes in for those necessities are restricted, and cluttered with middle men demanding bribe money and holding everything up. So some people are by-passing the Tsar's Technical Department and doing business through me, and others. Those boxes contain machine tool parts. We get them in through Sweden.'

'Machine tool parts!' Helen's face dropped with disappointment. 'And I had imagined other things, more exotic! All those tales my mother told me.'

He smiled. 'Much of it was cheap foreign cloth in those days. But sometimes my father took in rifles. They ran rifles in during the winter of 1905. And great bundles of the underground newspapers printed abroad, though they usually did that for nothing. Vladimir Ilyich Ulyanov who calls himself Lenin crossed over from here once.' And he paused, reflecting. 'Now there are big profits with the war, but it won't last for ever. Paul and I will have to make our pile now.'

She wanted to ask just how large the profits were but thought perhaps she shouldn't. 'How do you get your contraband to the city?'

'We use the sleigh.'

He stood and looked out across the grey-white stillness of the frozen Gulf. He frowned to himself, all the joking and flirting momentarily gone from him. 'It is a great white desert out there. Thirty miles to Petersburg. The first ten are safe. The sleigh runners sing on the ice. After that it is bad.'

Helen sensed uneasiness — almost fear in the set of his broad back. She rose and stood with him.

'You approach Kronstadt and the line of forts,' he said. 'They stick up out of the ice like a row of teeth, and their searchlights scan, looking for people like me. Sometimes the mist comes and you can lose yourself in it. But the mist crowds in on you and that great white desert has an awful sameness that confuses the memory. Funny. I can never get used to it.'

He frowned again and pushed his fingers through his thick hair as he peered out over the Terioki crossing.

13

High blind brick walls of the Deryabinsky prison yard permitted only a squared off view of the night sky. Bulky-coated guards with rifles slung stood hunched, watching the twenty prisoners formed up in two ragged lines.

'No talking!'

Nobody took the command seriously, and it hardly mattered now. The prisoners shivered in the cold and muttered softly, speculating on their destination. Peter Koltsov had saved half a cigarette for this day and he lit it with his last match. The sudden surge of nicotine made him light-headed. He coughed and his cracked ribs hurt.

'It hasn't been so bad here.' The rat-faced man next to him looked longingly at the stub of cigarette.

Koltsov dragged in smoke again then passed the cigarette to him. 'Finish it.'

'Thanks brother. Better here than the Schlusselburg. I did five there.'

'What for?'

'I'm a thief.' Rat-face shrugged. 'I'll miss this place, the food wasn't bad.'

A trusty moved along the line, dropping a thick padded coat in front of each prisoner. 'Wear it all the time or somebody will steal it.'

'We're going somewhere cold.' Rat-face looked anxious.

Koltsov pulled the coat on, glad of its warmth. It smelled of its previous owner. Somewhere cold. That could mean a penal colony in Siberia, or a camp far to the north.

'Better than the copper mines, brother, they are certain death.'

Koltsov nodded. Some men are perpetual optimists.

Rat-face drew on the cigarette until it burned his fingers, then crushed it out. 'What are you in for?'

'Treason.' Koltsov buttoned the coat. It had no pockets.

'Then you're a "political". You're lucky. "Politicals" get better treatment. What are you doing here with us criminals?'

'They got me for murder as well.'

'What did it fetch you?'

'Twenty years at forced labour.' He couldn't comprehend it. That night they'd arrested him he'd still believed he could give meaning to whatever they did to him. They could destroy him as a gesture but they'd lose in the end. After the casual beating he'd lain on the hard mattress of the prison cell and felt at peace. And he'd thought of that nurse who was a countess; face calm, hands gentle as she'd bandaged his ribs. She'd felt disgust — he'd sensed it. But even that hadn't mattered. Nothing had really mattered. He'd slept well for the first time in months, and dozed through the days that followed, sometimes wondering about her. Then they'd sentenced him. Numbed him with that figure.

'Twenty years, eh.' Even Rat-face was lost for a moment. 'But you might get amnesty.'

No. There would be no amnesty for him while the Romanovs ruled. Nor even the silent seclusion of a cell. They'd work him to death.

The guards were suddenly brisk, bawling at them to straighten the lines. An officer with major's insignia on his shoulder boards walked across the yard, gloved hands clasped behind him, and stood watching.

A sergeant called the roll of prisoners and the major stared at the trampled snow, bored until Koltsov's name was called. He looked up quickly but his face remained expressionless.

Another trusty moved along, handing each man a paper parcel of food.

'Eat some of it in the Raven before we reach the train,' Rat-face murmured, 'in case the guards take it from us.'

'Quiet! Straighten yourselves.' The sergeant glared at them while they shuffled into a semblance of order, then he turned and saluted the major.

The major nodded and paused before addressing them. His voice was unexpectedly soft.

'You are the refuse of our society, and society must be protected from you. To keep prisoners is costly so you must earn your daily bread. Your lives will be hard, but the Tsar in his mercy gives you time in which to atone. You can still be of service to Russia. Forget the past. Do not think of the future. Tonight you begin your journey. Do not ask, to where? For you that is of no importance. For you there is only work.'

Koltsov heard the clinking of chains. The hasp of an iron ring snapped tight on his left ankle and chain was strung through the staple. He could feel its heaviness but the weight seemed inside him. Twenty years!

'Right turn!'

The chains clattered.

'It's just the journey that's bad,' Rat-face muttered. 'When we get there we'll have a place to sleep, food. We'll be all right, brother.'

A guard shouted at him. 'What did you say?'

'I was praying, Your Honour.'

The guard laughed. 'This is heaven to where you're going. Start saying your prayers when you get off the train.'

I'll spare myself that ultimate human indignity. Koltsov bit back his crawling hopelessness and shuffled forward as the line began to move towards the Raven — a metal container, horse-drawn — waiting with its rear doors open. There is no God, no mercy, only the here and now of brutality, back-breaking toil, and then oblivion. He climbed awkwardly into the metal box, his chain dragging on the iron ring, and he stood in the press of men. Eight, ten, twelve of us. They can't get any more in. But the guards pushed them back. Fifteen, sixteen. We won't be able to breathe! Eighteen, nineteen, twenty. The steel door was forced in on them and locked. Darkness complete.

'For the love of Christ! We'll suffocate!'

'Shut up, you're using up air!'

The Raven jolted and began to move. They couldn't fall. If any of them fainted he'd be held up by the press of bodies. Already the air was foul and hot. Someone near the door shouted in panic 'Oh, God forgive me! I'll die!'

'Quiet, you fool, and listen! See if you can hear where we are.'

Koltsov strained his ears for last familiar sounds. They'd crossed a bridge, he could tell by the hollow sounds of the steel-rimmed wheels, and now the road surface was different. His tightly bandaged ribs ached and sweat streamed down his face.

'Try and eat some of the food,' Rat-face whispered. But they couldn't move their arms.

Would I have done it all; the subversion, incitement, and then the murder? Would I have done it if I'd known this would follow? Koltsov could taste the salt sweat on his lips. He didn't know. He knew only a black despair threatening to engulf him. I'll *live*. He arched his back and gasped for air. Somehow I'll live. Think of something to hang on to! Think of the city. Think of the comrades. But their faces had blurred into one like his own. A woman — think of that woman who bandaged you — she's life!

The Raven rattled on, a stifling container of collective despair, barely noticed by people trudging along the snow-covered paving. It moved towards the railway depot and was caught up in the traffic of theatre-goers returning home, or on their way to the clubs and smart restaurants. A cab driver cursed its slowness and edged past, and the shining black carriage with its Meretskov crest moved up behind.

Peter Petrovich anxiously judged the distance. His eyes were no longer so good and he didn't like driving at night — he'd avoided the heavier traffic on Sadovaya Street. Gauging the moment he steered the Meretskov horses round the slow-moving Raven. It was all wrong, the roads too cluttered at night. And why couldn't the young mistresses use the automobile?

Natalya and Anna had been to the Maryinsky.

'You must make an effort and get out more. It's good for you.' Anna's firm mouth tightened. 'Don't you feel better?'

'Yes. Much better.' Easier to agree. Though Natalya hadn't really enjoyed the ballet. She had been unable to adjust to its exquisiteness, and audiences were so over-enthusiastic these days. But at least it had taken her mind off Malenkov's letter.

'This is your first day off for two weeks,' Anna said. 'And you are losing weight. Madame Brissac will have to alter all your dresses.'

'Pointless. I don't yet know how thin I shall become. I may eventually disappear.' Natalya peered out at the tall, graceful spire of the Admiralty black against the milky white night.

'It is merely your waist.'

Lights across the river were pinpoints low down on the vast backdrop of the night sky and Natalya felt herself momentarily lost in the immensity of it all.

'Did you notice the number of officers in the audience?' Anna was frowning. 'It is shameful. Some openly boast of their intention not to return to the front.'

Her mind was seldom far from Rykov. Natalya pressed her forehead to the cold glass of the window. 'Look, Anna. Look at the stars.'

But Anna wasn't really listening. 'Of course, one has to be

fair. Many of the officers are convalescent.'

I don't look at the night often enough, Natalya thought. So engrossed in my own affairs. 'And many will never come back to us.' All those young men who had danced with her. There must be a star up there for each one of them.

'I looked along our line of boxes at the Maryinsky,' Anna was saying, 'Lena Orlenova's husband dead. Vikentia Strogonov, her father. There is barely a family untouched by the war. Our own father. Countess Elizabeth Dobronskya lost a brother at Tannenburg and two sons in the retreat. Did you notice her, sitting proudly alone?'

'She's very brave.' And Natalya had also noticed Madame Malnekov with a young man obviously her son, resplendent in his lieutenant's uniform of the Caucasus Squadron of the Guard. One sleeve empty, arm lost in Brusilov's campaign. And as they left the theatre, the boy had used his left hand awkwardly, adjusting the ermine cape over his mother's shoulders. How alike they are, Natalya thought. And why did I feel so envious?

There was shouting from the road ahead, and somebody blew a trumpet — an ugly comic sound. Peter Petrovich called down to them. 'A demonstration, young mistresses — the mob blocks our path.' And the carriage came to a stop, unable to turn into the broad thoroughfare.

Youths in student caps paraded past, some carrying banners denouncing the war, and others held torches. They joked and sang, huddled close to each other because of the coldness of the night.

'I've never seen so many.'

'They shouldn't do this,' Anna said. 'It is disloyal to those who are dead, held captive, and it encourages the Bolshevik agitators. How many demonstrations have there been this week?'

And this was why Malnekov was returning, with six hundred seasoned Cossacks to help keep order in the city streets. His letter had sounded bitter, sensing recent defeat and orders to return as cause and effect. But he needed her, he needed her. Natalya bit her lip.

'Why do they protest like this?' Anna looked puzzled. 'The war has to be won.'

'Maybe it can't be won.'

Faint strains of La Marseillaise filtered through the window of the carriage. Anna pressed next to Natalya and watched as one of the youths took off his cap and bowed low to the carriage. Then grinning broadly he winked at the sisters before moving on.

Anna laughed. 'How impertinent!'

'Don't you sometimes wish you were a student?' Natalya smiled as the youth turned briefly to wave to her. 'I think about it often — just recently. How different our lives would have been. Perhaps happier.'

'Their demonstration seems more like a carnival.'

Some of the young men were glancing back anxiously. A patrol of dark-clad Uhlans was moving up behind them at a slow trot, steam of the horses visible as they passed under a street lamp. A student ran in front of the carriage, and turning, raised his arm as a horseman drew his sabre and casually cut him down.

'My God!' Anna pressed her hand to her mouth.

Police moved in making random arrests, and one, still brandishing his revolver, hastily directed the traffic, waving on the carriages and automobiles held up at the intersection.

Peter Petrovich called down urgently. 'I'm sorry, young mistresses, I'll get you home.'

And a few minutes later the Nevsky was back to normal; vehicles moving again and horsemen and students gone. There remained only a student's cap and a dark red stain on the trampled snow, just under the street lamp.

14

Petrograd was besieged by blizzards, Arctic winds whipping the snow. Workmen in shaggy coats shovelled to clear the paving of the broad, fashionable avenues. Side streets of the poorer areas were left.

In early morning darkness, queues had begun to form outside bread shops. Men and women bundled up shapelessly stood huddled in the biting wind. Helen Mirsky had managed to edge herself back to the wall. She pulled her scarf up over her nose and mouth and held the collar of her coat with her gloved hand. I am beyond feeling depressed, she thought. Just numbly indifferently enduring — going on from day to day and waiting for the spring.

The queue now stretched back almost half the block. Ahead somebody banged on the baker's closed door and shouted to him. Helen didn't even look up. Would the baker sell out before she reached the shop? She sank herself deeper into her coat. I've lost sight of why I came to Petrograd and why I studied and schemed so hard. How magic the city had seemed. She tried thrusting her hands in her pockets and the chilblains on her fingers burned again. How long could the wretched winter last? The degree was now hers — confirmed two weeks before in a hurried, wartime ceremony. But what use was it? Nobody needed arts graduates at a time like this. It had led to nothing more dramatic than a modest position as clerk to Professor Zubov.

The crowd was becoming restive. A woman in front of Helen aired her anger. 'God punishes us. It's the fault of the Empress. She copulated with the *moujik* and that's why we have no bread.'

Somebody laughed — a harsh, strident, menacing sound, and the two policemen eyed the queue anxiously. They expected trouble these days. Helen made herself as inconspicuous as possible. Please let them start the riot *after* I have purchased the bread. God knows, there would be little enough to eat today. Her teeth chattered behind the scarf.

She must resist the temptation to feel sorry for herself. Petrograd had become appalling, but she was here because she chose to be here. One could be dishonest with others but not with oneself. God knows why I stay, she thought, and moved her toes inside her boots to see if she could still feel them. No, she couldn't. The clock at St Anne's struck the quarter hour. If the shop didn't open soon she would be late for work again.

There was a sudden disturbance at the head of the queue and the two policemen hitched up their belts and moved quickly. In the same moment glass clattered into the street as the shop window shattered, and Helen heard the harsh, strident laugh again. The crowd surged forward carrying her along, and even in her panic she cursed silently. Now she would have no bread. One of the policemen fired his revolver into the air and was promptly swept aside as the mob burst into the shop. More police would soon arrive and there would be arrests. Helen pushed her way clear and ran — frozen feet hurting — until she reached the Liteyny Prospect, and there she stopped and leaned against a wall. She felt dizzy. All that queuing for nothing. Near to tears she leaned for a moment longer then began walking towards the Nevsky intersection. It was pointless to let emotion get the better of one. She would borrow bread from Misha and queue again tomorrow.

Martin Baumler had risen early and gone to the consulate's office at the Singer Building — mainly to vent his disgust. Hal Winthrop sat back with his heels on his desk and waited for Baumler to pause.

' . . . so this guy at the Ministry of Communications asked me if I'd got a permit from the Vologda office for exporting the flax, and I said I'd filed one in Petrograd, and if they pulped down all the damned permits they wouldn't have a paper shortage. And he said . . .'

Winthrop interrupted. 'Jesus, Martin! They don't *trust* you. And neither do I when you wheel and deal. One of your couriers was picked up with precision lenses and a very cunningly altered import document. You may end up in court if I can't pull the right strings. And I hear a nasty little rumour that you brought drugs in from Finland.'

'I'm sorry, Hal. I'm sorry I'm making life difficult for you. But I've been waiting for four months for those lenses — Voldin *needs* them.'

Winthrop's eyes narrowed. 'What about the drugs?'

'Morphine. My small contribution to the wounded. God in heaven! Did you know that surgeons sometimes operate without anaesthetics? Not even a whiff of ether! I don't even charge for the stuff. I just pass it on to the Meretskov hospital.'

Winthrop nodded. 'Good of you, Martin, but the authorities — and particularly the Technical Department — are getting a bit sick of the ways you find of bucking the system.' And he paused, curious. 'Does the Countess know how you get the drugs in?'

'No. I figure how I do it is my own business.' He got up from his chair and walked restlessly over to the window. 'I'll be honest with you, Hal. Smuggling the morphine in is the one thing I don't feel guilty about. I've done nothing else worth while this last year.'

Winthrop frowned at his hand-made English shoes. 'All right. But I'm not getting you off the hook again.'

'You don't have to worry.' Baumler sighed. 'I'm so closely watched I've got no choice. I couldn't smuggle in a safety pin.' Unless I can find another route, he thought. 'Damn it, though, doesn't it make you want to puke?'

Winthrop swung his heels off his desk and sat thinking for a moment. Baumler was getting very touchy these days. 'Things may improve. Golitsyn says he's going to minimize corruption on the Murmansk line.'

'Golitsyn couldn't make a cat house pay its way. The Murmansk line is a gigantic bluff.' He thought briefly about Michael Stern, up there in the Arctic somewhere, trying to make the railway a reality. 'Do you ever wonder how Russia keeps going?'

Winthrop lit an expensive cigar and puffed a smoke ring into the air. 'Habit I guess.'

Baumler continued to stare out of the window. Cossacks of the City Garrison were patrolling slowly along the Nevsky. Maybe Russia couldn't keep going much longer. Maybe the long awaited revolution would really come. He turned. 'Sorry I chewed your ears off, Hal.' And he started to pull on his overcoat. 'I've got a case of rye whisky for you — no, it's not a bribe.'

Winthrop smiled. 'Stick around for a minute or two and I'll take you out and buy you lunch.'

'No, I'd better go.' Baumler frowned again. 'I'm bad company today.' And he left the tall Singer Building.

He walked along the Nevsky, past the Meretskov palace and on towards the Liteyny Prospect. I complain out of habit, he thought. I need something to lift my spirits. A bright red tram clanged slowly by, its overhead arm sparking on the cable. He was so preoccupied with his thoughts he didn't see Helen Mirsky approaching on the same side.

Helen had recovered from the incident at the baker's shop. But cold, and still a little dizzy, the thought of going to work at Zubov's draughty office in the university depressed her further. I shall give up the struggle for today, she decided. I'll telephone the Professor and tell him I have one of my sick headaches. Then I'll go home and try to get warm in bed.

A frozen beggar sidled up to her and moaned a petition. She shook her head, barely noticing him. Her breath steamed in the biting air. I do feel rather odd, she thought, and leaned momentarily on a shop window to steady herself. It is the cold. Just the cold.

A woman draped in heavy furs, and followed by a coachman carrying several boxes, emerged from the shop. Helen watched them as they mounted the coach. She didn't really resent others having more of the world's goods. Inequality was, after all, a fact of life, despite what the Bolsheviks might think. On the whole she preferred a social order where some were well off, because at least that suggested hope. One had to look on the positive side. She was about to move on when she saw Baumler, deep in thought, walking towards her.

It was the first time she had seen the wealthy American since that lunch at the Europe Hotel. Should she greet him? Helen paused. No, perhaps he wouldn't recognize her and that would be embarrassing. He was already passing. There was time only for improvisation. Helen fainted decorously.

Baumler felt useless. He knelt in the snow and lifted Helen's head. Damn, what did you do when a girl faints — loosen her collar? No, she'd freeze to death. A crowd had formed, curious and concerned. Baumler lifted the girl in his arms, surprised at how light she was. Somebody called a cab for him. He put her in the cab and gave the driver his address.

The girl seemed to be recovering very quickly, and Baumler had his first suspicions. I was not born yesterday, he thought. But there was no denying she looked thin, and she was probably hungry. Helen smiled and assumed her fragile pose — it came quite easily to her. And she really did feel light-headed. 'How very fortunate for me that you, of all people, should be passing at that precise moment, Mister Baumler.' She touched her hair with her slim fingers. 'I am normally in robust good health. I don't know what came over me.'

'Don't worry about it, Miss . . . er . . .'

So he *had* forgotten her name. 'Mirsky.'

'That's right. Helen Mirsky. You probably just need feeding.'

When they reached his apartment, Helen excused herself, and in the bathroom she worked frantically at making herself presentable. God! My hair! Baumler had good soap. Would he miss it? Yes, he might.

Baumler briefly considered calling his doctor to her, but his suspicion that Helen had engineered the whole thing was confirmed by her appetite. Nobody could eat with such evident pleasure and be ill.

Helen had not eaten so much since her last visit to Terioki. Baumler had real butter. And coffee, with sugar in it! A quick appraisal of the apartment had reinforced her impression that he was rich. She paused between mouthfuls ' . . . and somebody broke the shop window so I thought it prudent to leave without the bread. However, it has occurred to me that I could perhaps make some under-the-counter arrangement with the bakery that supplies the university refectory . . .'

Baumler sprawled back in his chair and smiled to himself. There was something very engaging about Helen — a combination of femininity, toughness and guile. She was small; five feet three or thereabouts, but clearly a survivor. 'I seem to remember that you were a student, Helen. What are you doing now?'

'I work in Professor Zubov's office at the university.' She considered for a moment. 'I am an extremely poor typist. But then, an academic education hardly prepares one for life's great struggle. After a day's work there never seems to be enough time to queue for necessities. And even queuing presents hazards. I hear of agitators joining queues to ferment riots, and police agents fermenting riots as an excuse to root out agitators. One wonders where it will all end.' She glanced quickly at the long mirror beside the bookshelves. I'm caught looking like a hag again. If only I'd worn the red dress. 'It is all so much more difficult being alone in the city.'

Baumler poured more coffee. 'Wouldn't you be better off at home with your family, rather than cold and hungry here in Petrograd?'

'My home is in Uleaborg.' And nothing would drag me back there, she thought. 'It is a small provincial town, with very little work. I would rather not return and be a burden to my family. Father has such high hopes for me now that I have graduated. I must not disappoint him. He is in poor health.' She touched her hair and smiled bravely.

'I'm sorry.' Baumler felt a little ashamed of his earlier suspicion. He screwed up his face in a frown. I'm still not entirely convinced. But she's got nerve, facing life in this city on her own. 'Maybe I should mind my own business.' Damn it, now he felt embarrassed. 'Clearly things are not going so well for you right at this moment. If you need some money — a loan. No strings,' he added quickly.

'No strings?'

He shrugged. 'It's an Americanism. It means I offer it without expectations.'

Helen hesitated. How good it would be to accept. She could buy some sugar again, and maybe some new gloves. Baumler was clearly an open-handed person when he wasn't trading. But people who gave, of themselves, their wealth, or their time, always put her at a disadvantage. It is safer to be with people who take, she thought, because they are easier to understand. And she decided that tactically it might be better to decline the offer — for the time being. 'Thank you, but no.' She lowered her eyes modestly. 'I really couldn't.'

'Well, let me know if you change your mind. My number is in the telephone book.' Baumler went over to his jacket draped over a chair and he took a cigar from his case.

Helen glanced at his broad back and athletic figure. He really might do, she thought. 'Where is your friend, Captain Stern?'

'Michael? He's in the wilderness, rebuilding a bridge at a place called Pitkul. I can't even find it on the map.'

'Will he be returning to Petrograd?'

'I don't know.' Baumler lit the cigar. 'I hope so.'

'You miss him?'

'Yes.' He narrowed his eyes and smiled to himself. 'Though I'm damned if I really know why. He's an odd fellow. He shares his wry good humour with you but saves his harshness for himself.'

'Something in his past troubles him.'

Baumler looked at her quickly. 'Woman's intuition?'

'I had thought it was obvious.'

'You may be close to the truth.' Baumler smiled. 'You're full of surprises, Helen Mirsky.'

Helen decided that she must establish a slightly stronger link with Baumler before she left. 'That was an excellent meal.' She leaned back, tensing her figure, and ran her hands over her waist. 'I am quite ashamed of eating so much. Do you trade in food supplies also?'

Watching her, Baumler was aware of a small surge of interest. 'No. I haven't got round to organizing the food. God knows, I've got trouble enough. But I handle just about everything else, when I get a chance.' And back with his problems he frowned and walked over to the window. 'Trading used to be easy in the old days.' Beyond the window demonstrators were moving slowly down the Liteyny. He noticed the slogan again — BREAD PEACE FREEDOM.

Helen continued to observe Baumler. He has a fine profile, she thought. And he is rich, generous and determined. Eminently acceptable, even desirable. She made up her mind to follow his interests. 'Yes. It must be very difficult trading, with so much of the world involved in this awful war.'

'It's supply that is the real nightmare.' He turned back to her. 'I spend most of my time and energy trying to get things in and out of Russia. I've got a hundred and thirty bales of flax waiting at Vologda for the spring thaw; forty of my motor cycles for the Artillery Department still stuck at Archangel. My agents in Stockholm have sent a freighter packed with aeroplane parts and it's anchored off Murmansk, unable to unload. There's a hundred thousand tons of war materials tied up there at Murmansk and the new railway line can only shift three thousand tons a day.' He paused, momentarily lost in his thoughts. I'm bitching again. I do it all the time. His attention was jerked back by something Helen was saying. 'I beg your pardon?'

'I said, have you tried the sledge routes?'

He was surprised that she should know about them. 'Yes. I've used them. But sledges can't carry that much — not like a train. The Lapps move about a hundred tons each day.'

'And the Finnish route from Skibotten?'

He was even more surprised. 'I've tried that too. Same problems. I have to compete for limited sledge carrying capacity.' And he tilted his head questioningly. 'How do you know so much about this business?'

Helen tensed slightly. Perhaps she had gone a little too fast. She answered as casually as she could. 'Oh, I have two cousins in Finland who talk about these things.' And she paused. 'Could you not change the nature of your imports, to less bulky items that take up only a small space?'

Shrewd as well, he thought. 'I'm trying to do that. But I still have to bid against others who are doing the same thing. And I have to contend with the corruption of the Technical Department.'

Helen was well aware that many men resent knowledgeable women. She moistened her lips slightly and thought for a moment. Baumler wasn't the kind to be affronted, and at least *some* of his trading requirements were suited to the activities of cousins Erik and Paul. Dare she suggest it? If he accepted the suggestion she would have established the basis of further meetings. She began hesitantly, as if merely speculating on things she knew little about. 'You said you have an agent in Stockholm. Supposing you could import into neutral Sweden. And somebody could arrange transhipment from Sweden to Finland, and then into Russia . . . .perhaps without the Technical Department even knowing?'

Baumler was startled. He laughed. 'You mean professional smugglers!' I don't know anybody who is really reliable in that kind of business, and the border patrols are pretty tough when they catch them.' He looked at her carefully. Her expression hadn't altered and he thought, by God, *she* knows somebody! 'Go on,' he said. 'You are about to suggest something.'

At that moment Helen almost drew back. She felt a sudden quickening of her heart — a presentiment perhaps, almost discerned and just as hurriedly dismissed. Of course

154

she couldn't let this opportunity pass, the possibilities were immense. She leaned forward, watching his face.

'Have you ever heard of the Terioki crossing, Mr Baumler?'

15

In the half darkness of the northern winter day Stern stood watching the line of chained convicts dragging logs onto the ice-covered river. The convicts did the heaviest work. Above the labouring men towered the rebuilt Pitkul bridge — his bridge — creaking under its own weight. A massive scaffolding of crossed timbers spidering up eighty feet above the ice, and spanning a hundred and fifty yards from bank to bank. It was a miracle of hasty improvisation. Like the whole bloody single track railway twisting off into the forest, and on and on across the most awful country he could ever have envisaged. Seven hundred and seven miles of it, nearly half its length curving to avoid treacherous marshes. And this far northerly stretch of one hundred and ninety miles was above the Arctic Circle where nature conspired with climate to create every conceivable hazard.

Stern waited until the convicts were clear of the bridge, and he pulled away the flap covering his nose and mouth and shouted to a man with a signalling flag. Breath turned to ice on the rim of his hood. He listened for the train labouring into motion. It shunted into view round the bend in the line and gasped up the slight incline — headlight lighting up the bridge. Not enough steam. It slid back to try again.

The train had priority. One waggon contained wooden cases, like the ones Stern had seen at the Murmansk depot months before. Now he waited as the engine appeared again, hauling the heavy trucks onto the swaying wooden structure and trundling slowly across. He watched as the red tail-light on the rear waggon diminished in the near darkness. Follow those tracks and he could walk all the way to Petrograd. And damn me, I wish I could, he thought. Just walk away from this place, and back to the city. And what would he do there?

He hadn't seen the Countess Natalya Meretskova since that New Year's Eve, in the dispensary of St Saviour's when she had bandaged the ribs of the Bolshevik agitator. He scowled to himself. I must be getting soft in the head.

How do you determine the point at which interest in a woman turns to — what? He pondered, remembering fragments of detail. Her face seen suddenly across the room after weeks of wondering about her. Her surprise at finding them there in the hospital and her weary irritation at his clumsy lie. Again her face in close up as she took something from a cupboard.

Only later, when he was alone, had he realized that the day was marked indelibly on his thoughts. It was of course because of her, but he could think of no single thing that she had said or done of which he could say — it was *then* — it was that moment when she turned her head, or her slight frown as he spoke to her. He knew only that at some time during the meeting he had become suddenly shy of her. I'm a fool of the oldest kind, he thought, mind drifting repeatedly to a woman who isn't for me. And I can't even be sure she's worth it. Years of duty meticulously observed have left me unstable — temporarily. I suppose I'll get over thinking about her. I don't want to but I suppose I will.

He turned his attention back to the bridge. A team of waiting men climbed up onto the massive creaking structure as the train disappeared into the forest.

Two things I've never been short of, Stern thought. Men and timber. Over seventy thousand had toiled building the Murmansk railway; Letts, Russians, Chinese had stayed or deserted. Here on the worst section they used Finns on six-month contracts, and God knows how many Austrian prisoners of war. And there were the convicts.

He scowled with disgust as he trudged through the snow towards the log hut he used as his living quarters and office. He'd save his anger over the treatment of the convicts until Southgate's arrival. An hour. Southgate should be here in an hour, providing the bloody train was on time.

The hut smelled of woodsmoke and lamp oil, and an overriding pervasive aroma of dried fish. A large stove burned in the centre, black chimney pipe slanting up through the wood- and moss-covered roof. On one of the makeshift benches he had set up a plan of the bridge, with loading and stress figures pencilled down one side. He frowned at it is he pulled off his sheepskin coat. It was incredible. He and the Russian engineers had rebuilt sixteen yards of bridge for every two thousand yards of track on the northern stretch. Seven weeks on the Pitkul. The test would come in the spring, when the rivers raged, smashing ice and washed-down trees against those wooden piles.

He groped for the bottle hidden behind books, but paused before opening it, staring again at the plan. That bridge will hold; even if the spring flood exceeds its 1906 peak. He peered at the neat amendments to his pencilled figures. Each one represented hours of calculations. And how many men had died turning the drawing and the figures into a reality? The whole damned structure haunted his sleep.

He splashed a drink into a tin mug. Where next? The bridge was finished. The cutting at Soroka? — they needed an engineer there. Track ballasting above Imandra? It couldn't be worse than here though it wasn't much better. He allowed himself a brief fantasy. Petrograd. Maybe they'd send him back to the capital. And maybe he'd see her again.

The second train of the day was making good time from Murmansk, averaging twenty miles an hour through the forest and round the frozen marshes. Pulled by two worn engines, it clattered into Imandra, twenty-two miles north of Stern's bridge, and there it made a brief halt to refuel.

From the single passenger car at the rear of the line of freight wagons, viewers could see shackled, bearded scarecrows in tattered padded coats. They dragged baulks of timber for the wood-burning engines, shuffling, feet covered in rags, oblivious to the curious stares of the passengers. The train began to move again and Lett guards, casually brutal, prodded the convicts with their rifles, returning them to work.

The train rumbled on, ten miles edging round a long, frozen lake, then twelve more miles of forest until it reached Stern's bridge at Pitkul. Colonel Henry Southgate alighted and pulled up the collar of his greatcoat against the cruel wind.

He looked round in the grey Arctic light at the rough wooden huts and mounds of snow-covered logs. What a God-awful place. A man clad in a thick, ragged fur coat approached and saluted stiffly. There was ice on his grey beard. 'Excellency. Captain Stern sent me to bring you to him.' He drew himself up and added, 'I am his assistant.'

Southgate sniffed. The man looked scruffy, like Stern. And why hadn't Stern come himself? 'Are you now. And what do they call you?'

'I am Rantalla, Excellency. Late of the Finland Regiment.'

'Lead on, Rantalla.'

Southgate was surprised by the change in Stern. No, he'd go further. He was shocked. Stern looked like a man who has worked too long without sleep. And something else — that hardness about his mouth hadn't been there before. And the bloody man still hadn't shaved off that beard. 'Going native are we, Michael? — succumbing to the climate?'

'A beard's warmer up here.'

Rantalla offered a meal and Southgate was appalled. 'Dried herrings! Good God! No, I'll wait until I get to Kandalaksha. Major Borlov's cook does a rather nice *cotletki*.' And glancing sideways at Stern he added, 'I'll have to send you some decent grub from Murmansk when I get back, Michael. We can't have you subsisting on bloody herrings — and cheap spirit.'

Stern shrugged. He was indifferent to what he ate. 'I assumed I would be moving on from here.'

'Ah!' Southgate sat before the stove and undid his greatcoat. 'That's something we have to talk about, Michael. But leave it for a minute.' He took the mug of tea from Rantalla then lit a cigarette, and as an afterthought he offered the packet to Stern. 'First I want to tell you how pleased I am — we all are — with your work. One of the most difficult bridges . . .'

'*The* most difficult bridge.'

'Very well, *the* most difficult bridge on the northern section. Splendid. Quite splendid. I might add that even I was beginning to wonder if it could be finished before the thaw. I suspect only you could have done it.' His eyes narrowed. Stern was angry, he could see it in the set of his jaw. Time to offer something. So he assumed his most sincere expression. 'Our masters have told me to thank you formally for them. And I'll go further, Michael. They are definitely considering something for you — a decoration, and perhaps promotion.' He paused, slightly embarrassed by Stern's gaze. 'You have been rather harshly treated in the past.'

'And my new posting?'

Southgate became brisk, leaning forward and rubbing his hands. 'We-ll, you are damned useful up here, Michael. The Pitkul bridge is crucial. And the Russians are so pleased with your work. We'd rather like you to hang on here for a while. The railway is working, but only just. When the thaw comes there are certain to be problems.' And he quickly added, 'Oh, I know this is a God-forsaken place, but I can promise you are not forgotten, and I intend seeing that you get some decent grub and comforts . . .'

'It's not the *place* so much!' Stern got up and began pacing the hut. 'It's what *happens* here. I can't turn a blind eye to it. You must know that twenty-five thousand prisoners of war have died building the line. And have you seen the convicts? I do what I can for the poor devils on this section and the Lett guards are careful when I'm around. But they are worked worse than animals and indifferently done to death when they can no longer stand. It's quite clear that the Tsar and his government don't give a damn about the captive labour.'

'Be reasonable, Michael. The Tsar was very distressed when he was informed. He ordered the evacuation of the prisoners of war to camps in Russia.'

'Distressed!' Stern gaped incredulously. 'The Tsar and his officials knew all along! They are only evacuating the prisoners of war because of pressure from the protecting powers. And what happens when they are gone? They'll send in more convicts. Sixteen hours a day they work. Convicts make up over half my labour force. And I feel dirty!'

Southgate's expression hardened. 'How the Russians treat their convicts is none of our affair. They either die here or at the front. And you are here because the War Office wants you here — needs you here. So here you bloody well stay until the War Office says otherwise. Got it? Now get us both a drink for God's sake.'

Stern bit back his icy anger. He couldn't argue with those faceless men fifteen hundred miles away. He fetched the bottle from its hiding place and poured the fierce spirit into two glasses.

Southgate sat with his glass held loosely in his hand, watching, curious as Stern swallowed the drink down in one gulp. 'Look, Michael. We've got fresh trouble. Even up here you must have heard the rumours. In Petrograd things are getting very sticky; strikes, the Duma demanding the resignation of the Tsar's government, plots to remove the Tsar even. There's talk of revolution. Our task is more important now than it has ever been. No matter what happens we've got to keep Russia in the war. And that means getting this railway working properly. That's why you have to stay.'

Stern stared at the fire. He'd known it all along. Even when he was speculating where they'd send him next. He'd known they wouldn't let him go from this bridge. And even if he left, turning his back on those prisoners, they'd still haunt him. 'Right. I stay,' he said. 'But damn our people for condoning this.'

Southgate breathed an almost imperceptible sigh of relief. He sipped the spirit and gasped, eyes watering. 'God in heaven! What is it, varnish remover?' And recovering, 'We'll see that you get some decent whisky as well. But first I think you should have a spot of leave — only a couple of weeks mind — then you get back here in time for the spring thaw. Now, where would you like to go; Helsingfors, Stockholm?'

Stern shook his head. 'Petrograd,' he said.

'Petrograd? But why? Nothing but shortages, and the damned city is like a powder keg.' But seeing Stern's implacable expression he sighed. 'Very well. I'll arrange it. But if there's trouble, don't get involved. And don't arrive in Petrograd with that beard. As it is Hanbury-Williams thinks you look a mess.'

'So what might he do? There's nowhere else to send me.'

Stern saw Southgate off on the late afternoon train to Kandalaksha, and he walked back towards his hut. Rantalla was waiting for him near the bridge and walked with him. He seemed concerned about something, but not yet quite ready to talk about it. 'Bad news, Excellency?'

Stern shrugged, his hands deep in his pockets. 'I stay, old man. But you can leave if you wish.'

'No, Excellency.' Rantalla moved with a swinging stride. 'I think I should remain with you.'

'I value your friendship. At least we can go to Petrograd for two weeks. We'll get drunk.'

'Yes. I have a great thirst.' Rantalla looked back at the bridge. 'How did we do it, Excellency? We've helped build a railway across God's most fearful wasteland. I cannot think He meant us to do so unnatural a thing. It seems almost blasphemous. And so many have died.'

The old corporal paused. 'Many more will die. These poor devils of convicts only last a month or two. When I was a boy it was the custom to leave a small piece of bread on the

161

doorstep each night, for runaway convicts. But where can they run to from here?'

'You are trying to tell me something. Say it directly — or as directly as you can.'

Rantalla sniffed and glanced around. 'Here is living death for them. What we have been party to is an offence against God and humanity.'

'Go on.'

Some Finnish contract workers were on their way to the bridge. Rantalla waited until they had passed.

'An escaped convict, Excellency — not one of ours. It is Peter Koltsov.'

'Koltsov!'

'I found him in the waggon workshop, more dead than alive. I think he must have come from Imandra.'

Stern stared. 'And what did you do with him?'

'I put him in the blanket and clothing store.' Rantalla rubbed his fingers through his grey beard. 'An impulse, Excellency. I didn't know what else to do with him.'

'To aid an escaping convict could mean that you end up as one yourself.'

'Quite so, Excellency. But I did not feel I could do less.'

Stern nodded slowly. 'Then neither can I, old man. We'll wait until the shift has changed, then we'll go and look at him.'

They returned to Stern's hut and waited. Rantalla put food in a sack, then glancing at Stern he added a hacksaw. Stern took the bottle of spirit and slid it into his pocket.

All movement to and from the bridge had ceased. They could hear loud laughter from the Finlanders' long mess hut behind the wood stacks. Rantalla led the way to the store and lit a lantern. Together they groped between the high racks stacked with clothing.

'He is here, Excellency.' Rantalla lifted the lamp to throw a large circle of light, and Stern looked down at the gaunt, verminous animal of a man laying under sacking in the corner.

'Koltsov?'

The creature blinked and held a thin, filthy hand to his eyes, shielding them against the light. Stern knelt next to him.

'From which convict gang have you escaped?'

'Imandra.' The voice was almost inaudible.

'Where were you heading?'

'South.' Koltsov sat up slowly and his ankle shackles clinked.

'Here, drink this. It'll warm you. No, not too much.' Stern took the bottle and sat back on the sacking. Rantalla gave Koltsov bread and dried herrings. He ate like a wolf, forcing the food into his mouth and swallowing quickly. 'I never thought to see you again, Englishman.'

'They send men here without expectation of their return. They must want you dead.'

Koltsov nodded. 'I'm convicted of murder.' And he went on eating.

There lies the difference, Stern thought. I was never convicted. But we are both here for the same crime.

'Do we help him, Excellency?' Rantalla stood poised with the hacksaw.

Koltsov's eyes were on Stern's face. Stern hesitated, then nodded. 'Yes. We help.'

They took turns with the hacksaw, cutting through the ankle shackle.

'How do we get him away, Excellency?' Rantalla tested the shackle to see if it would come apart.

'The guards at Imandra will have missed him by now.' He frowned and took another turn with the saw. 'All stations along the line will be alerted by telegraph. All trains will be searched.' The leg iron came off and Stern winced at the festering sores on Koltsov's ankle. 'If we send him to Murmansk the British naval units will pick him up and they will be forced to send him back. What we must do is make the guards along the line *think* he's going to Murmansk.' Stern's eyes narrowed. 'We'll put some of his clothing and the saw and shackle on a train moving north.'

Rantalla went back to Stern's hut for soap and a razor.

Koltsov pulled off his filthy rags. His harsh voice grated. 'You are taking great risks for me, Englishman.'

'Rantalla and I have seen too many men die here.'

They found some respectable clothes among those on the racks. Rantalla contributed a pair of his own boots that almost fitted. Using headed notepaper from the telegraph office, Stern typed a document identifying Konstantin Stashensky of Kandalaksha as a line repair worker employed by the Ministry of Ways and Communications. Then he used his own rubber stamp, but blurred it so that it was illegible, and he scratched an unreadable signature across it. Maybe it would convince semi-literate guards.

They each examined the document in turn. Rantalla considered, head on one side. 'Put a bold stroke under the signature, Excellency. It always intimidates. Then crumple the paper a little.'

It was now early in the morning. Koltsov, clean-shaven, and wearing a woollen hat and a ragged overcoat, looked almost believable. They gave him a tool box to carry.

'He might do, Excellency.'

'Yes, old man. He might just pass.'

Koltsov examined himself. 'If I am taken I will say I stole these things.'

Stern nodded. Nobody would believe it. They'd beat the truth out of him. But it didn't do to think about that. 'I'll take you over the bridge — south to Nivazya. From there you must walk to Kandalaksha, getting to the station before six. You will buy a ticket to Petrozavodsk just before the train is due. Here's some money.' And to Rantalla he said, 'Wait till the five twenty-two arrives going north. Put the clothes and the leg iron in the last waggon where they are sure to be found. But make sure you are not caught with them.'

Rantalla sniffed. 'Excellency, you are talking to an old smuggler.'

Koltsov's harsh voice grated, 'My thanks to you both. One day I may be able to repay you.'

'Our lives are full of debts. We are repaying one.'

Koltsov's mouth twisted. 'That may be true. But not many would acknowledge it. Most would not dare do this, even for a friend.'

'Then perhaps this makes us more than friends.'

'If I get clear I'll keep going south, to Petrograd.' Koltsov looked at them both. 'And if ever I can help you, you'll find me there.'

'It's getting late,' Stern said. 'We'd better leave.'

In the semi-darkness he walked with Koltsov as far as the bridge.

'They don't even guard it,' he said. 'Even wolves have got more sense than to come this far north. Just keep going. Move as fast as you can.'

Koltsov held out his hand. 'What is your name?'

'Michael.' Stern was surprised at the power in Koltsov's grip.

And Koltsov nodded. 'I am Peter.' He said it awkwardly, as if unused to using his first name. 'Goodbye.'

'Good luck.'

He watched until Koltsov's shape merged with the darkness. Now I've really bloody well done it, he thought.

The train bearing Koltsov was searched twice, and both times his identity document was examined and handed back to him. At Petrozavodsk he bought another railway ticket and watched curiously from a safe distance along the Petrograd platform as two ragged suspects were forced to remove their boots. Guards examined the men's ankles for shackle marks and, disgusted, let them go.

The Petrograd train arrived an hour late. Koltsov climbed on. Snow began falling again. At the rear, station staff hoisted the heavy crates of Vickers machine guns destined for the Petrograd Prefecture and stacked them in the last waggon. The train moved off.

Telegraph messages, that Koltsov had escaped, crackled along the cables south and were relayed on to the capital. There, the night telegraphist read the cable back to himself. He yawned and stretched and glanced out at the snow in St

Isaac's Square. God help the poor devil, on the run in weather like this. But with all the trouble in Petrograd maybe the police wouldn't have time to search for an escaped convict. He worked the morse key, acknowledging the message, then stopped and listened. There was a sharp cracking sound somewhere out there in the night. Like a rifle shot. And he continued to listen for a moment, then shrugged to himself. In these times the nights were full of sounds he would rather not hear.

16

The café was dirty, smelling of cockroaches.

Zubov glanced round at the working men eating with their fingers and he pushed his glass aside. Why do they offend me? They are honest Russians — the substance of my speeches in the Duma. But they smell. He quickly suppressed the thought that his obsession with cleanliness compensated for his self-disgust. No, it wasn't that at all. As a civilized being he hated dirt and disorder. He wanted orderly progress. And why hadn't Popov arrived? He stared at the wooden table. He'd felt so good last week. Then Madame Zubov found the contraceptives, her round flat face hurt and accusing.

He reflected that a small disaster invariably led to others, worse. Helen was becoming increasingly evasive; her sick headaches, her period — for God's sake how long could that last? And now the food shortage reaching crisis point just as the Tsar had ordered the disbanding of the Duma. Power sliding to the streets. He frowned at his coat cuff, grease-stained from contact with the table. And where the hell is Popov?

The fat little Okhrana agent appeared in the doorway,

peering myopically. Zubov raised his hand slightly.

'My profuse apologies, Professor. And you with so many grave responsibilities.'

'I can give you only five minutes.' Zubov glanced at his watch. 'So I would be grateful if for once you would come directly to the point. Why did you ask to meet me?'

Popov blinked, slightly offended, and sat himself down. 'Difficult, Professor. Things have come to a pretty pass. I need information. You have many contacts among the factions of the city.'

'I am not a common informer.'

The Okhrana agent nodded. 'But you told us about Koltsov. And we got a conviction — twenty years.'

'I saw that as a public duty.' Zubov groaned inwardly. Why do I lie so?

'We are looking for Koltsov again.'

'You mean he has escaped!' Zubov was shocked. 'I didn't know that!' He leaned forward and spoke softly. 'How could he escape from northern Karelia?'

'Somebody must have helped him. He has reached the city, I know it — I feel it here,' Popov indicated his stomach. 'But he is not with any of his known accomplices. You hear things, Professor. Where might he be — where might he go?'

Zubov shook his head. 'I don't know,' And he felt a growing alarm. Koltsov loose in Petrograd, and at a time like this! 'Does he know? Could he suspect that . . .'

'That you betrayed him?'

'It was not a betrayal!' Zubov whispered hoarsely. And he thought for a moment. 'Could he have found out?'

'I told you, Professor. Your name would never be mentioned and I kept my word.' Popov paused and added gently, 'Of course, your signed statement is in our records.'

Zubov looked at him quickly. 'Are you trying to blackmail me?'

'No, no. I am merely suggesting that we look after each other's interests. Think, Professor, have you heard anything at all that might give me a lead?'

'Nothing. I swear I have heard nothing.'

Popov rose. 'Your secret is safe with us. You are a respected Duma member and eminent lecturer. As far as the world is concerned your association with Koltsov is slight. But you will let me know if you hear anything, won't you? — just a telephone call to Popov.' And he bowed and made his way out through the crowded café.

Zubov sat staring at the table. I did betray him. I did. I did.

Popov returned to Okhrana 2nd Section at Number Five Panteleimenskya Street. He went straight away to the basement, digging among the boxes until he found the file on Peter Koltsov. It disturbed him a little. There had been a completeness about the case; the patient watching and recording of Koltsov's associations and activities and the neat culmination of betrayal, arrest, conviction and transportation. And now Koltsov had upset it all by escaping.

Popov concerned himself with the minutiae of human weakness and motivation. He was a man perfectly adapted to his task of winkling out the Tsar's enemies here in the capital — like a small, successful creature of antiquity beavering away in the hot sand, unaware of a possible approaching ice age.

He refreshed his memory, carefully examining each item in the thick manilla folder. The brothers, Dmitry and Peter Koltsov, had taken up much of his time in the past ten years. He paused, listening for a moment to the chants of demonstrators on the Liteyny Prospect fifty yards up the street, then he returned his attention to the documents. Some had faded a little, they extended over the whole of Peter Koltsov's adult life. Popov's eyes opened wide. There was a brief report on Koltsov's zealous pursuit of God, 1902. To have walked so far, and to so little purpose. Army Mutiny, 1905, extracts from the findings of the military tribunal, and sentence. Suspected complicity in the Tiflis bank raid, 1907. Trade union activity, 1908 to 1910. Formal but fruitless enquiry into the murder of Okhrana agent Zasulich. Popov moistened his lips nervously. Possible instigation of

Aboukov foundry strike, 1913. Membership of Workers' War Relief Committee. Statement by Zubov. Evidence of the manager of the Murmansk freight depot. And Popov frowned to himself. That was where Koltsov had associated with the tall, fair-haired English captain whose father played chess with Dmitry. And the report on Koltsov's arrest indicated the presence of two tall men in St Saviour's Hospital, one old and the other young and fair-haired. He scanned the testimony of Police Inspector Kazimov, Rozhdestvenskya District, and carefully noted the name, Countess Natalya Alexandrovna Meretskova. Could she have known who she was tending that night? It seemed unlikely, but Kazimov thought so and he was no fool. Popov closed his notebook. He'd got nothing else to go on. He'd start with the Countess and work backwards.

He sat for a moment, thinking. No woman in Koltsov's life, just arid documents revealing nothing of the inner man after 1902. No normal human weaknesses — they'd got Dmitry once on a drunk charge. No hobbies, no diversions, no friends. He sighed to himself.

There was a telephone in the basement. Popov lifted the earpiece and cranked the handle. The operator connected him with the Meretskov palace and a servant answered. Could he speak with the Countess? Official business. Ministry of the Interior. He frowned and waited anxiously, the palms of his hands moistening. Politicians, businessmen, university lecturers he could deal with, but the old aristocracy was another thing again. And when he heard the young woman's voice he gabbled hurriedly. It was late, of course, and he was reluctant to inconvenience so distinguished a person. Would he please state his business? Yes, he would, immediately.

And when Popov put the telephone earpiece back on its hook he almost sighed with relief. She would see him. She had an important engagement later, but if he came now she could talk to him for a few minutes.

He pulled on his coat ready to leave, but paused. Could something on Peter Koltsov have been put in Dmitry's file by mistake? It paid to be thorough. He found the file with Dmitry's name on it and held it almost fondly. All those hours he'd spent on this one. He opened it and blinked with surprise. A green sheet on top of the neatly tied documents had been rubber stamped with the single word — DECEASED. Dmitry Koltsov had hung himself in his cell in the Trubetskoy Bastion of St Peter and St Paul only a week before. Popov rubbed his hand over his round moon face. Well, that was one he wouldn't have to worry about any more. But it was strange, that feeling of loss.

He left the Okhrana 2nd Section and walked towards the Meretskov palace. It was dark now. There were indications of a street clash on the Nevsky; smashed banners and a few broken windows, but Popov barely noticed. His work kept him remote from the larger issues, except when these impinged on the territory of Okhrana 2nd Section. He never concerned himself why Russia was fighting, and neither did he question the existing social order. It was, after all, none of his affair who ruled. Occasionally he reflected briefly on the miserable inadequacy of his salary, but there were casual, unofficial perquisites for Okhrana men that allowed the strident Madame Popov to indulge her passion for cheap and showy clothes and jewellery. Popov paused briefly at the gates of the Meretskov palace. The palms of his hands had begun to sweat again. One had to be so careful with aristocracy. The life of an Okhrana agent was full of small anxieties. But he couldn't complain, in all honesty. Where else would he find such satisfaction in his work? He rubbed the toes of his boots on his trouser legs and walked up the drive.

Natalya was nervously fastening the front of her dress when Vera announced the arrival of Popov.

'A shabby little man, madam.'

Natalya peered at herself in the mirror. 'Who?'

'Mr Popov, madam. I have left him in the hall.'

'Oh yes. Show him into the study. I'll be down in a moment.' She smoothed her hands over her hips and frowned. I've become thin. And pinched looking. Not at all as Paul Malnekov remembered me. What will be his verdict? Did it really matter? It was just vanity. Tonight she would end the affair. So why was she debating with herself which earrings best matched the dress?

Natalya went down to the study. 'Do sit, Mister Popov.' What a strange little man — so ill at ease. 'There now. I'll sit here, and you can tell me what I have done to upset the Minister of the Interior.'

Popov blinked several times very rapidly. 'Such a beautiful palace. I have often admired it as I passed.'

'Yes.' She clasped her hands together and looked at him expectantly.

But Popov seemed unable to begin without elaborate formality. He wiped the palms of his hands with a grubby hankerchief and peered at the portrait on the wall. 'Count Ivan Alexander Meretskov. A great soldier of Russia. My illustrious uncle served under his High Excellency in the war against the Turks.'

'Did he now?' Natalya waited.

'At Plevna.' Popov's eyes were unnaturally large behind his thick pebble spectacles. 'I have never been a soldier, Excellency. Just an honest servant of the Tsar.'

'And you are about to tell me why you are here.'

'Er — yes. My department is interested in a certain Peter Koltsov, arrested on New Year's Eve at St Saviour's Hospital. A dark, slim man with a scarred back. Possibly you recall him?'

How could she forget? 'The man had broken ribs. I believe he fell from a tram.'

'Yes?' Popov stared, and it seemed to Natalya that he had suddenly slipped into a more comfortable role. He took out a notebook and sat with his stub of pencil poised. She felt a slight apprehension.

'I really know nothing about him. I bandaged his ribs and the police arrived.'

'There were two men with Koltsov.' Popov's gentle voice was more insistent.

Natalya bit her lip. 'Were there?' She was aware that Popov had noticed her almost imperceptible pause. 'Doctor Strozhov and I were alone with Koltsov when the police arrested him.'

'Two tall men, Excellency.'

'I merely bandaged Peter Koltsov.'

'One was old, and the other young and fair-haired.'

This is ridiculous, Natalya thought. I am forced into a lie to protect the impetuous Captain Stern. And this strange little man is making me defensive. 'I know nothing about those who may have been with him.' She looked determinedly at the clock. 'And I do have an appointment.'

Popov switched immediately to deference. 'It is unforgivable that I should impose on Your Excellency in this way. Only the most pressing . . .'

If she didn't stop him he would go on all night. 'I had assumed that the matter was finished with now that this man Koltsov is arrested?'

'Alas no. He was of course convicted but he has escaped.' Popov rose and went to the window. 'He is out there in the city. I'm sure of it. I must find him, and those who assist him.' He turned suddenly. 'Do you know the Englishman — Captain Michael Stern?'

'Vaguely.' He has noticed me hesitate again, Natalya thought. Why don't I just order him out of the palace? But she was curious. 'Captain Stern could hardly be an accomplice. He left Petrograd at the beginning of the year.'

'Yes?' The stub of pencil was poised again.

'Captain Stern is an engineer. He is in northern Karelia I believe, working on the Murmansk railway.'

Popov slid his battered notebook into his pocket. 'Thank you, Excellency. I'll trouble you no more tonight.'

Why is he smiling? Natalya wondered as she led Popov across the hall. 'From where did Peter Koltsov escape?'

'Northern Karelia.' Popov bowed. 'The Murmansk railway. Goodnight, Your Excellency.'

And as Popov pulled up his collar against the cold wind he noticed the long black automobile waiting in the shadows.

172

Curtains on the rear windows. Cossack driver. Caucasian Corps penant. He blinked. So even the beautiful Countess has her indiscretions.

Natalya stood quite still in the hall. Could Captain Stern have helped Koltsov escape? Yes, she was ready to believe he could. He had his own odd set of rules to live by, just as Peter Koltsov lived by his.

She was barely aware of Vera helping her on with her coat. The fat little man had delayed her. She hurried down the steps, wondering why her nervousness over the meeting with Malnekov had left her.

The seemingly mute Cossack chauffeur assissted her into the automobile then drove towards the river, following the same route she had taken that last time with Rykov.

How changed everything is, and in such a short space of time. But it's not just the city racked by strikes, it's me as well. Natalya stared ahead. Would I have it all as it was three — four months ago? What an egocentric little world — I even thought my penance in the hospital was important.

They crossed the river. Police were stopping lorries and carts on their way in and out of the city but they waved the black automobile on. To the east the dark shape of St Peter and St Paul was silhouetted against an ugly red glow in the night sky. Natalya peered out. 'The fire seems to be in the Vyborg district. Do you know what caused it?'

Her chauffeur spoke for the first time. 'Textile workers have burned a mill, Your Excellency. Cossacks have dispersed them.' He relapsed into silence and the car turned off the University Quay.

What would it have been like to have lived as a student struggling for a degree? Natalya looked back at the Academy of Fine Arts. Until these last few months I've never wondered much about what might have been. What do I want? She huddled down in her fur coat, remembering suddenly the young man with his empty sleeve pinned to his tunic, watching the ballet with his mother. A well ordered life without deceit.

She could see students and workers massing ahead on the broad Angliyskya. Pamphlets were thrown at the windscreen. The driver said nothing, but accelerated, scattering the crowd and speeding northwards until they were across the far bridge to sparsely populated Krestovsky Island.

The road ahead was dark, lights of the city left behind them. Natalya eased back in her seat again. Here they were safe. The Malnekovs had a large house in the city but kept the Krestovsky villa for occasional use. Natalya could make out the darkened shapes of remote summer residences, many of them closed since the war.

The car crunched the hard snow on the drive up to the Malnekov villa. Natalya quickly rehearsed again. She would explain carefully to him; the guilt, her puzzled need to live by quite ordinary rules. He would probably be contemptuous but his pride would only be minimally offended. Whatever, she would end it tonight.

How seldom does life turn out quite as one expects.

Malnekov was unshaven. He smelled of dried sweat, still dressed as he had arrived in the city that morning. Natalya dined with him on cold food put out for them by his servant, and her resolve gave way to concern. The hard lines on his face had deepened and there was grey in his hair that she hadn't remembered. He talked steadily, moving from strategy in the Carpathians to the situation in Petrograd. He is completely out of touch with what is happening here, she thought. And how long since he has slept? She asked him and he waved his hand impatiently. 'I'm all right, Natalya.'

'We could just as easily have talked tomorrow.'

'How can you say that? It is more important that I see you. Isn't that how it has always been with us?'

Not quite. He had been glad enough to go off to the front. And that disastrous campaign has done something to him.

They went to the long room where he slept and worked, lit now by blazing logs in the stone fireplace. It was here, on that great bed, that she had become his — totally committed, or so it had then seemed. Now the familiar masculine furnishings and decorations seemed ordinary, rather dusty, their magic gone.

Malnekov moved about restlessly, his mind back on the campaign. 'Transport bedevilled us. The terrain is suitable only for goats. But I could see the high point of the pass through my field glasses, and I knew beyond it lay the Hungarian plain.'

'You should rest.'

'One determined thrust.' He frowned to himself and stretched out on the bed, hands behind his head. 'That was what we were there for, surely? I had no doubts then. It was only when we began the advance. I'd never had doubts before.'

And neither had he known defeat. Natalya stood at the window, looking out at the dead, white land and listening to the voice in the darkened room behind her.

'Some of those Carpathian ridges are seven thousand feet — hard going for even the youngest and fittest. Ninety miles of crest and forest we took and held.'

'I think I can see another fire,' she said.

'My Caucasians cleared the high pass.' She heard him move, lighting a cigarette. 'But Stavka refused me reinforcements — they would not accept the casualties and I was forced into bloody retreat.'

Forty per cent dead and wounded. All those hospital trains. 'What did it achieve in the end?'

'Nothing.' The cigarette glowed. 'If another general had planned the campaign I would have seen the mistakes instantly. They were all there, waiting to be made. Reaching the Hungarian plain had become an end in itself. One day, clever young men in university offices will write the episode into the history books. They will reach the inevitable conclusion that I wasted an army.'

She was aware of the silence beyond the window. 'What now?'

'Riot control for the ageing Khabalov, here in the city — I brought back six hundred of my own Cossacks. The Tsar has washed his hands of me. When the war ends I shall seek service abroad — China perhaps.' He paused and the cigarette glowed again. 'Will you come with me, Natalya?'

'The second fire is closer, in the dock area.' She turned and faced him across the room. 'No. I won't go with you.'

'You wash your hands of me also?' He nodded. 'We get what we deserve in the end. Tamara is returning to Paris for good. She has the boy — he is her life now. Too late I see how badly I have treated you.'

'I permitted it. I am just as much to blame.'

'You offered me your love and I traded it for a disastrous campaign.'

'You couldn't wait to leave! As soon as the field command was offered you. Was what I offered not enough? You ran from me!'

'Ran? Yes, I did.' He crushed out the cigarette and frowned at the ceiling. 'I suppose I was running from your youth. Too many years have passed — you couldn't give me those back. In the Carpathians my bones ached. And I felt the cold — for the first time I really felt the cold. But I was with my Cossacks and I was *alive* again.' He turned his head. 'Do you know what I am saying?'

'I think so.'

'No, you don't. But it doesn't matter.' He held out his hand.

She crossed the room and knelt next to him. 'What will you do?'

'I'll start again. There is always work for professional soldiers somewhere in the world.' He touched her hair with his fingertips.

'What of you, Natalya — is there another man in your life?'

'No. There is nobody.'

'You are young.' He stroked her hair. 'It is spring for you. What do you want?'

'I don't know.' A tall son sitting with me at the ballet sometimes when I am old. 'I really don't know.'

'And you'll never come back here?'

'No. I won't come back.'

176

He smiled. 'Then we'll meet sometime, just by chance. And you will tell me that your life has begun once more.'

'Perhaps.'

'And I promise I will love you for what is left of my life.'

'Don't! Don't say it.' She squeezed his hand. 'After tonight I'll give nothing back.'

'But you are here now. Will you love me one last time?'

'Yes.' She nodded. 'Yes. For one last time.'

17

It was still dark as the early morning tram clanked its way up the Nevsky Prospect towards the Admiralty, laying bare the tracks covered over by the snowfall of the previous night. Near the turning at Nikolayevskya Street a van halted and well-overcoated men hauled out a wooden case draped with sacking. Their breath steamed. Two of them carried the case and the others followed, up the steps and into the high building. They had trouble negotiating the stairs, grunting and cursing as they edged the case up the last narrow flight and out onto the flat section of roof. On the landing below a woman was looking up the stairs, worried because of the noise. One of the men called to her, 'Police business.' She hurriedly closed her door. On the roof the two bearing the case set it down and began to open it. The others walked to the edge and peered cautiously down at Petrograd slowly stirring, then they turned back, slapping their arms around themselves. By God, it was going to be a cold watch. The two lifted the heavy Vickers machine gun from the case and set it on its tripod. One sat behind it, flicked up the rear sight and squinted along the barrel. They'd picked a good position. The view was unrestricted right up the Nevsky.

*　　*　　*

At the Prefecture building on Gorokhavaya Street dismounted Cossacks of Malnekov's IXth Caucasian Corps were casually guarding and warming themselves at an open brazier. Their mode of dress separated them from the other garrison troops — overcoats worn thin in the campaign in the Carpathians, and home-made expediencies to keep out the cold, they looked more like bandits. Lights were burning in the office windows behind them. General Malnekov had been in the building since before dawn, studying Khabalov's orders for crowd control.

He was already tired. How many of the one hundred and sixty thousand garrison troops could be trusted? He could count on his own Cossacks but there weren't nearly enough of them. Frowning, he went over to the large wall map of the city and he spoke to his aide without turning his head.

'The Ismailovsky Regiment?'

'They will remain in barracks, High Excellency, ready to be deployed along the embankment — from the Troitsky to the Dvortzovi. Cossacks — not our own — will patrol the north and eastern approaches to the city centre. Shall I alert the Volinsky Regiment to guard the Alexandrovsky Bridge?'

The reliability of the Volinsky was already in doubt. 'No. Use the Preobrazhensky Guard.' Malnekov pondered. Which regiments were loyal and which might break? There was no sure way of knowing. Positioning them was like playing chess with pieces of indeterminate colour — a significant defection at any critical point and he'd lose the game. 'We'll use two companies of the Volinsky at Znamenskya Square to cover the approach to the station. Our own Cossacks can stiffen them.' There was nothing more he could do now but wait. He turned to his aide. 'Are you happy that we are back in Petrograd, Major?'

Major Krasnov touched the prematurely grey streak in his hair. 'It gives a small respite from the front, High Excellency.' He smiled. 'And Petrograd still has its diversions.'

'Ah, you are young.' Malnekov went over to the window. In the street below, groups of demonstrators were passing, idly watched by his Cossacks as they blew on their hands and stamped their feet in the snow. 'And what do you do for diversion?'

Krasnov considered. 'In what other city would one find such beautiful women?' And he glanced curiously at the older man. Malnekov was frowning, lost now in his own thoughts. 'Do you want me out there today, High Excellency?'

'I beg your pardon?'

'Znamenskya Square. Our Cossacks to stiffen the Volinsky. Will you leave the matter to me?'

'Yes, Krasnov. You deal with it.' He remembered 1905, and the armoured trains pushing east through the snow drifts to Chitra. Those mutineers had been rabble too. And he, Malnekov, had crushed them with consummate ease. A Guard regiment and a few hundred Cossacks, that's all he'd had. He turned to Krasnov. 'No. I've changed my mind. The task of dealing with city rabble is humiliating for soldiers. But those Cossacks out there are mine — from my own district. Tell them that I will be with them at Znamenskya Square.' And he looked down at the street again.

Krasnov's eyebrow lifted very slightly. 'As you wish, sir. I will tell them.'

By midday there were large crowds converging on the city centre. Soldiers stopped many at the bridges but others streamed over the ice-covered river. At the Nevsky, women machinists from the Kazakhov mill joined with men from Aboukov's and the Narvskaya Zastava. They laughed and sang as they marched. Young Cossacks of the garrison rode slowly, jostling their small ponies through the press of people. A woman in the crowd shouted, 'We are not Germans. What do you need guns for?' And a Cossack called back 'Don't worry, we won't shoot.'

From high office windows all along the route, hundreds of typists watched the dark tide moving down the Nevsky towards Znamenskya Square.

179

Two companies of the Volinsky had arrived half an hour before. Long greatcoats fastened at the neck and feet already frozen inside their boots, they formed a line in front of the Nicholas rail terminus. They held their rifles across their bodies, and they watched and waited.

The touting *droshky* drivers lined along the station exit sensed trouble and they left, sleigh runners hissing on the snow, and travellers arriving from the east had to make their own way. Hauling their bags they passed anxiously through the evenly spaced soldiers and hurried across the square to safety.

The train from Murmansk was late as usual, delayed by heavy snow. An engine had had to be changed at Petrozavodsk, and passengers picked up the first hints of trouble. The telegraph clicked, relaying messages north through Zvanka. Rumours grew as the train crept towards the capital. Michael Stern huddled deep in his greatcoat and scowled out at the white land. Forest and snow. Mile after mile of it. A sameness that disturbed. He had intended to sleep but he'd felt half frozen ever since he and Rantalla had boarded the train at Pitkul. The heating system was faulty, cold air trickling through the vent beneath his seat.

He tapped Rantalla's leg with the toe of his boot. 'What do you say, old man? A bit too cold out there for a revolution?'

Rantalla opened his eyes. 'We'll find out soon enough, Excellency.' And he closed his eyes again.

Stern stared at him. 'Damn it, you could venture an opinion.'

'We should have gone to Stockholm as the English colonel suggested.'

The old man thinks I'm mad. Still scowling, Stern rubbed at the ice crusting on the window. Scattered houses with fences. A wide road. 'We're nearing Petrograd.'

Rantalla abandoned his doze and peered out. 'The Neva, Excellency, to our right.'

The train clanked, slowing through industrial suburbs. A pall of greasy smoke drifted over the railway tracks from the smouldering fretted ruin of the Berezin chemical works. Stern covered his nose and mouth with his scarf. 'Sulphur! For God's sake!'

'It smells of trouble.' Rantalla frowned.

The train moved at snail's pace into the vast network of sidings on the south of the city, and there it stopped for ten minutes. 'God, I'm cold.' Stern rubbed the steamed-up window. 'What the hell are they up to?' And in that moment the carriages juddered, and they began moving back the way they had come.

'We are being diverted, Excellency.'

'I wonder why?'

Ugly, squared off slabs of brickwork stained with smoke. Close-packed slums. They passed under signal gantries and rumbled between workshops. The gold dome of St Isaac's loomed ahead and the train crept into the Nicholas rail terminus. Rantalla pulled his shoulder pack from the rack. 'Now we'll see.'

Almost immediately Stern could feel the tension in the huge, glass-covered station. They had difficulty getting through the barrier. Travellers packed the exit, unwilling to venture out. Stern edged forward, his valise catching on suitcases and coats, and even before he reached the Znamenskya he could hear the voices. Thousands of people were filling the square.

'We'll never get through, Excellency.'

'We'll have to try.'

The infantrymen fronting the station had fixed their bayonets.

'Volinsky Regiment.'

Stern peered over the shoulders of the riflemen. An anxious Volinsky captain was pacing up and down, watching the crowd grow by the minute. On the right of the square, spread out to give adequate cross fire, were dismounted Cossacks, carbines held loosely.

Rantalla adjusted his shoulder pack for easy movement. 'It doesn't look good, Excellency.'

A setting for disaster. Stern noticed the tall, slim figure of

181

General Malnekov standing quite relaxed with his Cossacks. 'Take my valise, old man, and stick close behind me. We'll see if we can reach the Nevsky.' And he pushed his way between the line of soldiers. My timing is perfect, as usual, he thought. Just as the trouble is starting.

The crowd was largely good-humoured, and with all the thousands filling the square there were still spaces, odd patches not yet occupied. But peering over heads, Stern could see more people converging on the long open side of the Znamenskya. They were chanting in unison, 'Bread! Peace! Freedom!'

'Try that way, Excellency, to the Ligovskya Prospect!'

And they shouldered and pushed towards the north side. A mistake! Massed banners of Putilov workers from the south west of the city filled the Ligovskya. Stern's thoughts quickened, weighing the implications. He and Rantalla were only half way across, and the pressure of workers entering the square was edging the crowd towards the Volinsky bayonets. He glanced round, aware of sharp detail. A worker in a ragged coat, mouthing obscenities. A girl's frightened face over her red scarf as she clung to a young man. The peaked caps of the Volinsky riflemen. All hell was going to break loose any minute. He shouted round, knowing that it was pointless. 'Back! Get back!'

And with his Cossacks on the far side, Malnekov assessed the size of the crowd. He watched the captain commanding the two companies of Volinsky and his jaw tightened. Do it *now*, he thought, before the rabble get out of hand.

The Volinsky captain was still hesitating, then he gave the order, repeated by his huge, bearded sergeant. Rifles were raised, pointing up over the crowd. The soldiers fired a ragged volley into the air, shots echoing off the high buildings and disturbing a few startled birds. Immediately, panicking demonstrators tried to force their way back, but the great tide pushed them closer to the line of bayonets.

The moment of decision had come for the Volinsky captain. He gave the order to fire into the crowd. The bearded sergeant shook his head and one by one the rifles wavered. It could end here and now, Malnekov thought. One display of strength and purpose. The captain repeated the order, then he struck the sergeant across the mouth with the back of his hand. Blood spurted from the sergeant's split lips and splashed onto the snow.

Malnekov felt a release of tension as he saw the Volinsky riflemen backing uncertainly towards the station. And he was fleetingly aware of something almost forgotten. He drew his sword, and arm outstretched he gave the order. Cossack carbines came up. I'm young again, he thought, and swung his sword down. The carbines crashed.

Stern saw the girl with the red scarf crumple, sliding down still clutching her young man, and his hoarse cry was drowned in the shrieks of terrified demonstrators. Stern stood astride the girl and Rantalla crouched, shielding her head as boots scuffed the snow around them. The young man sobbed, staring down at the girl's blood on his coat.

'Protect her legs, damn you!' Stern shouted at him.

The carbines crashed again and blood gouted from the man's mouth. Eyes wide with shock he turned, staggered, bumping off scrambling workers and sank to his knees.

People streamed outwards, thinning the square. Stern waited, then picked the girl up. Her boot slid off, and he ran with Rantalla ahead forcing a way through. They reached the Ligovskya and he sank to his knees, gasping for breath. An ugly crackle of a machine gun sounded from further up the Nevsky on their right. He laid the girl on the paving.

'She's dead, Excellency.' Rantalla peered at her closely then crossed himself.

Stern remained kneeling next to the girl. She looked surprised; eyes open, lips slightly parted as though about to speak. I wonder what she was going to say? He covered her face with her red scarf. A running man threw aside a banner, catching him on the side of the mouth. 'God damn it!' He spat out a piece of broken tooth.

Ambulances were arriving, and lorries packed with uniformed police.

'We'd better leave her, Excellency.'

Two policemen, revolvers in their hands, approached. 'Stand up!' But seeing Stern's unRussian uniform and hard expression they were instantly deferential. 'Was she with you, sir? Don't concern yourself. We'll take care of her.'

He rubbed his aching jaw. 'A shade late for that,' he said, and watched as they lifted the girl and carried her away.

The square was like a battlefield. Twenty or more bodies still lay among smashed banners in the snow. Malnekov's Cossacks stood easy, their brief decisive function fulfilled. The two Volinsky companies were re-forming their line as the huge bearded sergeant bawled at them through lips still bleeding.

Stern looked around in disgust then took his valise from Rantalla. 'Right. Let us leave here, old man.'

And they made their way cautiously along the Nevsky, sheltering in doorways each time the rooftop machine gunners opened up.

Later, in the crowded dining-room of the Europe Hotel, the events of the afternoon seemed strangely unreal. Stern observed. An ancient waiter frowned, concerned, while a fat Russian complained. And two young Americans, slightly the worse for drink, were trying to catch the attention of an attractive girl alone at a nearby table. She had taken out a small hand-mirror and was examining her lips. Behind the murmur of voices were soft sounds of gypsy music from the cluster of potted palms.

'I can barely believe it all happened.' Stern ate carefully, avoiding his broken tooth.

Rantalla paused and took a spent carbine bullet from his pocket. 'Cossack, Excellency. I found it embedded in a book in my shoulder pack. It happened all right.' And he returned his attention to his plate.

Do revolutions begin like this? The fat Russian had ordered champagne, and the girl alone at the nearby table slid her tiny mirror into her bag as a middle-aged man crossed the dining-room and joined her. But it seemed now that waiters were listening for sounds outside in the street.

Stern frowned to himself. He'd tried to telephone Baumler but the lines were dead.

'The crowds have dispersed. Maybe it's all over.'

'They will be back tomorrow, Excellency,' Rantalla shovelled more food into his mouth. 'We should have gone to Stockholm.'

No. Stockholm would have been the sensible decision. Why break habit? He'd had to come back to Petrograd; to shake the kaleidoscope and see if the Countess appeared in the pattern. 'Admit that you're curious, old man.' He refilled Rantalla's glass. 'And isn't this more interesting than walking round Stockholm with a tourist guide book in your hand?'

Rantalla belched softly and pushed his plate back. 'I am an old dog, Excellency. I can smell more trouble. But I am certainly curious about what you will do.'

'What makes you think I'm going to do anything?'

'Your Excellency worries me a little.' Rantalla leaned forward, folded arms on the table. 'If you will forgive my saying, you have the temperament of a solitary man. You seem driven by something, and in a direction I cannot predict.'

'You're crazy. I have a crazy assistant.' Stern lit a cigarette. But he had become a solitary man, hadn't he, over those five years since the drowning of the Russian officer? And he remembered the journey back, and the old holy man squatting near naked in the dust on the road to Simla. He fingered his broken tooth and frowned. 'Damned thing. Tomorrow I'll have to find a dentist.'

'You want me with you?'

'No. We'll meet up later. Search out your cousin, the cab driver, and see what he has to say.'

'He'll know a little about everything, and nothing of real importance.'

'Let's go to our beds. I've had enough of today.'

'My bed is too soft, Excellency. I'll sleep on the floor.'

Back in his room, Stern dozed uneasily. Sharp images of the day kept intruding. Blood splashing on the snow as the Volinsky captain struck his sergeant across the face. Carbine

185

shots and the startled birds fluttering over the great square. The girl crumpling.

He rolled onto his back. God's teeth, the old man is right, the beds are too soft. Was the Countess asleep in her bed, just a mile away? He suppressed the perception of long blond hair, and her face, softened. A relationship beyond the formally informal was hardly likely. He couldn't think that far. A threadbare captain of engineers — that's what he was — and back to some fever-ridden outpost of India in a few months' time. But there was still the debt to pay, wasn't there? He lay on his back, frowning into the darkness.

Garrison Cossacks patrolled the street outside. He could hear the soft sound of hooves on snow. The city was quiet again. Snow had damped down the fires in the Vyborg district. Police and soldiers had dismantled barricades. At the Radziwill mansion on the Nevsky, lights of a gala party blazed until well after midnight.

At four o'clock in the morning, Sergeant Timofeyev Kirpichnikov of the Volinsky Regiment rose from his bunk and took his rifle from the rack. He went out into the darkness and crossed the barrack square to the quarters of his captain, and he lit the lamp. The captain had only a moment to feel surprise as he peered up at the bearded face with its split lips, and the rifle pointed at his head. Then, Sergeant Kirpichnikov blew his brains out.

18

As the morning slowly grew lighter the snow came again.

Peter Koltsov ventured out for the first time since his return to Petrograd. He felt strange, slightly dizzy. It's all the noise and movement, he thought. He'd been cooped up in a back room for too long. He sank his hands deep in the pockets of the old coat that Stern had given him when he'd escaped. At the late night meeting of the Petrograd Bolsheviks he had proposed they offer leadership on the streets. Only the fat, moustached Zersky had agreed.

Zersky was waiting for him on the wide, snow-covered steps of St Sampson's Cathedral. Together they joined a group of chanting workers moving towards the city centre. Some of them recognized Koltsov, and he nodded and waved as he carefully gauged their mood. Zersky was right — yesterday they had seen too many dead. Today they were making a lot of noise but they were nervous. Already his limbs ached but he increased his pace, walking ahead of them towards the frozen river.

They reached the Alexandrovsky Bridge where a large crowd had formed, peering through the fast-falling white flakes at the long grey line of soldiers facing them on the far embankment. Koltsov blew on his hands and glanced quickly round at the mill girls and factory hands. About a thousand — enough to storm the bridge. How afraid were they? The city was finely balanced, ready to be tilted.

Zersky looked worried. 'Too many soldiers,' he murmured.

'It depends on whose side they're on.' Koltsov blew on his hands again. 'We must try today. By tomorrow it may be too late.'

'It's too big a risk. If the soldiers shoot we'll lose hundreds.'

'If we don't take risks we'll never win.' Koltsov weighed the chances again then faced the crowd. The decision was made. 'What are we waiting for?' he shouted, his voice harsh.

A man in a ragged coat was watching him carefully and he sneered. 'You want to kill all these people? The soldiers will shoot us down as we step onto the bridge. No. I say we go back.'

Koltsov looked at the man's boots. They're too good, he's no worker. An Okhrana man maybe. 'Come on, comrades. Don't draw back now.'

But the mood had changed. Nobody was singing and the faces were anxious. Koltsov stared across the ice at the soldiers evenly spaced and perfectly still. If he could get just one regiment to defect. He'd have to try it alone. And he shouted at the demonstrators again. 'I tell you they are workers over there, just like us. I'll go and talk to them.'

The crowd watched in silence as he stepped onto the bridge and began to cross. His knees felt weak. It's because I'm tired. If I had one man beside me — just one shoulder next to my own. Dmitry — and the thought surprised him — or Michael Stern.

He'd gone a dozen paces and his mouth dried up as he heard a shouted order and saw the long rifles come up, pointing at him. Would they shoot? Only a few weeks before he would have welcomed an obliterating bullet to end his servitude as a convict, but now he wanted to live. He reached the centre of the bridge and paused. I can't go any further, he thought, my legs won't carry me. And he called to the soldiers. 'Our comrades back there behind me think you will shoot them. I said you won't because you are workers like us.'

An officer bawled 'Fire!'

Koltsov flinched.

Nobody had obeyed!

He stared as one by one the rifles were lowered.

The officer shouted, pointing to the crowd on the far bank, and the grey-clad infantrymen wavered uncertainly.

This damned snow, I can barely see. Koltsov brushed it from his face, peering across the bridge, and hope rising he saw a stocky corporal step forward and lift the officer bodily from the ground. He carried him quite gently to the embankment wall and sat him on it. For a few seconds there was silence, then the long grey line broke, men shouting and laughing. 'Revolution!'

Koltsov's eyes opened wide. They're coming over to us!

The soldiers cheered and surged onto the bridge, and workers came running to join them. Two foundrymen hoisted Koltsov and sat him on their shoulders.

I feel ridiculous, he thought, and struggled to keep his balance as he was carried to the city side of the river. He glanced to the east. The fortress of St Peter and St Paul was grey in the falling snow. Dmitry should have been here to see this. All that struggle. All those risks and hardships ending on a tightened rope. And now the Petrograd workers are making a choice. They set him down. Mill girls were embracing Aboukov foundrymen and soldiers were firing their rifles into the air. A waste of good cartridges. Koltsov scowled and climbed wearily onto the embankment wall. Now they are committed, he thought, and there can be no turning back. He raised his hand impatiently and Zersky bellowed for silence.

'This is just the beginning!' he shouted, looking round at the sea of upturned excited faces. 'We will sweep away the corrupt government. Petrograd will be ours. Russia will be ours. Bread! Peace! Freedom! There are no options!' His harsh voice was carried on the wind far across the crowd. 'All power to the workers and soldiers!'

The rest of his words were drowned. He climbed down and leaned against the wall, waiting for the noise to subside. 'What are we waiting for? Let us claim our city.' And leading them he moved off down the Liteyny Prospect.

They were held up by a machine gun at the Basseynaya turning. Koltsov directed the answering fire from a plundered shoe shop. Would the other troops come over? If they didn't it could die here in the space of an hour or so. He watched as a dozen Aboukov workers climbed over the high roof opposite and threw the police machine gunners into the street below.

At their barracks the Volinsky Regiment had again formed up. Band playing they marched out behind Sergeant Timofeyev Kirpichnikov and joined the revolution. There were savage exchanges on the Nevsky but one by one the police machine guns fell silent. Peter Koltsov watched as a small, immensely dignified student with a red armband led a huge, almost silent crowd along the centre of the broad thoroughfare. It's happening, he thought. The Tsar's rule is collapsing like a rotten house. And it's taken us by surprise.

Sure now of the capture of the city centre, he walked back up the Nevsky Prospect with Zersky. I'm so tired, he thought. 'Get the agents circulating. Sokolov, Iuranov and the others will want to know what's happening. I'll be at the Aliuyev house.' He paused outside the Meretskov palace. A mob was looting. 'The workers have begun the revolution almost without our help. They need leadership.' Windows shattered and curtains were being dragged down. Where is the woman? he wondered. And he returned to the Vyborg to begin the count.

The Aliuyev women kept a constant supply of tea for the agents. They came in one by one and reported to Koltsov on the defecting regiments. They were laughing, drunk with success. Koltsov frowned as he checked off his list. 'The revolution is here but it isn't won yet. We need barricades out there on the streets — good ones. The Tsar may be on his way back with an army of loyal troops.'

A man with a shaggy coat cut short at the waist carried in a Vickers machine gun. He grunted, setting it down on the floor. 'We took it from a rooftop on the Liteyny. The police used it quite effectively so we shot them with it. I think they are on our side now.' He pushed his way through the others and squatted on his haunches next to Koltsov. 'How many of the regiments are for us, comrade?'

Koltsov called for silence and read off the list. 'Volinsky, Preobrazhensky Guard, Pavlovsky, Oranienbaum Machine Gun Regiment, and the Semionovsky. That's up to now. Most of the Cossacks are neutral.'

'What of Malnekov?'

'He's with Khabalov. They have a thousand or more loyal troops holding out in the Winter Palace. It's only a matter of time.' Koltsov waved his hand impatiently. The reckoning with Malnekov would come later. 'We've got other things to worry about.'

The squatting man lit a cigarette and passed the packet to Koltsov. 'What now?'

'It's all happened faster than we thought. It will take our leaders time to get back from exile.' He smiled thinly. 'I wish I could see Lenin's face when he hears the news. In the meantime the Duma have the advantage. They have no legal authority but they've reconvened at the Tauride Palace. They intend establishing an interim government and as Bolsheviks we must have no part in it.'

'Why not?' The squatting man peered up, puzzled. 'We're fighting the same revolution as them.'

'Because they'll sell out.' Koltsov stared round, his face hard. 'When have workers ever been able to trust the bourgeois? Sooner or later the Duma will make a deal with the Tsar and the revolution will be lost.'

He stood and leaned on the table. Every small movement tires me, he thought. 'Eventually it comes to this — the Duma or us. We must establish our own alternative structures — the soviets.' He started to pace the room and ran his fingers lightly along the barrel of the machine gun. 'Remember, history is on our side. We'll win in the end. Sokolov has called for a meeting of soldier and worker deputies, tonight, in the chamber adjoining the Duma at the Tauride Palace. I'll be there.' And he paused, frowning. 'We will see who is on which side.'

When the others left, Koltsov sat and allowed himself to go limp. They'd won the first round. But he was as weak as a kitten. Everything, even thinking, called for immense effort. He examined the shackle scars on his ankles. One of them had opened again and was festering. That accursed railway had drained him. Dmitry dead, and I'm only half alive. Time. Perhaps I just need time. I have the Party, and the revolution. That's been my life. He lit a cheap cigarette and started going through his lists again. Why would I need anything more?

Zersky peered round the door. 'The word is out. We've got the crowds constructing barricades on the roads to the south and west.' His large face creased in a frown. 'The mob is emptying the prisons — politicals and criminals alike.'

Groups with red armbands hunted through the streets. They found police hiding in a tailor's shop off Sadovaya Street and promptly hanged them from lamp posts. District police stations were ransacked and burned. Train loads of troops were arriving at the Warsaw Station, and bewildered, they went over to the revolution — whole regiments intact.

At the university refectory, Helen Mirsky paused from ladling soup and stretched her back, glancing at the long line of soldiers moving patiently towards the tables. Students and administrative staff handed them bread and filled their mess tins. They are so touchingly grateful, Helen thought, and she smiled and scooped up soup for a boy who looked no more than sixteen. The boy smiled hesitantly and moved on to collect his wedge of coarse bread. Some of the soldiers were wearing red armbands and their expressions of hard satisfaction disturbed her a little. It was not that she resented the workers having their revolution, if that's what they wanted. But it leaves one in a quandary, she thought. Which side is going to come out on top?

She emptied her bucket and went back to the kitchen to refill it. Zubov had frequently said that she was politically naive. But, she reflected, I am not so naive as to commit myself to the losing side. The fervour of some of the students seemed slightly ridiculous to her. Where would they be if the Tsar arrived tomorrow with an army? She took her bucket back to the line of tables. No, for the time being it might be best to smile quite impartially and refrain from political comment. She ladled more soup. We-ll, it made a change from typing Zubov's letters. The Professor had been absent all the morning and returned from the emergency session of the Duma only an hour before. Soon he would be gone again and she could return and have the office to herself.

Helen glanced across at the handsome young officer who was standing apart, watching the queue. He wore a small red cockade pinned to the shoulder of his tunic. Some of his men shouted boisterously to the girl students. Frowning slightly, he shook his head, and they desisted. And he smiled at Helen. She smiled back hesitantly and wondered. For how long would the officers be able to maintain their authority?

Zubov appeared, pushing his way through the press of people until he reached Helen's side. 'How perfectly you fit the part of ministering angel,' he whispered.

Helen reflected briefly that Zubov had been a little acid since she had begun to find excuses why he should no longer call at her room. She lowered her eyes modestly. 'One must help where one can.'

'Yes? I do not really see you manning a barricade.'

She smiled and ladled soup, and said softly, 'Nor I you, Professor.'

'We are two of a kind, Helen. I am on my way back to the Duma. Can you leave this now and return to the office? The telephone is working again.'

'Certainly, Professor.' She had grown tired of dispensing soup and the refectory had begun to smell badly of unwashed bodies.

'I do not know when I shall be back. There is much to be done.' He lowered his voice. 'I haven't seen you for so long, Helen. If I manage to leave the Tauride Palace tonight I would like to feel that I could come to your room and rest there.'

Helen sighed to herself. Who knows what might happen in the next few months? Maybe Zubov would be on the winning side. But she surprised herself by whispering, 'Perhaps you should save your ardour for the revolution?'

Zubov hissed, 'I do not know why you are treating me this way!' And he turned and left, pushing through the crowd to the exit.

Helen returned to the office. *She* knew why she was treating Zubov this way. She sat at her desk and stared down. It was because of Martin Baumler.

For the first time in years, Helen felt the need to place virtue before expedience. She sighed. It is all that moral and religious training of my childhood, she thought. It goes on simmering away in the subconscious. On that day in Baumler's apartment, when he had fed her and she'd told him about the contraband route from Terioki, she'd made up her mind that she would do all she could to get him. And with that decision made, there had come the vague awareness that she must deserve him — perhaps even that God must first agree that she deserved him. She glanced up at the ceiling, as though maybe He was aware of her thoughts. One had to be particularly careful when one was playing with those whose rules were not one's own. Quite ridiculous of course. She'd even given a beggar a small coin the other day. Just in case.

A head appeared round the door. 'The Duma is forming a provisional government! Isn't it splendid?' And before she could work her face into a quick smile, the door closed again.

That Baumler seemed at present more interested in their business arrangements had not deterred Helen. She felt reasonably confident that given a little time, a little determination on her part, he could be persuaded where his best interests lay. In all honesty, she thought, I am exactly what he needs. She did not love him of course, but she admired and respected him. And he was rich. That was surely sufficient.

She began to type Zubov's hastily prepared speech but with only half her mind on the task. The business possibilities of her involvement with Baumler already seemed promising. Carefully worded letters from Cousin Erik indicated that the first shipment would be made over the ice tomorrow night. Drugs and precision lenses would fetch a price no matter what happened here in the capital, and the upheavals would merely serve to make the transhipment easier. For a while at least there would be no border guards to watch the Terioki crossing, and the sailors at Kronstadt could hardly interest themselves in a lone contrabandist at a time like this. Helen continued to type, then struck a wrong key. Erasing errors neatly was not one of her particular skills. She cursed softly, then glanced up at the ceiling and apologized.

In the late afternoon when Helen left the university to make her way home, there were fires burning all over the city.

She could see St Isaac's silhouetted against an angry red glow, and another orange fire just beginning, in the direction of the Segievskya where the mobs were burning the Law Courts. Army lorries garishly painted with slogans and packed with shouting soldiers roared along the University Quay. Helen walked quickly. A breakdown of order leaves women particularly vulnerable. Twice was it? No, three times that day she had been embraced in the most familiar fashion by exuberant guardsmen of the city garrison, flushed with their success. Didn't they ever wash?

Helen reached the area of decaying terraces where she lived. What a strange thing a revolution is. The Law Courts and prison burning, ugly rumours of soldiers lining up their officers and shooting them, yet the workmen's café is open for business. Relieved, Helen passed the lighted window and hurried home.

When night came the city smelled of smoke. Bands of men roamed the streets, looting and looking for police. Some just looted. On rooftops of the Nevsky Prospect policemen were found frozen to death by their machine guns. The Imperial flag fluttering over St Peter and St Paul had been hauled down when rebel troops threatened to shell the fortress. Khabalov and his loyalists surrendered. The crowd wanted Malnekov but he had already slipped away.

In Panteleimenskya Street hundreds of people had gathered at the headquarters of the Okhrana 2nd Section. A small fat man with pebble glasses was shrieking, 'Burn it down! Smash in the door and burn everything!' And the enthusiastic crowd complied. Filing cabinets crashed out of windows into the street. The small fat man had made himself a red armband. He piled bulging manilla files into a huge heap and soaked them with paraffin, then he set fire to them while he called for more. 'Collect them all up! We'll burn the lot!' And the crowd delightedly obliged. The fire roared, sparks and ashes rising in the cold night air. The small fat man stood back and wiped his spectacles, and he blinked as all the records of Okhrana special agents went up in smoke.

Professor Zubov had been at the Tauride Palace since early in the afternoon. The entrance to the colonnaded building looked out on a courtyard filled with army lorries parked haphazardly. Zubov stood on the steps and breathed in the biting air. He'd spent hours talking with deputations, and petitioners swarming freely through the unguarded corridors and chambers. At seven o'clock he'd been hurriedly elected to the temporary committee for restoring order, and now, exhausted, he was taking a short rest. He was numb. He must find somewhere to sit and think. He'd made too many hasty decisions, offered too much advice and encouragement, and he was not too sure about some of the executives they'd elected. He went back inside.

The building had become more like an armed camp than a solemn legislature. Boxes of ammunition, stacks of rifles and machine guns cluttered the corridors, and there were soldiers everywhere, sleeping on benches and even on the floor. Zubov found a darkened, empty office and sat with his feet up. The exercise of authority had been a heady experience. And now the suggestion that he should join the Provisional Government! He reflected for just a moment that Helen should have been here to see his success, then he frowned sourly.

But Zubov was really a cautious man and he wished that power could have come to the Duma by a more ordered process. He liked certainties. And what had come easily to them could just as easily be lost. He heard Kerensky's voice outside, still issuing instructions as he passed along the corridor. The man was a dynamo and already emerging as leader. But Zubov was uneasy. There was something ephemeral about Kerensky — a belief in the omnipotence of the spoken word. More sounds in the corridor. Zubov swung his feet off the desk but continued to sit for a moment longer. Words, high sounding phrases, even good intentions may not be enough unless they coincide with what the great masses out there want.

Wearily he left the darkened office and began his way back.

He knew there were others who wanted to use the power unleashed on the streets. Had the Duma really won? During the day word had gone out, to workers' committees, barracks, groups of the far Left, and a hurriedly convened rival group — the Executive Committee of the Soviet — was to meet in the old budget room at nine o'clock. He pondered, frowning. Before he returned to the chamber he'd take a look to see who would be sitting with the Soviet. He walked to the budget room antechamber.

Soldiers from the defecting regiments, and workers in rough clothes. They don't look much, Zubov thought. Some of them were talking loudly but most seemed awed as they filed through the door. There were others though, conversing quickly before the Soviet convened. Zubov assessed the group. Chkheidze was with them, and Sukhanov, and Molotov. There were a number of his old political enemies, but more friends. Yes, more friends than he'd expected. Was he perhaps in the wrong camp? They had begun to move towards the door of the budget room, and in that moment one of the group looked in his direction. Koltsov — the man he'd betrayed! And guilt turned to apprehension as Koltsov paused.

'Zubov?'

Zubov knew of the spirit-breaking toil of convicts on the Murmansk line, but he was still shocked by Koltsov's appearance. He'd barely recognized him, so thin and deathly pale. Masking his feelings he stepped forward and held out his hand.

'I was delighted to hear of your escape.' He smiled. I lie all the time. Koltsov would be a formidable rival. 'You are with the Soviet?'

'Of course. And you are with *them*.' Koltsov indicated towards the Duma members entering the other chamber.

'Yes. We shall form the Provisional Government.'

Koltsov's thin lips curved slightly. 'The Duma has no more authority than us — now.'

Zubov felt a surge of relief. He has no idea, no inkling that it was my testimony that sent him to the wilderness.

197

'The people of Petrograd think otherwise.'

'The people of Petrograd may change their minds.' Koltsov glanced quickly round at the two distinct flows of people. 'You really have more in common with us, Zubov. But you've always given in to your bourgeois inclinations.' He frowned. 'The Soviet could use you. You've many contacts and you're a good organizer. Some of your friends have come over. Join us. Power will ultimately slide to the Soviet.'

If only he could be sure. Zubov felt his hands moistening. And aware that he was possibly committing political suicide, he shook his head.

Koltsov watched him, expressionless. 'One day I will remind you of this moment.' And he turned and followed a newly arrived group of ragged workers into the budget committee room.

Zubov agonized. Other people were always so sure, whereas he had to pretend certainty. He could still change his mind. But no. Koltsov, Chkheidze, Molotov. And those shabby exiles: Lenin, Trotsky, Zinoviev. They couldn't win.

The budget room door closed.

19

'Damned thing! It aches like the devil.' Stern crossed the hotel room and peered at his broken tooth in the mirror. 'I eventually found a dentist — on Sadovaya Street. I even got as far as sitting in his chair.' He turned briefly. 'Do dentist's chairs worry you? Then a machine gun opened up a mile or more away and the bloody tooth-puller scuttled down to his basement. Left me sitting there like an idiot. So I gave up.' He scowled, touching his face gently. 'I can't eat. What did you do with your day?'

Rantalla sprawled wearily in the chair. 'I searched for my

cousin. I saw two dead policemen in the snow on the Liteyny. They'd been pushed off the roof. But further along, some of the kiosks of the arcade were open for business.' He paused. 'Odd, isn't it, Excellency? I do not know which side I am on.'

Stern wandered to the window. He hadn't found the Countess. The Meretskov palace was looted — servants gone, and no sign of the sisters. He frowned out at the night. Maybe they'd left the city? He winced at another surge of pain. 'You found your cousin?'

'Yes. He has an injury — caught in the crossfire on the embankment.' Rantalla rose and joined Stern, peering at the jagged eye tooth. 'You are perhaps close to a nerve, Excellency. Wait. I have a soldier's remedy.'

And he went to his room and returned with his shoulder pack. 'Cloves.' He opened a small tin. 'Place one under your lip. I could, of course, extract the tooth if Your Excellency wishes. I have a small pair of pincers.'

Stern thought not. 'Thanks. I'll live with it. Is your cousin badly hurt?'

'A flesh wound. Not critical, but serious enough to put him to bed.'

The clove worked! Stern sucked on it. 'I'm damned if I know what I'd do without you, old man. Does your cousin need anything?'

'Somebody to complain to, and to bring him gossip.' Rantalla pondered. 'The cab horse needs attention. There's precious little food for the poor animal. I'll see to it tomorrow.'

Stern paced up and down. Tomorrow he would have to find out what had happened to the sisters. Where to begin? He turned at a light tap on the door. 'Who the hell? . . .' And he opened it and took the envelope from the green-bloused hotel boy.

'Attaché's Office. "Urgent"?'

He handed the boy a coin and closed the door. 'Who would want to contact me here?' And he frowned, toying with the envelope.

'If Your Excellency opens it we will find out.'

He crossed back to the light and tore the flap. Rantalla watched him as he read the brief typewritten message.

'God in heaven!' he shouted. 'Listen to this, old man. "Loparskya Bridge destroyed by fire. Proceed directly to Murmansk on receipt of this cable. Southgate." ' He stared at it again. Yes, he had read it right. 'Seven hundred miles we've come, and just to get a train back!'

Rantalla sighed. 'And I was going to try sleeping in that soft bed tonight.'

He crumpled the cable. He'd win a knighthood for Southgate — that's what the swine was after. And a fat pension for his old age, and access to all those doors closed to him because of his slimy dealing. 'To hell with the man!' Southgate was as much of a leper as he was. 'I won't go.'

'A direct order, Excellency?' Rantalla looked at him levelly. 'We are professional soldiers. Not like that rabble out there.'

'Don't be so bloody reasonable! I hate it when you're reasonable. Seven hundred miles!'

'Your Excellency is a master engineer. Understandable that you should be upset, but who else would they turn to?'

'And don't bloody well humour me!' Stern threw the cable into the waste bin. His tooth had started to ache again. 'All right. So I'm going. But I'm not going tonight. And you don't have to come with me, you've got your cousin to look after.'

The old man considered. 'He lives alone. He has no friends, only acquaintances.'

'Stay as long as you need to.'

'Thank you, Excellency. I'll see him on his feet, then I'll rejoin you.' And he frowned. 'I should cross the city — make the poor devil some soup.'

'Do you need company?'

'No. I'll manage.'

'It will be bad out there tonight. The prisons are emptied. Have you a weapon?'

'Automatic pistol, Excellency.' He rummaged in his

shoulder pack. The pistol was wrapped in a clean rag. 'I took it from a Japanese officer in 1905. He had no further use for it.' And Rantalla squinted along the barrel. 'He had no further use for anything. Has Your Excellency ever killed a man?'

'One. A long time ago.'

The old man glanced at Stern. 'God forgives us if we have no choice.'

He didn't answer, and Rantalla changed the subject. 'I'll pack for you in the morning. You are staying in the hotel tonight?'

'No. There is something I have to do.'

'I wish you would stay, Excellency. But I know you have reasons of your own for being here. Take my gun.'

'Thanks, old man. I have my own.'

'Use it if you have to — don't hesitate.'

That holy man at Simla had said he would kill twice, and he'd wondered ever since who the second one would be. 'Don't worry. Ask your cousin for the name of a good dentist.'

The erratic telephone system was working again. After Rantalla left, Stern asked the operator to connect him with Martin Baumler.

'Michael! Where have you been, for God's sake? I tried your hotel twice.'

'I was looking for a dentist.'

'A what?'

'Never mind. How are you?'

'I've been with Hal Winthrop in the Singer Building most of the day, watching the battles from a nice high window. When can we meet?'

'I'm ordered back to Murmansk. I'll have to go tomorrow.'

'Tomorrow! Good God! Look, Michael. I'm going to be tied up for an hour or two — maybe longer. I've — er — I've got a consignment coming in tonight. I want to tell you about it. I'll be back at my apartment later. The janitor has a key. Let yourself in.'

'I'll be there if I can.' And Stern hesitated, reluctant to reveal his intention, even to Baumler. 'The Meretskov palace is looted. Do you know what's happened to the Countess and her sister?'

'They're almost certainly at the charity hospital. I saw the carriage in the yard when I passed there earlier.'

So she *was* here.

'I might look by the hospital, on my way to your apartment.' He tried to sound casual. 'Maybe there's something I can do.'

'The hospital! On your way here?'

He scowled. 'It's only a short distance from the Liteyny.'

'Yeah, right. Absolutely right.' Baumler rapidly changed tack. 'Offer your services — no harm in that. No harm at all. See you later, Michael. Take care out there on the streets tonight.'

Stern put the telephone earpiece back on its hook. He imagined Baumler smiling to himself. No point in wondering if Baumler thought he was just a bit crazy. He'd only got this one night left. And anyway, what was his small insanity compared with what was going on out there?

He took his service revolver from the valise, and sitting by the window he carefully cleaned and oiled it. Then he slid the cartridges back in their chambers and lit a cigarette. Why am I suddenly nervous? he wondered.

The snow had stopped falling. Far over the roofs the dome of St Isaac's was silhouetted against a crimson glow. A machine gun chattered briefly. The square below was almost deserted — just one or two small figures hurrying, staying close to the shelter of doorways.

He looked at his watch and crushed out the cigarette. Time to go and find her.

Natalya and Anna had been at the hospital since early the previous morning. Wounded from the street battles crowded the wards and corridors — two had bled to death before anybody could tend them. Volunteers worked in the

202

kitchen and fed the queues in a haphazard fashion. For all but the critical cases there was little time for more than first aid.

Natalya returned to her small room adjoining the administration offices. Peter Petrovich, tired and bewildered, followed her.

'I would have defended the palace with my life, young mistress, if you or your sister had been there. Mindless vandalism! It is shameful that men should behave like animals.'

'Sit down and rest.' Natalya put the kettle on the small burner. 'It doesn't matter. We are safe and so are you. The palace can look after itself.' How odd that she should care so little. 'Palaces are just buildings.' It was never home, like Ustreka, or even this small room.

A lorry roared past in the street outside and seconds later there were more rifle shots.

The old man was angry and confused. 'I have heard dreadful stories, young mistress. At Kronstadt the sailors buried their officers alive. And yesterday one hundred people were shot down in Znamenskya Square.'

'It wasn't a hundred.' Natalya made the tea and paused. 'General Malnekov and his Cossacks killed fifty-three unarmed demonstrators, and the wounded fill our corridors.' How could she have pitied him? She stared expressionlessly into the mirror. I should have known what he was capable of. How could I have let him . . . She bit her lip. I don't know myself. I enjoyed it. She handed the old man the tea. 'Stay here and rest.'

She returned to the dispensary where Anna was assisting Doctor Strozhov. Casualties straggled back beyond the outer door, and mattresses lined one wall of the adjoining corridor. Noise and smell. I ought to be used to it, she thought.

Strozhov straightened his back wearily and prodded a youth with his finger. 'No, we cannot spare space for this one.' And he peered down at the boy's stomach. 'He is shamming. He has only a slight flesh wound. How did you get that, *yoonasha*? Riding a whore with stays on?'

'No, Comrade Doctor.' The youth drew himself up. 'I killed a Tsarist lackey when we burned the Assize Court.'

'You should be ashamed of yourself. What will your mother think?' And the elderly doctor let his wire-rimmed spectacles slide down his nose. He bent over a casualty who had at that moment been carried in from the street. The man's face was as pale as death. 'Quick, Anna. Press your thumb here to stop the bleeding. And I . . .' Strozhov smiled gently at the white face. 'I will work a small miracle.'

Anna pressed and stopped the bright red pulsing flow. And while she pressed she averted her eyes. The small room was filthy again and spattered with blood. An orderly was swabbing the floor with disinfectant. He called to Natalya. 'We have used nearly all the dressings, Sister.'

'Tear up sheets.' Natalya knelt next to a seated soldier. His battered cap was on his knees. It bore the badge of the Semionovsky Regiment. His overcoat was ragged, worn thin at the elbows and he had sacking wrapped round his legs. A straggling beard and long hair lapped over his collar. She looked at him curiously. He couldn't have got like that in just the last few days. 'What is wrong, soldier?'

'My feet, I have frost bite, little sister.' He had a dreamy, lost look.

'Where are you from?'

'Austria. I escaped from Austria with the captain. We reached Petrograd this morning. The captain — His Excellency — told me to come here.'

'The captain? What is his name?'

'Rykov, little sister. Captain Rykov. He told me to find the charity hospital of St Saviour.'

Rykov! 'Where is he? Where is Captain Rykov?'

'They have locked him up.'

'But why?'

The soldier looked dreamy again. 'We escaped and crossed the front many days ago.' He frowned, trying to remember. 'Two weeks — perhaps three. Nobody stopped us. We just walked. The Commander of the Military District of Sarni wanted His Excellency to go to hospital. But His Excellency asked if he could go to Petrograd and the Commander gave him papers — for me also. We travelled for more days, held up by the bitter weather, and we reached Petrograd today as it became light.'

'But why is Captain Rykov locked up?'

'His Excellency has had a bad fever and I took him to the barracks — it is the only place I know. A young ensign with a red armband now commands the regiment. He told Captain Rykov that everything has changed and that regular officers are no longer wanted unless they support the soldiers and the workers in their struggle against the Tsar.'

'The captain has a fever, you say.' Natalya tried to hurry him.

'Yes, he is very sick, and sweating. He became angry. He told the young ensign to go to the Carpathians and talk of struggle, and he tore the St George Cross from his neck and threw it in the ensign's face.'

'And that is when they locked him up?'

'Yes.' The soldier turned his dreamy eyes to her. 'The ensign called guards. But before they dragged His Excellency away he said that I should come to you.' He paused. 'I think His Excellency has the lung sickness. He spits blood. He said you would help me.'

Natalya stared. Poor Rykov. Always a better man than he thought he was. 'Come with me.' She helped the soldier as he hobbled into the dispensary. Doctor Strozhov glanced up. 'Who have we here?'

'The soldier has frost bite. Please let him stay. I have to leave for a while.' And Natalya took her army greatcoat from the locker.

Anna paused from tearing up old sheets. 'Where on earth do you think you are going?'

Natalya had already decided that it would be better if Anna didn't know — for the time being. 'I have to hurry.'

'But it isn't safe out on the streets!'

'I will be all right. I will take Peter Petrovich and the carriage. Stay here.'

'But Natalya . . .'

Natalya was already hurrying along the corridor. She called back to Anna. 'Don't worry. I shall be back soon.' And she returned to the small room and woke Peter Petrovich.

The old man was reluctant, grumbling as he followed Natalya down the stairs and out into the yard at the back of the hospital.

'But the Semionovsky barracks is on Zagorodny Prospect, across the city!'

'It is *urgent*, Peter Petrovich. Captain Rykov is there, ill.'

He continued to grumble. 'If any *man* had asked me I would refuse. There are ruffians out there who would slit your throat for a kopek. You have been headstrong all your life, young mistress. Your father, God rest his soul, always said so.'

'Yes, yes! But hurry!' Natalya climbed into the carriage and buttoned her overcoat against the cold.

Peter Petrovich finished harnessing the horses, and still muttering he climbed up to his bench. 'I am too old. I have spent my life in the service of a mad family.' He flicked the whip and drove out of the yard.

The night air smelled of smoke. Natalya could see the ugly glow over the rooftops. The carriage moved along Shpalernaya Street. It seemed quiet enough. She peered out anxiously as the old coachman drove on.

As they passed the Church of All Sorrows thick smoke drifted towards them. Peter Petrovich sensed danger. One wing of the prison was burning. Men were moving ahead, silhouettes against the red glare. They shouted to each other as the prison roof collapsed with a dull rumble, and some mindlessly hurled debris at the windows. Glass tinkled. A burning timber crashed into the street in front of the carriage.

Peter Petrovich hauled on the reins and the horses reared, snorting with fear, and slithered to a stop. A dark shape, running, stooped, reached up dragging on a horse's head and the coachman shouted, 'Let us through. We are from the hospital.'

Men clawed at the carriage door. Natalya was afraid. How arrogantly stupid she had been to venture out. She could hear Peter Petrovich calling to her to run. A heavily bearded face was peering in at her. 'Who have we caught here?'

She tried to sound authoritative. 'I am a nursing sister from St Saviour's Hospital. Please let us through.'

The bearded man climbed in. 'A nurse! In a fine carriage! You're a Tsarist bitch!' He seized her by the lapels of her coat and hauled her face into the light. She struggled, sick with loathing and fear. An animal! He's a filthy animal! And she hit him in the mouth. He grabbed her wrists, holding them easily with one hand. 'Let's see what you look like under that coat.'

Natalya squirmed, trying to wrench herself free. Surely the others wouldn't let this happen! But the faces peering in were excited. 'I'm first.' The bearded brute smelled of sweat and urine. He pressed her down onto the carriage seat and ripped at the buttons on her coat, slapping her hard across the face as she writhed. 'You must be a princess — fine soft clothes.' And he tore her dress open. 'Go on, struggle harder!'

She felt helpless despair and hate as his free hand moved over her body.

Stern had reached the west end of Shpalernaya Street. Further on he could see the burning prison, and the crowd gathered round a coach. Fire flared up, roaring through the gaping hole in the roof, and through gusts of smoke he saw the coachman lash out with his whip, then slump on his bench as he was hit from behind. The horses dragged the carriage half-round before their heads were seized again and held. Dark shapes of men peering through the carriage door were shouting excitedly as one leaned in and dragged out a strip of clothing.

Stern felt a surge of disgust. He pulled out his revolver and fired twice in the air, then ran towards the group. They fell back and scattered as he fired again. Through the open door he saw the vague shape of a girl, her dress ripped, and the bearded man straddled over her.

His disgust turned to rage. He found release, swinging the barrel of the revolver across the bearded startled face. 'Out!' And he jerked the man by the collar, throwing him down onto the snow.

The rabble returned, advancing cautiously like dogs. One threw a blazing brand of timber, showering red embers as it hit the door and bounced into the carriage. Stern groped frantically, burning his hand as he dragged it out, and in that moment he saw that the girl pulling her coat together was Natalya. He turned back to face the mob and fired the revolver again, this time at their legs. Horses reared, almost overturning the carriage. He stooped and scooped up the reins. The bearded man was on his knees, spitting blood and broken teeth. Stern kicked him hard in the ribs and hauled himself up onto the coachman's bench. He shouted, flicking the reins, and the horses bolted back along Shpalernaya Street. Bricks and burning wood thumped against the rear of the carriage.

Peter Petrovich groaned and stirred. His face and beard were streaked with blood. 'Faster, Excellency!'

Natalya groped slowly upright, aware of the intense cold on her body. Her mouth was bleeding. She held the army greatcoat together at the neck and tried to control her violent retching. But sick waves of outrage kept welling in her. She leaned forward and vomited. I'd have the brute hanged! Grandfather would have in his day. She retched again and gasped for breath. Flogged as that agitator Koltsov was flogged, then hanged. And I would have watched. Slowly her breathing became more regular. It's over. And she was shocked by the savagery of her own response. Scratch the surface and I'm not so different from my Meretskov ancestors. The carriage clattered into the yard of St Saviour's Hospital. But we don't parade our feelings. She pressed the back of her hand to her mouth to stem the flow of blood.

Michael Stern helped her out.

'The ubiquitous Captain Stern. Where will you turn up next?'

'Allow me to assist you.' He was astonished at how calm she seemed.

'No. But help my coachman if you will.'

The old man had eased himself down and was leaning, holding his head with his hands. 'I am sorry, Your Excellency.

'Don't be. It was my fault. My own stupid fault.'

Supporting the old man, Stern followed her into the hospital. Anna ran to assist them.

'The Englishman was like a lion, young mistresses. He threw that hog out of the carriage like a sack of rubbish.'

Stern half-carried the coachman to a bed and lowered him onto it. And still dazed, the old man peered up at Natalya. 'I was like a lion once, when I served with your father against the Turks.'

She leaned over and kissed his forehead. 'You are still like a lion. An old, tough lion. Rest now.'

They left Peter Petrovich and went upstairs to the administration quarters. Stern couldn't get over how composed the Countess seemed, but he noticed that her knuckles were white as she held the army greatcoat together. 'I'm perfectly all right, Anna. Don't fuss.' She paused at the door of her small room. 'You can make some tea — for Captain Stern as well. I haven't yet thanked him.' And she turned. 'Allow my sister and me a few minutes alone, Captain.'

Alone in the corridor, Stern was aware of the quiet. Only faint sounds of trolleys, and doors opening and closing on the floor below. He sat on a bench. His tooth had stopped aching. He looked down at his hands, they were still shaking. I'm no lion, he thought. But I should have thrust the revolver into that bearded face and pulled the trigger — killed the second man. He would have been no loss, and for her I would do that. He'd never come upon a woman like her before.

But almost immediately the frown crossed his thoughts. What did he really know about women? A few brief affairs, none of them particularly satisfactory and ending when he moved on. Then five years out of civilized company. He was perhaps vulnerable to this apparent conjunction of the elements of high romance. Life wasn't like that. And was the woman what he thought she was? He pondered the enigma of her relationship with Malnekov. Cool, imperious beauty giving herself freely to the beast? He hadn't been able to equate it until now. He suppressed the image of her: dress ripped, hastily covering herself. Until tonight he'd separated romance from desire. An obsolete idealist, Baumler had once called him. Quixote with a slide rule inside his head.

He went to the window, opening it slightly and breathing the cold air. What she was, he didn't know. He knew only that he'd shaken the kaleidoscope and she had re-emerged in the pattern. Inevitably. He could believe that now. Threads of lives converged here. He stared out at the dark, fevered city.

Natalya had changed her dress. It was clear to Stern that she and Anna had discussed something other than the encounter on Shpalernaya Street. Anna's face was tense. She handed him a glass of tea then sat rigidly upright. And he thought she was having difficulty controlling herself. Natalya was in front of the mirror, peering at the ugly cut on her lip.

'Peter Petrovich and I probably owe you our lives.'

Only probably. The debt wasn't yet paid. 'I regret that I arrived a shade late,' he said.

She glanced round at him, one eyebrow raised, then turned back. 'You were not *too* late, Captain. I certainly cannot complain of your timing.'

Damn, now he felt embarrassed, and he wondered why she wasn't. 'It will probably be dangerous on the streets for some days. You should stay here where you are safe until the trouble dies down.'

'We cannot!' Anna said quickly.

Natalya explained. 'I was attempting to reach the Semionovsky barracks where Captain Rykov is imprisoned. We believe he is very sick. Tomorrow I must go again, and secure his release.'

'*We* must go,' Anna said.

'No!' Natalya shook her head. 'Two of us would be a pointless risk, and there is little that you could do. The new commandant of the Semionovsky Regiment will have to listen to me.' She pressed her handkerchief to her lip. 'After all, he is a mere ensign.' And she frowned into the mirror.

Stern smiled to himself. The events of the night hadn't shaken her imperious certainty of what she was. 'I don't think that is a very good idea,' he said. 'For the time being everything is upside down. If this ensign has command of the regiment he has considerable power. Your status may even antagonize him.'

She looked round at him. 'Are you saying he will not listen to me?'

'You will need some kind of release document,' he said gently. 'Something the ensign cannot choose to ignore. Do you know any Duma members?'

'A few — Rodzianko, Shulgin, Mazurev.' And she looked doubtful. 'I have met Zubov at official functions.'

'Then it is to the Duma that we must go first.' He drank down the tea and stood. 'I will be here at eight o'clock tomorrow morning.'

'You are offering to come with me?'

He nodded. 'I think it best. You shouldn't cross the city on your own. And I can perhaps talk to the ensign as a fellow soldier.'

'Your government isn't involved in what is happening here, Captain.' She looked puzzled. 'They may not approve of what you are doing.'

'They never do.'

'I shouldn't ask you to help.'

'You didn't.'

'I'm already indebted to you.'

Not so. Her steady gaze was disconcerting. I wish she wouldn't do that, he thought.

'Will you tell me why you are offering your services, Captain?'

'I'm afraid I can't do that right now,' he said. 'One day, perhaps.'

20

When morning came the streets were calmer and some of the trams were running. On the Liteyny Prospect a bank had opened for business.

At the Tauride Palace, Duma committees had been in session through the night. Zubov's eyes were red-rimmed from smoke and weariness. He was too tired to do any more and he made his way to the improvised canteen where he was served with bread and tea. He rested his head against the wall behind him and closed his eyes. During the night's rambling discussion of priorities his flashes of insight had all been ominous. The Duma wanted restoration of order so that the country could get on with the war — the honour of Russia demanded it. All right and proper, he thought, but is it what the people want?

He scowled to himself. I doubt because I'm tired. A few hours' sleep and I'll feel confident again. Yet instincts for survival nagged at him. The slogan of the Soviet — BREAD, PEACE, FREEDOM. That's what the people want. Not the honour of Russia.

He drank the tea but left the bread, and he rose wearily. Now for discussion on what to do with the Tsar. Kerensky was absolutely right, of course, capital punishment was barbarous. The Duma wanted the Tsar arrested and held in protective custody. The Soviet wanted his head. And wasn't that what many of the people out there were calling for?

Zubov passed through a long chamber. Maybe he should change sides while there was yet time? But no, he thought. The Duma is where I belong. Peter Koltsov was right about me. My bourgeois inclinations are too strong. He grimaced slightly at the floor scuffed by boots and littered with cigarette ends. He knew it wasn't important right now, but why did the workers have to turn the palace into a pigsty?

The building was already crowded and the air smelled stale. Zubov smiled, patted shoulders and murmured greetings as he moved on towards the corridor leading to the Catherine Chamber. And then he stopped, surprised. The Countess Natalya Alexandrovna Meretskova had risen from a bench and was standing in his path. What on earth was she doing here?

'Deputy Zubov?'

Zubov wondered momentarily how her lip had been split, and he glanced round. He would prefer not to be seen talking to one of the richest members of the old aristocracy. She was dressed in an ordinary soldier's greatcoat, unbuttoned, and even in his anxiety his eyes were drawn to her figure. 'You need me?'

'Yes.' Natalya nervously moistened her lips. 'A captain in the Semionovsky Regiment is being held prisoner in his barracks. He is very sick and needs urgent attention. We wish to take him to the hospital of St Saviour. We need a paper — just a scribbled note for his release.'

Zubov was aware of the foreign-looking officer and the tough old man in the sheepskin coat. He allowed himself one more quick appraisal of the Countess. What a superb woman she is, he thought. No wonder Malnekov wanted her. But it would be wiser to decline. He didn't want to get mixed up with her kind at a time like this. 'I regret that I have no power to interfere in matters of military justice.' He smiled and adopted his most sincere expression. 'Be assured that if the captain is innocent no harm will come to him.'

The foreign officer was nodding. 'We believe you, of course, Deputy Zubov. But the captain needs urgent medical treatment. We merely ask that he be transferred to the custody of the staff of the hospital. A note from you and we'll manage the rest.'

English, Zubov thought. In no other people did you find that combination of modest, self-effacing audacity. 'I wish that I could help.' He glanced quickly round again. 'We must assume that the officer commanding the Semionovsky has a reason for what he does. And now, if you will excuse me.'

As he turned to go he felt the Englishman's grip tight on his arm. 'Deputy Zubov, the officer in question has escaped from an Austrian prison camp. He reached Petrograd only yesterday. Surely there is something you can do — merely an indication that you are worried about his condition?'

Zubov was tired and angry. He pulled his arm free. 'I think not. I have more important matters.' He bowed briefly to Natalya. What a pity, he thought. I would like to bed her. And he turned and entered the room given over to the Extraordinary Commission of Inquiry into the Activities of Former Ministers and Dignitaries.

Rantalla sighed and watched Zubov's departing back. 'A dog dressed up as a man, Excellency. He is looking after himself.'

'You're right, old man.' What now? Zubov was the fifth Duma member they'd tried.

Natalya sat on a bench. She looked defeated. 'Could we try Colonel Englehardt?'

Stern shook his head. 'Englehardt has left to talk to the railway troops.' He frowned to himself. If the Duma members of her acquaintance could do nothing then he would have to try elsewhere. She was looking down, her slim hand covering the cut on her lips. Why did that sadden him? He lightly touched her shoulder. 'We're not beaten yet.'

She turned her head slightly, glancing at his hand. He withdrew it and spoke to Rantalla. 'Stay with the Countess. I will find somebody from the British Military Attaché's office.'

Rantalla nodded. 'I will look after the Countess.

Remember you have little time left, Excellency.'

'There's time enough, old man.' And he moved off quickly through the crowded chamber. To hell with Southgate's order, he thought. I'll leave when I've got Rykov out of jail for her and not before. He searched for British officers among the foreign observers. General Knox had been and gone. Hanbury-Williams was at the front. And nobody else here with sufficient pull. Where next?

He moved along corridors trying offices. Then he realized that he'd toured most of the palace and was back in the chamber adjoining the budget committee room. There he paused, frowning at the committee room door. He couldn't believe that the Petrograd Soviet would help. So there remained only one course of action. He would have to go to the Semionovsky barracks alone.

At that moment a slender man in a black trenchcoat left the chamber. Stern stared. 'Peter Koltsov!'

The man glanced in his direction, then stopped, surprised.

'Good God!' Stern felt a surge of pleasure at seeing Koltsov free. He stood looking at him, shaking his head in amazement. 'Old Rantalla and I kept wondering what had happened to you.'

'Michael!'

The name came awkwardly and Stern smiled. 'Man, I'm glad to see you.' He clasped Koltsov's hand. 'To meet here of all places! Are you trying to find somebody to listen to you too?'

Koltsov smiled very slightly. 'No. But tell me why *you* are here.'

Tired, Stern leaned against the wall. 'Damn it, I'm beginning to wonder. I'm with a lady, the Countess Natalya Meretskova. We are trying to secure the release of an officer imprisoned in the Semionovsky barracks. The poor devil is very sick.'

Koltsov pulled a packet of cheap cigarettes from his pocket and lit one. 'Perhaps I can help.'

'I doubt it. I can't even get to Englehardt.'

Soldiers and shabbily dressed workers began emerging from the chamber. Some wore red armbands. One of them paused briefly, his hand on Koltsov's shoulder, and murmured congratulations.

Stern watched. Of course that's why he is here, he thought. Where else would Koltsov be? 'You're a member of the Soviet!'

Koltsov nodded. 'Military Section. Let us find the woman, who is a countess.' His mouth curved momentarily. 'And a nurse.'

They began walking back towards the Catherine Chamber. As Stern talked he wondered at how ill Koltsov still looked. ' . . . and when we heard nothing we assumed you'd reached the city. I was worried in case that forged document let you down.'

Koltsov rasped short answers. 'No. The forgery got me all the way down the line to Zvanka . . .'

'You kept the telegraph operators busy — the line fairly crackled.' Stern laughed. 'And Rantalla and I kept those Lett guards searching woodpiles for two days.'

He saw Natalya across the hall. She was still seated on the bench, nodding as Rantalla spoke to her. Odd, he thought, that I should feel that small shock of pleasure each time I see her face.

Rantalla glanced up as they approached, and he stood and offered his hand to Koltsov. 'You reached freedom, thank God.'

Koltsov shook his head. 'You and Michael got me out, not God.'

'Perhaps He helped a little.' Rantalla smiled, white teeth showing.

'You see, Countess,' Stern turned to Natalya. 'We have an ally after all. Peter Koltsov is a member of the Petrograd Soviet. He may be able to help us.'

Her jaw tightened almost imperceptibly as she stood and faced Koltsov. 'Does the Soviet lead the rabble on the streets and in the barracks?'

'Nobody leads them yet.' Koltsov smiled to himself.

'That is why they are rabble.' And he glanced round at the ornate clock over the doorway to the Catherine Chamber. 'I'll go to the Semionovsky barracks with you, but I must be back here within two hours. Do you have transport?'

Rantalla nodded. 'I have my cousin's cab. The horse is hungry.' He frowned to himself.

The cab was old and smelled as if each of its past users had contributed to its stale mustiness. Rantalla drove through the snow-covered streets littered with debris and broken glass. Buildings were still smouldering. Men and women were scavenging, carrying armfuls of books from a shop. Natalya stared out and spoke without turning her head. 'They cannot possibly want them. Why do they steal them?'

'It's a bad winter.' Stern watched a man pushing encyclopaedias into a sack. 'They'll burn well.'

'Or perhaps he has a hunger to learn,' Koltsov said.

Natalya didn't answer.

Stern noticed Koltsov's eyes on Natalya. She must know it, he thought. She's quick at knowing things like that.

'This Semionovsky officer, held prisoner at the barracks. He is a friend of yours?'

Natalya turned suddenly and caught Koltsov looking at her. 'Captain Rykov was attached to our household. He was appointed by the Tsar.'

'Ah, you mean Citizen Romanov.' Koltsov smiled faintly.

She stared at him. 'His Imperial Majesty decorated Captain Rykov for gallantry at Tannenberg. The captain has been shamefully treated by a junior officer of his own regiment. I am astonished that a mere ensign can exercise such authority.'

'Casual, blunt use of power shouldn't surprise you. It has been a tradition with the ruling class for centuries.' Koltsov leaned wearily back in his seat.

Stern didn't like the drift of the conversation. 'Well, let's hope the new leaders learn the fine balance between authority and freedom,' he said, and smiled at Peter Koltsov. 'Of course, it takes time and practice.'

217

'Russia doesn't have time, Michael. We've got our revolution. Now we must survive.'

'Then we must thank you for sparing us two precious hours.'

'Debts.' Koltsov's mouth curved briefly.

He smiled back and felt Natalya's curious glance.

The old cab rattled through the gates of the barracks. Soldiers were warming themselves by a fire in the middle of the yard. They glanced indifferently as Stern helped Natalya out. One of them slouched ahead, leading the way to the office of the ensign commanding the regiment. He knocked on the door and went in, closing it behind him.

They waited in silence. The room was small, sparsely furnished with a desk and filing cabinets. An orderly found a chair for Natalya and she sat stiffly. Stern went to the window where Rantalla was looking out over the vast drill square.

'Does all this stir your memory, old man?'

Rantalla shrugged. 'It was a way of life, Excellency.' And he frowned as if wondering about the years.

Only Koltsov seemed quite unconcerned. Stern watched him as he peered at the notice board, slowly reading the regimental bulletins. His lips moved as he silently said the words over to himself, like somebody who has learned to read late in life. Natalya was watching him as well. The office door opened and the soldier beckoned with a jerk of his head.

Stern was surprised. The ensign sitting behind the desk was no more than twenty. His uniform was new, decorated only by a red cockade pinned to his shoulder. He looked more like a university student than a Russian officer.

The ensign quickly appraised Natalya before taking off his wire-rimmed spectacles. 'State your business.' His tone was aggressive, as though he felt it necessary to indicate his authority.

'Certainly.' Stern adopted the same tone. 'A Captain Rykov of this regiment returned here from an Austrian prison camp. We hear that because of some misunderstanding he is being held. He is clearly out of touch with recent events and has perhaps unwittingly offended. But he is sick — perhaps very sick, and we would be grateful if you would allow him medical attention at St Saviour's Hospital.'

The ensign looked at him coldly. 'You are a foreigner. Your papers?' And he held out his hand. He examined the documents carefully and then placed them on his desk. 'The prisoner, Rykov, will not be released. He has expressed counter-revolutionary opinions and insulted the courageous struggle of our soldiers here in the streets of the capital. His case will be brought before a tribunal of soldiers of this regiment.'

No. His aggression is natural to him, Stern thought. He's enjoying it.

Natalya started to speak. 'But Captain Rykov has fought and suffered for Russia . . .'

The ensign was shaking his head impatiently. 'We know only that the captain allowed himself to be captured.'

A pontificating pig. Stern suppressed his anger. 'The captain wears the Cross of St George. Come, man, he deserves hospital treatment.'

The ensign rose to his feet, knuckles pressed on the desk. 'You are English,' he rapped. 'It is not for you to question what we do. The prisoner stays in the cells and your business here is at an end. You will leave.'

Peter Koltsov had said nothing. Now he leaned across the desk and took a typed paper from the ensign's tray and with the stub of a pencil began to write on the back of it. The ensign stared at him incredulously, then blurted out. 'Return that! I could have you shot!'

Expressionless, Koltsov scratched his signature and handed the paper back. 'This is an order from the Military Section of the Soviet.' He walked to the window, staring out at the drill square, and he lit a cheap cigarette.

Eyes wide behind his glasses, the ensign read Koltsov's pencilled scrawl. He licked his lips. 'I had not understood, Comrade Koltsov. My apologies. The prisoner will of course be released immediately.'

Koltsov remained looking out of the window, and he merely nodded.

Even Stern was astonished. The ease of it! Koltsov had secured the release of Rykov and badly frightened the new commander of the Semionovsky Regiment. And he hadn't even raised his voice.

Rykov was brought up from the cells. He was dirty and unshaven, his face flushed with fever. He stood supported by a soldier and blinked slowly as if unaccustomed to the light. Then he saw Natalya. He squeezed his eyes tightly and lowered his head. A single tear ran down his face. Natalya took his hand. 'Welcome home, Captain Rykov.'

Peter Koltsov turned and observed the scene. He looks puzzled — just as he does when he reads a word he hasn't come upon before, Stern thought, and he took Rykov's arm. 'Lean on me, Captain.' Damn, his tooth had started to ache again.

They went out to the cab and settled Rykov, his head resting on Natalya's shoulder. The cab moved off, through the gates of the barracks and east along Zagorodny Street. They rode in silence for a while. Koltsov stared out at the city, but from time to time he glanced at Natalya. She was as he remembered her before his servitude as a convict — a lifetime ago.

Rykov coughed, then tried to sit upright. Natalya murmured to him and he closed his eyes again.

It was late. Stern touched his aching tooth with his tongue then called up to Rantalla. 'Hurry, old man. Peter Koltsov must be at the Tauride Palace in five minutes.'

'The horse and I are doing our best, Excellency.'

'Will the revolution wait for that poor, overworked nag?' Stern smiled at Koltsov. 'We've barely had time to talk.'

'But it's good that we met again, Michael.'

Lives touch and separate. Stern pondered. 'Your brother, Dmitry, knew my father — they played chess together. Did you know that?'

'No, I didn't.'

'Odd, isn't it?' He shrugged. 'My father is dead now.'

'And so is Dmitry.'

Natalya was watching them both.

'We must get together, Michael.'

'I have orders for Murmansk.'

'Ah. Orders.' Koltsov smiled. 'Then you have no time either.'

The cab had reached the Tauride Palace. Koltsov climbed down, and Natalya leaned forward a little. 'Thank you, Mister Koltsov, for Captain Rykov.'

Thanking him doesn't come easily to her, Stern thought.

Koltsov nodded. 'Mistakes are made. But the revolution is not unjust.' He stared at her. 'Captain Rykov is fortunate to have a friend as loyal as you. Tomorrow they would probably have shot him.' He grasped Stern's hand and shook it. 'If you get back to Petrograd you'll find me?'

'Of course. We'll drink cheap spirit and eat dried herrings — for old time's sake.'

'Perhaps it's just as well that you're leaving, Michael. Rescuing people is becoming a habit with you.' He laughed harshly. 'Where might it end? I promise I'll miss you.' He reached up and squeezed Rantalla's hand, then walked slouch-shouldered like a man very tired towards the broad steps of the colonnaded palace.

Rantalla clicked at the horse and the cab moved on. Stern watched Koltsov's departing back. 'I'm not at all sure what we would have done without his help.'

Natalya eased Rykov forward as he coughed. 'You think of him as a friend?'

Friend? You have to define your terms and decide on your criteria. The word didn't seem adequate. 'Yes. Something like that.' And he shrugged slightly. 'He's a strange fellow.'

And frightening. Natalya remembered suddenly a wolf in winter on the estate at Ustreka. It had stared up at her window, then loped off through the snow. She rested Rykov's head against her shoulder again and wiped the beads of sweat from his forehead.

'You've a bit of a fever, Captain.' Stern took off his greatcoat and wrapped it over Rykov's lap. 'It's old but it's warm.'

Rykov smiled faintly. 'And I thought you were just another badly dressed Englishman.'

Stern looked down at the frayed cuff of his shirt. 'And you were right. I never seem to find time to do something about it.' He smiled back. 'I'm damned if I know what I've become.'

'A knight errant?' Natalya looked out at Shpalernaya Street. 'We're nearly there.'

They reached the hospital and Rantalla climbed down to help with Rykov. 'You have little time, Excellency.'

'I know it. Get my valise, old man. We'll meet up at the station.'

'There is only one hour.'

'Don't worry. I'll be there.'

Anna was waiting as Stern aided Rykov up the hospital steps. He saw the shock in her face. Rykov drew himself up and smiled — a hint of his old self. 'I must apologize for my unmilitary appearance. The Austrians drew lots for my spurs.'

Anna had control again, forcing the corners of her mouth up. 'You keep such bad company, Captain.'

And she and Natalya took Rykov to a small, private ward.

Stern went to telephone Baumler, fingering his aching tooth as he waited for a line. The service was poor but at least it was working.

'I'm catching a train, Martin.'

'Hey, I'm sorry I missed you last night. I was late getting back to the apartment.'

'Don't apologize. I never got that far.'

'I was at Staraya Derevnya. By God, it's bleak out there. I had some morphine coming in. What happened to you — did you find the Countess?'

'Yes. I found her. She and her sister are staying at the hospital. The palace is looted.'

'But they're all right?'

'Yes. They've got Rykov. He's very sick. Listen, are you staying on in the city?'

'Sure I'm staying. Certainly I'm staying. Trade continues though governments topple. And I've got myself a new trading route.' Baumler sounded excited. 'I'm bringing stuff in over the ice. Even with a revolution the possibilities are wide open.' He paused. 'And it's not just the trade, Michael. My life's here and I kind of want to see how it all turns out.'

'Write to me, will you? I can be reached through the Military Mission in Murmansk.'

'Yes. I'll write. And as you seem to have an obsessive interest in the aristocracy I'll let you know what I hear about the house of Meretskov.'

'Thanks.'

'Though to tell you the truth, Michael, if I was a member of the old elite I'd think about getting out.'

'Maybe things will settle down in a week or two.' He frowned to himself.

'Don't count on it. It's really only just begun here. Now comes the struggle for power. The Provisional Government of the Duma won't last, take my word for it. And next time I hear gunfire in this city I'm gonna wear a red armband. It will be the only safe colour.'

'Take care, Martin. I've got to go now.'

He was still frowning as he hung up the receiver. They'd deposed the Tsar. How long would it be before they turned on the aristocracy? He went back to wait outside the small ward. Forty minutes left.

As soon as he saw Natalya and Anna emerge he knew the verdict on Rykov was bad.

'Tuberculosis,' Natalya said. 'Both lungs are badly infected.'

Anna was pale. 'He came all this way back just to be told that.' She took a long breath and set her face determinedly. 'Captain Rykov will not die, Natalya. I will not allow him to die.' And she walked quickly away.

Natalya started to follow, then stopped and stared after

her. 'My sister will have to face the truth. Captain Rykov is mortally ill. Doctor Strozhov gives him a month, perhaps two.'

He can't know that for sure. Stern groped with the thought. 'Nobody can know that for sure. There's more to Rykov than a pair of diseased lungs. What about his will? He's tough — he must be to have got himself this far. And if your sister says she won't let him die, then by God maybe he'll live.'

Natalya looked at him. 'You are full of surprises, Captain.'

They walked together along the corridor. 'What time is your train?'

'I leave within the hour, Countess.'

'Another bridge to build?'

'Yes.' How could he warn her against what might happen here in the city? 'The old man, Rantalla, is staying for a while. He's a good friend; tough, brave as a lion — if you need help.' He stopped to face her as they reached the main entrance hall. 'And if there is ever anything I can do . . .' What the hell could he do for her up in the Arctic?

'Gallant Captain Stern.' She fastened the button on his breast pocket. 'The threadbare hero. We are already indebted to you.'

There was still a life to be paid for. He pulled on his greatcoat. 'Countess, it might be wise to take a holiday — out of the city.' He tried not to sound urgent. 'Or better still; you and your sister go to Norway or Sweden for a while.'

'But I couldn't possibly do that.' She glanced round the busy entrance hall. 'There's so much to be done. And what of Captain Rykov? He cannot travel, and we cannot leave him.'

No. She wouldn't do that. 'Then I can only urge you to take great care.'

'You are concerning yourself with my life again, Captain.' She smiled and held out her hand. 'I'm grateful, but you really don't need to. We'll manage now.'

He took her hand and bowed, some part of his mind recording that this was the first time that he had felt the physical warmth of her body. Maybe he'd never see her again. 'Goodbye, madam.'

'Goodbye, Captain.'

He glanced back as he reached the door. But she was already engrossed; giving instructions to a nurse, and signalling to a porter.

Rantalla was waiting for him at the station buffet. 'You have fourteen minutes, Excellency.' He pushed a glass of weak, tepid tea across the table. 'It is tasteless but it's all there is. I've packed a flask for your journey.'

He watched as Stern drank the tea. 'You never said why you wanted to come to Petrograd, Excellency. Would you like me to keep an eye out for the woman — the Countess?'

'Yes, old man, I would.'

'She has a way with her.' Rantalla pondered. 'I have Your Excellency's interests at heart and I will do whatever you wish. But she is not for you. It might be wiser to forget her.'

'Wiser?' Why break the habits of a lifetime? 'Then who is she for, old man?'

'A prince. A grand duke. A general perhaps.' Rantalla paused. 'Certainly someone of a different temperament. Your Excellency is a solitary, driven by motives no woman ever really understands.'

'I'm tired of being a solitary.' He remembered the warmth of her.

'God made us what we are, and we have to live with it. If you had her you would still be alone.'

'But you'll watch out for her anyway?'

'Yes.' The old man frowned. 'Peter Koltsov is also attracted to the Countess.'

'I thought they disliked each other.'

Rantalla shrugged as if it made no difference. 'Maybe.' And he turned as the door opened, letting in the harsh sounds of the station. A group of men wearing rough factory clothes entered. They were strung with bandoliers and each carried a rifle.

'People's Militia, Excellency. They take their orders from the Soviet.'

Stern half-watched them as they stood at the counter drinking tea. Then he heard the train blasting steam and he stood and buttoned up his greatcoat. 'Time to go.'

They walked to the barrier. Militia men were checking identity papers as passengers passed through. One of them peered suspiciously at Stern's uniform, but the leader said, 'Leave him. He's an Englishman.' And he grinned. 'We're looking for Tsarists. The Soviet has no quarrel with you.'

'I thought authority rested with the Duma?'

'Temporarily.' He grinned again and eased the rifle sling on his shoulder. 'You'd better hurry. The train's waiting.'

Rantalla found him a carriage.

'Well, old man.' And he smiled.

Rantalla sniffed and his leathery face creased in a frown. 'You have the cloves, Excellency, for your tooth?'

'Yes.'

'You will let me know when you reach Murmansk?'

'Yes. And now our paths separate for a while. But we'll meet again soon.'

'God is gracious, Excellency.'

PART TWO

21

Seen from the Kola inlet the town of Murmansk suggested impermanence, as if its raw shape would soon dissolve into the backdrop of fir slopes and ragged heights beyond. Unpaved tracks littered with rubbish ran between rows of rough log dwellings cluttered up close to the wooden quays at the harbour's edge. More huts and shanties straggled out along the first few hundred yards of the single track railway. The port was ice free all the year round, and the railway linking it with Petrograd was the sole reason for Murmansk's existence.

Michael Stern slouched along the timber quay, reflecting with disgust on the miserable, squalid town. Night — day, it made no bloody difference. The grey half-light would remain constant until spring. He'd shaved off his beard and the cold wind off the inlet froze his face. He reached the end of the quay and a marine of the British Military Mission saluted. He nodded back and climbed down into the waiting naval tender. He wasn't used to boats. A sailor cast off and the diesel engine roared, propeller churning. Stern steadied himself. All that dark water. The Gulf far to the south would still be frozen, ice fingering in along the river and canals of the city. Again no word from Petrograd. He frowned to himself. Maybe Rantalla had trouble.

He adjusted to the slight pitching as the tender moved out across the harbour. Rantalla had intended coming north six or seven weeks ago, and here it was, nearly spring. Damn it, why worry about the old man — he's tough, he can look after himself. He's got a reason for not writing. But I want news of her, he thought.

There were numerous small craft anchored in the

fairway, and a freighter, dirty and rust streaked, had turned the headland approach, smoke drifting back from its single funnel. HMS Glory lay in midstream. Stern stared at the dark shape. Now he was going to find out why he'd been kept here.

The tender passed the repair vessel, Xenia, and the Russian warship Chesma, firmly aground. It had been there for months with its skeleton crew. They leaned, bored, against the rail, looking down at the tender. One of them grinned at Stern and gave the clenched fist Bolshevik salute. He waved back and glanced at the ship's rusting side, and the red flag hanging limply. Baumler had been right all those months ago. Red was the only safe colour in Russia. The Provisional Government of the Duma was out and Lenin and his Bolsheviks were in. His attention shifted as the tender caught the wash of the freighter then edged alongside the high, dark side of the British cruiser.

A young naval officer led the way down narrow steel steps and along a passageway. 'Colonel Southgate is expecting you, sir.' And he ushered him into a large cabin.

Southgate and three men in civilian clothes were grouped around a table on which was spread a map. Southgate turned. 'Ah, Michael! How good to see you again.'

The greeting was a little too cordial and Stern felt wary.

'Now, Michael, this is Major Krasnov, late of His Imperial Majesty's Cossacks and now on the staff of General Malnekov.'

Where had he seen him before?

'And this is Monsieur André Bourges of the French Diplomatic Corps.' Southgate's smile was fixed and icy as he turned. 'And this gentleman is Mr Hashimoto from Yokohama in Japan.'

Mr Hashimoto smiled and lisped a greeting as he shook Stern's hand.

'Well now, everybody knows everybody. Come and join us at this map, Michael. I'd rather like your opinion.'

He felt more on his guard. Asking for his opinion was a trick Southgate had, of buttering him up before disclosing a

228

dirty job. And more, it was an insult to his intelligence. He stared down at the large scale map of the Russian Empire stretching from Europe to the Pacific.

Southgate placed his hand over European Russia. 'The Bolsheviks are now in power here. By the Treaty of Brest Litovsk they've taken Russia out of the war and made their separate and tentative peace with Germany and Austria. Officially we accept this. But unofficially it is the job of each of us here to get Russia back into the fighting.' He paused, frowning. 'And of course, this means toppling Lenin and the Bolsheviks.'

Stern felt his eyes open wide. He's mad! But the others seemed neither surprised nor concerned. Southgate's squat hand made sweeping motions across the map. 'As you know, Michael, the Bolshevik hold is very shaky and doesn't extend over the whole of Russia. They have enemies on all sides; Germany has occupied the Ukraine and is still a threat to Lenin. Here, at Orenburg, the Cossacks refuse to recognise Lenin's government. And the "White" Volunteer Army of General Alexiev is actively co-operating with the Don Cossacks against the Bolshevik Red armies.' He moved his hand further to the east. 'And here, on the Manchurian frontier, General Malnekov is raising another "White" army to oppose the Bolsheviks and harass the Trans-Siberian Railway. If the White armies defeat the Bolshevik Red armies, Lenin's government will fall. And the Whites will resume the war against Germany and re-open the Eastern Front. The White interests, then, coincide with ours.'

What exactly is the swine up to now? Stern wondered, remembering that other briefing delivered in the same matter-of-fact tone, just before they'd crossed the Hindu Kush for the boundary survey. 'I thought our government just agreed to co-operate with Lenin's government,' he said.

'Yes, yes. Quite.' The Colonel looked impatient, leaning over the map and frowning. 'Governments agree all kinds of things. Naturally we must maintain normal relations with the Bolsheviks for as long as we can, but at the same time offer under-the-counter support to their enemies — the White armies. Which brings us to the substance of this meeting.'

The others stirred very slightly.

'We are committed to helping Malnekov build up his irregulars — mainly cavalry — on the Manchurian border. But we've got a problem, Michael.'

Stern felt his gut tightening. He'd already begun to guess.

'The governments represented by Monsieur Bourges and Mr Hashimoto have agreed to supply six light field guns and three thousand Japanese service rifles, with appropriate quantities of ammunition. And Major Krasnov here is negotiating the sale of Tsarist jewellery in New York to pay for the purchase of horses. Unfortunately the British Government is committed here at Murmansk — a heavy expense — so we have no funds available for Malnekov.'

The Frenchman sighed to himself. How typical of the British to arrange that others meet the expense. 'So may I enquire of the British contribution to this endeavour?'

'Ah! We are now at the crux of the matter.' Southgate allowed a small, almost theatrical pause and his pale blue eyes assumed deep concern. 'Our contribution will be vital. Malnekov is reluctant to begin operations while a lady who was known to be close to him is still in Petrograd and able to be used as a hostage by the Bolsheviks. We will arrange for her exit from Russia.'

Just as he'd thought. Stern didn't allow his expression to change.

Krasnov glanced quickly at him then smiled at the others. 'If this is to be done it must be done quickly. The lady in question is a liability. Our White army will be on the defensive — exposed to risk until she is brought out.'

Znamenskya Square. That's where I saw him, Stern thought. He was with Malnekov that day.

The Frenchman was looking thoughtful. 'If your irregulars are at risk because of this woman, then so also is our expensive equipment. Is there no way round this?'

Krasnov stroked the single grey streak in his hair and raised one eyebrow very slightly. 'Not while General Malnekov commands.'

The others debated the operation and Stern watched them shrewdly assessing the possibility of losing their stakes. Finally the Frenchman nodded. 'We are agreed. Go ahead with your plan to rescue the General's woman.'

'Well done! A noble decision! What do you think of that, Michael?'

'The age of chivalry isn't dead,' he said.

Mr Hashimoto smiled as if enjoying some secret thought of his own.

Krasnov smiled also. 'Captain Stern has a wry sense of humour.'

'Yes, hasn't he.' Southgate's mouth curved but his pale eyes remained expressionless. 'Well, now it's all settled.'

The others left for the tender, Krasnov pausing at the door. 'We'll meet again soon, Captain Stern.'

He smiles too much, Stern thought.

When they'd gone, Southgate rubbed his hands together. 'I handled that rather well. Don't you think so, Michael? Bloody clever of me to lumber the others with the expense.'

'And I'm to fetch the Countess Meretskova out of Russia.'

'That's right. You and Krasnov should be able to manage it between you.' The Colonel splashed whisky into two glasses.

'Of course, I can't make you go. You're an engineering officer. But you're the ideal man, in the present circumstances. It would take weeks to get one of the cloak and dagger brigade here. And you've met the Countess. You know the city and you speak the language. Best of all, you have a legitimate reason for being in the capital. When were you last in Petrograd?'

'At the beginning of the revolution.'

'Ah, yes. It's all changed of course. I was there a week or so ago.' He frowned. 'Couldn't get a decent meal. Damned

231

shortages. Not that that will worry you — you've always been indifferent to civilized food. And anyway, you and Krasnov should be back here inside a week.'

'I don't want him with me.'

Southgate stared. 'What do you mean, you don't want him with you? He's tough and resourceful.'

'I mean I don't trust him.'

'Trust? Malnekov wants it this way.' And the Colonel looked edgy. 'Our masters have agreed. Krasnov goes with you.'

In the end it comes down to instinct. Stern watched the older man's face. Assume a catch, as he should have done that other time, now six years ago. Assume that Krasnov and Southgate have got something else going between them.

'You need me in Petrograd and I'll go,' he said. 'But send that slimy swine back to Manchuria — or New York as that's where he seems to be doing his soldiering. I mean it. He's not coming with me.'

'Damn you! Quirky as ever!' Southgate's cold eyes briefly registered anger. He thought for a moment, chewing his thumbnail. 'Very well, Michael. If that's what you want. Krasnov can return to New York to negotiate the sale of Tsarist trinkets. But you'll need somebody to help you.'

'I'll use Rantalla — the old man. I trust him.'

'Fine.' Southgate was still frowning slightly. 'There is one other thing, Michael. The Countess had a large fortune in personal jewellery. Most of it was confiscated by the Bolsheviks, but some of the known items haven't appeared in the published lists. Krasnov hoped to bring these out also.' And he smiled suddenly. 'After all, the young woman will need something to live on, and she might even want to contribute to the White cause. Are you getting the drift?'

'Yes,' he said. 'I'm getting the drift.'

'Jewellery belonging to the old Russian aristocracy is fetching a high price.'

'I can imagine.'

'So you'll do your best?'

'Yes.'

'And you'll keep it — er — high on your list of priorities?'

'I'll give it a lot of thought.'

'Splendid!' Southgate continued to smile. 'Pull this off, Michael, and that other business six years ago will be far behind you. Oh, I know you've not had the recognition you deserve for all your work here, but believe me it hasn't gone unnoticed. Had a word with General Poole the other day. A citation is definitely being considered.'

He wasn't listening. 'If I bring the Countess out, the sister, Anna, will have to come also.'

'Only if it's absolutely essential. The sister has no trading value.'

'Do you know the condition of Captain Rykov?'

'Rykov?' Southgate stared. 'Oh, *Rykov*. The consumptive. He shares an apartment with them, but last we heard he was being moved to a soldiers' hospital. Should be there by now. He's been seen out and about sometimes. Now look, you concentrate on the main issues. The sister and Rykov are not important to us. You'll need some authentic looking papers.'

'For both sisters.'

'Very well, for both sisters — leave it to me to arrange. They are living in rather reduced circumstances. And because of her past association with Malnekov, the Countess is in a difficult position — our sources suggest that the Petrograd Cheka is taking an interest in her. You know about the Cheka? It is the counter-revolutionary executive — a sort of Bolshevik equivalent to the Tsar's old Okhrana. Now if the Bolsheviks get wind that Malnekov is preparing to move, they will certainly arrest the Countess and use her as a pawn in the game. Malnekov is very attached to the lady and might even be persuaded to delay his operations if her life is threatened. And that wouldn't suit us at all.' Southgate paused. 'Now, is there anything you want?'

'The old man, Rantalla. If I use him he won't be able to remain in Russia. Can you arrange British nationality for him and a pension?'

'I suppose so. Anything else? I mean for yourself,

Michael. It's not often I ask a man to do a job like this.'

'Nothing.' He downed the whisky. 'There's nothing you can do for me.'

Southgate was watching him, eyes narrowed. 'Do I detect a personal interest — in the Countess? Not a good idea, Michael — you could come to grief there.'

'I hardly know her,' he said. 'When do I leave?'

'As soon as possible. Your official reason for being in Petrograd will be consultation with the Commissar for Ways and Communications, I'll cable him that you are going. And I'll set up a meeting for you with Kirilin at the Academy of Science. He worked on the Trans-Siberian. We'll give you enough bridge and railway problems to keep you in the city for about a week. That should do you. I don't anticipate any serious problems.' And he poured himself another drink. 'By the way, I wouldn't look up your friend Baumler if I were you.'

'Why not?'

'Well, there's an outside chance that you might get caught.' Southgate smiled as if the possibility was so remote as to be almost non-existent. 'Best not to involve anybody else. We don't want to upset the American government, do we?' He swallowed the whisky and hissed inwards. 'And of course, Baumler has a way of attracting the wrong kind of attention. He's into all kinds of things with his wheeling and dealing — so we hear. Smuggling and God knows what else.'

Stern nodded and looked at the bland face of his superior, certain already that there were yet other things he wasn't being told. 'Just supposing I'm caught?'

'I'm afraid I'd have to disown you, Michael, as a lone Pimpernel.'

Well, he hadn't expected anything else.

'So it's all settled then,' and Southgate looked brisk. 'I'm glad you and I are dealing with this end of it, Michael. After all, we can't trust these damned foreigners. Now you'll have to keep a sharp lookout for these Cheka people, they are a tiny bit dangerous.'

Stern left, returning on the tender to the quay, and he walked back towards his quarters. Images and questions crowded his mind and he felt an unaccustomed sick excitement.

He reached the railway line and paused, waiting while the night train rumbled slowly past; boxcars, flatcars, filthy and worn from over-use, miles of it strung out behind the huge American locomotive, its fire box deep red in the half light. Four days to Petrograd. He'd be there himself in a week — maybe less. He still owed the Countess a life, and hers was threatened. He'd have gone anyway — debt or no debt. This is what he'd come all the way from India for. It had all been there in the cards waiting to be played. There was no possibility of retreat, though perhaps a Cheka bullet through the back of his head if he was caught.

The tail light of the train diminished in the south. Across the tracks Lett railway workers were painting over the markings on boxes of British ammunition. He watched them for a moment. What would they now be labelled? Nothing was quite what is seemed.

22

Martin Baumler wasn't happy. No, he'd go further. He felt like some old dinosaur wondering where all the ice had come from.

It was another raw day. He trudged through the filthy snow. Have trouble and you could be sure that more would follow; the Pierce Arrow, gleaming and useless, had been stuck outside the apartment for two days — petrol quota used up and nobody to bribe. Not a cab in sight. He scowled. And who was taking so much interest in his letters? One had been clumsily re-sealed and that had made him look carefully at the others. And today there was the matter of the so-called tax inspector checking his bank accounts.

The snow was deeper in the side street. And if the Bolsheviks ever managed to feel secure, maybe they'd manage to get the rubbish cleared again. Though one had to be fair. They'd got a lot of problems; like trying to keep everybody fed, coping with the typhus outbreak, and apportioning out the fuel and petrol so that people like him got only their fair share. And checking on bank accounts! He wouldn't have known about that but for the whispered warning of the bank teller. All in all it didn't look good, and perhaps he should seriously consider transferring his business interests to Sweden? His thoughts turned briefly on Helen Mirsky.

He reached the Morskaya. A huge red flag draped the balcony of the Ministry of State Domains. On the outside wall, tattered proclamations of the old Provisional Government had been plastered over with posters of square-jawed workers building the promised land. I'm a stranger here, he thought. Something corrupt but wondrous had gone out of the city. There was still a night life. He'd gone to the Lantern a week back; champagne, girls and gambling, but it had a precarious feel, a hanging on until somebody found time to sweep it all away. There'd been a few people he knew, mainly foreigners, and old Tsarists playing for low stakes, and he'd left depressed, wishing that he'd taken Helen to the ballet instead.

Baumler walked up the steps and entered the sumptuous foyer of the Astoria. Here at least was more his style, though it had come to bore him a little. He was still feeling low as the hotel boy took his coat. I guess I've become too used to winning in a game going stale, he thought. The older you get the more you ponder it. You can't quit the game and in the end you have to lose. He found a vacant chair near the entrance to the dining-room. Ultimately we are all losers -- every damned one of us.

Baumler was awaiting the arrival of Natalya Meretskova, and he was curious. He hadn't seen her for several weeks. Some people adapt — lately he'd been noticing those who

236

did and those who didn't — and she and Anna were managing much better than he'd thought they would. In their circumstances would he have coped as well? He stared at the edict of the Central Committee of the Petrograd Soviet, prominently displayed near the dining-room entrance. Patrons were to refrain from affronting the dignity of hotel staff by offering them tips. No bread was to be served with main meals. The purchase of more than one meal per person was an offence. I've lived too long with corruption, he thought. I'll never change. I'm permanently tainted.

And damn it, there across the dining-room, half-hidden behind a jungle of potted plants, was the short fat man with the thick spectacles. That was the third time he'd seen him in two days, turning up in unexpected places. And what had seemed like a joke a week ago had now become slightly menacing. He glanced across again and the potted plants moved very slightly.

Then he saw Natalya Meretskova.

She was flushed from the cold outside. If it had been another woman anywhere near as attractive he might have whistled softly and appreciatively to himself. Was it with an eye for effect or was it natural of her to stand, framed as it were by the gilt doorway that almost matched her hair?

He rose and went over to her. 'War, revolution, bitter weather, and you continue to look beautiful, Countess Meretskova.'

She smiled as he shook her hand. 'I'm merely Citizeness Meretskova. And you can feel how cold I am.'

'They still have a wine here that makes the winter seem quite mellow.'

'Will it make me more forgiving of the Soviet?'

'Two glasses and even the Tsar would embrace Comrade Lenin.'

He led the way to the dining-room where a table was reserved for him. 'This time you must try the *koulebiaka*. I hear that Georgy Mikhaylovich's chef is working here now.'

Without her old army greatcoat he could see that Natalya

was slimmer, almost thin, though the curves of her body still pleased him. 'You've been toiling?' He looked at her hands and immediately she half-concealed them. They were raw, fingernails broken by her work at the hospital.

She glanced down and unclenched her fingers. 'Hard work makes the days pass quickly — sometimes. I haven't been waited on since I last lunched with you. Odd how one gets used to doing things for oneself. Anna and I take turns at cooking — surprisingly she is much better at it than I.' She ate hurriedly, as though accustomed to having little time to spare. 'Captain Rykov tries to cook sometimes but he burns everything, poor man.'

Baumler was embarrassed at still having money, even though he knew she wouldn't accept anything but an occasional meal from him. He sighed, suddenly feeling like a glutton. 'We learn all kinds of things about ourselves.'

'Don't we though.' Her face was expressionless.

'I come here less frequently.' He glanced round. 'Too many new faces, I guess. How's your wine?'

'You were right. I'm mellowing, though not yet quite ready to embrace Comrade Lenin.' She raised her glass and smiled slowly.

She doesn't have to do that, he thought. She doesn't need to charm me. I admire her enough. 'It's good business practice to wine and dine the clients.'

'I'm not a client. You only pretend to make a profit from my sister and me.'

'A few pieces of jewellery.'

She had turned to look at the musicians and he noticed her dress pulled tightly over her breasts. How did she still manage to look so beautiful?

Natalya seemed to sense his glance and she turned back, her eyes questioning. 'You take chances for us.'

She'd finished her meal so he lit a cigar. 'I must admit I take a devious pleasure in smuggling.' He looked towards the potted plants. The fat little man was still watching. Who the hell is he? 'The Bolsheviks are ruining my business in the name of equality. I can't even bribe officials any more — most of them are so damned fervent. So I amuse myself, and make some profit, playing out the role of gentleman contrabandist. The jewellery I smuggle out would otherwise be confiscated from you Tsarists — I don't feel I'm doing anybody any harm.' And he shrugged. 'Things are getting difficult though and I don't know how long I can hang on here. But I promise you that your diamond clasp will reach Sweden before I finally pack my bags.' Frowning, he remembered. She'd worn that star clasp at the last Meretskov ball, a lifetime ago. 'Why do you want it deposited in a bank in Stockholm rather than London or Paris?'

'It's the only good piece I managed to save.' Natalya shook her head incredulously. 'Do you know? Anna and I had drawers full — we didn't even lock it up. We had no appreciation of its value. Anyway, the clasp is no use to us here, and inevitably it would be taken from us. Better that you get it to Stockholm. Perhaps Anna and Captain Rykov can leave Russia one day. Sweden has a healthy climate — he might recover there. They would need money from the sale of the clasp to start their lives again.'

Baumler nodded. 'What about yourself?'

'My first concern is for them.'

'That's very noble of you.'

'It only seems so.'

He wasn't sure what she meant, but something about the set of her face suggested that he'd be wiser not to probe. 'And how is Captain Rykov?' he asked.

She frowned. 'Sometimes he seems to improve, then he is ill again — it is the nature of the sickness. But worse for Anna, he tries to hide his condition. He is the one who is noble. We have only two small rooms. One of them is very damp and we cannot afford to heat it, so Captain Rykov must share with us. We have curtained off part of our room for him.' She added lightly, 'Many are far worse off.'

'I thought Rykov was being moved to a hospital.'

'Have you seen them? They are dreadfully overcrowded. He would surely die.' She bit her lip. 'We have resisted any attempt to move him. Our hope is that when the summer comes he will be well enough. And maybe — just maybe, he and Anna can cross the frontier.' And she pondered, still frowning to herself. 'Strange, when I reflect on the illusion of security. We thought our world would last another hundred years — even a year ago we owned a palace, and estates we seldom visited. Now we share a room with a sick officer and the day to day struggle to keep ourselves has made us almost indifferent to delicacy.'

'Look, Countess! Have some of my money for God's sake!'

'No.' Her face softened. 'Thank you. Money might make life easier for a while but it wouldn't really solve the problem. As it is, Anna and I have employment as nurses and that means we have food permits. We cannot in all honesty, complain. We even manage to work opposite shifts so that Captain Rykov is never left for too long. We'll manage. It's really amazing how we manage.' She smiled. 'And as you said, we are learning all kinds of things about ourselves.'

She doesn't distance herself any more, he thought. And he pondered the enigma of her. She was still a mystery to him. If he propositioned her, would she smile slowly and agree, or would she slap his face? He really hadn't the faintest idea.

Now she was looking at the clock. 'I must leave or I will be late for work. Thank you so much. A meal and conversation is so —' she tilted her head on one side and her eyes lit up in that way that warmed him, '— so comforting.' As she rose she paused, remembering. 'Your friend, Captain Stern. How is he?'

'Michael? He's still up in the frozen north, I think. I write to him but I'm not sure my letters are getting there.'

She frowned. 'I thought I saw him yesterday, from the window of the hospital.'

'I guess it was somebody else.'

He walked with her to the steps of the hotel. 'I'll see you again soon,' he called, and waved to her as she hurried off in the direction of the embankment. Then he turned quickly

240

back into the hotel and waited, half-concealed near the entrance to the dining-room. The small fat man emerged, blowing his nose, and he stood for a moment glancing towards the doorway. Baumler sidled up to him. 'I'm not out there, I'm here.'

Popov jumped, then clutched at his glasses and blinked. 'I beg your pardon, sir.'

'You've been following me again.'

'I swear on my mother's grave! I have never . . .'

'Oh, don't give me that,' Baumler interupted. 'Let's you and me have a little drink. I'll tell you where I'm going next, and how long I'll be there. It might save you a lot of trouble.' He gripped Popov's arm. 'Well, come *on*. I haven't got all day.'

Popov began to sweat, then he sneezed. '*Please*, Mr Baumler!' he hissed. 'This is most irregular!'

Baumler led him protesting into the long Astoria bar. 'See, I'm making life easy for you. You want to know more about me, don't you? And it's quite safe in here. Now what do you drink?'

Popov glanced around despairingly. 'Brandy,' he said.

Baumler had almost begun to enjoy himself. 'It must be a dog's life, following me around in weather like this. Come to think of it, you don't look too well, Mr . . .'

'Popov.' He blew his nose and blinked unhappily.

'Well, Mr Popov. That's a very nasty cold you've got there. You'll get pneumonia, trailing round the streets after me. Can't you find some other kind of job?'

Popov drew himself up. 'I have been in this profession all my life.' Then he sagged and sniffed. 'It is all I know.'

'All your life? Then you were with the Tsar's Okhrana?'

'Yes.' He sneezed again. 'It was my proud privilege to serve His Imperial Majesty.' The brandy was beginning to work and Popov was relaxing a little. 'I shall not see such noble times again.'

'And now you work for the Cheka.'

'Shh!' Popov peered around then sipped his drink. 'I didn't want to work for the Cheka, Mr Baumler,' he whispered. 'But what else could I *do*?' He paused. 'They frighten me.'

'I take your point,' Baumler nodded. 'But why the hell are you following me?' He signalled to the waiter and pointed at the glasses.

Popov's gloom deepened. 'I cannot tell you that, Mr Baumler. It wouldn't be proper.' He glanced at Baumler's well-filled wallet as the other man paid for the drinks. 'No, it wouldn't be proper, even though I am miserably paid and my poor wife is sick.'

Baumler held the wallet open in his hand and looked sympathetically at Popov. 'You mean the ethics of the profession?'

'Quite so.'

'Well, if you really feel you can't . . .' and he started to replace the wallet in his pocket.

Popov grasped his arm and muttered quickly. 'They know that you smuggle, Mr Baumler. And your name has been linked with the drugs found in the coach at the Hospital of the Heroes of the Revolution.'

'You mean the charity hospital?'

Popov shook his head impatiently. 'It has been renamed.'

Baumler lowered his voice. 'But the drugs were months ago. And if they think I smuggle, why haven't they called me in for questioning?' He had another thought. 'And why are *your* people interested in drugs and smuggling? I thought the Cheka was only concerned with counter-revolutionary activity.'

Popov whispered urgently, 'Because the Cheka believe you are smuggling out jewellery for members of the old aristocracy. Tsarist jewellery is being sold in London and New York and the money is being used to support counter-revolutionary groups inside and outside Russia. A necklace belonging to the late Princess Vyazemskovna was auctioned in New York last month and the money paid over to an agent of the White armies. Believe me, Mr Baumler, you are playing a dangerous game. The only reason you have not been arrested is because they want to find out who you deal with and how you get the jewellery out. You are being watched all the time!'

Baumler felt a sharp twinge of alarm. He hadn't been told that the necklace was being sold to support counter-revolution. With the alarm came anger at being duped. He frowned. This was an altogether different ball game, and now he was involved in conspiracy against the new government. 'Somebody is taking an unhealthy interest in my financial arrangements, Mr Popov. What do you know about that?'

'Your trading accounts revealed nothing, so copies of your bank statements have been sent to the Cheka building for scrutiny.'

'Can you intercept them — hold them up for a while?'

'Difficult, Mr Baumler. The risks I would run!'

Baumler took out his wallet and peeled off some notes.

'No, no. That is far too much. I couldn't,' Popov said, quickly sliding the notes into his pocket. Then, curious, he looked sideways at Baumler. 'As one professional man to another, Mr Baumler, tell me how *did* you smuggle the necklace out?'

Baumler downed his drink. 'As a professional, Mr Popov, I am not even prepared to admit that I smuggle. You keep in touch.' And he left, walking quickly back to the Nevsky Prospect.

The time had definitely come for decision. He'd have to start thinking about how to get himself and his money out of Russia. It wouldn't be easy, with that tax man snooping into his finances, but there were ways and means. He frowned as he walked. What about Helen? Damn it, he'd become very fond of her, schemer that she was, and the thought of going off and not seeing her again depressed him. A few people you care about in your life, he thought. Michael Stern, Hal Winthrop maybe. And Helen. They get fewer as you get older. And that's the crux of the matter — I'm damned near old enough to be her father. And I've never been really sure which she wanted, me or my money.

Did it matter any more? If he could shift his wealth to Stockholm there would be enough to live well and make a fresh start. God knows, he'd held on to his freedom for long enough. Helen could marry him *and* his money if that's what she wanted. He'd have to put out some feelers — discreetly test the idea on her.

In point of fact, Helen Mirsky had been carefully instilling the notion of matrimony into Baumler's head for some time. It had required infinite patience, evasion, tactical withdrawals; and a constant reappraisal of his interests. But the time and trouble were surely well spent. She was aware that he was taking the bait, entirely convinced that it was his idea.

Helen hurried through the arched doorway and along the main corridor of the university. The student population had changed in the last year. Some were middle-aged workers, still self-conscious at being in such an illustrious centre of higher learning. And there were the sons and daughters of peasants, sent by rural soviets. Helen moved among them and caught her reflection in the glass panel of a door. How drab I've become, she thought. Even the Professor will find me less interesting if I don't put some weight on. Zubov had a penchant for bosomy creatures.

She reached the office and found Zubov pacing up and down, nervously smoking a cigarette.

'I'm sorry I'm late.'

He waved impatiently. 'It doesn't matter.' And frowning he turned to the window. She glanced at the ashtray on his desk. It was already full of stubs. What could be worrying him?

'It is quite ridiculous,' she said. 'Why cannot our Bolshevik government do something about the trams? There are so few running, they become hopelessly over-crowded. I nearly suffocated on the return journey from the city and the boy pressed against me could not lift a finger without inviting a charge of indecent assault. He kept mumbling apologies because he wanted to wipe his nose.'

244

She pulled a tiny mirror from her bag and began fiercely combing her long hair. 'In the end I became so irritated I said, "Please feel free to take out your hankerchief, the Bolsheviks have not yet passed an edict against their use".' Helen fastened her hair back with a clip. 'But of course he didn't have a handkerchief and merely wished to wipe his nose with his sleeve.'

She glanced at Zubov's back. Yes, he's worried. 'The winter does drag on so. How long will it be before the Gulf unfreezes?'

He didn't answer.

'I have the notes for your Thursday lecture. I'm afraid I still have a tendency to type "g" for "h". I hope this will not confuse you too much. And if I may remind you, Professor, you have a tutorial at two-fifteen.'

Zubov still had his back to her, his shoulders tightened slightly. 'Cancel the tutorial. And get Yefremov to take my seminar.' He turned. 'I have to see an official at Gorokhavaya Street. It is probably about one of the students.' 'I should be back to chair the meeting on the revised curriculum.'

Helen watched Zubov pulling on his overcoat. His movements were hurried and tense. He left the office without a word, and she sat thinking for a moment. Gorokhavaya Street. Was Zubov going to the Cheka building? She suppressed a small shiver. Russia isn't red, she thought. It is grey; with shortages and suspicion, and the possibility of civil war. And fear of the Cheka.

As Helen began to work she reconsidered the notion of leaving Petrograd, and her thoughts returned to Baumler.

Professor Zubov reached the forbidding Cheka building in Gorokhavaya Street. He took a deep breath and entered, moving through the grimy entrance hall to the general office. A wooden counter separated the public area from the clerks and typists crammed desk to desk. Zubov tried to act casually. He leaned on the counter and waited to be attended to. Behind him, others who had been summoned to the building sat silently staring ahead of them, afraid to speak to each other. Their fear depressed Zubov. I'm not like them, he thought, trying to reassure himself. I have no reason to be afraid. That matter of betraying Koltsov is far behind me. I am a respected member of the university faculty. I have status. Yet he felt diminished, vulnerable, waiting. Finally an overworked clerk came to him. 'State your name and business, comrade.'

'My name is Zubov. I have come to see Commissar Koltsov.' And he hastily added, 'The Commissar is a good aquaintance of mine.'

The clerk was unimpressed. 'Were you sent for?'

Zubov bit his lip. 'Yes. I was sent for.'

'Sit over there with the others.' The clerk indicated with a nod of his head.

Zubov couldn't. He stood on his own. I *am* different, he kept telling himself. I need not fear. But a dark, shapeless, nameless dormant thing was stirring within him, crawling across his thoughts and turning the ordinariness of his surroundings into the substance of a bad dream. A gas lamp high on the wall hissed. Damn Koltsov, he thought. At least the man could have spared me this.

Peter Koltsov knew that Zubov was waiting, and that waiting would make him more pliable. He stared down through the grimy window of his third floor office at small figures in the street below. Some must be guilty, some innocent, you couldn't tell from here. He'd let Zubov stew for a few more minutes. He watched a man glancing anxiously at the Cheka building before crossing the street to pass on the other side. That one must be guilty of something — some dark secret tucked away inside his head. He has learned to fear us. Who would have thought it possible? Who would have thought we could take over the revolution with such fabulous ease? A few ministers arrested. A blank shot fired from the Aurora, and Kerensky's Provisional Government had collapsed even more quickly than the Tsar's. And now Russia is ours to remake — if we can hold on to it. He frowned to himself. We got more than I ever dreamed for my lifetime. But I never anticipated this flat feeling that catches me unawares sometimes — the ultimate futility of all human endeavour. I learned that on the railway.

He went back to his desk and lifted the telephone. 'Send Zubov up.'

The office was carpetless. Apart from the large desk there were just three chairs — one had a broken back rest and served as a stool. But Koltsov was indifferent to the austerity of his surroundings. He wore a plain uniform fastened at the neck, and no insignia to suggest his rank or function. He leaned back in his chair and waited. I'll have to crack Zubov, he thought.

Zubov was shown up the stairs. They were littered with cigarette ends and small rubbish, as if the demands on the staff and the comings and goings of users left no time for routine cleaning. Even in his anxiety Zubov wrinkled his nose with distaste. He reached the third floor and was shown into Koltsov's office.

And he was surprised. 'I am happy to see you looking so much fitter, Comrade Commissar,' he began, anxious to establish a personal relationship. 'May I smoke?'

Koltsov nodded. 'Sit down. And yes, smoke if you want to,' and he waved Zubov's cigarette packet aside. 'No, I have given up the habit.'

He would, Zubov thought, and he lit the cigarette and looked for somewhere to drop the spent match. Finding nowhere, he put the match back in the box, aware that Koltsov was watching him. Damn the man — he always had a way of making one feel ill at ease. 'I must confess to my curiosity, Commissar. Your summons worried me a little.' He frowned down at the cigarette.

Koltsov continued to watch him. 'Go on. You were saying that you feel worried.'

Zubov glanced up quickly. 'Well, naturally, as we of the Provisional Government opposed the Bolshevik takeover of power — right as that now seems to me,' he hastily added. 'It is perhaps understandable that some of us are perhaps a little . . . er . . .'

'Suspect?'

'I was going to say, out of favour.'

'You feel out of favour — a little bitter perhaps?'

'No, of course not.' Zubov licked his lips and glanced round again for an ashtray. Now he felt irritated as well as nervous. 'Why should I feel bitter? I have renounced political work, realizing that my true vocation lies in the academic life.'

'You feel you were wrong in your previous beliefs?'

'Perhaps slightly.' Zubov tapped the ash from the cigarette into his open hand.

'Only slightly wrong?'

He squirmed in his chair. 'Comrade Commissar, if you would please tell me what you want of me?'

Koltsov looked at him steadily. 'Yes. But first I will remind you of the day I asked you to join with us. You believed that the bourgeois Provisional Government would hold on to power and you rejected my offer. You backed the wrong horse. So now you are suspect.'

Zubov's hands had begun to sweat. 'But you know that I am loyal to the new regime, and I am no longer active in politics.' The cigarette was burning his fingers and he dropped it with a mumbled apology, feeling ridiculous. 'You know I'm not a threat to the government.'

'Yes. I know it, Zubov.' Koltsov sat back in his chair and placed his finger tips together. 'But think how it looks on paper. We do not have time to separate sheep from goats.' He sighed. 'I might have left you to your lecturing if I had not heard that you associate with people who are against us.'

'No! I associate with no enemies of the Bolshevik government. If anybody has said so they are lying!'

Koltsov leaned forward, aware of the effect. Another turn of the screw and Zubov would do anything he was told. 'You know Baumler, the American.'

'But only very slightly.' Zubov looked startled. 'Is he an enemy?'

'Yes. And you are on close terms with an intimate of Baumler's.'

'No!' Zubov thought frantically. Who could it be? 'No, I'm sure I'm not.'

'The girl in your office, Helen Mirsky. She has been seen with Baumler on a number of occasions; sometimes in crowded restaurants, sometimes in discreet cafés. And Baumler is working for the counter-revolutionaries.' Koltsov clenched his fists. 'Just think how it looks — you, a member of the old Kerensky government associating with these people.'

Zubov was shocked. He hadn't even known that Helen knew Baumler. 'But it cannot be! The girl hasn't a serious political thought in her head!' And seeing Koltsov's cold expression he added, 'Surely you believe me?'

'Whether I believe you or not is quite irrelevant. The evidence against you is damning.'

Zubov wasn't a fool. He summoned what dignity he could. 'You want something of me. Please end this cat and mouse game, Commissar, and tell me what it is.'

Koltsov leaned back again and allowed himself a thin smile. 'Information. That's all. Just a little information on what your colleagues at the university say, do, think. And particularly I want information on Baumler and this girl, Helen Mirsky.'

Zubov jerked upright in his chair. 'Are you suggesting that I become a spy — an informer against those of my own profession?'

'I suspect that it is a role not entirely unfamiliar to you.'

What had he meant by that? He couldn't possibly know. Zubov shook his head. 'No. I cannot do it.'

Koltsov didn't even change his expression. 'Yes, you will.'

Zubov sat staring at him for a moment. He had heard of what happened. A Cheka squad, and interrogation in a harshly lit room smelling of fear and vomit. His shoulders sagged and he nodded slowly.

'Very well,' he said softly.

After Zubov left, Peter Koltsov went along the corridor to the small toilet with its chipped sink, and he scrubbed his hands carefully. You can't make an omelette without cracking eggs.

He dried his hands and examined his finger nails. Who was he to be squeamish? He was merely a tool of the revolution — it mattered nothing that he hated what he did. It mattered only that the work was done.

He went back to his office and took a duster from his desk drawer. His heavy weariness began to leave him. It was time to visit the woman. He placed one foot on the edge of the broken chair and started to polish his calf length boots. Eight days since he'd last seen her, the woman once a countess. A small mark on the left boot stubbornly resisted the duster. He frowned. I'm becoming fastidious. Since when have clean boots been a necessity for revolution?

23

A single gas lamp cast a pale circle of light halfway along the row of high, ugly terrace houses. Stoliarny Street. Stern could just make out the name almost merging with the snow-flecked brickwork. He'd followed Rantalla's directions — 'Your nose will find it, Excellency. Walk briskly. Don't pause, the house is watched.'

Stern glanced neither to left nor right but he counted the houses. Sixteen, Seventeen, Number Eighteen — that was the one. He kept walking, into the circle of light, and on until he'd crossed Sadovaya Street running at right angles. The watcher had been there, in a doorway almost opposite Number Eighteen. The poor devil looked half-frozen — a penalty for such an unsavoury occupation.

From the café on the corner of Sadovaya, Stern could observe the house. He ordered lemon tea and sat near the window, rubbing the steamed up glass with the sleeve of his leather coat. The watcher wasn't visible from here, but it didn't matter. And there was plenty of time. Natalya

Meretskova would leave the hospital at seven thirty, catching the Voznesenskaya-bound tram on the embankment. The journey would take her twenty-two minutes — Rantalla's observations were meticulous. She would alight just sixty paces further up Sadovaya at the Gorokhavaya intersection. He could just see that from here. A Cheka man would alight also and follow her, relieving the watcher opposite Number Eighteen. They were uncommonly efficient.

Stern frowned. The rescue was going to be much more difficult than he'd thought — more difficult than Southgate had suggested. He spread the newspaper on the table but kept his eye on Number Eighteen. There appeared to be no way of entering the house without being seen, and no way of approaching Natalya Meretskova at the hospital. He lit a cigarette and casually rubbed the window again. There remained the journey to and from her work. She took longer going; Rantalla said she used a different route, spending ten minutes at St Isaac's Cathedral before continuing on to the embankment. He sucked smoke and pondered the possibilities. He hadn't even seen her yet to test that feeling of months ago. Another fourteen minutes and she would walk past the café and cross over to Stoliarny Street.

There was a light burning in the window on the third floor of Number Eighteen. Rykov was waiting for her to come home. Southgate's intelligence was faulty. Rykov hadn't been moved to a hospital — he never left the house. And there was that feeling of unease. Why had the Colonel said that? In Murmansk the difficulties had been played down. Deliberately? But it made no kind of sense, even allowing for Southgate's habitual double-dealing. What would be the point of making the rescue seem easier than it really was?

He glanced out again, his attention caught by a black automobile pulling in to the kerb outside the café. Damn, now he couldn't see. A Red Guard driver got out and opened the door for the slightly-built passenger. Stern watched the man straightening his peaked cap and pulling up the fur collar of his greatcoat. Peter Koltsov!

A raw wind lifted paper, plastering it against the front of

the car. Koltsov said something to his Red Guard, who nodded and drove off through the slushy snow, then he crossed the road and walked down Stoliarny Street. He didn't pause to check numbers but went directly to Number Eighteen and climbed the steps.

Stern crushed out the cigarette. His shocked surprise was followed by an uncomfortable feeling of incompetence. He hadn't the faintest idea what was going on, and Natalya Meretskova would be alighting from the tram sixty paces along Sadovaya in just three minutes.

He left the café but stood waiting in the doorway. A crawling doubt crossed his thoughts. What did he really know about her? He'd made assumptions, but what did he know for sure? She'd been the mistress of a general who was prepared to delay his offensive because of her. And now she was being visited by a Bolshevik commissar whose familiarity with the street suggested he'd been there before. Maybe I'm the world's biggest fool, he thought. And did Southgate know that Koltsov visits her?

He pulled up his collar against the wind. The tram appeared in the distance, dimly lit, clanking along Sadovaya Street. He felt a knot in his stomach. Blue sparks crackled on the tram's overhead arm. It slowed and juddered to a halt. Two men got off. Then Stern saw her in the dim light as she stepped down from the platform.

She was just as he remembered her. But different. Her hair was hidden under her fur hat. A scarf draped twice round her neck hung down over the shoulder of her old army greatcoat. Something in the set of her face suggested the surrendering of illusions. Another man had alighted and was following her.

She walked past the café doorway — he could have stretched out his hand and touched her. What was going on inside her head? He watched her cross the road, hurrying to get home. She passed under the circle of light in Stoliarny Street and climbed the steps of Number Eighteen. A Soviet commissar need not be less vulnerable than a Cossack general. Or a captain of engineers for that matter.

* * *

Natalya groped along the dimly lit hallway of the house. Paper peeled where the walls were damp but she'd stopped noticing that. Two youths were sitting at the bottom of the stairs, and they stood quickly to let her pass. She smiled briefly. They looked at her in the same way each night and she'd almost stopped noticing that as well.

By the time she reached the first floor landing her calf muscles ached. The Vanovsky family were quarrelling behind their closed door. A smell of cabbage soup lingered on the stairway. She climbed, slower now, to the third floor. Glotsin the furnaceman clumped down from the top of the house, on his way to the night shift at Putilov's. He nodded to her as he passed. Apart from the janitor, who was an informer, the people who were her neighbours were generally friendly. It was a puzzle to Natalya that they seemed to feel no resentment towards her and Anna. She paused to get her breath. The moment before entering the room was always the worst. Would Rykov be struggling to appear well, just so that she wouldn't worry? A brief, wordless prayer, and Natalya turned the key in the lock and opened the door.

She remained quite still, almost too weary to feel surprise. Commissar Peter Koltsov was standing with his back to her, examining the titles on the single bookshelf.

He turned as she closed the door behind her. 'Good evening, citizeness. I see you read English.' And he peered down at the book, his forehead wrinkling as he slowly deciphered the name. 'Dickens. I have heard of him. He identifies the conditions of the English working classes — so I have read.'

Natalya glanced quickly at Rykov, sitting in his chair and looking bitter and feverish. Koltsov's presence always made him worse. She turned back to Koltsov. 'Why have you come here again, Commissar?'

Rykov began to cough. 'I have already asked him that.'

Koltsov carefully, almost reverently replaced the book. 'I was passing. I came to enquire after the health of Captain Rykov.'

'You can see he is ill, and that visitors disturb him.'
Natalya leaned with her back against the door and let her
body go limp.

Koltsov looked at her. 'It occurred to me that as Captain
Rykov has not been officially discharged from the army he is
still entitled to soldiers' rations — considerably more than
he gets at the moment. Perhaps I can arrange that.'

Rykov wiped the damp sweat from his forehead. 'I am
not one of your Red Guards, Commissar. How will you
square such a deception with your Bolshevik conscience?'

Koltsov sighed to himself. 'We are not monsters, Rykov.
Rules must occasionally be bent to fit needs. The fact that
many are ill and hungry is not our fault. Blame our
enemies.' He glanced at Natalya. 'Blame the Malnekovs
who harrass the supply routes. As it is we distribute the food
as fairly as we can. Those who do the heavy work get more
than those who do light work. Those who choose not to work
get nothing. Isn't that a more reasonable arrangement than
existed under the Tsar? The sick get special rations when
these are available. You are still listed as a soldier, and you
are sick.'

Rykov started to speak but Natalya quickly interrupted
him. 'We would be grateful for the soldiers' rations for
Captain Rykov — if that is what he is entitled to.'

Koltsov glanced round at the sparsely furnished room
and his eyes rested on the damp patches on the wall. 'You
are officially overcrowded, but it is unlikely that the Commissar for Health can do anything about that. We have too
many problems with the typhus epidemic and not enough
resources.'

'We can manage, Commissar.' Natalya's voice was flat
and unresponsive. She straightened herself slowly, limbs
aching. If only he would leave her alone.

'Yes. You are a very determined person, Natalya
Alexandrovna.'

Natalya watched his face. He had other purposes in coming here — one she could guess. His quick, appraising
glance at her body made her feel sick. 'I am very tired,

254

Commissar, and I have to prepare a meal for Captain Rykov. If you have no other business with us I would be grateful if you would leave now.'

Koltsov pondered. 'I would like a few words with you — alone.'

She stared at him, one eyebrow slightly raised. 'Very well.' And taking a small bag of vegetables from the cupboard she led the way to the kitchen shared by the occupants of the third floor.

Koltsov was frowning. 'Rykov has tuberculosis and in these conditions you and your sister could also become infected. He should be in a hospital.'

'No!' And she shook her head. 'He would die, you know it.'

'What if you become sick also?'

Sometimes, when she least expected it, her emotions would surface. She suddenly felt close to tears. 'Can it really matter to you? Oh, why do you come here? Does it matter to the Bolsheviks if we die?'

He stared at her. 'It must matter to *you*, Natalya Alexandrovna. This life is all. We have only the here and now.' He paused. 'And your life matters to me.'

She was barely able to control her anger. 'Is that why I am followed, my every movement watched? Is that supposed to be a demonstration of your concern for me?'

'You are watched because the criminal, Malnekov, may try to make further contact with you. He is an enemy of the state, supported even by people within this city.' And stung by her obvious contempt he added, 'Your previous association with Malnekov is of course known to us.'

'I do not know where General Malnekov is. I have not seen him or heard from him for months.' She tipped two of the carrots into the sink.

'Has any of the Meretskov jewellery been used to buy him support?'

'No.'

'You would not lie to me?'

'I am not lying to you.'

He sat on the corner of the table and frowned down at his polished boot. 'Then your association with Malnekov is in the past — finished?'

Was it? Natalya didn't really know. She began washing the vegetables. 'Let us say that at this time in my life General Malnekov is not uppermost in my thoughts. I have too many pressing problems.'

Koltsov's jaw tightened. 'The struggle for survival can drain one of all feeling.'

What did he know of feelings? He was coldly, soullessly efficient. But she remembered the scars on his back — Malnekov had ordered that punishment all those years ago. *He at least knows about suffering.* She paused, looking down at her hands in the water. 'You have indicated concern for Captain Rykov. You know that my sister and I cannot allow him to go to hospital because he would die. Perhaps he will die anyway. But if . . .' She turned, 'If he and my sister could leave Petrograd — go north to Finland or Sweden where the climate is dry, he *might* recover.'

'It's possible.' Koltsov nodded. 'Men can survive almost anything if they have the will.'

Michael Stern had said that, on the day Rykov had been taken from the Semionovsky barracks. Sometimes she'd watched Rykov struggle for breath, knowing that it was only his burning resolve that kept him going. She glanced round for the kitchen knife.

Koltsov picked it up and handed it to her. 'You know, don't you, that even if Rykov and your sister had exit papers, there could be no question of you leaving. The revolution imposes its own demands. Malnekov must be stopped somehow. I must keep you here.'

Natalya began to scrape the vegetables. What of his other reasons? Revenge for that scarred back? Desire for her? 'Does the Commissar concern himself only with state security? No hint of self interest?' She turned and saw the surge of anger in his eyes. 'I'm sorry. I shouldn't have said that.'

'Think what you wish. You must remain in the city.'

'I know it.' She bit her lip. 'I've known all along. But

Rykov and my sister, they cannot be used. Surely you could let them go even though I must stay.'

'It is difficult.' He frowned. 'Few are allowed to leave. And what of you? You would be alone here.'

'That wouldn't matter.'

'You think of them and not yourself. You are a noble person, Natalya Alexandrovna.'

Natalya turned back to the sink. 'No, Commissar. I want them to be safe so that for a while — just a while — I do not have to feel constant concern for them. I want a little peace in my life. It isn't because I am noble, if that is really what you have chosen to believe. It is because I am tired and because I am selfish.'

Koltsov watched her slumped shoulders as she stared down into the sink. 'We don't always know our own motives.' He shrugged. 'How can anyone know another? I will leave now. And I will see to the matter of extra rations for Rykov.' He began buttoning his coat. 'As for Rykov and your sister journeying to Finland or Sweden . . . I do not know.'

'If it is at all possible . . .' Natalya blurted out, then stopped herself.

Koltsov stared at her. 'I will have to think about it. Goodnight, Natalya Alexandrovna.'

She returned to scraping the vegetables. 'Goodnight, Commissar.'

Rykov ate the small meal. 'Excellent!' he said. 'You should become a cook. In Paris perhaps. I'm feeling much better but I'm a little tired.'

Maybe he is slightly better, Natalya thought. 'Yes. Go to bed. I'll wait for Anna.'

He rose slowly. 'You and Anna are very good to me.' He stretched out and lightly touched the back of her hand. 'You could have left — got out of Russia if it were not for this sick and useless officer.'

'You were never useless. You keep up our spirits.' She wondered if he'd overheard any of the conversation with

Koltsov. 'Anna loves you, and you would have done at least as much for us.'

'Yes. Anna loves me. But . . .' He paused, frowning. 'I am prepared to do whatever you think best for her; stay here, go to the hospital, try for the frontier.' He smiled and added lightly, 'Or simply remove myself from your lives.'

She looked at him quickly. 'Don't say it. Don't even think it.' And she forced a smile. 'Go to bed. We want you well again.'

Rykov pulled the curtain that separated his small part of the room from theirs. He undressed slowly and lowered himself into his bed. He was very weary, but maybe the soldiers' rations would give him sufficient strength to get across the frontier. And if not, there is always the revolver, he thought. He'd hidden it under the mattress. One obliterating moment and they would be free of him. But Anna loved him. He stared up at the ceiling. Beyond the curtain he could hear soft sounds of Natalya washing.

He wondered what she looked like with the glow of the fire on her body. He'd lived in close proximity with the sisters for months. There was little about them that he didn't know, yet this intimacy had been curiously detached from his true feelings for them — until now.

He listened for the sounds of the sponge being squeezed into the bowl. I must be getting better, he thought.

Natalya rubbed herself with the towel, remembering Koltsov's eyes on her hips as she had turned to him. Unused assets? He'd said it was possible for Anna and Rykov to leave the country. What would persuade him to arrange that for her?

She smoothed her hands over her slim waist, then shivered slightly.

24

'We haven't talked enough lately, Martin.' Hal Winthrop stood at the window of his comfortable office high up in the Singer building. 'You're sure you won't dine with me this evening?'

'I have to see somebody — fat little guy with glasses.' Baumler grinned. 'I'll buy you lunch tomorrow — that is if I'm not in jail.'

Winthrop sighed and stared down at the Nevsky Prospect. 'I love this view, even in drab winter.' He spoke without turning his head. 'Why don't you go home to the States? You're finished here, Martin, you know that.'

'I know it.' Baumler crushed out his cigar. 'If I go for a pee I rub shoulders with a Cheka agent.' He paused. 'And I can't go back to the States. I'd be arrested.'

'All those stories about you are true?' Winthrop turned his head.

'No. Just some of them.'

'Go to Sweden then. Slip over on a business trip while the going's good, then stay there. You've got money in Sweden, haven't you?'

'Not much. Nearly all I've got is here.'

'God Almighty!'

Baumler frowned. He'd started withdrawing cash from his accounts, smallish sums just in case.

Winthrop sat himself at his oak desk. 'Five hundred roubles. That's the limit. You can't take more than that out of the country.'

'I'm trying to figure a way round it, Hal, but the Cheka have taken an interest in my banking arrangements.'

'Then there's no way round it, for Christ's sake!' Winthrop leaned forward. 'Look, we've been friends for a long time, and you've done me some favours. I don't want to talk to you through bars or preside at your funeral. Take the five hundred — in Swedish kroner — and clear out.'

'I'll give it serious thought.' Baumler grinned wryly. 'Have a cake ready with a file in it. So long, Hal.'

Winthrop looked defeated. 'Take care, Martin.'

Midday had passed and the temperature was dropping again. Baumler felt the cold, but more, he felt that gnawing unease. Hal's advice was too negative. Damn it, I need Michael Stern and his slide rule mind to think this through with. He huddled deeper into his coat. Hal Winthrop is certainly right about me being finished here, it's time to start packing. But how do I get my money out? I've been rich all these years, he thought. And all these years I've talked, boasted even about what it was like to be poor when I was young, scraping for dimes. It was just talk of the distant past, I can't remember it clearly. And now, in middle age, I'm not ready to face poverty in a new country.

He'd been a fool, keeping nearly all his money here. But until very recently he'd never anticipated leaving Russia — it had been his home for twenty-two years. He'd thought he'd die in Petrograd, a rich old man. Now all his assets might just as well be frozen. He daren't draw heavily on his account while the Cheka was watching it.

Frowning, he crossed the Alexander Gardens. There are ways round it, there *must* be. I could call in debts in cash, but nobody has ready money these days — it would take too long. There remained the account in the name of Larsen in the Rozhdestvenskaya bank down town. He'd opened it when he first came to the city twenty-two years ago, and he'd kept it going out of sentiment, or habit, he wasn't sure which. There wasn't much there — a couple of thousand roubles. Supposing he transferred credit from the North Baltic account then drew it out in cash in the name of Larsen?

He could see Popov, waiting for him by the bronze horseman. Even from twenty yards away it was evident that the little man was very cold, blowing on his fat fingers and glancing round. 'Not here, Mr Baumler,' he murmured. 'Follow me at a safe distance.'

And he followed, still pondering the Larsen account. Even if he could get cash that way, how would he get it out of the country with that five hundred rouble limit? He noticed debris on the ice of the river. Another two weeks maybe before the thaw. Why not smuggle out cash over the Terioki route? He and Helen could leave a day or so later, pick up the money then cross into Sweden.

Popov had reached the Dvortovi Bridge and was waiting half-way across. He looked frightened. Baumler took up a position a few paces away, leaning on the iron rail and watching the sea birds scavenging on the ice. 'Those copies of my bank statements, Mister Popov. Have you managed to delay passing them on?'

'Yes. I have them. And I've studied them, Mister Baumler.' Popov's eyes were wide. 'Regular large sums have been deposited over the last year and they do not relate to your sales!'

'I'm not paying you to study them. Just keep them out of sight for a while.'

Popov shook his head. 'It will not *do*. My employers are not stupid! They know you smuggle and they know you are wanted in your own country. Commissar Koltsov already has enough to make an arrest.'

How had they discovered he was a fugitive from the States?

'If the Commissar orders your arrest they will force you to tell everything, Mr Baumler. And worse, far worse, they will compel you to reveal that I aided you!' Popov wrung his fat hands in anguish. 'Oh God! — if there is a God. I should never have allowed my natural greed to get the better of my judgement.' And he whispered hoarsely, 'You have been withdrawing cash over the last month — twenty thousand roubles. It is there in the statements. Why cash, Mr Baumler?'

Baumler rubbed his jaw. I'm a dinosaur, he thought, and the cavemen are closing in with their bows and arrows. 'The jig is up, that's why.'

'Jig?' Popov stared, uncomprehending.

'I mean the game is over.' Popov was in deep now so he might as well tell him. 'I'm getting out of Russia. But twenty thousand roubles isn't enough to get started again. There's more in this for you, providing you keep those bank statements out of sight until I've transferred credit from my trading account to my bank down town. That should take . . .'

'Impossible!' Popov interrupted. 'I beg of you! Don't even think about it. Commissar Koltsov knows your real name is Larsen. If you withdraw a large sum in cash under that name he will realize you are planning to run!'

There was that feeling of being cornered.

'Five days — a week at the outside, Mr Baumler. Then I must pass those bank statements on. You must leave before then.' Popov blinked uncontrollably. 'Oh, if only I could leave Russia. My employers terrify me. The Commissar is a devil. Promise you will leave soon. You must not get caught — for *my* sake.' He groaned softly and glanced sideways at Baumler. 'You at least have status and a passport. I am just a poor man with a saintly invalid wife.'

Baumler sighed and reached for his wallet.

Evening was approaching. Already office workers were streaming home over the bridge. Popov slipped the bundle of roubles into his pocket. 'Go back towards the city, Mr Baumler. I will follow in a few moments.'

Baumler set off against the tide of people. Twenty thousand roubles, and a few thousand more in Stockholm. It wouldn't go far. Even if he could get out of Russia it would be back to lean times.

He reached the Nevsky. Palaces and mansions, requisitioned or boarded up. He didn't look at them. A few months ago there was hardly a door closed to him. Where were all those rich, charming, idle people? Those who'd stayed were penniless — the debris of the revolution — avoiding your eye if you saw them on the street, or embarrassed, asking for a loan.

Baumler's jaw tightened. And what was he now? A middle-aged trader with few assets and not much going for him but his wits. What about Helen? Without money she would soon become disenchanted, and at his age he couldn't afford that kind of failure. I can't take her with me, he thought. I'll have to go alone.

Popov had followed Baumler as far as the Stroganov palace, and there he paused, watching as the tall American merged with the crowds on the Nevsky. There would be no security, no proper sleep while Baumler remained in the city. It might be safer to arrange an accident; he still had contacts who would do that sort of work. But it was expensive, and Baumler was tough and unpredictable — he might not acquiesce in being pushed under the ice. Better to hasten his departure. Ideally, Baumler should be separated from his twenty thousand roubles just before he crossed the frontier.

Popov turned along the Moika towards Gorokhavaya Street. He was unable to shake off his heavy gloom. That morning, Madame Popov had begun shouting at him as soon as he woke. There had been dried herrings for breakfast, and no bread — she'd eaten it all, the insufferable old whore. Was it right, was it just, that he, Popov, who had once served the Tsar, should find himself in such depressed circumstances? What had happened to the world? In the old days you knew where you were. You did your job and made what you could on the side. You kept your nose clean and collected your pension at the end of it all. Now nothing was certain and any small indiscretion could lead to nine grammes of lead in the back of the head. And look where my natural greed has led me, he thought. He blinked several times. I'll change. Once Baumler is out of the country I'll be safe — all those old Okhrana records destroyed and nothing to connect me with my past. Once I'm safe again I'll change.

He crossed the street. And, oh God! There was retribution! The connecting link with his past. Natalya Meretskova was standing on the steps of the Cheka building.

Engrossed in her thoughts, she hadn't noticed him. Popov hurried through the door. He went straight to his desk in the crowded general office and sagged. What had she come here for? He kept his head down but watched the entrance. Please God, don't let her meet Commissar Koltsov. I'll change, I promise.

People came and went. The Cheka building was busy at all times of the day and night. Natalya had paused twice on the steps, trying to pluck up courage to go in. Still undecided, she walked to the embankment and looked out over the frozen river at the thousands of lights on the far bank. Even in the darkness birds screeched and flapped over the ice. How fortunate they are, she thought. They just respond to their needs and never have to make decisions. And they are innocent.

For her there really was no choice. She knew it. But to go back there and face Peter Koltsov with that proposition! Her breath steamed in the cold air. The overheard conversation of early morning had made her ache inside. Yes, I actually hurt, with love for Anna and her sad Rykov. And it hurts more than any love for a man. Anna had made fairy tale plans while Rykov coughed. Someday they would go to Finland. Or would Sweden be better for his health? A small house among fir trees. He'd get well. And perhaps I'll become a writer, he'd said. She would encourage him. He would become famous. And neither of them believes any of it, Natalya thought. Rykov would never manage the scramble over the frontier, he'd have to be taken out by train and with proper exit papers. Commissar Koltsov was the only man she knew who could arrange that. She took a deep breath and turned back to the Cheka building.

Peter Koltsov was shaving with tepid water in the small toilet at the end of the third floor corridor. He flicked the bright blade over his face and stared at himself in the mirror. Thirty-one years, but he looked older. What should he expect? He'd helped to turn the world upside down. He pulled his tunic on and buttoned it at the throat. Some jaw stubble had escaped the razor. He frowned and carefully scraped it off. Why had he become so concerned over his appearance? The hard lines of his face softened momentarily. Natalya Meretskova had a way of slipping insidiously into his thoughts. It was a puzzle how such a corrupt class could produce such a woman. Frowning, he picked up the razor to clean it. She could have left, probably in some style. Instead she stayed to live in squalor with her sister and the consumptive. He turned on the tap. It hissed and a small trickle of water began then stopped. Koltsov sighed to himself. One day they'd get the water supply working properly. And the food. One day there might even be time to be happy. He walked back along the corridor, passing an elderly cleaner suddenly busy with his broom. And he stopped in his tracks, startled by the slight catch in his breath. Natalya Meretskova was seated on the wooden bench outside his office.

'You wish to speak to me, citizeness?' My official tone, my official manner. It's like tough armour. Wearing it I can say, do, witness anything.

She rose from the bench. She looked pale. 'Yes, Commissar — if you can spare me the time.'

He opened the office door, wondering what had brought her here to this place. She's edgy, so she wants something hard to ask for. He tried to sound friendly but was aware of the habitual harshness of his voice. 'You have difficulties? The men detailed to follow you — are they showing respect? I can always replace . . .'

'It is an urgent personal matter.'

He placed one of the chairs opposite his desk and motioned her to sit. 'An urgent personal matter. Continue.'

Natalya moistened her lips. The proposal now seemed outrageous to her. She fumbled for other things to say. 'I — I wanted to thank you for your humane consideration for Captain Rykov. The card for extra rations arrived this morning.'

'You needn't thank me. Rykov is a citizen like any other.' Koltsov paused. She had some other purpose in coming. Or could it really be that she wished, urgently and personally to thank him? He leaned forward and lowered his voice, hoping to put her at her ease. 'I remain concerned for you and your sister.'

To Natalya, Koltsov's shift in position seemed more menacing than reassuring. Despite his slim build his shoulders suggested latent power. He began toying with a paperweight, passing it from one hand to the other. He saw her watching his hands and he carefully put the weight down and shrugged. 'I have given up smoking, so I compensate. How are you and your sister now?'

'Oh, we are well enough.' How could she work her way round to the proposition? The thought of it brought a quick surge of near panic and revulsion.

'I could arrange for an army doctor to examine Rykov.' He frowned. 'Yes. I think that should be possible, though it will take a few days.'

She nodded, watching his face. There was still time to retreat. 'That is extremely good of you.' How could she think of offering herself to him?

'It has been nearly a year, hasn't it?' He pondered. 'A year since we fetched Rykov from the Semionovsky barracks.' That was before divisions became chasms. He rose and went to the window, frowning out at the dark sky and groping in his mind for some common ground. 'That English captain, Michael Stern — with us that day. He saved my life once. Did you know that?'

Natalya was puzzled. Why was he telling her this?

'Tsarist justice consigned me to a living death as a convict on the Murmansk railway. I reached a point where a bullet seemed preferable, and I ran, half-hoping that I would be shot. I reached Pitkul in a freight car. Michael Stern and the old man found me. Stern gave me money, and clothes, forged a paper and put me on a train going south, to Petrograd.' He paused. 'I have great respect and fondness for Stern.' He continued to look out of the window, waiting for her to say something.

Fondness? How strange to hear him use such a word. Natalya didn't reply.

He turned. 'Do you ever hear from Michael Stern?'

Perhaps there was some Cheka purpose behind the question. She shook her head.

Koltsov sighed to himself, aware that conversation without a direct material purpose came clumsily to him. And people are defensive when they step through this door, he thought. So what has she really come here for? He needed a cigarette — there was a full packet in his drawer. Instead he toyed with the paper-weight. 'I'll see what else can be done for Rykov. Is there anything I can do for you, Natalya Alexandrovna?'

She must either thank him again and leave, or make it quite clear why she had come. Natalya glanced at him quickly. 'There is something. If my sister and Captain Rykov could be sent to Finland, I would consider myself greatly in your debt.' She spoke hurriedly, anxious now to have it said and done with. 'I would feel obliged to repay the debt in some way acceptable to you.' And she faltered to a stop, astonished at the change in his expression.

Koltsov stared at her and felt the anger welling up inside him. How could he have been such a fool? She was just an aristocratic whore after all, quick to know that he wanted her and now ready to trade on it. His anger made his voice harsher. 'What do you think their freedom is worth — one night of your favours — two?'

Her face burned. 'I thought — I know that you . . .'

'I had valued you more highly, citizeness.' He stood. 'I had thought it necessary to match your integrity.'

Too late she realized what she had done. The possibility that respect for her had been important to him hadn't occurred to her. She looked down at her clenched hands. 'But perhaps the — the proposition is still of interest to you, Commissar?'

Koltsov's head swam. He took the packet of cigarettes from his drawer and lit one. 'Yes. It interests me.' He sucked down smoke and stared at her. 'Even women of your class can serve a useful function.'

Stung, she forced herself to look directly at his face. It doesn't matter what he thinks, as long as he does what I want of him. 'Then it only remains for us to arrange a time and place.'

As Natalya walked out of the building she felt slightly giddy, and she leaned against a wall for a moment before continuing along Gorokhavaya Street. Now the contract was arranged. Others must have done the same — traded what assets they still had. She forced herself to visualize Koltsov's scarred body pressed to hers, and she felt sick. But shame nagged at her and her face burned as she recalled his bitter contempt.

Popov had watched Natalya leave. His relief was dogged by doubt. What might follow from her meeting with Koltsov — had they discussed the past? If it was ever even suspected that he had had some part in Koltsov's arrest and conviction, interrogation would swiftly follow. His hands sweated. Oh God! — if there is a God. I walk a tightrope over an abyss. Who could he betray to save his skin? Zubov? Maybe, but not yet. He forced himself to think like a professional. Nobody had come to arrest him, no summons from the Commissar. Some indication of what Natalya Meretskova had come to the Cheka building for might be in Koltsov's office — a file on the desk, a note on a pad, something in the waste basket. He needed a routine excuse to visit the Commissar.

Popov edged his way between the close-packed desks, to the typist who each evening updated the list of foreigners in the capital. He peered myopically over her shoulder at the paper still in her typewriter. She half-turned her body, distracting him. He blinked. She smiled, noticing his eyes drawn to her large breasts. Even in his anxiety, Popov found a moment to regret Madame Popov and the bonds of matrimony. 'I'm going upstairs. May I take the list to Commissar Koltsov's office for you?'

The girl looked relieved. 'If you would, comrade.' Koltsov frightened her.

'A great pleasure.' Popov waited for her to finish then pulled the sheet of paper from the machine and, stomach churning, he ascended to the third floor.

Koltsov was pacing his office, unable to work. She's just a

woman after all, no different from other members of her corrupt class. Why then did he feel the sick excitement at the bargain they'd struck? I should get myself a whore from the Seinnaya to drain the lust from me. But he knew that he wouldn't do that. No, he needed one night to purge himself of her. That she found the bargain acutely distasteful added to his desire. He would take from her what she had so willingly given to Malnekov. He glanced round at the light tapping sound on the door. Popov came in with the list.

'Put it on the desk.'

'Yes, Comrade Commissar.' Popov quickly surveyed the desk top. Nothing. A paper-weight. Not a scrap of paper.

Koltsov forced himself to think of work. 'What do you have on the American, Baumler?'

Popov was expressionless. How to be evasive without sounding incompetent? 'There are irregularities in his finances, Commissar.'

'I know that, you idiot!' Koltsov scowled. 'What else have you managed to unearth?'

'Most of his trade is centred here in Russia, but he has a small agency in Stockholm. The North Baltic Company takes care of his New York interests.'

'What about his smuggling? Tsarist jewellery fetched sixty thousand dollars in New York last month.'

Popov speculated for the hundredth time. Which would be the wiser course; to squeeze more money from Baumler then arrange an accident or to think in larger terms — of a future far away from Russia and Madame Popov? 'I have leads, Commissar. The American's legitimate trade has shrunk. He is increasingly dependent on smuggling but I do not yet have enough evidence to ensure a conviction.'

'You were supposed to find the route he uses and who his contacts are.'

Popov looked earnest. He bent to scratch his leg and glanced in the waste basket. An almost full packet of cigarettes! Nothing else. 'There are several distinct possibilities,

Commissar. I am sure that another week — ten days perhaps . . .'

'Then at the moment we are no further ahead than we were before. Have you studied his bank statements for patterns?' Koltsov rubbed his hand over his jaw, barely listening to Popov.

'. . . we have the American under constant surveillance, Commissar. Everything that can be done . . .'

One night with Natalya Meretskova. He'd never allowed himself to think about it before. His lust disgusted him and he turned savagely on Popov.

'I'm surrounded by idiots! Must I do everything myself? I'll give you until the twentieth of the month to find out exactly how Baumler is smuggling jewellery out of Russia.'

'But Commissar, it could take longer. There are . . .'

'There are no options.' Koltsov stared at him. The twentieth. 'If you fail I'll have somebody dig back into *your* past.'

Popov shuddered. 'My life is an open book.' He began to retreat towards the door. 'But I assure you, Commissar, that no stone will be left unturned . . .'

Peter Koltsov had picked up the list of foreigners that the myopic agent had placed on his desk and he ran his eye down it, pausing startled at Stern's name.

'. . . I will find out everything, Comrade Commissar. By the twentieth. You have my word as an honest servant of the Soviet.'

Koltsov interrupted him. 'Forget that for a moment.'

Popov blinked. 'I beg your pardon, Commissar.'

'There is an Englishman at the Europe Hotel.' Koltsov leaned back in his chair and chewed his thumbnail. 'His name is Michael Stern. He is possibly accompanied by an old Finlander called Rantalla. Find out what Stern is doing in Petrograd. Use whatever men you need, but understand this, no harm must come to either of them.'

'Certainly, Comrade Commissar. It shall be done. Goodnight, Comrade Commissar.' And Popov backed out of the door, amazed that nothing awful had happened to him.

Alone, Koltsov stared at the list again, remembering Pitkul, and Stern and Rantalla taking turns at sawing through his shackles. It had all been so simple then. Escape or die, no other options. He took the cigarette packet from the waste basket and lit one.

25

A brief thaw had cracked water pipes all over the city. Out at the Baltic shipyards dock workers were laying bets on when the ice would start to break up on the Gulf. The weather was capricious at this time of the year; an hour or two of hard bright sunlight tantalizingly suggesting the coming spring.

It would freeze again tonight. Stern pulled up the collar of his leather coat. He walked warily. Every vagary of the bloody climate brought some hazard. He listened for the dull roar of loosened snow sliding from the rooftops above. Three days in the city and he still hadn't made contact with Natalya Meretskova. He crossed to the north side of Mikhailovskya Square.

Southgate had indicated urgency in getting the Countess out, but how to begin if he couldn't get near her? He followed the ornamental railing fronting the Alexander Museum. Would it all have been easier if he'd had Krasnov with him? No, damn it. He scowled to himself. That swine was more interested in the jewellery — he'd have had to watch him all the time.

The museum had opened its doors at ten a.m. It was cold inside, little fuel to spare for heating. Already there were people, heavily clad, moving softly, pausing before paintings and icons, then moving on. It was a puzzle, why they came. Stern watched a young man who'd followed him in. Stoop-shouldered in his shabby coat, he took a paper bag from his pocket and broke off a piece of bread, chewing it slowly as he peered up at a Shubin sculpture. A freezing, hungry city, in a country racked by revolution and the beginnings of civil war, and they come here to stand in wonder before the art of their ancestors.

Stern moved to the south wing. He couldn't altogether discount the possibility that he was being followed — it was a feeling he'd had since he'd left the Europe Hotel. Nothing that he could positively identify but rather a slight tingling in the back of his neck. He ascended to the next floor and paused in front of the large canvas of Christ and the Sinner at the top of the staircase. He engrossed himself in it for a moment then glanced casually back. And there was a surprise. The young man with the paper bag was right behind him.

'An interesting work.'

The young man chewed another piece of bread. 'I prefer Repin.'

'His paintings are further on.'

'Yes.'

Stern watched him as he moved off slowly. Unlikely, but you could never be sure.

Rantalla was waiting for him in Room 92. There was nobody else there. The old man's jaw was set hard. 'This is going to be no picnic, Excellency,' he murmured. 'The Countess went to the Cheka building on Gorokhavaya Street yesterday.'

'What time?' He spoke softly, watching the door.

'Six fifteen, on her way home from the hospital.'

What the hell was she up to? He frowned. 'How long was she there?'

'Nearly an hour.' Rantalla's leathery face creased with concern.

'It is very puzzling, Excellency. Even the man following her was confused. I have to watch both of them.'

'Did she look anxious — afraid perhaps?'

'Not as far as I could tell, Excellency.' The old man glanced at him quickly then appeared to interest himself in a heavily-framed landscape. 'Possibly the situation is different from what you had been led to believe?'

'Possibly.'

'And the English colonel has minimized the difficulties, for some reason of his own.'

'Probably.'

'Call it off, Excellency!' Rantalla murmured.

'I can't do that, old man.'

'You have a personal interest, and that's dangerous. I fear you are being used.'

'Maybe she's being used.' He frowned again. 'Whatever, I was sent to get her out of Russia and that's what I must do.'

'There is another game going on. I'm an old dog. I *feel* it! And if you get her out she will not be yours. She'll go to that Cossack general.'

'It makes no difference.'

Rantalla's eyes narrowed. 'Something else drives you. Something apart from your interest in the woman.'

'Call it a debt.'

'You could pay it with your life.'

'Let's hope it won't come to that.' He smiled thinly and looked quickly round to see if they were being watched. 'The Countess will be working from midday. She goes to St Isaac's, breaking her journey to the hospital.'

'She rarely misses, Excellency.'

'Do Cheka men follow her into the Cathedral?'

'It depends. The man on duty today is often lax.' Rantalla pondered. 'Or perhaps he retains some religious scruples. He usually remains in the square and follows her again when she comes out.'

'I'll get there first today and wait inside for her.'

Rantalla sighed softly. 'Your Excellency enjoys a challenge.'

The stoop shouldered man with the paper bag was near the door, looking at a Kandinsky. Stern signalled with his eye and whispered. 'You go, old man. I'll be at the Academy of Science this afternoon. We'll meet at the workmen's café at five. Take care.'

273

After Rantalla left, Stern moved slowly towards the door, and he paused in front of the Kandinsky. 'Intriguing, isn't it?'

The young man looked round quickly then frowned back at the oddly arresting cluster of coloured shapes. 'It doesn't tell me anything. It's meaningless.'

'The meaning is in the colour.' Stern grinned at him. 'Try Surikov. Room 72. He tells you something.'

Stern left the museum and walked towards the Morskya, wondering if the young man was following. There wasn't much time to spare but it would be better to take no chances. On the Nevsky he entered the Silver Bazaar, left by another exit, then doubled back through a crowded arcade. At the Stroganov palace he turned left. A road gang was clearing the paving of snow. Some of them were ex-officers, great-coats stripped of their proud epaulettes. They sweated over their shovels.

He crossed St Isaac's Square and entered through the great bronze doors of the Cathedral. He walked softly, following the richly decorated northern wall. There were few people in the vast building at this hour. Just to his right an old woman in rags bowed low, almost prostrate on the cold slabs. He waited, hidden from the main doors by a broad malachite column. Perhaps she wouldn't come today, that being the way of things. Light was tinged blue through the stained glass in the depth of the sanctuary. He wondered why she came here so often — he hadn't thought of her as religious. But then, how little he really knew about her.

And there she was, a small figure across the interior of the huge cathedral. She was wearing the soldier's greatcoat and the fur hat. He watched to see if she was being followed. She paused to kneel before a smoke-blackened icon, and he waited a moment longer then crossed until he was behind a column only a few paces from her.

'Countess. No! Don't look round!'

Her back stiffened and her head rose. She stared up at the icon.

'It's Stern, Countess. Listen carefully. I have been sent from Murmansk. I have forged papers to get you and your sister across the frontier.'

He thought he detected an almost imperceptible sigh in the slight movement of her shoulders. 'We cannot go with you. Captain Rykov is dependent on us.'

'I know that!' he whispered urgently. 'But you, Countess, will be in the greatest danger from the moment General Malnekov is ready to begin his operations along the eastern railway. Nothing will save you then.'

A fat priest, still sleepy, glanced at them and walked on towards the great doors.

Natalya's voice was almost inaudible. 'Go back to Murmansk, Captain. Your government will pursue its own interests, as governments always do. And General Malnekov will raid and plunder because that is his nature. I must stay.' She stood quickly and stared fixedly at the icon. 'I think I am safe for a while. If those who sent you are in any way interested in two people they cannot use, tell them I have arranged for my sister and Rykov to leave Russia.'

'Wait! Don't tell me what to tell them! I haven't come nearly a thousand miles for that. What arrangements have you made? Who here do you trust?'

She stared at him incredulously. 'We don't trust. We *trade*. Commissar Koltsov will ensure Anna and Rykov reach Helsingfors.'

'Trade? What are you up to?' he whispered savagely. 'What did Koltsov make you promise in return for their freedom?' He gripped her wrist tightly. 'I want an answer, madam!'

'Let go!'

'Tell me.'

'It has nothing to do with you!'

'Give me an answer.'

'Peter Koltsov exacted no promise from me. I went to him!' She winced. 'You are *hurting* me!' She glanced fearfully round. 'Please! The priest will see us!'

Slowly he released her. 'Supposing I can take you, your

sister and Rykov out by train, in three days' time?'

'It's impossible. Leave me alone, you are interfering in my life.' She rubbed her wrist. 'Three days' time would be too late anyway.'

'Tomorrow night then?'

Her voice was flat. 'Go back, Captain. I'm not responsible for you but I don't want you caught.'

'I'll be here tomorrow morning at the same time. Say you'll be here also.'

She shrugged hopelessly. 'I come here each day.' And she turned and started to walk to the great doors.

'I'll make the arrangements,' he whispered.

She didn't look back.

He allowed five minutes then left, walking towards the Nikolayevsky Bridge, barely aware of those he passed. The anger hit him in waves but he didn't know whom to direct it against. Koltsov? No, she'd shown her distaste for him then offered herself — how could he reject so complete a vengeance? Should he blame her?

It did no good to think about it. He crossed the dirty rutted snow to the bridge. No matter how hopeless it looked he'd still have to play out his role of visiting engineer. Kirilin was expecting him for two hours of discussion at the Academy of Science. How in the name of God could he talk of track ballasting on this of all days?

Ragged children were skimming stones across the frozen Neva. Two or three weeks and the ice breakers would begin smashing a passage through the Gulf. And with the coming of spring, General Malnekov's White army of irregulars would move into Manchuria. What would happen to her then, if he didn't get her out of Russia? He reached the north bank of the Neva. There was a chance she'd change her mind — back away from her pact with Koltsov. He'd have to allow for that and have a plan ready. It would mean using the railway — he wasn't even sure it could be done.

Kirilin had specified twelve thirty for the meeting and it was nearly that now. He increased his pace along the University Quay. The Academy of Science was at the Strelka end, past the university. He had three track ballasting problems (two of which he'd already half solved) to put to Kirilin, an old, shrewd specialist of Trans-Siberian experience. Would it seem odd if he cut the discussion short?

Frowning with his thoughts, Stern passed the front of the university and almost encountered Helen Mirsky. Good God! Could it have been her? He glanced at her back as she climbed the broad steps to the university entrance. And yes, it was. No other woman he knew walked quite like that. He wished he could have talked to her.

Kirilin was all he'd been told; old, impatient and derisive. He smelled of stale tobacco. 'Sixteen yards of bridge for every thousand yards of track.' He lit his pipe, hands arthritic. 'Forty per cent of the track laid in curves to avoid marsh. I told them the route was wrong. They should have surveyed west of Lake Ukhtinsya.'

Stern shook his head. 'They'd have lost the advantage of a sea link at Kem. And the line would have run within a few miles of the Finland frontier.'

Pipe smoke filled the office. 'What's wrong with that?'

'It's strategically unsound.'

The older man scowled. 'Soldiers had too much hand in the decision making.' And he stared at Stern through narrowed eyes. 'You rebuilt the bridge at Pitkul. I've seen the report. A fine piece of imaginative engineering. You and I have a lot to talk about.'

Stern sighed to himself.

Helen Mirsky couldn't quite make up her mind. Was it Stern whom she'd seen? Perhaps she was mistaken. And one never knew these days whether people wanted to be recognized. It was bad enough meeting old student friends, embarrassed, pretending enthusiastic republicanism.

Her black market expedition had taken longer than her lunch hour. She'd crossed the river because of the rumoured illicit sale of fur gloves, brought in by 'bag men' from outside the city and now being hawked in the Siennaya market. She'd had to guess the size, measuring the gloves against her own slim hand and imagining them worn by Baumler. We-ll, where was the harm in buying him a birthday present? After all, his trade had been extremely lucrative to her, and to Cousins Erik and Paul. And — and this was the crux of the matter — she had enjoyed that moment of purchasing the gloves. It was as if buying something for Baumler had made him hers in some way.

Zubov hadn't yet gone to lunch. As Helen entered the office he glanced up, closing the file he was reading, and then he locked it in his desk drawer. And she was curious. Until a month ago he'd never locked anything; letters, lecture notes left anywhere. Now he was becoming — what? — secretive. Listlessly he picked up a typed report and stared at it.

Helen sat at her own desk but kept her heavy coat on. 'It is impossible to type if the heating keeps going off, Professor.' She blew on her hands to warm them.

'Coal shortage,' Zubov muttered. 'The Student Action Committee is considering ways and means.' And he continued to stare at the report.

He isn't really reading it, she thought. 'This morning, while you were out, the pipes made an obscene gurgling noise, then the radiators cooled quite rapidly.' She tried putting her hands under her armpits. 'Spring seems so long away. When do you think the thaw will come?'

He looked at her. 'You really are cold — and a little pale. I will bring a small oil heater from home for you.'

Helen pondered. Zubov had undergone a complete change since that visit to the Cheka building. He'd become almost apologetic, as if trying to make amends for something. And he'd stopped brushing against her, which was a relief, but slightly disconcerting because now she didn't know what he was thinking. And why had he started locking files away?

'I have gone to bed almost fully dressed for almost a month. How I long for the most elementary comfort of sleeping in a thin nightdress again.' She glanced at him. He didn't even look up. Not a suggestion of arousal. Helen

278

began to type, her cold fingers clumsy. If she played her cards shrewdly she wouldn't have to concern herself with Zubov's unaccountable self-searching for much longer. Sweden beckons, she thought. Tonight she would see Baumler again and work a little magic.

Zubov stirred slowly and tried to concentrate on the report, but his mind kept drifting to the files locked in his drawer. Nine were headed with the initials of academic colleagues, the tenth inscribed 'H.M.' He looked across to where Helen Mirsky sat. Desire for her was deadened by his guilt. He noted things she said and eavesdropped on her telephone conversations with Baumler. Fear and self-loathing alternated with a nagging anxiety that his treachery would be discovered and the whole façade of his life collapse. 'I have to attend the meeting of the Student Action Committee, Helen.' He was unaware that she had been watching him. 'It will probably go on until at least four thirty. The chairman usually has a lot to say.'

'The fervent boy with the appalling acne?'

Zubov stared at her. 'It *is* cold in here. The winter seems endless. Go a little early this afternoon if you wish.' He took up his notes and left.

Helen sat quite still for a moment. Why did she always end up feeling a little sorry for him? And what was in those files?

She remained long enough for Zubov to reach the upper floor where the Student Action Committee was to discuss the fuel economy programme, then she took the gloves purchased for Baumler and went home.

The evening required elaborate preparation. Baumler had responded satisfactorily on the last occasion she had worn the low cut dress. So now it hung, sponged and pressed, shining as she smoothed it with her fingers. But wasn't it outrageous that with Russia out of the European war there was still insufficient fuel in the city for her to take a hot bath? Helen shivered as she washed in front of the fire. She hadn't seen Baumler for a week and knew only that he was preparing to transfer his business operations to

Sweden. Sweden would suit her quite nicely. She paused from drying herself. And he needs me, she thought. It was all quite unexpected, that realization as she'd crossed the Vena restaurant, seeing his face before he saw her. If she hadn't turned up he would have gone on sitting there, gloomily smoking another cigar.

She began dressing with care. Petrograd was becoming unendurable; the cold damp and the hunger. And worse, that feeling of loneliness at night when the mist from the river rubbed against the window. She hadn't been consciously aware of it until that day — seeing Baumler across the restaurant. Had she been lonely all along and not known it — his need triggering something in herself?

A last look in the mirror. She was not displeased. In this dress I could surely raise Lazarus from the dead, she thought. Though a small prayer might propitiate Him. Dear God, maybe I don't deserve it, but let me win this time.

Her cab moved slowly with the night traffic along the south embankment, past the high-spired Admiralty and the Winter Palace. The buildings were still the same but the feeling of permanence had gone. And for those of us who have lived through the last three years in Petrograd, nothing will ever seem certain again, she thought. The cab turned right at the parade ground and moved eastwards towards the Liteyny Prospect.

Baumler looked harassed as he opened the door for her. 'I nearly had the whole damned kitchen in flames. Do you want a drink? Here, let me take your coat.' He paused, eyes wide, and whistled softly. 'That dress!'

'I wear it only because it is warm. Today the heating has been cut at the university. I was frozen to my remotest extremity.'

He nodded slowly. 'I'll bet the Professor was warm. Sit down. I'd better get back to the food before I burn it again. You know where everything is.'

Baumler's apartment was well heated. Helen took off her boots and sat on the massive old sofa, her feet curled beneath her. She winced slightly and smiled at the sound of loud clattering in the kitchen. He'd dropped something. He seemed nervous. Perhaps the dress was already working its magic.

And Baumler *was* nervous. The omens were worse today and Popov had wept, begging him to get across the frontier. But how to break the news of his impending departure to Helen? He scalded his fingers and blew on them, cursing softly. Could he change his mind — take her with him? No, it would be a weak indulgence. Facts had to be faced. He was hard up, middle-aged, and with a very uncertain future.

She called to him. 'What are we eating?'

'It was to be beef Stroganov,' he called back. 'But I couldn't get the beef. In fact I could hardly get anything. Even the black market is drying up. So we'll have to have omelette à la Baumler. You like mushrooms?'

'Very much.' A lie. She hated mushrooms.

'It will be ready in a few minutes.' She'll manage, Baumler thought. She hasn't done too badly — a little money stashed away in Finland, and now there would be her share of the cash profit of the next and last run from Terioki. 'I did manage to get a good Moselle to go with it. The fellow who sold it to me said it came from the cellars of Prince Yusupov.'

'You are incorrigible.'

'Hell, it's for sale, isn't it? At least I appreciate what I'm drinking.' Baumler came in with a large silver dish. He was still in his shirt sleeves, an incongruous white apron draped round his waist. He glanced at her as he passed. God's teeth! In that dress she looked very desirable. He lit candles on the table in the alcove and poured wine into long-stemmed tinted glasses. 'Damn! I forgot the tarragon. You need tarragon on the omelette.' And he went back to the kitchen.

Helen sat at the table. Next to her plate was a small, expensively-wrapped package. She picked it up, testing its weight, then put it back. Perhaps she wouldn't have to work too hard after all.

Baumler reappeared with the tarragon but minus the white apron. 'Don't open the present yet. Save it until the end of the meal.'

Helen sampled the omelette. It was very good, despite the mushrooms. 'You constantly amaze me. I cannot keep up with your many facets.' She began to eat. 'Do you cook for yourself all the time?'

'Mostly I eat out.'

'With such culinary talents I am astonished that one of the gourmet ladies of Petrograd has not trapped you into matrimony.'

Baumler grunted, then swallowed and poured more wine. 'There is no permanent woman in my life. I guess I've never had that kind of time to spare, I'd make a very bad husband.'

Helen was slightly puzzled. Why the change in his mood since last time? Perhaps he had momentarily lost his nerve. But she could cure that if he would only relax for a minute. She assumed her warmest smile. 'Yes. I can imagine that you would be quite difficult to live with.'

'Absolutely right.' Baumler went on eating. 'Now I'm stuck as a bachelor.'

Helen pondered. Why the game? She decided to change her tack. 'How fortunate to be so self-contained, able to face the years alone.' And she leaned forward, holding out her glass for Baumler to fill and at the same time allowing him a protracted view of the deep cleavage of her dress. Smiling lazily, she leaned back again. He'd weakened then. Just one night. That's all she needed. And she'd have him hooked. His common sense must surely prevail. He would be insane to reject the obvious advantages and delights of marriage to her.

Baumler felt a huge sadness. Supposing he did it — married her? What happens when the dream time ends and she wakes up one morning in a seedy hotel in Stockholm, looking across the room to a middle-aged man frowning at himself in the mirror? No. He was crazy to let her go, but let her go he must.

'Tell me, Helen, aren't there dozens of young university students after you?'

Helen reflected. 'Not *dozens*. Actually I see very little of them. I am incarcerated all day in the office.'

'Ah, yes, with Zubov.' A slight frown crossed Baumler's thoughts. 'When the Professor answers the telephone he seems anxious to keep me talking. Affable, but he asks a lot of questions.'

'Really?'

'Perhaps he wants you for himself,' Baumler joked.

Helen was expressionless. 'The thought had never occurred to me.' And anxious to change the subject, she leaned down to the floor beside her for the gloves, carefully wrapped. 'I am a day early.'

Baumler was startled. 'But how did you know my birthday is tomorrow?'

'You mentioned it on the night you took me to the ballet.'

'But that was — what? — over a month ago.'

'I have an inconsequential talent for remembering dates and details.'

Baumler shook his head. 'You shouldn't have. Can I open it now?'

'Please do.'

He stripped the wrapping and took out the gloves. 'These are superb!' He tried one on. 'Perfect fit!'

She watched him, a slight smile on her face.

'Thanks, Helen. Thanks very much.' He hadn't seen gloves like this since early in the war. She had a way of disarming him and he couldn't afford the price. 'You might as well open your present now.'

Helen picked up the package and carefully unwrapped it, saving the paper. She looked at the small, gilt-embossed leather-bound box.

'It once belonged to a grand duchess,' he said.

Helen opened the box and stared down at the emerald brooch, and she gasped softly. The stone was set in finely-worked silver — unmistakably the skills of Fabergé's. 'It is so beautiful!'

283

'Put it on.'

'Shall I? Yes, I will.' She rose quickly and went to the mirror, fastening the brooch at the low neck of her dress. 'You are too generous!' And she had a sudden small presentiment. It was too expensive. 'But why? It isn't *my* birthday.'

Now he would have to tell her. He screwed up his face in a frown. 'It's a sort of goodbye present, Helen.'

'A goodbye present?' Helen froze but continued to look into the mirror.

He groped for a cigar. 'You and that young scoundrel — Erik — have been very useful to me over the last few months. But it's all getting a bit dangerous. The Bolsheviks don't like the way I do business. I have one last consignment coming in from Terioki before the ice starts to break up, and I'm hoping to get a little of my money out on the return run. Then I'm getting out.'

'Yes. Perhaps it would be wise to start again elsewhere.' She turned to him. 'I also would like to leave.'

'Well, we could talk about that.' He felt embarrassed.

She sat again, leaning forward on the table, her chin cupped in her hands. 'Yes. Do let's talk about it.'

'You're a very smart young woman.' He scratched a match and lit his cigar. 'It's an obvious waste of your talents just typing letters and speeches for Zubov, and I'll be frank with you. I don't trust that guy. Now, you are half-Finlander. I can fix you a job with Grasbeck in Helsingfors — well paid.'

Helen's expression didn't alter. 'First a brooch, now a job.'

Baumler groaned to himself. She was going to make it difficult for him. 'Grasbeck is doing well and he's a good man. You've got your share of the Terioki profits stashed in Finland. You could start again — a new life.'

How could he be so stupid? Helen resumed eating, quite slowly until the impulse to throw the food at him subsided. Her anger gave way to a feeling of emptiness. 'Will I see you again before you leave?'

284

'Hell, I have to be gone by the twentieth. Safer that we don't meet.' Baumler frowned. 'A Cheka guy keeps following me. Better that you don't get too involved in my life.'

She carefully put the fork down. 'But I'm already involved in your life.'

He took a deep breath. 'Well, now comes the parting of the ways.'

Helen continued to look at him for a moment. Then she bit her lip and stood. 'I think I should go home now.'

As they crossed the city to Vassili Island, she sat silently staring ahead while Baumler drove. His face wore a gloomy scowl. Reality had to be faced. He could almost have had a daughter her age. And she's a schemer. What the hell did she really want with him apart from money he no longer had? But the thought was there in the back of his mind. Maybe I'm just glad of an excuse. A middle-aged bachelor scared because he was very nearly hooked. Deep down I'm relieved.

He stopped the car outside her house and sat for a moment. 'I'm very fond of you, Helen. I really am. But I'm too old . . .' He tailed off, glancing at her quickly. And by God, she looked beautiful now that she was sad. For the first time since he'd met her over a year ago, the little adding machine behind her eyes wasn't working.

Helen unclipped the brooch and handed it to him. 'It really is much too expensive. Goodbye, Martin.' And she got out of the car.

'But Helen! . . .'

She was already hurrying up the steps and into the house.

He continued to sit, holding the brooch. Women! They knew every trick of putting you in the wrong. But damn it, he'd done it now — finished it before it really started. Just over a week and he'd be out of Russia. She'd forget him — the young always do. And suddenly he was impatient to be gone.

Helen heard the car start and move away. She took off her dress and carefully draped it on its hanger. It wasn't the end of the world. She picked up stockings from the end of the bed and began washing them in the cracked sink. How quiet the house is tonight, she thought. Beyond the window a cold mist from the Gulf shrouded the buildings opposite. I'm not lonely. Not really.

26

After the encounter in St Isaac's Cathedral, Natalya set herself determinedly against Michael Stern's offer of rescue. He is far too impetuous, she thought. How could he possibly get three of us out of Russia by train, and at such short notice? But she felt unsettled. Why, in the name of God, had he reappeared now?

She moved between the close-packed beds. Only lice had prospered during the winter. Fevered typhus victims, breath corrupt, filled the ward. Natalya's back ached from bending to wash blotched, emaciated bodies.

'Will·I recover, little sister?' The man tried to moisten his cracked lips. She gave him a sip of water and looked at the board over his bed. A Red Guard. 'Yes. You'll recover.' The epidemic was almost over, cut short by the rigorous measures of the Petrograd Soviet. 'One more day and your fever should begin to subside — you'll feel much better.'

One more day and she would fulfil the bargain made with Koltsov. She turned to the next bed. A sick anxiety caught up with her again. What would Peter Koltsov expect of her? She'd only known Malnekov.

Until that morning Natalya hadn't given serious thought to what she would say to Anna and Rykov. Deception was inevitable. During the day she fabricated a story. And it was quite convincing — even I would believe it, she thought. Tonight she would have to tell them.

The long hours of duty in the hospital ward had the

essence of an unpleasant dream, clock time moving with a slowness unrelated to time in her head. But at odd moments, remembering Stern's anger, she felt oddly touched that he should concern himself so over her honour. The marks of his grip were still visible on her wrist. A strange, outdated young man, she thought, moving around in the middle of revolution and confident only in his own code of values. It would be better not to go to the cathedral tomorrow. He would wait, and then finally give up. Safer for him. And less worrying for her. Tomorrow would be difficult enough, knowing that Koltsov's harsh eyes were watching the clock, anticipating his satisfaction.

On the tram returning home, Natalya rehearsed the story of why Anna and Rykov must leave the city separately from her. It wasn't quite as believable now. She pondered. They'd be concerned, but she had talked them into believing things before. The story would need to be told with enthusiasm and great conviction.

Rykov was by no means convinced. 'Natalya, what are you saying?'

She sighed, as if explaining something to a child who chooses not to understand. 'It is perfectly straightforward. Finland has its own internal problems, made marginally worse by the exiles. Commissar Koltsov doesn't care to risk the Tsarist Russians in Finland sending word to General Malnekov that I am free. On the promise that you will both say nothing of my release, he has agreed that I should leave quietly through Murmansk. For my part I have given my word that I will have no contact with Russian emigrés. There is really no need to concern yourselves. I shall be quite safe. In Murmansk the British will protect me. And I shall join you later.'

Anna frowned. 'But we always agreed that when we left we would stay together.'

'We didn't know this opportunity would present itself.' Natalya pretended impatience. 'Heaven knows when we might have another chance.'

'We shouldn't separate. Why can't we all go to Murmansk together?'

'Oh, do be sensible! Captain Rykov is hardly fit to make the long journey to the Arctic. It is better that we separate for a while than stay in Petrograd. Commissar Koltsov needn't let us go at all. We should be thankful.'

Rykov's face had tightened. 'Koltsov! Do you really believe that we would leave you, knowing that your release from this city is dependent upon the word of that Bolshevik!'

'Don't forget that it was Peter Koltsov who got you out of the Semionovsky barracks.' And I trust him, Natalya thought. He disgusts me but I don't doubt his word.

'I'm not blind,' Rykov said. 'Koltsov always has a purpose of his own for everything he does. I have seen the way he looks at you.'

Anna glanced quickly at his face, suddenly aware of what he was thinking, and she said fiercely, 'Gregory is right, Natalya. We all go together, or not at all.'

She felt a weary anger. All her worrying and planning to be ruined by them. 'You *must* go. Can't you understand? To have *papers* — genuine papers that allow you to cross frontiers! There are members of the Imperial family who would give anything for this opportunity.'

'Anything?' Rykov snarled. He turned and grasped Anna's hand. 'You could both have left months ago. There are ways over the frontier for those who are fit and strong. It is I who have prevented this. You are squandering your lives on me. I shall leave the apartment immediately and present myself to the hospital of St Paul. My life is no longer in your hands. You are both free to seek some other means of escape.' He went quickly to his small part of the room and pulled out a travelling bag.

'But you can't!' Anna exclaimed. 'St Paul is overcrowded and fever ridden — they can't look after you. You will die there!'

'So I *die* there,' he shouted. 'The world will not come to an end!'

'Oh God!' Anna grasped Rykov's wrist, but he pulled himself free. Then he gently held her shoulders. 'No, Anna. It is a matter of honour.'

Natalya sat and closed her eyes, resting her head in her hands. Honour! I should have foreseen this. Rykov is as outdated as Captain Stern. As if honour could possibly be of any importance now.

Anna was still begging Rykov. 'If you die, I will die also.'

'You will not! You will live — millions do. Go to Finland with Natalya, for *my* sake.'

'Stop it!' Natalya opened her eyes and leaned forward on the table. 'Stop it, both of you.'

And they turned to her.

She looked at Rykov. 'Wait until tomorrow. You say we are squandering our lives for you. So please do this one thing for me. Promise you will wait until tomorrow. And then if you want to go you must do so.'

'Very well. How can I refuse you?'

Natalya took a deep breath. Tomorrow morning she would have to go to the cathedral after all.

They went to bed, and for a long while they each lay silent, unsleeping in the darkness. Rykov groped softly for the revolver under his mattress. It was still there, safe with its possibility of honourable oblivion. And beyond the curtain, Anna slid her hand to Natalya's and squeezed it hard. The night seemed endless. Natalya dozed then jerked awake at the sudden image of rifles in a mist, then she slept until Anna woke her in the morning.

The Cheka had changed their watch. From the high window Natalya could see the men of the morning shift stamping their feet, trying to keep warm. One would follow her when she left and the other would watch the house. She left at the usual time, walking to St Isaac's. She never hurried or looked back. It was odd to have adjusted to someone behind her all the time. Sometimes, in a crowded street, she even slowed her pace unconsciously, so that he shouldn't lose her. I wonder what he thinks? He's familiar with the whole pattern of my movements. Does he make assumptions about me? Can he guess my mood from some slight change, perhaps in the way I'm walking? Tomorrow he'll wait again outside the house, but I won't be there.

She reached the cathedral and entered, moving quietly under the vast dome and following the southern wall to the smoke-blackened icon. A pretence of prayer, she knelt and stared at the sad face in the painting. Perhaps Michael Stern wouldn't come. A door slammed somewhere and the sound echoed hollowly. Supposing he doesn't come — what then? Rykov will leave, or do something worse, and it will all be for nothing. Minutes passed. Oh God, what do I do? If I stay much longer it will look suspicious. Then she was aware of Stern close by, standing in the half-light behind the ornamented column.

'No — don't turn your head!' he whispered. 'You were followed into the cathedral.'

She stiffened but kept her eyes fixed on the icon.

'Just one word, Countess. Have you reconsidered — could the three of you be ready to leave at nine tonight?'

'Yes.' Her heart was thumping painfully.

'I'll get instructions to your sister. Just do what you always do.' She heard him move slightly. 'Don't glance in my direction. Go now.'

Natalya crossed herself and rose, and she walked back under the dome to the bronze doors. Her relief was enormous. Succeed or fail — the responsibility was no longer hers. She paused briefly on the broad steps and peered up at the grey day. I didn't pray, she thought. I'll pray tomorrow in Finland, God willing.

Natalya walked through the Alexander Gardens on her way to the embankment. Children were running between gaunt trees and the statues of Gogol and Lermontov were encrusted with ice. The path leading across to the Admiralty had been cleared of snow. Perhaps after today she would see this no more — Petrograd behind her for ever. At the embankment she looked out across the river to Dvortovi Bridge, and she was aware of a small, nagging guilt. Koltsov would be waiting tonight, expecting that she'd keep her part of the bargain. She'd given her word. What would he think of her?

She continued along the embankment to the tram stop, her breath turning to tiny icy drops on her scarf.

The brief thaw of the previous day had flooded an office block on Gorokhavaya Street. Now it had frozen again. By evening long icicles hung from the balconies. The Cheka building at Number Two stood only a few yards from where Rasputin had lived, but now the monk was almost forgotten and people passed his house with barely a glance. There was, though, a tendency to cross the road and avoid the unimposing grey entrance of Number Two. Those who walked through those doors didn't always come out. Even at night lights burned in many of the windows.

Commissar Peter Koltsov had worked since seven in the morning and now he was preparing to leave for a late session of the Petrograd Soviet. Tired, he leaned back in his chair and rubbed his jaw. The cigarette packet lay half-concealed under papers on the desk. He scowled at it. Damn, he was addicted again. Slowly he lit one, smoke harsh on his throat, and allowed himself to go limp. The woman would come to him tonight. Long hours of work had almost purged him of desire. He sucked in smoke and toyed with the matchbox. Desire dormant, he could think straight again. He'd handled the matter badly.

He rose and pulled on his greatcoat. Natalya Meretskova was trading with the only asset left to her. It couldn't have been easy, he thought. She doesn't want me, I fill her with distaste. And what do I really want from her? It was strange, that need for someone so different. He picked up his cap, setting it squarely on his head. I have purpose in my life — the Party to serve. That should be enough. Right at this moment I would rather just talk to the woman — try to bridge that chasm. And he frowned, groping with the thought. Once we must all have been innocent — I'd like to find that feeling again. He crushed out the half-smoked cigarette. Perhaps that is what I'll do — just talk to her. That might give me more lasting satisfaction than briefly possessing her body. And even if she doesn't understand, it will not matter.

He tidied his desk, scooping up the surveillance report on Michael Stern, and still frowning to himself he stuffed it into his coat pocket.

As Koltsov's car crossed Petrograd towards the Smolny Institute he puzzled over Stern. The information that Popov's subordinates had collected that day seemed innocent enough, yet it *felt* wrong. Stern had visited St Isaac's Cathedral before going on to the offices of the Commissar for Ways and Communications. In the evening he had met the old man Rantalla, then returned to the Europe Hotel. Why St Isaac's? — hundreds went there of course, but Stern wasn't Orthodox or a tourist. And why had he applied for an exit visa to Finland when it was quicker to get to Murmansk by the Karelian route? None of Stern's activities since he'd arrived in Russia could in any way be called suspicious. In fact it was almost the other way round; he did his job thoroughly, met the old man, walked sometimes. And Koltsov knew that other officials wouldn't have taken a second look at that surveillance report. But there was that nagging question. Why had Michael Stern made no attempt to contact him?

The car moved along Sadovaya and Koltsov could see the Europe Hotel set back in Mikhailovskaya Square. Perhaps Stern had been warned off by the British Military Mission — they had no great liking for the Bolsheviks. Or perhaps he had realized he was being followed and felt offended, the English were strange about things like that. So I'll call on him tomorrow, Koltsov thought to himself and smiled. I'll take a bottle of cheap spirit and some dried herrings to remind him of Pitkul. And when we've drunk enough I'll tell him about the woman, and how I nearly made a mistake. He shifted uneasily. Stern had made no attempt to see Natalya Meretskova either — or so it seemed. Now why was that?

At Number Eighteen Stoliarny Street, Natalya was anxiously rearranging the contents of three travelling bags. She folded Anna's dress, noticing for the first time how worn the cuffs were. There will be other dresses, she thought — in Finland.

Somebody flushed the lavatory upstairs and water gushed down the pipe outside the room. Nervous, the night sounds of the house assumed a significance of their own to her. She paused and looked around the room. 'How little we are leaving behind.'

'We shall start again.' Rykov toyed with the revolver for a moment, and frowning he slid it back under the mattress.

'Anna and I had so much. But we never really *owned* anything. Apart from Ustreka, the palace and the estates were merely places we lived in — too big to possess.' And my furs seemed no warmer than this old army greatcoat. She laid it over the foot of the bed and smoothed it. One becomes attached to the most unlikely things.

Another twenty minutes before Stern would arrive. The tension was making time drag. 'I wonder who lives at Ustreka now? Perhaps the local Soviet has turned it into a hospital or a school. I remember my brother returning from the hunt with the dogs. Last night I tried to visualize each room in turn, but I couldn't recall the shape of the study.'

Rykov smiled. 'I remember it. I also remember you there, reading the books. You were very gawky and thin, with your hair in plaits. Always asking questions.'

'Was I really thin? Yes, I suppose I was. And rather foolish.'

Rykov continued to smile. 'Oh, infinitely foolish. But with a charm that completely captivated me.' He paused. Something in Natalya's expression suggested to him that he shouldn't continue. He looked at the clock and took a deep breath. There was little time left. 'You had a determined incorruptibility that you have retained despite everything, Natalya.'

That wasn't true. Natalya bit her lip. What of Peter Koltsov waiting tonight? He needed something from her, she knew it. He had tentatively reached out to her, before she had proposed that bargain.

She busied herself again. How could she have given him

293

'what he needed just with her body? And it was too late to think about it now. 'Is the Cheka man still walking up and down?'

Rykov went to the window. 'No. He is in a doorway.' He stared down at the street. This had been his only view of Petrograd for months. And there were times when he had been very happy in this room. He was half afraid to leave. How would he manage the climb over the rooftops? 'Is Anna all right? — she hasn't taken her scarf.'

'It is quite warm under the door to the roof, heat from the house rises. Don't worry about her. Captain Stern will be here at eight o'clock.' Natalya paused. 'You *do* love her, don't you?'

'Yes.' Rykov looked again at small figures moving in the street below. In a way he did love Anna.

'And will you go on loving her?'

'As long as it makes her happy. Though God knows why she should go on wanting half a man.'

'You have always been very much a man.' Natalya looked at his back. 'Better than most, and better than you think you are.'

Rykov didn't reply.

Anna's key sounded in the lock. She entered with Michael Stern behind her.

At the Smolny Institute in the Rozhdestvenskya District, members of the Petrograd Soviet took their seats for the late meeting. Peter Koltsov sat in his usual place, only half listening as Saratov read endlessly from his pages of statistics on the coal shortage.

Koltsov was still puzzled, frowning, and doodling on the blotting paper. The room filled with tobacco smoke and Kalinin the chairman rose and slightly opened a window, letting in the muted murmur of the city. A train whistle shrieked in the distance. Koltsov looked down at the scribble on the blotting pad. He'd drawn the dome of St Isaac's Cathedral, and a question mark next to it.

He forced himself to listen to Saratov, but after a minute

or two his mind drifted. Why had Stern visited St Isaac's? There was no reason why he shouldn't, but . . . He leaned sideways and whispered to Kalinin that he would be back in a moment, then he went to the next room and telephoned the Europe Hotel. Was Captain Stern there?

'No, Commissar. The English captain paid his bill and left an hour ago. Is there anything I can do?'

'No.' And he put the telephone down. Something *was* wrong. He could feel it. He picked up the phone again and asked the operator to connect him with the Cheka building, and he waited impatiently, drumming his fingers until he was answered.

'What were Natalya Meretskova's movements today?'

There was a pause. 'The citizeness went to the hospital in the usual way, Commissar. She returned to her rooms in Stoliarny Street at six thirty this evening.'

'Nothing different?'

'Nothing different, Commissar.'

Koltsov pondered. 'She spoke to nobody on her way to the hospital or on the return?'

'No, Commissar. She stopped briefly at St Isaac's Cathedral whilst going . . .'

Koltsov slammed the telephone down.

Where was Stern now? Losing the surveillance man, no doubt. He chewed his thumbnail for a moment, then he snatched his coat and cap from the rack. Stern had a visa for Finland.

Across the city, Michael Stern was leading the way over the roofs of Stoliarny Street and stumbling clumsily in the darkness. God Almighty! The snow kept sliding away under him. He turned to help Rykov who was already gasping for breath, and they continued, edging their way to the fire escape that gave access to the alleyway at the rear of the houses. Stern paused, waiting for Anna and Natalya to join them. Could they manage the next part? He peered over the roof's edge. Why does ascent seem easier? — you fall just as far.

The fire escape was old, rusting. It creaked on its crumbling mountings as he swung himself out over the edge and began his way down. Near the bottom he paused and listened, then dropped the last seven feet. The others followed and he supported each of them in turn as they lowered themselves down to the alleyway. Whispering to them to remain silent, he walked quickly to the corner and looked to where Rantalla was waiting with the cab.

'Hurry, Excellency!' The old man hissed. 'We have little time.'

As the cab moved through the streets towards the Alexandrovsky Bridge, Rykov slowly recovered his breath. He looked down at himself. Stern's uniform was a little too big for him, but it was unlikely that anybody would notice. The city confused him. He glanced out of the window. Months in that quiet room, and now he felt dizzy from the sounds and movement. He clenched his teeth as a lorry rumbled noisily past.

Stern was watching him. Rykov would have to walk through the crowds of the Finland Station. 'Are you all right, Captain?'

Rykov nodded.

'Very well, we'll go through it all once more. The ladies have excellent forged papers — nobody will question them. And you, Captain, have my passport with an exit visa for Finland. Rantalla has purchased four railway tickets. We will wait at the entrance to the station while he parks the cab where his cousin will find it. When he joins us we walk to the barrier. I have a platform ticket and I'll carry the two biggest bags — the railway officials and Red Guards will assume that I am the English officer's servant.'

He glanced reassuringly at Rykov. 'The English behave with polite arrogance, as if the train really belongs to them. Walk slightly ahead with Rantalla and Anna until you find a first class carriage. I will follow with the Countess. When the train leaves, trust Rantalla. He will look after you all.'

The cab moved slowly in the night traffic, then they crossed the river to the Vyborg side. Soon the Finland

Station loomed ahead and Rantalla called down to them. 'We are nearly there.'

Now the dangerous part. Stern looked at them each in turn. 'When we leave the cab, act naturally; talk, laugh, you are going on a visit.'

'You haven't yet told us how *you* intend to escape, Captain.' Natalya said.

He smiled. 'Are you concerning yourself in my life, madam? Don't worry. I'll leave the city by the Vyborg Road and walk. It is seventeen miles to Bielostorov just this side of the frontier. The River Sestro will be frozen. I'll cross and be in Raiaioko in Finland before dawn.'

'What then?'

'Why, madam, I'll just keep walking until I catch up with you.'

She frowned. 'I think it is a little more dangerous than that. Even for a knight errant.' The cab stopped.

They climbed down and waited at the station entrance. Stern stood slightly apart from the others, guarding the bags. He glanced round, noting the militia men some twenty yards away. He tried to look like an officer's servant, but felt like a British officer clumsily disguised and wearing a placard announcing his true intentions. Nobody even glanced at him. The old coat belonging to Rantalla's cousin smelt of the cab horse, and the soft cap was a shade too small for his head. He watched Natalya out of the corner of his eye. She was managing to look quite calm and appeared to be recounting an anecdote of the day. Anna wore a frozen smile and Rykov's jaw was set hard.

The station was crowded. Somewhere a train shunted and blasted steam. Rantalla reappeared, walking towards them with his long loose stride.

'Well, we are ready, Excellency,' he murmured.

'Right. Now let us play out our roles.'

'I'll not see you until Finland, Excellency. God be with you.'

'And you, old man.'

They walked across the station to the barrier of the

Helsingfors platform. No militia! Stern could barely believe their luck. 'Smile,' he whispered to Natalya. 'You are going on holiday.'

Rykov's foreign uniform seemed of brief interest to the railway officials, but they casually examined the tickets and papers then nodded.

Miraculously they had passed onto the platform without question. The express train was waiting, second and third class carriages already filling. Night mist merged with steam from the engine, curling slowly under the hissing orange lamps, and in the spaces between, the platform was shadowy, shapes indeterminate.

Stern slowed his pace. His heart was thumping unpleasantly. He allowed Anna, Rykov and Rantalla to get twenty yards ahead and shifted the heaviest bag to his other hand. 'You are frowning again,' he murmured to Natalya.

'I keep expecting somebody to call to us to stop,' she whispered. 'And we are actually about to board a train for Finland!'

It's all too easy, he thought. 'We are not safe yet, Countess.'

Rantalla had found a first class carriage and he was helping Anna and Rykov into it. He looked back, waiting for Natalya and Stern.

Only a few more yards. Stern breathed deeply. Once they are on the train they'll be safe — half an hour to the frontier. The debt will be paid and it doesn't matter a damn what happens to me. 'When we reach the carriage, get straight into it, Countess. Don't delay. Don't say anything.'

'I'll not rest until you reach Helsingfors, Captain.'

He felt his face whiten with shock and he stopped. 'Alas, Countess. None of us may reach there.'

Peter Koltsov had moved out of the shadows into the circle of yellow light cast by the hissing platform lamp. Behind him were six Red Guards with rifles. Mist shrouded them and Natalya remembered her dream of the previous night. She gripped Stern's arm tightly. He slowly lowered the bags. 'Oh God!' he said.

Koltsov stepped forward and stood, expressionless, in front of Natalya. 'Citizeness Natalya Alexandrovna Meretskova, you are under arrest.'

Stern held her hand. 'Don't do it, Peter! Let her go.'

Koltsov shook his head.

'But it's no good, Peter. She's no real use to the Cheka — or you.'

Koltsov spoke softly so that the guards wouldn't hear. 'You and the others may go, Michael. Natalya Meretskova stays. There are no options.'

'Please, Peter. I saved you once.'

Koltsov's face softened momentarily. 'And now I'm saving you. Board the train quickly.'

Natalya pulled herself free from Stern and turned to face him. Her face was pale. 'Don't blame yourself, Captain. You did your best — the best that could be done.'

'I'm so very sorry,' he said.

'Debts have to be paid, one way or another. Please go. Look after Anna and Rykov.' And she turned to Peter Koltsov.

Two of the guards edged Stern towards the carriage. He pushed their rifles aside, but Koltsov shook his head. 'No options. Go now.'

'Damn you and your Cheka!' His shoulders sagged and he gave up. The train juddered and began to move, and he climbed up onto the step.

Koltsov raised his hand in a small gesture of farewell. 'Don't come back, Michael.'

Stern remained on the step as the long line of carriages clanked slowly out of the station. Soon the figure of Natalya was small in the circle of light. She stood quite still, flanked by Red Gaurds, watching the receding train.

27

'How long has he been drinking like this?'

'Since we arrived in Helsingfors, Your Honour.' Rantalla led the way, half-supporting Stern up the stairs and into the hotel bedroom. Stern swayed for a moment then crashed backwards into a chair. Colonel Southgate scowled at him.

'His Excellency doesn't like himself very much, if you understand me.' The old man bent and pulled off Stern's boots.

'He's going to like himself even less when I get through with him.' Southgate cupped his hand under the younger man's jaw, lifting it into the light. 'Well now, Michael. This is all a bit excessive, isn't it?'

Stern opened his eyes cautiously. He recognized the Colonel and jerked his head free. 'Go to hell!'

'This is not quite our style, Michael. I didn't expect to find you looking like a derelict seaman.'

He stared up at Southgate through bloodshot eyes. 'You tricked us. You knew all along that the Countess wouldn't leave without Rykov, and you knew Koltsov would never let her go. You expected us to fail.'

'And you did. So my expectations were met.'

'It was all a gesture.' He rested his aching head. 'A gesture to convince the French and the Japanese and get them to commit themselves.'

'Blame yourself, Michael. I needed a week, that's all. I was sure that you'd go to Petrograd, see that it was impossible, then return — perhaps with some of the jewellery. I didn't think that even you would go ahead with the escape bid after you'd seen what you were up against. That attempt of yours wasn't just foolhardy, it was ridiculous.'

He felt more than ridiculous. 'They'll shoot her, won't they?'

'Damn it! How do I know!' The Colonel looked uneasy and suddenly old. 'It's no longer our problem. We can tell the French we did our best. And the Japanese are losing interest — they've decided to support Semenov instead. He's another Cossack with a band of cutthroats, so it doesn't matter any more what Malnekov does, or what happens to him.'

'And the Countess was just an expendable pawn in a game we are no longer playing.' Stern got unsteadily to his feet. 'Because of our meddling she is now in a Cheka cell.'

'Oh, for God's sake! She never stood much of a chance anyway. The Bolsheviks would have arrested her sooner or later. You got the sister and Rykov out so you achieved something.'

'I didn't even do that. Koltsov let them go.'

Southgate had had enough soul-searching for one night. 'We can't win every battle. Rantalla will take Rykov and the sister to Stockholm — they can't stay here in Helsingfors with the damned Reds flexing their muscles. I tell you, Michael, the disorders in Finland are just additional evidence of the inability of foreigners to order their lives decently and efficiently.' He sniffed and watched Stern's face. 'You and I are returning to Murmansk in the morning. Go to bed. I'll see you at breakfast. Seven o'clock sharp. And I want you sober, shaved and respectably dressed. Got it?' He grunted to Rantalla and left the room.

'Damn him!' Stern paced up and down trying to clear his head. 'Was that escape bid so ridiculous, old man?'

'You very nearly made it work, Excellency.'

'Nearly? Peter Koltsov could have arrested us all.'

'Not you and I.' Rantalla considered. 'He owed us one favour.'

'Now he owes us nothing. And if I went back . . .'

'He would kill you,' Rantalla said quickly. 'Put the idea out of your head, Excellency.'

Southgate returned to his own room, and frowning he went to bed, moving around and trying to get comfortable on the unfamiliar mattress. Stern had always been a bit of an embarrassment. He continued to frown into the darkness. The army was commissioning most unlikely riff-raff these days. Oh, Stern was a good engineer, he'd concede that, and quite useful for certain jobs. But it went against the grain, having to use people like that. They should never have let the damned man out of India.

At seven next morning the Colonel waited impatiently for Stern to join him for breakfast in the crowded dining room. He started on his kipper but kept glancing at the clock. By seven fifteen he was angry, kipper ruined, and he left and went quickly to Stern's room. Empty! The bloody man had gone!

'Rantalla!' he roared and stumped next door, pushing in without knocking. 'Where is Captain Stern?'

'On his way to Petrograd, Your Honour.' Rantalla was hurriedly packing. 'I found this note under my door when I woke.'

> Old man,
>   Don't follow me. You are too good a friend to lose. Wait for me at Rautta this side of the frontier. I may need you.
>   Stern

Southgate cursed silently and he closed his eyes. If Stern ever got back he would pay for this. He'd have him sent to the filthiest outpost in the Empire. Rantalla had resumed his packing. 'Where the hell are you going?'

'To Rautta, Your Honour.'

'You're being paid by the British Government. Go to Rautta and you break your contract — you'll not get a penny.'

'Captain Stern may need me.'

'Are *you* insane as well?'

Rantalla screwed up his face and considered slowly. 'Yes. I think I am, Your Honour. It is an infection. I must have caught it off the British.'

Michael Stern knew better than to try entering Russia by the more obvious routes. He travelled to the Finnish town of Vyborg. From there a railway branch line straggled east-

302

wards to the frontier village of Rautta, and there it stopped.

He climbed down from the carriage and looked around in the faint light of the dying day. The single tracks of the railway ended a hundred yards further on among high timber stacks. He had bought a shaggy coat — fur turned inwards for warmth, and unshaven and with a soft cap he looked no different from the other arrivals who were swinging their bundles down from the train.

The village was small; log huts covered with snow and lit by oil lamps. Beyond the last dwellings the country was raw, dotted with frozen morass and small lakes. Now it was dead, white-covered, stretching off to forests of pine and fir. The frontier followed the frozen Sestro but the remaining twenty miles separating Russia from Finland was unmarked and with only occasional clusters of log dwellings for the border patrols. Wolves strayed south through the winter forest and at daylight their tracks were sometimes seen in the village. The chances of crossing safely into Russsia were better here.

Stern walked a little behind the other travellers. There was no hotel and he went to a drinking den lit by candles.

The drink served was fiery, warming him. I'll wait for the moon, he thought, then head for Grusino on the Russian side.

To Anna and Rykov he had described his plan of rescue as flexible, but that hardly disguised the uncertainties ahead of him. Their faith in his ability had surprised him. Anna had thrust all the money she had into his hands. But her money and his own would hardly be sufficient for bribery on the scale he envisaged.

He took another cautious sip of the spirit and kept his eyes on the other occupants of the dimly lit room. The border villages were part of a strange no-man's-land attracting a mix of spies, opportunist idealists and scoundrels. And Bolshevik agents? It would be wise to make sure he wasn't followed when he left.

He waited another hour then went out, buttoning his coat. And he stood for a moment, accustoming himself to the darkness and watching to see if anybody else emerged, then he set off, following the last hundred yards of railway track. The moon would be up soon. Six miles to the frontier, another seven to Grusino and the Russian railhead. Then Petrograd.

Even though it was nearly Spring, Petrograd was still dark at nine in the morning. For those in the cells of the Cheka building, time had a different meaning. It was measured by familiar sounds. Natalya knew the hour by the clanking of buckets in the passageway outside. Her pulse quickened as the key turned in the lock and she stood as the door swung open. 'Prisoner Meretskova, come with me.'

She followed the guard along a dark, stone corridor, then up narrow steps and past the communal cells. Twenty or so women were crowded in each cage. They glanced at her, listlessly indifferent. The guard led her along another now familiar passage that took them past the rear door of the general office crowded with typists and clerks. She had become used to the daily journey and slowed her pace as the guard reached the interrogation room.

He opened the door and jerked his head for her to enter, then locked it behind her. She stood quite still for a moment, listening. No sound ever penetrated the door. It was always the same room. To calm herself she tried to imagine the ordinariness of the daily procedure. Somewhere in the building there was a clerk whom she would never see. Each morning he must pencil her name on a list, allocating her an hour in this room.

It smelt of fear and disinfectant. The walls were bare brick. Once there had been a window high up, but it had been filled in leaving just a small metal grille leading to a ventilation shaft. A single bright bulb was set behind glass in the ceiling. It cast a harsh light on the wooden table and two hard chairs. The floor was wet by the far wall. Somebody had mopped it just before she had arrived. Natalya sat cautiously on the edge of a chair. A room is just a room, she thought. Bricks cannot retain fear.

It was altogether strange. Natalya knew that she would

feel calm again when Peter Koltsov arrived and resumed the investigation. The daily repetition of even her secret thoughts in an elaborate ritual of question and answer was like a Catholic confession. And peace came when Koltsov closed his note book and lit a cigarette. Strange also was the feeling that she had learned far more about him than he had ever intended; from the way he paused, rephrased, altered his expression, or toyed with the matchbox. Perhaps he wouldn't come today? The thought made her anxious. Perhaps it would be somebody else! She stood, nervously smoothing her hair. Please don't let it be anybody else.

Keys rattled. Peter Koltsov entered and closed the door behind him. 'Good morning. Please sit.' He placed the notebook on the table and took out his pen, carefully buttoning the pocket of his tunic before he took his place at the table.

She is less afraid today, he thought. And she works hard to hide her fear. His harsh voice grated. 'We shall go back over your statement of your relationship with the criminal, Malnekov.' He glanced at his notes, though he didn't really need to. 'You first met him the day before your nineteenth birthday, at the residence of the one-time Baroness Kleinmichael. You became his mistress six months later. Tell me about that. Did you admire him?'

'Yes.'

'Explain why.' Koltsov leaned back. It is like a drug, he thought, hearing her repeat it over and over again. But the frown was on his thoughts. This time he must take the questions to their conclusion.

Natalya began again. 'I was young. General Malnekov had authority and he was handsome. And I was flattered by his interest in me. I had never met anybody so certain — so sure of his opinions and abilities.'

He only half listened. He knew every opinion Malnekov had ever expressed to her. He watched her carefully, noting the slight movements of her hands. The cuffs of her dress were soiled, but he knew the cells were filthy — there was never time to clean them. She was looking down and there were shadows under her eyes, making her palely attractive. He felt a sharp pang of concern. Today he would have to persuade her to disown Malnekov. She had stopped speaking. 'Why have you paused?'

She hesitated. 'I had thought that you were no longer listening.'

'Continue.'

'General Malnekov's opinions hardened when it became clear that His Imperial Majesty's government was no longer capable of conducting the war. He continually urged . . .'

Koltsov glanced at his notes again. She had repeated the story so many times she had it word perfect. Now to break the pattern. He interrupted her. 'What did you think about the atrocity committed by Malnekov and his Cossacks in Znamenskya Square?'

She stopped, startled. The sudden deviation from the pattern confused her. 'I — I was shocked.'

'Shocked? Is that all? Come now. The man you thought you loved was suddenly revealed to you as a criminal.'

She squeezed her fingers together. 'I was shocked and disgusted. But later I wondered what pressures were on him to make him do such a thing.' And she continued, not waiting for Koltsov's questions. 'I wondered, you see, if it was in some way because of me. I had gone to him the night before and I told him the affair was over.'

Now Koltsov was anxious to steer her admissions. 'Malnekov's history reveals him for what he is; Chita, the useless and bloody campaign in the Carpathians, the massacre here in the city. You had realized that you could not love such a man. Answer, please.'

Natalya bit her lip. 'I felt sorry for him.'

'But you no longer loved him.'

'I no longer thought I loved him.'

Koltsov leaned forward. He must get her to say only what he wanted her to say — enough to persuade her to sign the statement. 'You are revolted by his actions against the Russian people.'

Natalya nodded.

'If you were free and Malnekov came to you, you would not be able to give yourself to him. You would reject him in disgust? Answer, please.'

'I would reject him,' she said softly.

We both disgust her, Koltsov thought, and for a moment he was almost able to identify with Malnekov. 'And you would now agree that Malnekov has, by his atrocities, placed himself outside existing law. And that by raising an army to plunder the country's communications on the Manchurian frontier he has become nothing more than a common bandit.'

Natalya nodded again.

'Then you would be prepared to sign a statement indicating your total rejection of the activities of Malnekov and other such Tsarist bandits. And that you align yourself with the struggle of the people against Tsarist tyranny?'

'No. I cannot say that! It isn't *all* true!' Natalya twisted her handkerchief in her fingers.

Koltsov sighed, then leaned forward again. 'Listen to me, Natalya Alexandrovna. You are already charged with treason. In the last few days, Peoples' Commissar Dzerzhinsky, Chairman of the Extraordinary Commission to Fight Counter Revolution, has taken an interest in your case. He has drawn the statement up. It would be useful to our cause if you signed it. If you do not sign it the matter will be taken out of my hands.' He stood and began walking up and down the room, frowning to himself. 'I don't want this to happen. You have agreed that Malnekov is a bandit. Sign the statement and I may be able to save you.' He turned to her. 'There is little time left.'

'I *do* loathe what he did!' Natalya cried passionately. 'But I think I loved him once. I cannot betray him. And I cannot say I align myself with you! You are doing the same things.' She looked quickly round the interrogation room. 'All the things that the old Tsarist police did in this building. You took it all over from them, and you use it as they did.'

'But only because of the most pressing necessity!' Koltsov

almost shouted. 'We are trying to claw our way up out of the rubble of the old corrupt rule. The revolution is precariously held. We are ringed round with enemies; the Volunteer Army in the south, Malnekov, Semenov and the Japanese in the east, Germany in the west. And the British, who say one thing but plot another in the north at Murmansk. And here in the city there are those who would betray us — sell us out to the foreign interventionists. We have to use whatever means we can to save the revolution. Can't you understand that?'

'Yes! I understand! I know you want to build a new and just world — but you cannot do it this way. If you do, you'll be no better than those who oppressed you. What you build will be different from what you intend. That is why I can't sign the statement. Can you understand *me*?'

Koltsov stared at her. She was lost.

Slowly he sat, and he lit a cigarette and blew smoke up at the light — it fanned out across the ceiling. She wouldn't change her mind, so there was nothing he could do for her. He felt a dull ache.

'That night I came to the hospital — you remember?'

'Yes.'

'You were very tired. You bound my ribs. I greatly admired you. Perhaps you sensed that?'

'No, I didn't.' Natalya smiled very slightly, surprised that she was at last able to talk to Peter Koltsov as a human being. 'You frightened me, but I saw what they had done to your back.'

Koltsov gestured almost impatiently, as if his wounds and scars had ceased to be of any significance. 'I was sentenced to twenty years as a convict. I thought I would die on that railway. Sometimes I had dreams of escaping — running to the south, free of my shackles. And I would reach a forest where I was safe. You were always there, somewhere in the dream.' He frowned. 'But I would wake, the shackles still on my ankles.'

Natalya nodded slowly. 'I dream too.'

'Of what?'

'Of this room.'

He leaned forward. 'Then I am in *your* dream.'

'Sometimes. Sometimes I am alone in the silence.'

Koltsov rubbed his hand over his eyes. 'Tell me. If Michael Stern had not tried to smuggle you out of Russia, would you have kept your word and come to me?'

'Yes.'

'Though the thought was distasteful to you?'

'Yes.'

He almost winced. 'The question is now academic. If I could offer you your freedom on the same terms, would you accept?'

'No, Commissar.'

'The thought is still distasteful to you?'

'No! It's not that. It's not like that at all.' She looked down. How could she explain to him? 'Strangely I wish that I could keep my word to you. But I know that I cannot compromise any more. Do you understand me?'

'Yes.' The dull ache within him had become a pain. She was again the woman who had bound his ribs — the woman of his dream when he was a convict. She had revealed that part of him that he had concealed even from himself, and given him the one thing the Party couldn't give. And he had lost her.

She sensed his thought. 'What will happen to me?'

He began pacing the room, unable to look at her. 'You will leave here in two days' time. There will be an administrative hearing at the Deryabinsky Prison — merely a formality.' He tailed off.

'Then I will be shot?'

He stopped in his tracks, staring at the wall in front of him. 'Yes.'

Her voice was small. 'Will I see you again?'

'Yes. In the afternoon before you leave here.' He turned to her, his face pale. 'Is there anything I can do for you?'

Bewildered, she shook her head, then looked down at her hands. 'I would be grateful for some water to wash with.'

'Yes,' he said. 'The cells are filthy.' And he rubbed his eyes, frowning to himself. 'There is never time, you see.'

'I understand.'

309

He grasped her hand tightly, unwilling to let her give up her life. 'Please think carefully. Reconsider. Sign the statement and I will see that you live. We have only the here and now and you are too young to throw it all away.'

Natalya looked at his hand clasping hers. Strange. I could stay like this, and never feel afraid. She shook her head. 'I cannot sign the statement.'

Koltsov released her and he turned to the door, hesitating before he opened it. 'Yours is a lost and discredited cause. Why must you die for it?'

'It had *some* nobility,' Natalya said.

The guard came and took her along the corridor. He paused for a moment and stuck his head into the rear door of the general office, speaking rapidly to the girl with the large breasts. Natalya had a brief glimpse of freedom beyond the office and entrance hall of the Cheka building, then the guard took her back to her cell where daylight never penetrated. The door slammed behind her, and she was alone again in the silence.

She sat on her hard bunk and rested her head in her hands. I'm afraid again now, she thought, strong only when I am with him.

The guard came back with a bucket of water and a small piece of hard soap. He seemed suddenly respectful. 'Orders of the Commissar.'

It would be better to fill the time until she was too tired to stay awake. Natalya washed herself and some of her clothes. Why was she being so sparing with the soap — it only had to last for two days? Such is human hope. She hung the clothes to dry on the iron frame of the bunk. Fear suddenly welled in her. She would sleep just two more times on that bunk. She took up the clothes and began washing each of them again, taking as long as she could.

28

Morning lectures had ended and students were streaming along the corridor and down the wide staircase to the university refectory. Helen could hear their voices as they passed Zubov's office. A girl laughed, then sang

'Out of the realms of blizzards, ice and snow
How fresh and pure your month of May leaps forth.'

Helen paused from typing. Had she ever been as young as them? That first student year seemed a lifetime ago. All those high hopes. Before Zubov. Before Baumler. A catalogue of failure. She finished typing the letter and put an envelope in the machine.

It was extremely odd the way she'd got through the last week in a quite mechanical fashion; work, and even conversation with Zubov, quite separate from her real thoughts. Zubov hadn't appeared to notice any change in her. Much of the time we are like a pair of sleepwalkers, she thought, making appropriate noises but barely aware of each other's presence.

Another half hour to her lunchtime. Helen put fresh paper into the typewriter. The question of what to do next had to be faced. Baumler had been extremely foolish to reject her. He needed her even though he hadn't yet realized it. But he wasn't going to change his mind, and the days were trickling away. She stared at the paper in the machine — she'd typed the same line twice.

Helen indicated to Zubov that she would be gone for a few moments. He merely nodded, preoccupied with his files, and she went across the hallway to the toilet to waste ten minutes. Combing her hair, she looked at herself in the mirror. Perhaps I should return to Terioki and marry Cousin Erik, she thought, that is if he hasn't already proposed to the mayor's daughter. She examined herself,

311

frowning slightly. Cousin Erik would do — he'd be rich one day. And sleepy as Terioki was, her nights would certainly not be dull. She pulled her hair back fiercely and clipped it. Why do I even hesitate?

She returned to the office, and entering quietly she could hear Professor Zubov speaking on the telephone.

'Yes, Commissar. Quite so, Commissar.'

The change in Zubov's expression was startling. Helen sat at her desk, tidying it before going to lunch, and half watching the Professor. His face was pale and his mouth twitched slightly.

He replaced the files in the drawer with his free hand. 'I understand, Commissar. But as the person in question is terminating business, I cannot see what I can do . . .' Zubov rested his head on his hand and listened, eyes widening. 'I would not want you to think . . . But, Commissar!'

Helen heard a distinct click.

Zubov continued to hold the telephone, staring at it, his face now an unhealthy colour. Then he put it down and suppressed a retch, stuffing his handkerchief into his mouth.

Helen watched astonished as he got up, almost running out of the door and across the hall to the toilets. He is demented, she thought. And he has gone out and left his drawer unlocked! Helen rose quickly and went over to Zubov's desk.

Zubov stood over the lavatory and was sick — stomach muscles contracting violently. Slowly he washed and got a grip on himself. Come what may, he'd have to keep going. He went back to the office, and he remembered the unlocked files.

Helen was busy typing. 'How does one spell perfidious, Professor? Is it one ''f'' or two?'

He looked at the files in the drawer. They were just as he'd left them. 'One ''f''.'

Helen smiled. 'Thank you.'

'I have a headache, Helen. I'll go out for a while.'

'Take care, Professor.'

Zubov walked in the cold afternoon. He crossed Vassili

312

Island, beyond the area of factories, slums and dockyards, until he came to where the hard, frozen marshlands merged with the ice-covered Gulf. Far across the white desolation lay the fortress of Kronstadt, barely visible. He peered into the fine, grey mist. What a sham his life had become. Even my wife has at last seen through me. And he reflected for a moment on the emptiness of his house since Madame Zubov had left, quite suddenly, with an ex-Tsarist cavalry officer. How can I blame her? Koltsov has exposed my true self. I might never have known what I really am. Perhaps I should feel grateful. Even if I had never betrayed anybody, I was guilty by inclination. If one day we are judged, surely we must answer for all the sins we would have committed if we'd had the opportunity. Perhaps I should end it all — now? The thought startled him with its sudden simplicity. Why not walk out onto the ice, and lie down, and sleep? All of his problems would be resolved and he would cheat Koltsov.

He stepped tentatively onto the ice, feeling its hardness under his feet, and he began to walk. A wilderness, he thought. It's like another world — grey and still, and with a knowledge of its own.

Soon the frozen marshlands were small behind him. Kneeling, he placed his hands on the cold surface, then stretched out face down. The ice was like fire. Who would write his epitaph? What would they say of him? He began to compose one inside his head. But God, that awful coldness was eating into him! How long would it take? They would find his body, decomposing, somewhere along the shore when summer came. Bloated and decomposing. By then the epitaph would be forgotten — and so also would he, quite quickly. He sat up. Oblivion had lost its brief appeal.

Somebody was shouting to him and he turned. A man on the marshlands waved and shouted again. Zubov got stiffly to his feet, his teeth chattering. Well, it hadn't really been such a good idea. Feeling foolish he began to walk back towards the man on the marshland. Who knows, the world might change. Maybe something would happen to Koltsov.

Glancing down he saw the broken-off head of a coach bolt ground into the ice. He bent down, and then he could see the very faint tracks of sleigh runners. How odd, he thought. Who would drive a sleigh in over the frozen Gulf? And he trudged on. The lights of the city were already appearing against the immensity of the grey twilight beyond.

Helen had waited, almost sick with anxiety, for five thirty to come. Never had an afternoon lasted so long. She crossed the Dvortzovi Bridge to the telegraph office in St Isaac's Square. Hastily she scribbled a cable, then she paused and slowly tore it up. It would have to be worded with extreme care. Who would have thought that Professor Zubov could be so treacherous! A file on her — all her telephone conversations with Martin Baumler. The Professor was obviously working for the Cheka. Her hands trembled. How inviting Terioki now seemed. But part Finlander as she was, the Petrograd Cheka would never willingly let her go — not now. Even now they could be waiting for just the right moment to pounce. She swallowed, suppressing her panic. There was only one possibility open to her. She must persuade Cousin Erik to make a final journey before the ice broke up on the Gulf. She began writing again, then paused to re-read the cable form.

PLEASE COME ONCE MORE BEFORE SPRING STOP I NEED YOU SO MUCH STOP HELEN

It looked innocuous enough. An impassioned cry to a lover perhaps. Cousin Erik was no fool. And he would come if he could. Helen bit her lip. If he could.

29

Sadovaya Street widens at Hay Square and the sprawling area of markets and filthy courts and alleyways. Dostoevsky had lived here fifty years before. There were hard traders selling pots and pans, old furniture, bric-à-brac, old books. And others, penniless, sold the clothes off their backs. It was said that souls could be bought here. Because of the 'bag men' profiteering in food from outside the city, the market was frequently raided. Popov glanced anxiously round and tried to keep up with the rapidly moving Baumler who was pushing his way through the crowds. He clutched Baumler's arm. 'But what did they say?'

'It's all settled. I've seen the American Consul again. I should get my visa tomorrow.'

'Promise you will go, Mr Baumler.'

'Oh, I'll go all right. Tomorrow night.' And he frowned to himself. Why did thoughts of Helen intrude every time he made another arrangement towards getting out? He looked around. 'Now where the hell are the second hand clothes sellers?'

'Over to the right. Why are we going there?'

'We are going to meet an old friend,' Baumler said, and pushed his way forward.

'I don't have any friends. I only have enemies.' Popov blinked and looked at Baumler suspiciously. 'Who is he?'

'An Englishman. Captain Stern.'

'Oh God! He's come back!' Popov halted and whispered frantically. 'You cannot *do* this to me, Mr Baumler. I will not move another step.'

Baumler grabbed his arm and hustled him on. 'You want to get out of Russia too, don't you — and with some money to make a new start?'

'Yes, yes! But what do I have to *do* for it?'

They reached a huge shed; just three walls and a roof.

People were milling around the traders, turning over the old clothes and shouting their offers. Baumler looked quickly round, and he stopped and smiled slightly in the direction of the tall young man in the shaggy sheepskin coat, yellow hair under his soft cap.

'There he is. Come on.'

'It is madness to talk to him here!' Popov murmured. 'Signal to him and I will lead the way to the house of my illustrious uncle.'

Stern had been waiting for over an hour. And now that old broken tooth was aching again. He trailed behind as the fat little agent led the way out of the market and into Zabalkansky Prospect. Glancing back briefly, Popov turned off into a reeking courtyard and climbed wooden steps to a door on which was chalked a number five.

Stern followed and entered, and when the door closed behind them Baumler clasped his shoulders then hugged him. 'By heavens! It's good to see you! But you're crazy to come back! When I got your telephone call I thought you were speaking from Helsingfors.' And he turned. 'You know Popov. And this is his uncle. We can talk here.'

Popov was torn between his fear and the demands of hospitality. He gestured to a very old man with no teeth, dressed incongruously in a worn astrakhan overcoat. 'Tea, uncle. Bring tea and then leave us.' He turned. 'Sit. Everybody sit and be comfortable.' Grunting, he dragged over two battered chairs for Stern and Baumler. 'We are safe. I took the precaution of never informing my employers of my illustrious uncle who fought with great distinction against the Turks, earning for himself the praise of His Imperial Majesty.'

The old man, mumbling and clattering the mugs, looked too frail to have ever taken up arms. The large, sparsely-furnished room smelt foul and there were mice droppings on the threadbare carpet.

Stern was weary. He opened his coat. A damned long journey, longer than he had expected, across the snow and through the forest, and his muscles ached. Fitful sleep in the crowded third class waggon on the line down from Grusino. He rubbed his hand over his jaw. Bloody tooth, he thought, and none of Rantalla's cloves to ease it.

The old soldier placed the samovar on the table. His voice was a high-pitched wail. 'If Your Excellencies have tobacco for a veteran of Plevna . . .' He tailed off and stood looking like Popov, with his hands clasped.

'Here, have these.' Baumler handed him two cigars. 'And some money for your trouble.'

Popov looked greedy as Baumler peeled off his thick roll and placed twenty roubles on the table. The old man ignored the money but sniffed the cigars, then shuffled off into the next room. Popov scooped up the twenty roubles. 'I will buy him food.' And turning urgently to Stern: 'If you are caught in the city you will certainly be shot, Captain. What possessed you to come back here?'

Stern frowned down at his grimy hands. 'Damned trains are filthy,' he said. 'How can I get the Countess Natalya Meretskova out of the Cheka building?'

If he had asked them how to bring her back from the moon he couldn't have shocked them both more.

Popov gasped. 'Impossible! I will have nothing to do with it! She is being moved to the Deryabinsky tomorrow for execution.' He blinked uncontrollably. 'Absolutely impossible. Even if you got her out of the Cheka building, there is nowhere you could take her.'

'I'd take her over the frontier by the same route I came in.'

'Impossible.'

'Don't keep saying that, Mr Popov. Start thinking positively.'

'You want to make a fresh start, don't you?' Baumler added. 'Far away, maybe in America or England.'

Popov groaned. 'But how will *I* get out of Russia?'

Stern leaned forward. 'If you help me get the Countess out of the Cheka building, I'll take you through the forest and into Finland.'

Popov had spent all his life in the city. 'There are wolves

in the forest.' He wrung his hands. 'And Red patrols.'

'I didn't see any.' Stern smiled. 'Not one wolf, or a Red patrol. Lies. We'll go to Grusino. Then we'll just walk. The frontier isn't even marked. And when we get to Rautta, a friend of mine — Rantalla — will be waiting. We'll be safe.'

Popov looked agitated. 'You make it sound so *easy*. To get the Countess out of the Cheka building I would have to take terrible risks.'

'For which you would be handsomely paid,' Baumler added.

'The Countess isn't just an ordinary prisoner.' Popov licked his dry lips. 'Commissar Koltsov has a personal interest in her. The expense of arranging an escape would be very heavy and still the chances would be slim.'

'Suggest a figure, Mr Popov,' Stern said.

'You would take me out anyway, even if we failed?'

'Yes.'

Popov took a deep breath. 'Thirty-five thousand roubles. Fifteen thousand now and the rest tomorrow after I have talked to some people.'

Stern paused. He didn't have anything like that much. 'I'll give you five thousand now and the other thirty thousand later.'

Popov looked incredulous. 'Five thousand! That will barely bribe one man!'

Baumler groaned and handed over another ten thousand. 'That's on account. See that you deliver.'

Popov did quick sums in his head. 'Then there is the matter of my professional fees. Shall we say another thirty thousand?

Even Baumler gasped. 'God's teeth!'

Stern didn't know where he would get the money, only that somehow he would. 'You shall have it, Mr Popov. When we reach Helsingfors. That is a promise.'

Popov looked surprised, then relieved. 'You are a gentleman, Captain Stern.' And he wrung Stern's hand. 'Your Excellency may remain here. My illustrious uncle will be proud to accommodate you.' He blinked, thinking hard. 'I will not be able to return here tonight. You must meet me at midday tomorrow, on the Yekaterinsky Quay, near the first bridge after the Church of St Saviour on the Blood.'

'I'll be there.' Stern pondered. 'If you succeed in getting the Countess out, I will have to hide her until nightfall — preferably somewhere on the north side of the city. And you will have to meet us.'

Baumler felt uneasy. He knew the safest place would be the run down bungalow he rented at Staraya Derevnya just along the coast where he met with the smuggler. But he was reluctant to disclose its whereabouts in front of Popov. What the hell? He was up to his neck anyway. The smuggler would never come again. 'I know of a place,' he said. He pulled out a scrap of paper and began drawing a map. How many times had he met Helen's cousin there? He scowled as he drew. With luck he'd be out of Russia by train tomorrow night — Petrograd behind him for ever. And Helen. He'd never see her again either — why did he have to keep suppressing that thought?

It was now near one o'clock in the afternoon and across the city Helen had gone to lunch in the university refectory. The queue was moving slowly. She leaned against the wall for a moment before edging forward again. The fair-haired student in front of her was reading a book, and pausing every few moments as if memorizing. Another engineer from the Academy of Science. He smiled at her shyly.

The effort of working as usual and pretending ignorance of Zubov's treachery was beginning to wear Helen down. She felt another surge of anxiety. Why hadn't Cousin Erik answered her cable? Perhaps she had left it too late and the ice was no longer safe.

She reached the counter and took a wedge of bread from the basket. Her bowl was filled with soup and she groped between the crowded tables, trying to find a space. Lenin's poster, flanked by red flags, looked down at them all from the wall. Was Comrade Lenin having cabbage soup today?

She squeezed onto the end of a bench. Yes, as an honest revolutionary, he probably was. Even the deposed Tsar would be having soup — though probably not from choice. So one had to concede that it was all much fairer. She sipped at the soup. It was also devastatingly dull, though she felt much too nervous to really care. Perhaps she should go home and see if Cousin Erik had sent an answering cable?

The young engineering student had searched for a place, and now seated himself opposite her. He smiled shyly again then dipped his bread into his bowl. Helen smiled back briefly. An innocent.

Professor Zubov had arrived and was taking his place at a slightly less crowded faculty table a few yards away. His colleagues were in conversation and Helen wondered if Zubov was once more eavesdropping. She felt disgust, then paused in her thoughts. She was not, after all, entirely blameless. Baumler was still moving about the city, unaware of Zubov's file and the Cheka interest in her and him — or so she had interpreted the situation. Now that the initial feeling of panic had subsided, the question of whether she should find Baumler and warn him was becoming more insistent. Helen ate the rest of her bread. The young engineering student's knee touched hers. Not quite so innocent, she thought, and she drew her knee back out of range. Clearly it would be safer to stay well away from Baumler and quietly leave the city, but there was no denying that the arrival of Bolshevism and its attendant threats posed some interesting ethical problems.

Helen was about to pick up her bowl and return it to the counter, but Zubov had seen her and he came over. 'Ah, Helen.' And he sat in the place vacated by the young engineering student.

She steeled herself and smiled at him. 'What dreadful soup today.' Then she hastily added, 'But of course we should all be thankful to Comrade Lenin.'

'Your landlady telephoned, just after you left the office. She said a cable had arrived for you, and she thought you would be anxious to know its contents.' Zubov glanced searchingly at her face.

Helen groaned inwardly. That *he* should find out about it! She didn't allow her expression to change.

'I took the message down.' He frowned earnestly as if anxious to please. 'Now let me see . . .' And he rumaged in his pocket. 'I had it here somewhere. Ah, yes.'

Whatever it says, I will not look surprised, Helen thought determinedly. And she read.

ARRIVING TWENTY THREE FORTY FIVE
THURSDAY STOP LOVE ERIK

Tomorrow!

'Good news?' Zubov was still watching her face.

'Yes. My cousin.' She folded the paper casually and put it in her bag. 'For months he has been saying in his letters that he will visit Petrograd for a few days.'

'Your cousin from Finland?'

She hesitated almost imperceptibly. 'Yes.' And she sighed. 'How typical of Cousin Erik to arrive on a late train. He is breathtakingly unworldly and impractical, and will of course expect me to have a hotel room booked for him.' Had that sounded convincing?

'But it will be pleasant for you to have news from . . . where is it that he lives?'

'Oh, indeed, it will be pleasant, and I shall enjoy showing him the city,' Helen said, deliberately evading the question. And she added, 'He has always expressed an interest in the arts. I must try to get tickets for the theatre.'

'Ah, perhaps your friend Baumler can help you there. He knows everybody, doesn't he?'

'He is hardly a friend — more an aquaintance,' she said. What a perfidious reptile the Professor was. She gave him her warmest smile.

They returned to the office. I mustn't make one slip, Helen thought. And she worked into the late afternoon, aware from time to time that Zubov was watching her. He's smoking too much again, and that means he's thinking hard.

'Ivan Gordeyev is giving a lecture on the epic poetry of

Finland, Helen — next Monday. Will your cousin still be here then?'

'I'm sure he'll want to stay for that, Professor.'

'I'd like to meet him.'

'He is a studious boy, always at his books.' She put the cover over the typewriter and took her coat from the rack. 'He'll be honoured to meet such a distinguished scholar as yourself.'

One more night to get through, and tomorrow.

As she left for home, Helen paused for just a moment at the embankment wall, looking down at the frozen river curving its way to the Gulf. Spring nearly here, and how strong is that ice?

The white desert of the Gulf stretched for hundreds of miles, far out beyond Terioki and Helsingfors to the distant Baltic. A silent wilderness for much of the year. Moonlit now, the Baltic tide and very slight variations in the temperature were weakening its solid form. Near its rim, where ice met open sea, the hard surface strained, splintering like thunder and a wide crack appeared, zigzagging back. A huge iceberg crumbled off and floated free. Then there was silence again.

At Terioki, thirty miles up the coast from Petrograd, Erik Halla was out in the night down by the harbour, hands deep in his pockets. He sniffed the air. It was still bitterly cold but the weather was on the turn, and not much time left. He calculated in his head the weight of the sleigh and its return load, and he frowned to himself and walked out onto the ice, testing it with his heel. It worried him. Tomorrow or not at all. The night was clear. Far off he could see pinpoints of light from the line of fortresses that he would have to pass, and to the left the single gleam from the coast guard station at Lissy Nos. He frowned to himself and watched for a while, counting the intervals between sudden sweeps of the Kronstadt searchlights probing the ice. One last time, and that would be the end of it. He'd never do it again. Still frowning he turned back to the village of Terioki.

30

Zubov hadn't slept well. His dreams of Helen had been faintly erotic — a confused jumble of impressions; the Finland Station and a man alighting from a night train. Then he had become the man, in Helen's room, groping for her in the darkness.

During the morning seminar with his third year students, he only half attended. Something was nagging at the back of his mind. Helen's cousin was a Finlander and for years the Finns had evaded customs by smuggling. Was the cousin the link in the contraband activities of Baumler?

Zubov pondered the matter as he returned to his office. Helen was filing and seemed preoccupied, frowning to herself. He pretended to work. Why had she evaded when he'd asked her where her cousin was coming from? She'd talked about him in the past — but of course I never really listened to her in those days, he thought. So all I have is a date and a time of arrival of a young man from somewhere in Finland.

'You seem a thousand miles away, Helen.' He smiled at her. 'A visitor coming — you must have a lot to do. Why don't you go to lunch, and take an extra hour?'

'That's very kind of you, Professor.' What is he thinking now? Helen wondered. 'I'll just finish the filing.' And after today I'll never again stand at this cabinet, or type his letters, or feel his eyes on me. Tonight I'll cross the ice, God willing, and the Professor will never see me again. She put the last letter in its folder. All those dreams she'd had of the great city, of wealth and romance. They were just dreams. I'll start a new life, and I'll be satisfied with less. But as she left the office her thoughts returned to Baumler. She wasn't really enjoying the idea of his impending comeuppance.

Alone in the office, Zubov telephoned the Finland Station and asked for the time of trains arriving that night. He waited impatiently, tapping his teeth with his pen until the station official answered. He scribbled the times down on the pad in front of him. 'But there is a train at eleven forty-five, surely?' He frowned. 'There isn't? — you are sure?'

He put the phone back on its hook and stared at it. So Helen had lied. Her cousin must be arriving by some other means — some other route. What route? Zubov chewed his finger nails. If he went to Commissar Koltsov with what he now knew, Helen would be arrested, this very day, and God knows what they would do to her to make her talk. Yet if he failed to reveal what he'd just learned, and somehow she escaped, Koltsov would certainly kill him. It was nearly midday — only a matter of hours before the man was due to arrive from Finland. Zubov pondered his own treacherous nature. What choices does a coward have?

Just before midday Michael Stern left the house of Popov's ancient uncle, and he walked to the Yekaterinsky Canal. There were few people on the quay. Bright hard sunlight reflected off the high, elegant buildings flanking the canal.

He'd spent much of the night working out the escape route, but after that he'd slept soundly. He could do nothing more. Everything hinged on Popov getting the Countess out of the Cheka building. From then on they'll have to kill me if they try to take her back, he thought. No options, Koltsov would say. He slowed his pace as he approached the Church of St Saviour on the Blood.

Popov's moon face was half hidden behind a newspaper. He was leaning against the wrought iron paling at the canal's edge. He didn't look round when Stern stopped a few paces away, casually resting his elbow on one of the stone pillars supporting the paling. Now was the moment Stern feared. Would Popov say that the task was impossible?

Popov lowered the newspaper very slightly and blinked down at the rubbish strewn, half-buried in the ice. 'I cannot stay long, Captain,' he murmured. 'The Countess is to be moved to the Deryabinsky at four o'clock. Before she leaves, Commissar Koltsov is seeing her in interrogation room Number Nine — from two o'clock until three. So we must make our move immediately after that time.'

Stern breathed a small sigh of relief. So Popov would do it.

Popov appeared to be feverish despite the cold. 'Captain, you cannot imagine the problems! The *timing*. I have had to pay four people, and if just one thing goes wrong . . .'

Stern interrupted, looking over Popov's shoulder. 'The arrangements, Mr Popov. Say them quickly. Militiamen are approaching.'

Popov gulped, then gabbled. 'I have done all I can. Be outside the Cheka building at exactly seven minutes past three. Have a warm cloak for the Countess.'

'Right.' Stern watched the militiamen now only thirty paces from them. 'Good fellow.'

And Popov whispered beseechingly, 'Promise you will not leave without me, Captain!'

'If I leave, you will leave with me. You have my word, Mr Popov.'

Popov nodded. 'I trust you, Captain Stern.' He folded his newspaper and returned towards the Cheka building. There are few whom I trust, he thought, but who has ever been able to trust me? Even my own mother — God rest her sanctimonious soul.

The clatter of typewriters in the crowded general office jangled at Popov's stretched nerves, and the girl with the large breasts wondered why he hadn't looked at her. Popov's agitation was such that he could only pretend to work, filling pages with meaningless scribble and trying not to look at the clock. The Countess should be in interrogation now. Oh God, if something should go wrong! Was there time to reverse it all? No, there wasn't. I will have a heart attack, he thought. And painfully slowly the minutes ticked by. Then it was two twenty — two thirty.

In the interrogation room, Peter Koltsov sat opposite Natalya. He had difficulty controlling the movements of his hands, toying first with the matchbox and then with his pen.

Natalya watched him and felt a numb compassion. It was both strange and awful to see him so distressed.

'I will not be kept waiting?'

He shook his head. 'No. The hearing is at seven.'

'And I will be shot immediately after?'

Koltsov nodded, unable to answer. For the first time in his life he wished there was a God.

'My sister. Have you news of her and Captain Rykov?'

He stood and began pacing the room. 'They are still in Helsingfors. Quite safe. The civil unrest has not touched them.'

'Will you please find some way of informing them of . . .'

'Yes.'

What had she not done? Natalya frowned to herself, trying to think of all the commitments of her short life. She had been unable to cry last night. One should at least be able to do that.

Koltsov sat opposite her again and stared down at his clenched hands. There was nothing in his philosophy that could help her through the next few hours. What could he say to her? That if there were more time and fewer threats to the state her death might not be necessary? But what comfort would that be for her to take to her end? He should tell her *something*. Something honest. He started to stretch out his hand to hers, then drew back. 'You have great courage,' he began and screwed up his face in an anguished frown. 'If you had been for *us* we would have been stronger in those early days.'

'A whole way of life divides us, so you have no choice but to shoot me.' Natalya smiled very slightly.

'Don't!' he said, then recovered his composure. 'No, you must say what you wish.' His voice became formal and flat. 'I would like you to know that nobody regrets this day more than I. Your loyalty to your own kind, and your integrity — these will remain an example against which I must measure my own future actions . . .' He stared hopelessly at her. 'That is not what I really wanted to say.'

Natalya suddenly realized how very tired she was. She

leaned across the table and touched his fingers with hers.

'If we could go back in time. Would you do it all again — arrest me?'

He pressed the tips of her fingers under his own, and he nodded slowly. 'Yes. I would do it all again. In the end there is only duty to one's ideals.' His harsh voice dropped to an urgent whisper. 'You see how painful is your example? And I must follow it. It means death for you and bleak years for me. I am cold and hard.' He shook his head, puzzled. 'Now I will turn to ice.'

Natalya felt tears burning her eyes. She *could* cry now. But she would spare him that. 'Do not turn to ice. We may meet again in some other time.'

'If only that were so. No, this life is all.'

'You cannot be sure of that.' Natalya swallowed back her tears.

Koltsov looked frantically at his watch. 'The hour has gone! Our time together has run out!'

'Goodbye, Peter Koltsov,' she whispered.

He stood and opened the door. 'Guard!' He turned and squeezed her hand as the man approached. 'Steel yourself. Your end will be quick and painless. Think of me as if I were by your side. I share this night with you.'

Natalya left the room, barely aware of direction. In a daze she followed the guard along the corridor. He glanced at a clock then indicated a bench. 'Sit there.' And she sat, staring down at her clenched hands. She must act with courage. Peter Koltsov would want to know how she had faced her end.

The guard seemed anxious, repeatedly glancing at the clock. 'Come,' he said. She followed him again. They turned the corner and he paused near the rear entrance of the general office. 'You wish to go to the toilet, miss?'

Natalya stared at him, unable to understand.

The guard looked quickly round, then back to her. 'You *do* wish to use the toilet, miss. Perfectly understandable. All prisoners want to go to the toilet after interrogation. Natural reaction.' And he nodded as though they were both now in agreement. 'I'll fetch one of the women.' He opened the general office door and signalled.

The young woman with the large breasts came out. She glanced at the guard then at Natalya. 'Another one? You think I have nothing else to do.'

The guard shrugged. 'It's regulations. Anyway, this one's for the Deryabinsky.' He eyed Natalya. 'Pity. She's not bad.' Then grinning at the other girl's breasts he added, 'Though you are more my sort — something to get hold of.'

The girl sighed but there was a flicker of interest in her eyes. She led Natalya along the corridor to the toilet. 'Go on. And hurry. You have two minutes.'

Natalya went in and leaned with her back against the door, her eyes closed. She heard the voice of the girl talking loudly to the guard, then the voices receded. Why had the man been so insistent? Perhaps because it gave him an opportunity to talk to the girl. Or maybe he was merely being thoughtful, assuming a need. What difference did it make?

She opened her eyes, and leaning forward, lifted the cover of the lavatory. A slip of paper was stuck to the underside. She stared, then pulled it off. The paper was typewritten under a printed heading. Part of the signature was obliterated by a rubber stamp.

Extraordinary Commission of the Central Executive Committee of the Petrograd Soviet of Workers and Red Army Deputies. 16th April 1918.

This is to certify that Anna Khitrova entered the Petrograd Headquarters of the Executive Committee at 2.30 p.m. and must leave the building by no later than 3.30 p.m.

Konstantin Mah. . . .

Natalya couldn't read the signature. She leaned back against the door again, breathing slowly and trying to calm herself. The girl had allowed her two minutes. How long had she been standing here in a daze? She fumbled quickly, opening the door. The girl was twenty paces along the

328

corridor, talking to the guard. And he was facing the girl so that her back was turned to Natalya. He glanced expressionless over the girl's shoulder, then grinned and reached out, touching her breasts. The girl laughed and slapped his hand away.

Natalya paused for just a second. How to get out? There was only one way. She would have to walk through that crowded office. Maybe they will shoot me, she thought, but they can only do it once.

She opened the office door and entered, hesitating before easing her way between desks and people. The other exit to the street seemed immeasurably far away. And dear God, any moment one of the typists or clerks would look up and recognize her. Now she was halfway to the gap in the long wooden counter. A man glanced at her as she passed but was distracted by the loud wailing of the old woman he was questioning. He turned back. 'Stop your noise, old mother. I'm not going to lock you up.'

Natalya walked on. Was it possible that she could pass through that gap in the counter and then out into the hall? Her knees would give way. She felt partly disembodied, as if watching herself as she moved towards the row of people seated on the wooden bench — each of them isolated by their fear. She reached the gap in the counter. Somebody would call to her to stop! Nobody did. A small fat man with a large moon face bumped into her. 'Excuse me.' And he muttered: 'Just go straight out.'

Now she was in the entrance hall, holding the pass for the bored guard as she reached the door. The guard took the pass and nodded.

Out on the steps, and the cold air and noises of Gorokhavaya Street were unbelievable. Natalya felt dizzy, swaying slightly. It could only be a dream. She would wake in a moment, back in her cell. No, it wasn't a dream. Captain Michael Stern was approaching up the steps. He gripped her arm, then smiled and put a cloak around her shoulders as he glanced quickly at the people coming and going through the doors of the Cheka building. And leading her down the steps he murmured, 'Welcome back to life, Countess.'

Professor Zubov had given in to his fear. He passed Natalya as she reached the bottom of the steps and he turned to her, slightly surprised to see that she had been released. But preoccupied with his own pressing problem, he hurried on with only a glance at the tall fair young man who was leading her away.

Peter Koltsov returned from the interrogation room to his office on the third floor. Zubov followed, talking rapidly. Koltsov went to the window and stared unseeing, biting his clenched fingers. It was worse than any pain. Blood from his fingers seeped over his hand. I am not yet turned to ice, he thought, and for God's sake what is that fool Zubov talking about?

'The girl, Helen Mirsky, Commissar.' Zubov stared at Koltsov and even in his anxiety he felt astonishment at the change in the man's face. 'She is meeting a man from Finland at eleven forty-five. But there is no train from Finland at eleven-forty-five!'

Koltsov rubbed the blood from his hand and forced himself to pay attention. 'What are you saying?'

Zubov licked his lips. He'd done it now. He'd betrayed Helen. 'The Finlander must be coming in by some other route.' He paused, waiting for Koltsov to comprehend, then he added, 'He must be the smuggler, Commissar — the one Baumler has dealings with.'

Koltsov sat at his desk and wrapped a handkerchief round his fingers. He tried to think. 'Eleven forty-five, you say?'

'Yes, Commissar.'

Eleven forty-five! She would be dead by then. He dragged his attention back to his duty. 'We have a few hours then, before Baumler and the girl rendezvous with this man from Finland.' And he scowled, puzzled. Why would Baumler risk dealing with the smuggler now, so close to his leaving the country? It made no sense. Baumler knew he was being watched — Popov had arranged constant surveillance. He shouted to his clerk in the next room. 'Send Popov to me.' Then, almost to himself he muttered, 'Why meet the smuggler now — what could Baumler be bringing in?' He paused. 'Or sending out?'

Zubov had waited anxiously. Surely Koltsov would now see that he had done his best. 'I don't know, Commissar. For years the American has had dealings with the Meretskov family.' He shrugged. 'Perhaps he intends smuggling Natalya Meretskova over the frontier.' He pulled out his cigarettes. 'May I smoke?'

Koltsov stared at him. 'Are you mad?' And he felt the sick anguish. 'Natalya Meretskova is to be shot tonight.'

Zubov had struck a match and now, surprised, he held it, forgetting the cigarette. Was this a joke? No, Commissar Koltsov never made jokes. 'But I saw the Countess — er, Citizeness Meretskova. She was leaving the building as I entered. A tall, fair-haired young man met her.'

Koltsov gaped. Zubov must be mistaken.

The clerk came in. 'I'm sorry, Commissar. I am unable to summon agent Popov for you. He left a few minutes after three o'clock. He said he felt unwell.'

'Never mind Popov. Have the guards check Natalya Meretskova's cell.' He glanced at the clock — it was nearly three twenty. 'She is due to leave for the Deryabinsky Prison at four.'

Zubov felt mounting unease. What was going on? He watched anxiously as Koltsov began pacing up and down.

'You say, Zubov, that you saw Natalya Meretskova met by a tall, fair-haired young man?'

'Yes, Commissar. I have the feeling I've seen him before.'

Stern! Was it possible? And she also knew Baumler. And Baumler was being investigated by Popov who had suddenly decided that he felt ill.

The clerk came back, almost running. 'Commissar! Natalya Meretskova is not in her cell!'

Somebody had allowed her to escape! Koltsov stared at the frightened clerk. And Zubov watched, fascinated and apprehensive.

Stern, Baumler, Popov, the girl — Helen Mirsky — and Natalya Meretskova Koltsov picked up the paper weight and snapped it in his hand. There must be no mercy shown — no weakening. 'Alert every militia unit in the city.' No bending to the demands of love or friendship. They must all be caught and shot.

31

The short daylight had almost ended as Helen, unaware that militia units were searching for her, hurried along the Liteyny Prospect towards Baumler's apartment.

She had weakened quite suddenly in the early afternoon, just after Zubov had left the office. She tried to telephone Baumler at his business address in the Schlusselburg Road. But of course, it being the way of things, he wasn't there, and the clerk had said to try his office later. So what had seemed to be a simply resolved ethical problem had become cause for gnawing anxiety. She couldn't just pack and leave. Foolish as Baumler had been to reject her, she would have to alert him to the Cheka interest. So I've a conscience after all, she thought, and much good may it do me. If he isn't at home I'll put a note under his door and then go. I can do neither more nor less than that.

As she neared the mosque opposite Baumler's apartment, she saw a black automobile pull up a few yards further on. And then a flurry of activity. Another car drew up behind it and large men in heavy greatcoats climbed out.

Helen stopped in her tracks. She watched the men as they stood for a moment in consultation, and she felt suddenly sick. She'd left it too late, and they had come for Baumler! She should turn straight round and go quickly away — across the islands to Staraya Derevnya to wait for Erik. But she knew she couldn't. Even in that moment she knew that Baumler had always been fair with her. Oh God! she thought feverishly. If I go now it will haunt me for the rest of my days.

She walked quickly past the heavily-overcoated men and then ran as fast as she could, across the courtyard and up the steps to Baumler's apartment. She rang the bell and beat the door with the flat of her hand, glancing frantically at the courtyard entrance.

'Wait, I'm *coming*.' She heard Baumler crossing the hall, and he opened the door. 'Helen!'

'Quickly!' She pushed him back and slammed the door behind her. 'You are about to be arrested. Oh, *hurry*, damn you!'

Baumler paused for only a second, then he pulled his coat and hat from the rack and grasped her hand. 'Out the back way.'

They had gone no more than twenty yards along Basseinaya Street when Baumler became aware of massive activity. Militia and Red Guards were everywhere. This surely couldn't be for *him* — he wasn't that important. He bundled Helen into a bookshop and they stood there, breathless. The shop was small and dusty, shelves packed together with barely room for movement between them. A wrought iron spiral staircase led up to the next floor. No assistant appeared. They went through the motions of examining books.

'Why did you risk your own freedom to warn me?' he whispered.

Helen was thoroughly frightened. 'An impulse, now regretted,' she murmured.

He grinned to himself. 'You keep surprising me. Has it occurred to you that all this huffing and puffing by the militia is really for somebody else?'

Helen's anger overcame her fear. She'd taken that awful chance merely to have him dismiss it! 'Then why don't you go out and ask them if it's you they want?' she hissed. 'For my part I have no intention of staying anywhere near you.'

And she left the shop and walked quickly through to Inzhenernaya Street. There was no denying she had been breathtakingly impetuous to come here and warn him. But that was the end of it. He could rot in a cell for all she cared.

Baumler had hurried out of the shop after her. For safety's sake he kept twenty yards behind. Obviously all this activity wasn't for him. Popov and Stern had got the Countess out, and the hunt for her was on. But Helen couldn't have known that. She'd really believed that the militia were after him. He was touched. No, he'd go further. He was truly moved by what she had done. Then he had a nasty shock. Red Guards had stopped a tall, middle-aged man — about the same build as himself. He hurried past.

Helen stumbled on the slushy paving then walked resolutely on, a small girl among the home-going Petrograders. I'll marry her, Baumler thought, and almost faltered in surprise. I'm broke and I don't care. I'll get her out of Russia and I'll marry her. He hurried and caught up with her just as she boarded a tram for the embankment and Vassili Island.

Seating himself next to her, he whispered, 'Where are we going?'

Helen stared ahead and murmured, '*I* am leaving Russia tonight with Cousin Erik. He is taking me across the ice. And you, Mr Baumler, can make your own arrangements.'

Baumler smiled to himself and squeezed up close to her as another man pushed onto the end of the seat. I'm happy, he thought. Despite the Cheka, and losing all my money — I'm happy. And he glanced sideways at Helen, feeling his thigh pressed to hers. She's beautiful, and come what may, she'll scheme me into being successful again.

The tram clattered across the Dvortzovi Bridge and on, past the end of the street where Helen lived. At the stop she climbed down.

'I don't know why you are trailing after me.' She walked quickly, looking straight ahead of her.

He grabbed her arm and turned her to him. 'Maybe I love you,' he said.

She stood quite still and looked up at his face. 'Do you?'

He sighed. The little adding machine behind her eyes was working again. 'I guess so.' He took her hand and they began to walk, slower now, towards her house. She didn't say anything but he could see that she was smiling to herself.

'How about you, Helen? Can you see yourself married to a tough old guy like me?'

She nodded.

'Of course,' he said, 'we'll have to start from scratch. And it will be hard going for a while.'

Helen nodded again. 'But we'll manage.'

They were nearly outside her house. He kept hold of her hand and said softly, 'There is somebody in your room. I just saw the curtain move. Keep walking.'

They passed the house. Baumler felt a tingling in the back of his neck as he steered Helen round the corner. He stopped and stared at her. So it was all true — her fears for him and herself. The militia were looking for both of them.

Her hand was trembling and he felt vulnerable. But it's because of Helen, he thought. All these years he'd needed somebody to worry about besides himself. He smiled grimly. Well now I've got somebody, and the chances are we'll both be dead by morning.

Under the single lamp further along the road, two militiamen were checking identities as people alighted from a tram.

'Come on,' he said, and he squeezed her hand tightly. 'We've a long way to go.'

32

Michael Stern stood at the window of the darkened bungalow. Clouds crossed the moon, shadowing the dismal marshes and flats edging onto the frozen Gulf. It had all seemed too easy; the rescue, a cab from the Cheka building, the tram journey and then the walk through the bleak wasteland of timber yards, logmen's huts and shabby rundown summer residences. He frowned out at the distant lights down the coast. What was happening there in the city itself?

A dog barked sharply some way off. He wondered what had disturbed it, and he listened intently, feeling for the slight bulge of the revolver under his coat.

Natalya stirred from her chair and groped across the dark room to join him at the window. 'I thought I heard something?'

'It was just a dog.'

I don't really know anything about dogs, he thought, but I always wanted one. And that cottage, remote, on the Sussex Downs and near the sea. In my mind I've walked those Downs a thousand times with the dog running in front of me. It seems unlikely now. 'Try to rest,' he said.

'I'm tired but I cannot rest.' Natalya pulled the cloak round herself. 'How dark the night is.'

'We'll leave soon. There is a local train from Novaya Derevnya to the Okhta Station. From there we'll go to Grusino, then through the forest.' He could feel her hand next to his on the window ledge.

'Is it a difficult journey?'

'Yes,' he said, 'but not too difficult. We'll take it as it comes.'

'Why did you come back for me, Captain Stern?'

For a moment he was silent, then he answered softly. 'Two reasons. I'll tell you when you are safe.'

She looked out at the darkness. He loves me, she thought.

Perhaps that would have some meaning at another time and in some other place. But she'd been too close to the Cheka firing squad. And too close to Peter Koltsov. Her hand trembled and Stern put his arm around her shoulder.

'Don't be afraid,' he said. 'Think of tomorrow. The past is dead.'

She rested her face against his coat. 'Yes. The past is dead.' The storm has swept away the corrupt, glittering splendour of the Romanov dynasty — my world. It was my world that created Peter Koltsov; scarred him, sharpened his vision but made him hard and cold. I warmed him a little, she thought, but now he will turn to ice.

She was aware of the pressure of Stern's hands on her shoulders. 'Your sister and Rykov are waiting for you. Twenty hours and you'll be safely in Finland.'

Twenty hours. How could she keep going for that long? She'd barely slept for two days and nights — already her weariness was complete. And another thought was in the back of her mind. Maybe I don't care enough for my life any more. She said something, murmuring into the shoulder of Stern's coat.

'I can't hear you,' he said.

She looked up. 'Perhaps one day I shall come back.'

'Perhaps.'

She lowered her head again, feeling some comfort from the closeness of him. And she wondered how Peter Koltsov would spend the rest of his life.

They remained holding each other, but distanced by their own thoughts. Stern stroked her hair and looked anxiously out as the moon emerged from behind cloud, palely illumining the wasteland stretching to the Gulf. We're not free yet, he thought. Not by a long way.

There was a slight sound outside. He stiffened and edged Natalya back from the window. 'Don't make a sound,' he whispered, and he went out onto the verandah, the revolver clasped lightly in his hand.

'Captain Stern? It is I, Popov.'

Stern pushed the revolver under his coat. 'Come in, Mr Popov.'

With Natalya they groped their way to the rear room, heavily curtained by Baumler months before. Stern lit candles. There were some old chairs and an empty packing case for a table. On a shelf they found blankets, tea, a primus stove and a bottle of brandy.

Popov was very agitated. 'There are militia and Red Guards everywhere, Captain.' And he hesitated, looking at Natalya and blinking. 'Your pardon, Countess. I do not wish to distress you.'

Natalya shook her head. 'Don't apologize. It is because of you and Captain Stern that I am free. You are both brave men.'

Popov blinked again, astonished. 'I — brave? Ah, quite so. The Countess is most gracious.' And he turned back to Stern. 'There were Red Guards at my house! I saw them from across the street. And my wife — a serpent, Captain — cackling and serving them tea! Then I went to the Siennaya market to buy food for the journey, and Red Guards were carrying out a raid. I was lucky to escape. You cannot imagine how big the hunt is.' He squeezed his fat hands together. 'We cannot possibly use the railway.'

Stern felt a surge of alarm for Natalya. 'Then we will have to wait for a day or two, until the hunt cools.'

'But to stay here would be dangerous! They will search this area also.'

'Then what choices are there?' Stern scowled. 'We cannot cross the ice on foot. So it's the frozen marshes as far as the Sestro River, or north through the forest to Grusino.'

'But I am a man of the city, Captain! What of the wolves?'

He'd seen wolves on his way into Russia — four of them, moving in file across the snow under the moon. He glanced at Natalya — she looked spent. She'll never make it to Grusino, he thought. 'The marsh route is the shortest.' He could carry her much of the way if he had to. 'We'll head for the Sestro River.'

338

'Oh, God! — if there is a god.'

Stern jerked round. 'Listen!'

Somebody was climbing the wooden steps of the verandah. Footsteps sounded outside. Stern pointed the revolver at the door, then lowered it, astonished. Baumler and Helen came in. And Baumler grinned around at them. 'Greetings, my children. God's teeth, Michael! You've certainly stirred things up in the city. You can't spit without hitting a Red Guard.'

Not since the collapse of the Provisional Government and the Bolshevik takeover had Petrograd known such a manhunt. Trains were held up, and blocks set up on all routes out. Ruins, churches, even cemeteries were searched by men with lanterns and torches.

Commissar Peter Koltsov had remained in his office in the Cheka building. Every few minutes the telephone rang as militia indicated another area of search completed. Koltsov marked them off with crosses on a map of the city.

Zubov sat on one of the hard chairs and chewed his finger nails.

'They are out there somewhere.' Koltsov frowned down at his map. 'Baumler, Helen Mirsky, Stern and Popov. And they must try to escape tonight, taking Natalya Meretskova with them.' His cold gaze rested on the other man. 'Now *think*, Zubov. Think hard. The Finlander is the key. Helen Mirsky must once have mentioned where her cousin comes from.'

'Yes. She mentioned it, but a long time ago.' Zubov groaned softly and rubbed his eyes. 'In those days I never more than half listened to her. There seemed no reason why I should remember anything that she said.'

'Nevertheless, it is there, somewhere inside your head,' Koltsov rasped. 'Dig it out.'

'The place cannot be far into Finland,' Zubov said. 'She told me once that the train journey took only two hours.'

Koltsov stared at him. 'You see? You are remembering things. And you would be surprised at what else you would remember — with a little pressure.' He lit a cheap cigarette, and as an afterthought he pushed the packet across to Zubov. 'You have another ten minutes. Then one of my best interrogators will see if he can open your memory.'

The telephone rang again and Koltsov answered, marking off another square of the map. At that moment the clerk entered with a bundle of papers. 'Commissar, we found these in agent Popov's desk. They are copies of Baumler's bank statements.'

Peter Koltsov took them and began going through each sheet. His face, half-shadowed in the light of the desk lamp, was curiously intent. There are no options, he thought. Natalya Meretskova's warmth reached me — revealed a small part of my being that I barely knew existed. I half want her to escape, but I must do everything in my power to prevent it.

But at the back of his thoughts there was a question. If I do everything possible to hunt her down, and she still escapes, will that small part of me remain alive? He knew that he wanted to believe that it would.

He paused over Popov's copies of the bank statements. There were pencilled rings round certain of the deposit figures. So Popov had known something but kept it to himself. The sums in question were large. Koltsov went back through sheet after sheet. Then he stopped. 'Deposits,' he said, and frowned, his eyes narrowing. 'Deposits at monthly intervals, but they fall only between the months of November and April. What does that suggest to you, Zubov?'

Zubov looked up, then he shrugged dejectedly. 'Half the year, Commissar. The cold half.'

'Yes. The cold half.' Koltsov's eyes widened. 'And the land routes over the frontier are used by smugglers all the year round. But Baumler has been paid for goods smuggled only during the cold half of the year — the months when the Gulf is frozen!' He jerked upright in his chair. 'The smuggler is coming in over the ice — and he's arriving at eleven forty-five!'

340

Zubov jumped to his feet, interrupting. '*Now* I remember! Helen Mirsky once said that she'd walked with her cousin down by the frozen sea. She said that from there she could see Fort Ino.' And he gabbled excitedly. 'Terioki! It must be Terioki.'

Koltsov swung his head round and looked at the clock. 'We have little time! We know that the smuggler is using a sleigh, and that he must be on his way if he is to reach Petrograd by eleven forty-five, but we do not know where he is making his landfall.' He stared down at the map again. 'It will be somewhere here, in the northern part — between Lakhta and Krestovsky.' He picked up the telephone. 'I will alert the coastguard at Lissy Nos.' '

Zubov waited anxiously. He was very tired and hungry, and his mouth was dried up from smoking too much. Worse, Koltsov frightened him. Yet there was something about Koltsov that was human and fallible after all. Zubov already half suspected the other man's internal struggle, and part of him wanted to stay and observe, to see if Koltsov would weaken.

Koltsov spoke hurriedly then put the phone down. He looked at Zubov. 'Red Guards will begin to search the shore area of Staraya Derevnya and Krestovsky Island. But if the smuggler moves quickly he may get our fugitives out before we find them.' He pointed at the map. 'Here, at Lissy Nos, troops from the Razdielnaya garrison will be waiting. They will have spare horses for us. We will ride out out onto the ice and intercept the sleigh before it reaches the open stretch of the Gulf.'

Zubov gaped. '*We?*'

Koltsov rose and snatched up his coat. He opened the door and shouted to the clerk. 'A fast car and a good driver! Outside in five minutes. Hurry!' And he turned to Professor Zubov. 'Yes. You are coming also. You have betrayed them as you once betrayed me — oh yes, Zubov, I guessed. And it seems appropriate that you should be there to see them caught.' He seized Zubov by the lapels of his coat and held him under the light. 'Tonight you will stare into the face of your own treachery. There are no options,' he added grimly.

Far out on the Gulf, Erik Halla's sleigh hissed over the ice. A cold wind whipped up the covering of snow, swirling it over the sweating horses. This was the bad stretch, just ahead. Erik peered through rime-rimmed eyes at the gleam of the beacon on Lissy Nos. Eight miles beyond that he could see the night glow of Petrograd. His hands were frozen, clenched over the reins, and he huddled deeper into his fur coat. He knew that the ice was dangerous in places — ready to crack under the weight of the sleigh. Gritting his teeth, he peered back as he dragged the horses round to follow the faint line of the coast. Let's hope that Cousin Helen is prepared to demonstrate her gratitude for this ride, he thought.

Kronstadt was behind him and he rested the horses, but harsh beams of the fortress searchlights were probing the whiteness. The next bit is easy, he told himself. All the way to Lakhta — just so long as the ice is still sound and nobody hears the hooves and the runners of the sleigh. He brushed rime from the edge of his fur cap and peered around again. This would be the last run he'd ever make. Even gold wasn't worth the risks. He'd slept badly for two nights, and he'd have nightmares if he ever got back. Cousin Helen would be his final contraband cargo over the Terioki crossing. Maybe he'd marry her and settle down.

Mile after mile, and now he steered by the red glow of the city, moving towards the north-western suburbs. There was another beacon on Krestovsky Island. He drove with it to his right. Ten more minutes and he would reach Staraya Derevnya.

The five fugitives in the bungalow had settled down to wait. Helen thought it tactically wise to take no part in the fierce argument between Baumler and Stern. By the flickering light of candles she poured oil into the primus stove and lit it. Cousin Erik would need hot tea when he arrived. She

342

glanced cautiously at Natalya, cloak draped round her. Helen had never before spoken to a member of the old aristocracy. But of course, we *are* all equal now, she thought.

Baumler frowningly continued with the argument. 'For God's sake, Michael! Popov is no fool. If he says the border guards will be waiting for you at the Sestro, take his word for it and come with us.'

'No!' Stern shook his head. 'Your smuggler is expecting one passenger. I'm grateful that you will take the Countess. Four of you will be his limit. Your chances will be a lot better without a fifth passenger. I'll take my chance here, and I'll try for the frontier in a day or two.'

'Don't be so damned British! Commissar Koltsov will have Red Guards swarming over these bungalows by dawn. Your life won't be worth a kopek. Even now he'll be drawing the net tightly round the whole area. Not even a mouse will get out by the land route.'

Natalya had listened carefully to the argument. Baumler was right. Peter Koltsov would seal off every exit then search and search, but not just to recapture her for the firing squad. He was tearing Petrograd apart to test his own integrity, and to prove to her that duty could not be put aside even though he loved her. Tonight the Cheka cells would be crammed with suspects. Should she offer herself back to the Cheka? — she was so tired the thought was seductive. And if she gave herself up maybe the hunt would be called off and the others could get to Finland. But Stern would never allow her to do it. He was as determinedly unyielding as Peter Koltsov. He would risk anything to get her out of Russia. She looked at him. He smiled reassuringly, and she thought, he will kill rather than let them take me. Her face softened.

The argument continued. Popov groaned out loud and rested his head on his fat hands. What a dreadful dilemma. If Stern stayed behind, the rest of them stood a better chance. But *who* then, would pay him, Popov? Better to risk all. 'Listen to Mister Baumler, Captain. The search for the Countess will go on for days. You must come with us.'

And Helen reflected. It was not that she begrudged the Countess her freedom — heaven forbid. But why had such an exalted person escaped from the Cheka building today, of all days, bringing militia and Red Guards out of every crack in the paving stones?

Baumler had momentarily given up the debate and was looking anxiously at his watch. He went to the darkened room at the front of the bungalow and sat by the window waiting. At eleven forty-five he flashed a pocket torch four times and waited again. Across the dark expanse of ice a faint light answered. Erik Halla had arrived.

Within minutes the smuggler hobbled into the candlelit room. 'My feet, quickly! I cannot feel them.' He fell into a chair. Helen knelt and took off Erik's boots, and she began rubbing his left foot. She was surprised when Natalya knelt and rubbed the other one.

'Harder!' Harder! Oh my God, they hurt!'

Stern handed him a mug of tea laced with brandy and Erik gulped noisily. 'I'm coming back to life.' He watched the two girls as they rubbed and he grinned wolfishly. 'That's better. By God, you should have seen me passing between that line of forts. I thought the sleigh would fly.' Then he looked around, and glanced back at Helen. 'Why so many people to see you off?'

Baumler pulled his wallet out. 'Here. You can have all of that if you take us with you.'

Erik jerked up. 'Five! You're crazy!'

'The Cheka want us all. They are out searching now.'

Erik shook his head. 'I can't take five.'

'Four then,' Stern said.

Baumler dropped the wallet in Erik's lap. 'I'll double that if we all reach Finland.'

Erik stood, wincing, balanced on one foot. 'You don't understand! The ice is already dangerous.' He picked up the wallet. 'I'll take double this for three of you.'

Popov had gone to the next room to listen. He ran back. 'Lanterns, Captain Stern! There are lanterns further along the point!'

Erik turned to Helen. 'Pull my boots on for me!' He leaned forward, speaking softly. 'Say the word and I'll take just you — we'd stand a better chance.'

Helen hesitated for just a second, then she shook her head.

Stern came back into the room. 'We no longer have any choice. Men are searching, moving rapidly in this direction. There are many of them.'

Erik fastened his boot and nodded grimly. 'Right. All of you then. Don't let good manners delay our departure.' He bounded out of the chair and through the door.

They followed, running to the sleigh, and they threw out everything that was loose, but it still creaked under the weight of Erik, Helen and Natalya huddled together in the front, with Popov crushed up behind them. Stern and Baumler ran, pushing on the struts. The sleigh moved slowly, gathering speed, and then Stern found that he was no longer pushing, but hanging on as the runners started to hiss over the ice. He leapt on the back, his knee just supporting him and his weight taken on his left foot riding on the runner. And he hung on and looked back at the dark line of the shore, and the dozens of searching lanterns.

The men on the shore had heard their movement and the thudding of hooves. A carbine cracked and a bullet whined over, then another far wide of them.

'Are we safe yet?' Baumler shouted.

Erik shook his head. 'Not until we are beyond Lissy Nos and the line of forts. Another seven miles.'

Stern cursed softly to himself as he clung precariously. In the scramble to get clear he'd lost his right glove. His hand was already numbing. Soon it would lose its strength.

The glow of Petrograd was already far behind and darkness lay over the vast stretches of ice ahead, pricked by small gleams of light from Kronstadt and the line of forts. The bright beacon of Lissy Nos indicated where the shore began.

Helen tugged Erik's coat and called to him. 'The ice, Erik! Will it support us?'

'I don't know.' His words were blurred by wind swirling up the snow and stinging their faces.

Stern changed his grip, trying to hold on with his left hand as the sleigh veered, heading for the gap between the forts. A searchlight on Kronstadt slashed the night, briefly turning the ice to gold.

The horses were tiring, Erik Halla knew it. 'We are nearly safe!' he shouted.

The searchlight went out and the ice shadowed again, pale white now from the moon half-hidden by cloud.

Another two miles and they were clear of the line of fortresses upjutting out of the wilderness. Sestroretsk, the last village on the Russian side of the frontier, gleamed distantly ahead and to their right. Popov laughed almost uncontrollably. 'See. We are nearly in Finnish territory!'

Stern knew that his grip was weakening. He looked back and felt a sudden bitter surge. 'Riders! Behind us!'

The sleigh moved faster again as Erik furiously drove the horses. Stern willed himself to hold on, but his numb fingers began to slip from the strut. Frantically he stretched out to Natalya. 'Grasp my hand!'

In the faint light from the moon he could see her eyes widen. She leaned back, clasping his hand between hers and looking over his shoulder at the distant riders gaining on them.

Stern felt the runner jar under his foot and he heard a sharp cracking sound.

'The ice!' Popov shouted. 'It's breaking!'

But still Erik drove the horses on. The black shapes of the pursuing horsemen were distinct now. Ten — no, a dozen of them. Now on the wide stretch of the Gulf, the wind howled, swirling the snow across the vast dead wilderness. Stern felt a sudden lurch as the surface beneath them cracked, then opened black with a loud splintering roar. They jumped, falling and rolling as the sleigh began to slide sideways. It tilted the ice, pulling the horses towards the jagged gap. The animals, wide-eyed, snorted with terror. Erik leapt up and slashed at the harness straps with his long knife, and the horses kicked clear and scrambled off. Their movement slewed the unstable surface. Erik groped for balance and with a despairing cry he fell back into the crack. He threshed the dark water as the ice crunched and closed over him.

'Erik! Erik!' Helen fell on her knees but Baumler dragged her up again. 'It's no use,' he shouted over the wind. 'He's gone!'

Stern clutched at the trailing harness straps of the terrified horses and was dragged flat across the ice. His frozen hands lost grip and he watched them gallop towards the lights far off. He staggered to his feet and pointed. 'Those lights ahead — that's Terioki in Finland! We've got to try for it.'

Natalya peered back at the approaching horsemen. 'They'll catch up with us long before we reach safety!' A gust of fine snow, carried on the wind, broke over them like a wave.

Stern tugged savagely at Natalya's wrists. 'Come *on!*' And he began to run clumsily, following Helen and Baumler and the gasping Popov.

Now less than a mile behind, Peter Koltsov dug his heels into the sides of his horse and shielded his eyes from the stinging snow.

The small figures running ahead of him seemed like children. There was no chance of their escape. As he steadily gained on them he could identify Natalya at the rear, being dragged on by Stern.

Koltsov's mount plunged through a snow drift. Only a few hundred yards separated him from the fugitives. Natalya had fallen and Stern was pulling her up. Pity for them jarred through his unguarded consciousness. But I play out the game to its bitter end this time, he thought, and lashed at the flanks of the straining animal. Then on his right a horse fell — ice breaking beneath it, and another reared up, throwing its rider as the surface split open. Koltsov hauled back on the horse's head and slithered to a stop. The others had halted, dismounting and hanging on to their terrified beasts.

And Zubov shouted as the ice began to slew beneath him.

He scrambled, dragging the horse round, and to Koltsov he called, 'We must go back!'

'No!' Koltsov stared frantically after Natalya. 'Leave the horses, all of you. We'll go on foot. Spread out and . . .' The shrieking wind drowned the rest of his words.

One of the horsemen shouted 'No, Commissar — it's too late! The surface is breaking up all around us. I beg you!' The others had already begun to retreat, leading their horses and groping with each step.

Shaking with fear, Zubov reached sound ice again. He knew that if Koltsov died he would be free. Why then did he want the man to fail but live — as other men do? He cupped his hands to his mouth and shouted. 'Koltsov! Don't go on! For the love of Christ, don't! It isn't worth it!' And almost to himself he shouted again, hopelessly, 'Nothing is worth this!'

Koltsov slapped the rump of his horse, sending it back, and alone he moved on after Natalya and Stern, stepping from one precarious footing to the next.

Baumler, unable to drag Helen any further, had picked her up and was carrying her towards Terioki. He turned and looked back at the others behind him. Popov was lurching on alone, but through swirls of snow he could see Stern dragging Natalya. 'Come on, Michael! We can make it now. There is only one of them following us.'

Stern shouted to him. 'Keep going!' And he bent over Natalya who had sunk to her knees. 'Up! You must try!' He looked back at Koltsov moving quickly behind them. It was too late to carry her now — they would soon be overtaken. He peered down at her, snow stinging his eyes. Her will to escape wasn't strong enough, and the insight that followed made him jerk his head round to the dark figure approaching. Part of her is really back there with Koltsov even though it means death. And he shouted at her through the wind, 'Get on your feet!'

She shook her head and her voice was faint. 'I can't go any further.'

'I owe you a life! I won't let you die!'

She stared at him, uncomprehending.

Koltsov was only fifty yards from them, his shape momentarily blurred by snow whipped back from a drift.

Stern bent and stroked Natalya's face. 'We will stay together then, and wait for Peter.'

Fumbling, his frozen hands clumsy, he pulled the revolver from under his coat.

Koltsov was also armed. He slowed, unclipping his holster. Then he stopped with his feet braced apart, and he faced Stern only twenty paces ahead.

Natalya dragged herself up and stood close to Michael Stern.

'The Countess is my prisoner, Michael,' Koltsov called.

'No!' Stern shook his head. 'If you try to take her back, either you or I must die.'

Glancing quickly round at the far-off lights on the bastions of Kronstadt, Koltsov ensured that he was alone. He turned again to Stern. 'What would you do? Take her away to *your* country? She doesn't really want that. We are Russians, she and I, and come what may our destinies lie here.' He started to move forward. 'The Countess and I each have a duty. Ask her, she will tell you.'

'To hell with your duty, Peter. I've said that she will live.' Stern raised the revolver in his frozen hands, his finger numb on the trigger. 'Don't come any further.'

Koltsov continued towards them. 'No compromises, Michael.'

Stern pointed the revolver at Koltsov's chest. 'Don't do this, Peter. Turn back!'

It seemed almost as if Koltsov hadn't heard. Quite slowly and deliberately he began to pull the heavy automatic pistol from its holster, and he looked past Stern to Natalya, his thin lips twisting into a smile. 'And so for each of us . . .'

'No! Don't!' Natalya seized Stern's arm as he squeezed the trigger. The gun roared sharply and leapt out of his numb hands, clattering onto the ice, and Koltsov sank to his knees, looking up at them.

'. . . there is a time,' he said, and slumped forward on his face.

'Oh, dear God, no!' Natalya fell on her knees next to Koltsov and turned him over, resting his head on her lap.

He looked at her, still smiling, and whispered, 'I said that I would share this night with you.'

'Do not die, Peter Koltsov! Please do not die! Not here in this awful wilderness!' She began to rip cloth from the lining of her cloak to staunch his wound.

Stern knelt and lowered his head against a gust of snow. Koltsov turned to face him and muttered, his harsh voice almost inaudible, 'Tell her, Michael. There are no options. And here . . .' he sighed, '. . . is all.'

Stern groped for Peter Koltsov's hand. It had gone limp. And already fine powdered snow was masking his face. Natalya kissed his cold lips and she looked up at Stern. 'I did not hear what he said.'

Stern stood. The revolver lay at his feet. He kicked it, spinning and clattering over the ice. He remembered the words of the holy man, that he would kill twice. And the debt is paid, he thought. Wind howled over the white waste, and to the south a searchlight probed briefly from Kronstadt.

'Come,' he said. 'Leave him.'

He grasped Natalya's shoulders, lifting her, and he pointed north. 'That is where we must go.'

She hesitated, staring down at Koltsov. Then she slowly turned away. They began to walk. Popov was limping ahead to where Baumler stood with his arm around Helen.

Natalya peered back. Koltsov's body was just a white shape, among other shapes and humps in the snow. She looked up at Stern. 'What did he say?'

'He said there are no options.' Stern stared determinedly ahead. 'And he said that here is all.'

'He cannot *know* that.' Natalya took his hand and they walked on towards the lights of Terioki.

'No. He cannot know that,' Stern said.

DIANE PEARSON

THE SUMMER OF THE BARSHINSKEYS

'Although the story of the Barshinskeys, which became our story too, stretched over many summers and winters, that golden time of 1902 was when our strange involved relationship began, when our youthful longing for the exotic took a solid and restless hold upon us . . .'

It is at this enchanted moment that *The Summer of the Barshinskeys* begins. A beautifully told, compelling story that moves from a small Kentish village to London, and from war-torn St Petersburg to a Quaker relief unit in the Volga provinces. It is the unforgettable story of two families, one English, the other Russian, who form a lifetime pattern of friendship, passion, hatred, and love.

'An engrossing saga . . . she evokes rural England at the turn of the century with her sure and skilful touch'
Barbara Taylor Bradford

'The Russian section is reminiscent of Pasternak's *Doctor Zhivago*, horrifying yet hauntingly beautiful'
New York Tribune

0 552 12641 1   £2.95

CORGI BOOKS

OTHER FINE NOVELS AVAILABLE FROM CORGI BOOKS

WHILE EVERY EFFORT IS MADE TO KEEP PRICES LOW, IT IS SOME-TIMES NECESSARY TO INCREASE PRICES AT SHORT NOTICE. CORGI BOOKS RESERVE THE RIGHT TO SHOW NEW RETAIL PRICES ON COVERS WHICH MAY DIFFER FROM THOSE PREVIOUSLY ADVER-TISED IN THE TEXT OR ELSEWHERE.

THE PRICES SHOWN BELOW WERE CORRECT AT THE TIME OF GOING TO PRESS (AUGUST '85).

☐	08615 0	**The Big Wind**	*Beatrice Coogan*	£2.50
☐	99019 1	**Zemindar**	*Valerie Fitzgerald*	£2.50
☐	12637 3	**Proud Mary**	*Iris Gower*	£2.50
☐	12387 0	**Copper Kingdom**	*Iris Gower*	£1.95
☐	12438 9	**Queen of The Lightning**	*Kathleen Herbert*	£2.50
☐	12508 3	**Unicorn Summer**	*Rhona Martin*	£1.95
☐	11037 X	**Gallows Wedding**	*Rhona Martin*	£1.95
☐	12503 2	**Three Girls**	*Frances Paige*	£1.95
☐	12641 1	**The Summer of The Barshinskeys**	*Diane Pearson*	£2.95
☐	10375 6	**Csardas**	*Diane Pearson*	£2.95
☐	09140 5	**Sarah Whitman**	*Diane Pearson*	£1.95
☐	10271 7	**The Marigold Field**	*Diane Pearson*	£1.95
☐	10249 0	**Bride of Tancred**	*Diane Pearson*	£1.75
☐	12607 1	**Doctor Rose**	*Elvi Rhodes*	£1.95
☐	12367 6	**Opal**	*Elvi Rhodes*	£1.75
☐	12579 2	**The Daffodils of Newent**	*Susan Sallis*	£1.75
☐	12375 7	**A Scattering of Daisies**	*Susan Sallis*	£1.95

All these books are available at your bookshop or newsagent, or can be ordered direct from the publisher. Just tick the titles you want and fill in the form below.

CORGI BOOKS, Cash Sales Department, P.O Box 11, Falmouth, Cornwall.

Please send cheque or postal order, no currency.

Please allow cost of book(s) plus the following for postage and packing:

U.K. CUSTOMERS – Allow 55p for the first book, 22p for the second book and 14p for each additional book ordered, to a maximum charge of £1.75.

B.F.P.O. & EIRE – Allow 55p for the first book, 22p for the second book plus 14p per copy for the next seven books, thereafter 8p per book.

OVERSEAS CUSTOMERS – Allow £1.00 for the first book and 25p per copy for each additional book.

NAME (Block Letters) ....

ADDRESS ....

....